CW00549398

MIDNIGHT MOON

By the same author

THE CLOCK TOWER

Midnight Moon

JEANNE MONTAGUE

CENTURY PUBLISHING

LONDON

First published in Great Britain in 1985
by Century Publishing Co. Ltd,
Portland House, 12–13 Greek Street, London WIV 5LE

ISBN 0 7126 0809 5

Photoset in Great Britain by
Rowland Phototypesetting Ltd, Bury St Edmunds, Suffolk
and printed by St Edmundsbury Press,
Bury St Edmunds, Suffolk
Bound by Butler & Tanner Ltd, Frome, Somerset

In homage to the composers Giacomo Puccini and Richard Wagner, whose operatic masterpieces are my greatest source of inspiration

BOOK ONE

The Finder

A sexless thing it was, and in its growth
It seemed to have developed no defect
Of either sex, yet all the grace of both, –
In gentleness and strength its limbs were decked;
The bosom swelling with its full youth,
The countenance was such as might select
Some artist that his skill should never die,
Imagining forth such perfect purity.

The Witch of Atlas. XXXVI, SHELLEY

Morocco. Winter 1792

The day had not fulfilled its early promise. It had become overcast, threatening a torrential, thundery downpour. Clouds obscured the sun, grey masses fringed with dull bronze, casting an unnatural radiance. The sea shimmered like pewter, and the wind whipped the waves into tossing white foam. It was a warm wind, although snow still capped the distant Rif Mountains, bringing with it a hint of spices and desert sand.

The triangular sails of the dhow strained beneath the pressure, the long narrow craft skimming over the water, leaving the sheltered harbour, heading out towards the Mediterranean Sea. The man at the helm cast an apprehensive eye at the silent, brooding figure of the tall Englishman who had hired his services. Behind him, his crew muttered amongst themselves, busy with the nets, subdued for once, jest and raillery hushed, awed by the stranger. Their swarthy faces were suspicious, dark eyes darting ever and again to the bow where the breeze tore at his long grey cloak and lifted the black curls away from his stern features. He ignored them, a faint smile on his arresting face, a cold smile which hinted at disdain and a passion for doing whatever he willed. The atmosphere was heavy with uneasiness.

The captain shrugged. His passenger had paid handsomely to be taken aboard. The fish could prove fickle and evade them for a week and he would still be in pocket. What harm to accommodate the mad English milord?

'Take me with you,' he had commanded, holding out a heavy purse. Why such a man should wish to voyage in a stinking fishing-boat was beyond the captain's comprehension. But the sight of gold was too tempting, and he had stifled memories of the rumours rife in the tiny port which clung like a fungus to the rocky Moroccan shore. These had begun as soon as the new owner came to the ancient palace which dominated the headland.

Tongues had wagged, and there was a plentiful supply of tidbits to whet the appetite of the most seasoned market-place gossip. The *effendi* was as rich as Solomon – his servants were without number – his women beautiful beyond compare – the friends of his bosom equally wealthy and of noble lineage. But after a while, a more sinister note had crept in, stories of unlimited licence taking place within the walls of El Skala, once the fortress of a high-born Berber, now a pleasure-palace. There were whispers about ungodliness and violence, and the raising of devils.

'So, what matters this to me?' the captain growled in his ferocious, red-hennaed beard. 'He may be a foreign sorcerer, but he's a generous one!' Yet he trembled as he scanned the lurid sky. Had his action offended some powerful genie? He was on the alert for the storm-demons with their devious tricks, those sudden, unexpected puffs exhaled from giant, super-natural lungs, which could topple the stoutest ship, consigning all to the deep.

The subject of his worried conjectures eased himself into a more comfortable position, wedging his wide shoulders against the mast, arms folded on his chest, balancing his legs to compensate for the lift and drop of the deck. He watched the coast receding, El Skala a gilded, domed mushroom sur-rounded by thick white walls. There had been nothing remark-able about his decision to sail that morning. He had acted purely on impulse. He chuckled as he imagined the pande-monium which would ensue when his guests awoke to find him missing. Let them fret. Let them fume. God damn them all!

He blotted them from his mind, half closing his eyes, concen-trating on the opalescent sheen of the water. There was a curiously emotional quality of colour, a sharpness of detail which fixed the attention with the uncompromising clarity of a vision. This was what he had needed, this physical sensation of the wind cooling his brow, and the tossing of the elements. Yet, at the same time, he was aware of the timelessness of it – the ship – the sea – the staggering vista of inlets and palm trees and the far off haze, blue over the Rif – the vast, dwarfing panoply of nature.

He dreamed, toying with the idea of ordering these seafaring rascals to pull in on the white sand of some remote island. They could shoot game for the pot, run lines and trap turtles. A simple life, sleeping under the stars, with himself happy in the company of plain men, leaving the complications of civilization for ever. But even as he visualized it, he was laughing cynically at himself. Lord, he could have had that back home in Wessex, if it was really what he wanted. He had sailed with other fishermen then, when he was a boy, rugged Dorset lads who risked life and limb to swell the coffers of their liege lord, as they had done time out of mind.

Suddenly the dreams vanished. He was wide awake, fully alert, his attention drawn to the water. He moved swiftly to the rail, leaning on it and staring hard. There was something amidst the swell, floating, half submerged, sometimes visible, sometimes not.

A frown drew his black brows together, eyes slitted. Then in a few strides he had reached the captain at the wheel, an impatient hand on the man's shoulder. He swung him round with a ruthless strength belied by his elegant appearance. 'Heave to!' he shouted. 'There's an object in the sea. Just over there. Look!' His tone brooked no disobedience.

The captain's eyes followed that stabbing gesture. He saw it, and his mouth dropped open in alarm. 'We must sail past it, *effendi*,' he spluttered, attempting to shake off that iron grip. 'It may be an *'efreet* – or a ghoul! We dare not take it aboard!'

The Englishman's jaw set grimly and his eyes glittered like chips of green ice. 'Fool! I think 'tis a body. We shall investigate.'

The captain threw himself on the deck near the booted feet, his hands clasped in supplication, eyes upraised to that hard face. 'Oh, honoured sir – I beg you – leave it be. If not a ghost, then it will be some accursed suicide, or even the victim of a cruel murder! There are pirates in these waters, *effendi* – we dare not meddle lest it be their wicked work. They will find us and slaughter us! We shall be tortured! They have horrible ways of making a man die slowly, inch by inch! Do not bring their wrath upon us!'

The Englishman looked down at him as if he were some disgusting insect. He lifted his lace-edged handkerchief to his nostrils. 'Not only a fool but a coward to boot! Keep your distance – you stink of rotting fish. Now, do as I say. Steer the vessel alongside the thing, whatever it may be.'

By now the crew had seen it, murmuring, gesticulating, their eyes round and scared. Their superstitious dread was like a plague, thick, grey, infectious, easily tipped over into panic. Even the Englishman felt a chill prickle down his spine. He gripped the rail till his knuckles turned white as they came ever closer to that bobbing bundle. It was like rags, yet rags turned solid, held rigid by that which they hid from sight. The thing was not easy to approach. It rolled and ducked, flirting coyly with the waves.

'Get a boathook!' He shouted, easing his troubled spirit by losing his temper.

The fishermen gibbered and shook their turbanned heads. With an oath, he grabbed it himself, leaning over the side and thrusting out the long pole. The hook bit home and he braced his feet, heaving at the heavy, water-logged thing, snarling out such a violent curse that the captain leapt to his side, fearing him more than ghosts or vengeful pirates. Together, they hauled it aboard.

It lay in the scuppers, an oozing lump which may once have been a living creature. The wrapping shrouded it, greyish, sodden, indeterminate. The Englishman went down on one knee, tugging at the covering. The top layer came off and there was a second's stunned silence.

The captain broke it, exclaiming: 'By the Beard of the Prophet! It is a stripling! Is he dead?'

The Englishman was aware of nothing but the vague outline of this curled heap which resembled nothing more than a pile of discarded garments. There was a faint movement, and then the body stretched, revealing hands, two thin arms, shoulders marked with criss-cross weals, and a thoroughly drenched head of cropped black hair.

'Get a blanket!' he snapped and, bending over, he raised the body in his arms, heedless of the water draining from it, folding it close to his own warm flesh.

The body was cold, as cold as the tomb. He could feel it soaking through his clothing, chilling his skin, penetrating his very bones. He wrapped the blanket round it, and put a wine-flask to the blue-white lips, forcing some into the mouth. There was a choking cough as the liquid caught in the throat, life returning as the twisting head sought to avoid more. The hands fluttered, and a long, shuddering sigh escaped through the lips.

Suddenly, the lids flew open and a pair of extraordinary eyes stared straight up into the Englishman's. They were steady, wide-spaced, darkly circled, like two pieces of burning coal. It was a level, unbending stare from which the blindness of near-death had completely vanished, moving over his face in a slow, blank inspection.

He recovered his equilibrium, saying quietly: 'You are safe. Can you understand me?'

The strange appraisal continued, and the bloodless lips did not answer. He tried to recall phrases of the local dialect but his brain refused to function, bewitched by those enormous eyes in that childish face. An eerie silence filled the boat.

The captain shook himself, perplexed, afraid. 'What shall we do with it, *effendi*? It is a runaway slave, perhaps – a rich man's catamite who has displeased his master, flogged and flung into the sea to drown. A wild thing, maybe – not of this earth. In either case, it would be prudent to throw it back.'

The Englishman rounded on him fiercely. 'No!'

'Then sir – I pray you – take it to the village and give it to the fishermen's wives. They will care for it and take steps against the evil eye.' The captain was a burly man with the strong, hawk features of his race. His hands were broad, calloused and strong; there were several long knives stuck in the red sash girding his middle and yet he was obviously terrified of their find.

The Englishman shook his head, hardly hearing him, moving like one in a trance. 'Don't be afraid,' he whispered to the creature he had rescued. 'Can you speak English? What is your name and from whence have you come?'

There was no response for a second then, almost shockingly, the lips curved slightly, a spark of amusement lighting the eyes. It passed in a flash, leaving him thinking that his imagination had been playing tricks.

The captain was glancing up at the sky. A dull grey vapour had overspread the entire western half; the heavens were inky black and that darkness brought a quiver of rain in the air. He had smelt it coming even before the first faint webs floated down from those lurid, orange-tipped clouds. 'We must return, *effendi*, ere the demons of the storm overwhelm us. If you insist on bringing that person ashore, then let it be on your own head.'

As he finished speaking, there came a tremendous flash of lightning, livid blue, covering the whole sky, followed by a distant roll of thunder which lasted for several seconds, ending with a succession of deep throbs. The heavens seemed to open and the rain came down in huge drops which fell straight through the gloomy air.

Then, with a savage howl, the wind was upon them. The sailors furled the canvas and it was indeed as if devils roared and screamed about the bare masts, every rope and plank groaning under the torturing onslaught as the vessel was carried towards the harbour.

The Englishman crouched in the limited shelter of a bulwark, a fold of his cloak held protectively over the youth. He looked up at the storm, responding to its fury, filled with a curious sense of elation, tinglingly alive. It was in this mood that he brought his trophy to El Skala – the creature whom the sea had swallowed and then spewed forth as if not strong enough to absorb it.

Chapter 1

Beaumaris Combe, Dorset
Spring 1793

Sally Anstey had just retired to rest when she was disturbed by a hammering on her bedroom door. Pulling a wrapper over her white lawn nightgown, she went to open it. The corridor was dark, but Meggy's face shone ghostly-white in the light of the candle weeping its waxen tears into the brass holder clenched in her hand.

'Oh, Miss Anstey . . . pardon me for disturbing you, but 'tis my sister, Dora – she's been took awful bad. Can you come?' she stammered, eyes wide and alarmed in her plump face. She was breathing hard, and most dishevelled, hair straggling untidily from beneath her mob cap.

'Really, Meggy. Why call me? Can't Mr Boxer attend to it?' Sally was tired and irritable. The children had been most taxing all day and she had been looking forward to reading for a while before sleeping. Now there was this nuisance, a matter for the housekeeper or the steward, surely?

Meggy shook her head earnestly, as solemn as an owl. 'Oh, no, miss, begging your pardon . . . she can't abide Mr Boxer, our Dora can't . . . won't let anyone go near her. I think she be adying, the way she's howling and carrying on.'

Crossly, Sally started to dress. 'Where is the wretched girl?' She hardly knew Dora. She was not one of the maidservants. Sally had seen her a few times in the village. Pretty face, sluttish appearance, a bold air. That was Dora, quite unlike the dim-witted Meggy.

Meggy crept into the room, eyes averted as Sally divested herself of night attire and put on her chemise, stockings, petticoat and long brown dress. 'She's in that cottage, down by the mill, what she shares with her friend Polly.'

'Why isn't she at home with her parents?' Sally asked, rolling up her thick, straight fair hair and pinning it into a coil at the nape of her neck.

'Pa's kicked her out, miss. She's a bad 'un, so they say. Won't have nothing to do with her.'

This is the price I have to pay for appearing to be so practical, sensible and independent, Sally thought as she filled her basket with jars of salves and bottles from the medicine chest. In fact, were I truly as sensible as people believe, I'd be devious enough to adopt that air of delicate, refined silliness which is so much admired in young ladies. It must be nice to be lovely, helpless and socially acceptable, loudly declaiming that my sole aim in life is to comfort and flatter the self-esteem of men. No one would dream of disturbing me in the dead of night to attend a sick peasant.

She flung her hooded cloak over her shoulders, tying the strings beneath her chin and then giving a final glance around the room to make certain that the fire was safely guarded and no candles left burning. It was a pleasant room with a four-poster bed which she wished she now occupied, deep chairs, a fine dressing-table and a writing-desk. Most comfortably carpeted and curtained, and panelled in dark, rich oak. Not too ornate and not too plain, most suitable for a twenty-four-year-old spinster who was neither quite a governess nor yet one of the family. Sally had becomed hardened to her unqualified position.

She and Meggy stood in the passageway like conspirators. The house was completely silent, except for the longcase clock ticking on the landing. 'We'll go out through the kitchen,' Sally said, 'and we must make no noise.' She did not want the fuss and bother of the watchman charging after them with his blunderbuss, mistaking them for prowlers.

They sped along shadowed corridors and down the wide, curving staircase. Sally had equipped herself with a lantern and its yellowish, uncertain beam played over the features of Beaumaris ancestors captured for posterity on canvases in carved, gilded frames. Those blank, painted, long-dead eyes appeared to follow her. She addressed them mentally as she hurried by. 'Don't look down your proud Wylde noses at me! You are my forebears too, you know.'

In the canopied stone fireplace in the Great Hall, the logs collapsed in a shower of sparks, the ruddy glow reflected in the armour, the shields and crossed pikes adorning the walls. Between them, the tapestries seemed alive, allegorical figures in swirling draperies set in a background of ruined temples and writhing foliage. Meggy gasped with fright as the fire died to sullen embers. The lantern did little to chase away the shadows as they went down the long, stone-flagged passage leading to the kitchen. Sally marched ahead, with Meggy scuttling behind, making for the scullery and the outhouse beyond, finally reaching the yard. The moon, a lopsided orb, hung in the indigo sky. Somewhere an owl screeched.

'Oh, miss, we must hurry,' Meggy whispered, terrified. 'There be bogles and witches abroad at this time of night.'

'I don't want to hear such rubbish,' Sally declared, stepping out firmly, pretending a confidence she was far from feeling. Old customs and superstitions held sway in that part of the country, and she had been brought up to believe in them, despite the logic she struggled to bring to bear. 'Where is the cottage?'

'It's near Old Scratch Mill,' Meggy breathed, a catch in her voice. 'I came through the village and we can go back that way.'

'But isn't there a short-cut?'

'Yes, miss, but we daren't use it. 'Tis bad enough in broad daylight – but after dark! Lor', miss – you surely won't take Skenkzies Lane!'

Sally was perfectly familiar with the legends attached to the spot. Picturesque though it was, a deep winding cut leading to where the stream raced and the mill-wheel churned, it yet maintained a gloomy air, even when the sun shone. Nightfall rendered it particularly dark and it was held in awe. There were stories of evil spirits lurking for the rash traveller.

Resolutely, Sally turned her steps towards it. 'Come along, Meggy.'

Meggy stopped dead. 'No, miss. I can't.'

Sally walked on, taking no notice. 'Your sister is ill. Have you forgotten? You said we must make all haste.'

Footsteps pattered behind her. Meggy was between the devil and the deep, frightened to go on yet scared to be left there alone. 'I dunno, miss,' she grumbled. 'We be taking our lives in our hands, and more than that – our souls too. Not that it matters to you – you aren't afeared of nothing or nobody.'

Ah, if that were only so, thought Sally ruefully. She did not fear the dead, only the living with their malice, their thoughtlessness. The manor house was behind them now, and they skirted a copse. Meggy was clutching nervously at Sally's cloak, and the moon kept disappearing, blanketed by heavy, drifting clouds which caused a fleeting confusion of light and shade as they sailed across.

17

Two fields had to be negotiated, and Sally kept close to the hedge. Brambles caught at her and the ground was uneven with stones and stubble. Through a gate, down a pathway which sloped sharply. Meggy was hanging back, whimpering. The black mouth of Skenkzies Lane yawned just ahead. The darkness looked solid. Sally felt sure that if she put out a hand, she would meet the resistance of a thick, invisible barrier. Pulling the trembling Meggy along with her, she advanced into the tunnel. The shadows parted to let them through, then closed again at their backs. Branches creaked over their heads. Leaves shivered and rustled, and the wind made a soft keening, gusting up from below.

With a mighty effort, Sally fought the panic which was threatening to swamp reason, but her pace quickened, feet slipping on muddied ruts. They were nearly at the bottom. She could hear the brook rushing, wild and menacing. It awakened a medley of other loud, ominous noises – whistling and booming and thudding, above, below and on every side.

The impetus of headlong flight brought her to the clearing beyond, but still she ran until the lane was far behind. She paused for a second, out of breath and with a madly pounding heart. Meggy collided with her, incoherent with terror. It took a while to calm her, and then they commenced following the course of the stream, coming to a break in the trees where, on the further bank, the mill itself could be seen. The moonlight, sharp as a blade, cut across it – the revolving wheel, the frothing water, the dark bulk of the house with a solitary light in a lower window.

In her eagerness to leave that haunted spot, Meggy was now in the lead, looking back as Sally hesitated. 'Miss – miss! Do come on!'

The masses of driving cloud hid the moon again. Sally's lamp had little effect in the darkness, but she was comforted to have it in her hand, for there was a chill sense of loneliness which gripped her heart and sent shivers through her. She was about to follow Meggy when she saw a movement in the mill garden. It was a figure, a dim white figure. At that instant a ray of moonlight penetrated the clouds, showing in startling prominence a woman darting furtively towards the building.

''Tis a witch!' A voice at her shoulder made Sally jump, but it was only Meggy.

'Don't be silly!' She could hear the hysterical sharpness in her response. 'That's only Mrs Smithers.'

'Same thing,' retorted Meggy, forgetting respect in this fraught moment.

Sally thought it much more likely that the notorious Mrs Smithers was involved in the smuggling activities of the area rather than black magic, but she said nothing and they went on their way. Soon the cottage came into view. It was tiny, little more than a tumbledown shack, set apart from the village like a leper's lair. A few mean boards held it together and turves formed the roof. A blood-chilling sound came from within, resembling the crying of a wild animal.

' 'Tis Dora,' sobbed Meggy. 'She's been hollering like that for hours.'

Visions of some dread infection – smallpox perhaps, even the plague, floated behind Sally's eyes. She had been a fool to come. The children – no harm must come to Guy's children! 'What ails her, Meggy?'

'Don't rightly know, miss – she's got these awful pains in her belly.' Meggy was heaving at the door which hung awkwardly from one broken hinge.

It was pitch-black inside. The lantern light did not find its way into the corners. Sally stumbled towards something writhing and moaning on a heap of rags. She tripped, stubbing her toe on some unseen, knobbly obstruction, giving vent to an unladylike curse. 'Damn it, Meggy, is there no fire here? The place is like an ice-box.'

She held the lantern high, the wick wavering and then growing steady. Fury raged through her. No person, no matter how debased, should be forced to live in such conditions, let alone be ill there. Dora lay humped on a filthy blanket, knees drawn up. Her cries had now dwindled to a monotonous, complaining: 'Ah – ah – ah –' She was squirming and clutching at her hair.

Meggy crouched by the blackened hearth, attempting to breathe life into the miserably few faggots. She had taken the flint and tinderbox from Sally's basket, and managed to coax a spark at last. Sally leaned over Dora and tried to push aside a strand of dark, greasy hair which was plastered over her open mouth. 'What is the matter? Have you been sick? Are you hot and feverish?'

Dora did not answer, turning her face to the wall. Sally took her by the shoulder, pulling her over on to her back, and then she knew. Dora's belly was grotesquely distended. Sally shrank from the task ahead. She had never witnessed childbirth.

She rounded on Meggy furiously. 'Why didn't you tell me she was in labour?'

Those wide, silly eyes were alarmed, the mouth open in shock. 'Labour? A babby, d'you mean? I didn't know, miss – I swear I didn't. She never said. She's been hiding here for weeks now.'

Exasperated by her stupidity, Sally took off her cloak, rolled up her sleeves and unpacked her basket, setting the contents on the earth floor. What she had brought would be of little use, except for some clean linen and a pair of scissors. 'Where is her friend – this Polly person?'

'Saw her go in the Barley Mow earlier, miss. I 'spect she went off with one of the lads. She's no good neither, gets drunk and lets any man who wills take her to the woods,' pronounced Meggy with prim disapproval.

'Don't stand there gawking like a barnyard goose! Run for Mother Trat, the midwife!' Sally shook out her apron and tied it round her waist. The fire was burning but there was very little wood. 'Stir yourself, Meggy, and you can collect some logs too.'

Meggy's mouth set mulishly. 'Mother Trat won't come to the likes of her,' she said with relish. 'None of the village folk'll come nigh her. Quite right too, the dirty slut!'

'Shut your spiteful mouth, Meggy!' Dora shouted, glaring at her and adding a stream of colourful abuse which ended in a howl of pain.

'Easy – easy, Dora.' Sally tried to make her lie back, but she persisted in propping herself up on her elbow, filthy oaths snarling from between her lips.

'Shame on you, our Dora,' Meggy reproved with a triumphant smirk. 'Don't you talk like that in front of Miss Anstey. Bless me, I can't understand why such a sweet lady is bothering with a sinner like you, be blowed if I can. Just you be civil to her, d'you hear?'

'Mother! I want my mother,' wept Dora, threshing from side to side in her agony.

'Pa's forbidden her to come to you, and now I knows why,' brayed Meggy, supremely happy at her sister's distress. 'If I'd knowed you was having a bastard, I'd not have troubled Miss Anstey. You could've died and rotted here for all I'd have cared – so there!'

'Be quiet, Meggy!' Sally vented her worried concern on the girl. What a heartless little beast! She sounded just like Cecily goading Barbara in the nursery of Wylde Court. 'Go and find some firewood at once!'

Meggy flounced out, wearing an air of saintly martyrdom. Dora gripped Sally's hand, making her wince under the fierce pressure. 'You won't let me die, will you, miss?' she implored. 'Nor my babby . . .'

Dora's eyes were desperate, set in dark, crêpey circles, her haggard face running with sweat. She could not have been more than sixteen but looked like an old, terrified woman. 'Of course I won't, Dora. Try to be calm,' she said, dipping a cloth in a chipped crock filled with rain-water and applying it to Dora's cheeks and brow.

She had never felt more helpless, and had no idea what to do. Well-bred unmarried ladies were not supposed to understand the basic facts of life, shielded until they were safely wed. Sally had always suspected this to be utter folly, and never more so than now. Fortunately, she had spent more time in the kitchen with the servants than would have been permitted had she been a daughter of the house, so was not entirely ignorant, but: 'Dora, do you know what we must do?' she asked, on her knees by the girl.

Dora gave a wry laugh. 'Oh, dear me – I might have guessed – you be too genteel for this job, miss. I'll wager that you don't even know for sure how a babby gets in there, leave alone how it comes out, eh? Poor Miss Anstey, I feels sorry for you. Never you mind. Don't fret. We'll manage fine.'

They exchanged a long look in the dim glow of lantern and firelight. A strange, guarded exploration of each other. There was nothing they could take for granted, no common experiences to share, women from different walks of life, as far removed as if they were denizens of alien planets. Yet Sally recognized a kindred loneliness, and although there was no solid foundation on which to build friendship, she wanted this to happen. She was filled with an overpowering determination that Dora and her child should survive the ordeal ahead.

It was a harrowing night, for the baby was a long time coming. Meggy was no help, though she did keep the fire blazing. When the actual moment of birth took place, it was as if Sally shared Dora's agony, finding a kind of frenzied exaltation in this primitive act where nature took over, magnificently cutting across all barriers of class, custom and behaviour. Dora squatted on her haunches, her back pressed against the wall, the hut resounding with her throaty grunts of expulsion. Sally, on her knees before Dora's spread thighs, received the wet, wrinkled head of the child in her hands. The body slithered after it, and she held him, red, squalling, his minute fists beating at the air in protest at being thrust out into the cold world.

Dora lay back, exhausted, her voice husky as she demanded: 'Give him to me.'

Sally obeyed her, laying him in her arms, covering them both with Meggy's shawl. Dora was transformed. She sat there rocking her infant, a beatific expression on her face – no longer Dora the Slut – now Dora the Mother.

Meggy was strutting around, taking the credit. 'There now, Dora – what a fuss! Wasn't as bad as all that, was it?'

Dora smiled. 'Not for you.'

'And you got a lovely little boy.' Meggy ignored her sister's sarcasm, poking a finger into the child's tiny hand.

'Your nephew,' reminded Dora drily.

Meggy frowned. 'I don't know about that. He's a bastard. Do that make him my kin?'

''Course it do, chicken-brain – that don't make no odds.'

Sally was wide awake, although she felt as if there was grit under her eyelids. She had just come through a shattering experience. A miracle had happened in that crude shack, the miracle of life renewed. Till now its true significance had never touched her, this event which took place at every moment of each day, somewhere on the earth. Babies were usually delivered in the privacy of bedchambers where the midwife held sway and were only presented in public when they had been washed and swaddled and generally civilized, looking as if the stork had brought them or they had been found, pink and perfect, under a gooseberry-bush.

The harsh reality had been an extraordinary revelation. Sally had acted almost by instinct, assisted by the race-memory of woman, heedless of the mess, the blood which had smeared her hands. Now she wanted to wash Dora and her baby but there was no water.

'Oh, my dear, this is a sorry place,' she said, shaking her head as she attempted to make Dora more comfortable with the limited resources to hand.

''Tis well enough.' Dora was smiling widely. No queen could have been more content. 'I've got my little 'un, that's all that matters. Thank you, miss, for all you've done for us.'

22

Humbled by such stoical acceptance of a wretched lot, Sally exclaimed: 'You can't stay here! Where is the child's father?'

Meggy gave an indignant snort, jealous of the attention being lavished on her sister, and from one of the gentry too! 'Reckon she don't know who he is. I've seen her with this fellow and that – dirty, she is, real dirty!'

'You're a bloody liar!' Dora was like a tigress defending its young. 'I know who the father is right enough.'

'Then let me fetch him,' begged Sally. 'Who is it? One of the farm hands? Tell me, Dora, so that he may accept his responsibility.'

'No, miss.'

'But, Dora – you must,' Sally insisted, and the argument continued as she took the baby and laid him on a piece of clean cloth while she prepared to sever the natal cord.

Dora was reluctant to let him go, even for a moment, watching anxiously, holding one small fist in hers. 'I can't tell you, miss. I promised. It isn't a farm boy, but I'll never breathe a word to no one – wouldn't be right and proper. I won't bring disgrace on him.'

'But what are you going to do?' Sally tied the cord in two places with a bit of twine and then cut between them with her scissors, binding a wide strip of linen round the baby's stomach. With a look of disgust, Meggy threw the afterbirth on the fire. Dora had nothing prepared. There were no baby garments, so Sally folded him in a blanket and carried him closer to the lantern.

'She'll be turned out of the village,' Meggy said in a pious, irritating voice. 'The parish won't support her brat.'

Sally did not answer, as she stared down into that newborn little face. He was quiet now, looking about him, his eyes drawn to the light. Sally drew in a sharp breath. Was it weariness, the flickering lamp, her own imagination which caused her to see something familiar in those infant features? It was reflected in Guy's daughters, and in every member of the family – strong, unmistakable – that nose, that crest of hair – an indefinable air which marked them as Wyldes.

Sally's heart sank. No wonder Dora was not prepared to speak. Someone was insisting that she hold her tongue. Someone powerful. She listed the possible suspects, mentally crossing them off as they paraded before her mind's eye. Not William, that plain-spoken, open-hearted friend, on whom she had always relied. Could it be Denzil? She knew that he was a flirt, but had been away at university and, when home, his time was dominated by his mother. Maybe Jack was the culprit, but she doubted such secrecy if he were to blame. He would have gone about openly boasting of yet another conquest. That left only Guy, and she knew him to be quite capable of such behaviour, yet why should he stoop to take a village drab when there were so many beautiful, highborn ladies clamouring to share his bed? Pain lanced her, as sharp as Dora's birth-pangs. It was as if she was bleeding to death inside.

In a sort of sick stupor, she came to a decision. 'Dora, I forbid you to stay here. You must come back with me to Wylde Court.'

'Oh, I couldn't, miss.' Dora was appalled at such a suggestion.

'You can. You will.' With the child held in one arm, Sally repacked the basket with her free hand, giving brisk orders to Meggy. 'Stay here with your sister while I go for the gig. There are a hundred rooms in the manor, Dora. I'll arrange matters with Miss Potter. You will be quite safe.'

'Please don't trouble yourself on my account, miss. You've done enough. Let me bide.'

'It wouldn't be healthy for the baby.' Sally settled the discussion once and for all. 'He must be somewhere clean and warm.'

'Well, if that's the case, then I'll do it,' Dora conceded reluctantly. 'Forget the gig. I can walk. Having a babby isn't an illness. I feel as fit as a flea, honest I do.' She was already struggling to her feet.

Sally had grave misgivings for Dora was swaying weakly, but she was afraid to leave her. Meggy could not be trusted to see that her sister did not slip away and hide whilst she was gone. Outside it was chilly, that damp, dark chill which precedes dawn. Quiet, so very quiet, as if the world waited, holding its breath for the arrival of the sun. That awesome feeling pervaded the three women as they hurried in the direction of the manor. Meggy became quite hysterical when Sally mentioned the short-cut and, indeed, she herself had no liking for the lane so with Dora's stout assertion that she could walk the extra distance, they took the path leading to the beach.

In that dim half light, everything was grey – grey sand, grey rocks, grey sky, save for a pink pearling in the east which gradually spread over the grey sea. It broke over the boulders, its roar muffled by the sea-mist drifting like smoke. The horizon did not exist in its trailing shrouds. The village was deserted.

No one was about yet, though smoke spiralled from one or two chimneys of the white-walled, thatched cottages. The cobbled street was steep, rising from the quay and beyond it was the hill road winding up to Wylde Court. The sun was coming up. Its light no more than grazed the world, gilding the crests of distant hills, picking out litle except the tallest trees from the hollows between them. Wisps of watery vapour hung everywhere.

Sally was bone-weary, walking as if in a dream, feeling the weight of the baby nestled close to her breast under her cloak. Another Beaumaris child given into her care. Was this to be her destiny? she wondered. This caring for children who were not her own? Guy's children. Even this little scrap of humanity – if it was Guy's. As always, bracing herself against the worst, she did not doubt it. How could he do it? It was an act of despicable irresponsibility. Yet even as she raged against him, she was already shaping excuses for him in her mind, as she always did – always would.

March had gone, with its brisk winds, greening buds and landscapes dappled with sunshine and moving cloud. Now it was April and on the slopes of the downs around Wylde Court, the fresh young green of the grass was starred with daisies, and along the lower hedges the tender blades were being attacked by hundreds of birds caught up in the frenzy of nest-building. Chaffinches sang in the fruit trees in the orchards at the rear of the kitchen garden. The banks were scented with clustering primroses.

Sally sniffed this perfume with a tingle of pleasure. She had made good her escape from the house by offering to fetch some of last year's apples from the big shed where they were stored on racks. She was almost running in her eagerness to get there, excited by the feel of the object in her pocket. It was as important to her as a holy relic and, very soon, she would be able to take it out and look at it, then play her secret game.

She had awakened that morning with spring-fever in her blood, firing her longings, making her restless as if waiting for chains to be removed, blown away by the wind or rusted by the rains. Dear God, there must be some change which would open the way to liberty and happiness? She had the urge to run far away from her duties, to seek out the wild, woodland creatures and ramble, day after day, forgetting Wylde Court, and herself.

She had risen and put on a lilac, flower-patterned dress of fine wool, the long skirt falling from a high waistline, and a lace fichu partly covering the deep oval of the neck. She had taken a final glance in the pier-glass and had been held by her sedate reflection. How well I conceal it, she had thought, this churning feeling which is making the sunny room throb. No one would suspect. No one must! Her excitement had been increasing by the second but she did not let it show.

There she had stood, the perfect picture of an impoverished relative who had been given shelter by the family and later become the governess of Guy's three daughters. Little did they know – little suspect that this stillness, this air of aloofness, had been carefully cultivated. Sally was not a conventional beauty, and there was a remoteness about her which frightened off most men, yet she was a striking girl. Small, slender, with large brown eyes and corn-coloured hair drawn back into a chignon, a severe style which was unflattering. Not for long, she had promised herself, soon, soon, I'll let it fall free – as soon as I reach the apple-loft.

It was quite hot in the orchard. Sally could feel that heat running through her, matching the pulsing of her blood. There were silvery fruit buds on the trees and new shoots showing amongst the long, yellowish tufts of wet grass. Sally shot a glance over her shoulder. All was well. The children had not followed her. Dora was keeping an eye on them – Dora, who understood her. Thank God for that at least. Love them Sally might, but they were demanding little tyrants and her life had been devoted to them since their mother died. Ah, had they only been hers – and Guy's. All she could do was love them because he was their father.

It would have been better for her had she been able to marry. She was now past the age when suitors came courting, and her spinsterhood was partly her fault. She had done nothing to encourage them, too aware that she had little to offer, no title, no dowry, no outstanding beauty, and must be eternally in the debt of the Wyldes for giving her a home. Her mother, old Lord Mark Beaumaris's half-sister, had committed the cardinal sin of marrying for love, running away with a penniless young lawyer. She was disowned for her folly, but when Sally had been left an orphan, her uncle had taken pity on her. She had been brought up with his own sons, and later filled an odd niche in the establishment, a general dog's-body.

And Guy hardly knows I'm here, she mused, her flat-heeled pumps making no sound on the gravelled path between the gnarled trees. I'm like a piece of furniture or a comfortable old coat. He probably thinks I have no opinions, no feelings – so accustomed to my presence, but at least he trusts me with his daughters.

With a quick glance round to make certain that she was unobserved, she slipped into the shed, making her way between the clutter of garden tools, glinting chains and wooden crates. It was intensely quiet, not a bird chirruped within earshot. With anticipation shivering through her, Sally climbed the rickety ladder to the loft. There was a heap of hay in one corner and she flung herself down on it. For a moment she sat erect, making sure that she was alone. The scent of hay was intoxicating, reminding her of what was to come for she had been there many times in the past. Somehow, what she was about to do was impossible in the house. There she assumed one personality, the woman of sound common sense, the practical helper – here, she became someone else, a dreamer, an abandoned creature allowing herself full rein to dwell on things far removed from her normal existence, wild things, vivid images which set her aflame.

She lifted her arms and pulled out the pins. Her hair took on a life of its own, uncoiling like a sensuous animal, flowing over her shoulders in a straight, shining curtain of gold. She shook her head, rejoicing in this freedom, remembering Miranda's words whenever the child saw her brushing it. 'You look like a princess with your hair down, Sally. Why don't you always have it like that?'

With reverent fingers she felt in her pocket, pulling out a large handkerchief, unfolding it lovingly, carefully, spreading out the creases. It was of the finest, most delicately woven white linen, trimmed with point lace, embroidered with the initials G.W. twining in one corner. Inside it lay a miniature of its owner, skilfully executed, set in a gold filigree frame. Sally held it up, studying it closely, her face rapt as she gloated on each angle of that painted face, treasuring it, caressing it with her fingertips. The artist had been faithful in his reproduction and it was Guy to the life, so handsome with that faintly mocking amusement in the green eyes which seemed to be looking directly at her. A sardonic smile played over his beautiful mouth, doing nothing to soften those arrogant features with the pronounced cheekbones, strong nose, and the deep cleft in the square chin. A lock of black hair curled over his brow, the rest waving over his well-shaped head.

Slowly, Sally lifted the locket to her lips, pressing them to the portrait, eyes half closed, a sweet languor stealing through her. The handkerchief had been soiled when she had taken it months before, and the faint perfume of musk, a trace of snuff, a hint of masculine sweat still lingered on it. This powerful combination seemed to break in a fiery foam of sensuality over her mind. Without a moment's hesitation, she had stolen the miniature too. Lady Charlotte had hunted for it for a while and then forgotten it. She did not like Guy much, so was hardly likely to mourn such a loss.

Sally's hands moved to her bodice, her fingers shaking as she unbuttoned the front, slipping the locket inside against her warm, firm breasts. As if in a trance, she felt it burning there, dreaming of him, images crowding in, and in this fevered state it seemed that Guy was making love to her. The sensations became more acute, culminating in an ache between her thighs. In her extremity, all thoughts of prudence had fled before the overwhelming current. She lay back on the hay, unable to express, even in thought, what was happening to her. Her movements seemed guided by someone other than herself. All the while it was as if Guy was with her, caressing her, handling her body till passion spilled over, a sweet suffocating anguish where everything bloomed magically for a split second, each corner of her being filled with a blinding explosion of light and heat.

She gasped, then slumped absolutely still, one arm thrown over her eyes, while the waves of feeling receded. At length she came back from that dream-world, awakening to see the dust motes dancing above, aware of the prickle of straw against her legs. She pulled down her skirt, calm and spent, resting there for a while before allowing everyday thoughts to intrude. 'Oh, Guy – Guy,' she whispered.

He had been a dashing young man of twenty when she was brought to Wylde Court, the family seat of the Lord of Beaumaris Combe. His brothers, William and Denzil, had been seventeen and eleven respectively. A girl in the house was a strange phenomenon, though they had sometimes been visited by various female cousins. They had teased her, those indulged Beaumaris brothers, heirs to a vast kingdom acquired by their Norman forebears who, once in England, had begun a ruthless appropriation of land from the rugged coast of Dorset to the chalky Wiltshire downs. Those fierce, haughty conquerors had made themselves masters of the sheep-farming communities, the weaving industries, the grazing and arable lands, shifting loyalties from one monarch to the next, conniving, murdering and plundering in the process. The family had long since become respectable, but they were proud of their freebooting ancestors, particularly Guy who relished power, wealth and authority.

Sally had seen little of him when a child. He had been a remote, fascinating figure who returned home infrequently yet set all afire with the excitement of his coming. On the death of his father, he became Lord Beaumaris, but this made scant difference to his life-style. He left the management of his estate to Boxer and William, who would have been quite happy to have been born a gentleman-farmer. Neither did he tame his wild ways by his marriage to Celeste Rotherly, a marriage of convenience, naturally. Sally had gained a scrap of comfort in realizing that it was no love match, purely a matter of money and property as was the custom. It had helped to numb the raw ache in her heart when she saw him with his pretty, vapid bride and to endure the torture when their children were born. She had been deeply shocked and ashamed by the rush of hope which had swept her when Celeste died in childbed; she spent hours on her knees, praying that God would forgive her for such wickedness. That was years ago. She no longer prayed at all, her faith corroded by countless disappointments.

Sally had no illusions about Guy Wylde, Lord Beaumaris. He was not really worth languishing over, so domineering and arrogant, and he had treated poor Celeste abominably. Yet there was something about him which roused Sally's compassion, this man who had everything. Perhaps that was the trouble. He had too much, leaving him nothing for which to strive, no goals save drifting from one magnificent establishment to another, from one lovely woman's bed to the warm welcome of the next, his life an endless round of pleasure, or so it seemed to her as she watched and listened as time went by.

Sally stood up, brushed bits of straw from her clothing and took a mirror from her drawstring bag. She peered into it. There was a touch of pink on her cheeks, a hint of something different about her eyes. Hopefully, she would not meet anyone on her way back to her room. She was calmer now, once more the demure relative on whom they relied, never guessing that in her daydreams, she was as shameless as any of the women whom Guy took, then casually cast aside.

Long ago, she had vowed that even were he to beckon her with his cold, mocking smile, she would never be his. He should never know of her secret game and the part he played in it. Never. The hot blood ran up into her face as she visualized him discovering her as she had been but a short time ago, lying there in wanton abandon. At the same time, the flashing image of his tall, muscular body and those compelling eyes watching her thus, sent a quiver of desire running along her nerves.

This was horrible. She pulled herself together sharply, scrambled down the ladder and picked up a trug, bundling in some apples to justify her visit there. No longer content, she longed to see him. And what then? she jeered at her foolish self. What will you do? Go against your principles? Run to his arms like the others? She wanted to – oh, how much she wanted that, but controlled this rampant longing, feeling disgust, as if caught in treachery, in shameful betrayal, looking into herself and finding loathsome weakness and corruption.

She was unwilling to take up the yoke so soon after the sensual release of the loft and her feet dragged as she returned. Wylde Court lay dozing under the warm sunshine, as it had done for centuries. It had begun as a turreted castle and was still surrounded by a moat, reached from the road by a double-arched bridge and ivy-covered gatehouse. The towers remained though the house had undergone changes, steeped in history. From a medieval dwelling, it had been embellished with the ornate comfort of the Tudors. Its Elizabethan owner had added wings; his Cavalier grandson had defended it against the Roundheads in 1645; in the middle of the present century, Mark Wylde had come back from his Grand Tour of Europe with a portfolio of sketches. Fired by the beautiful baroque architecture of France and the Doric columns of Italy, he had been unable to rest till some of this opulence had been incorporated in his manor house.

These alterations had not detracted from its grandeur, rather they had enhanced it and it had now mellowed into a delightful whole. The grounds were impressive, landscaped by Lord Mark's imported gardeners forty years before. A lake had come into being, complete with a mock-Grecian temple on its bank, a capital spot for picnics and late-night summer parties. There was a sunken grotto, complete with gushing spring and a waterfall, ruled over by a mighty bronze Titan, attended by nubile mermaids.

Sally loved every inch of it, admiring it afresh as she passed through the kitchen-garden where the newly-dug earth was ready for planting, and came to the area behind the stables. It was enclosed by stiff, clipped yews and fragrant borders, rioting with daffodils, tulips and narcissi. She paused, wondering whether to gather an armful for Lady Charlotte, but then baulked at the thought of having to spend a tedious hour with her, and continued along the path which led into the yard.

William was just coming out of the back door and her heart flipped over for an instant. He resembled his elder brother, and from that distance she had imagined – had thought – but as he waved and came closer she knew that she had been mistaken. It was true that they shared the same over-pronounced good looks, but in William every feature had been softened, his manner gentle, not overbearing, and he lacked that inner fire which roared through Guy's every action. He was thinner and not quite so tall; his hair was dark brown, not raven-black, and brushed back from his fine brow. Because he spent the majority of his time in the country, his clothing was simple and service-able. He wore a bottle-green tailed coat over a plain, dark waistcoat and his cravat was innocent of lace trimming. His muddied beige breeches and top-boots indicated that he had spent the morning riding round the farms, visiting the tenants.

His thoughtful hazel eyes lit up and he smiled widely, his hands outstretched towards Sally. 'At last! I've been searching everywhere for you.'

'What is it, William?' She disengaged her fingers from his and scanned his face anxiously. 'Has something happened to one of the children? Is Miranda missing again?' An uprush of guilt swept through her. Guy would never forgive her if –

He grinned reassuringly and shook his head. 'No. Nothing like that. Why do you always assume the worst? You'll go quite grey with worry one of these days and what a pity that would be.' His eyes were warm as they regarded her, filled with an intensity of feeling which disconcerted her. She cursed her own perversity. Here was a most personable man who showed, in a hundred little ways, that he was most fond of her. Yet, in all honesty, she could not bring herself to encourage him, hanker-ing after the unattainable.

'Why this urgency?' she asked. His answer had relieved her of one panic, but now she was plunged into something very akin to it as he said:

'It is good news. I've had a letter from Guy. He is on his way home.'

Always, that tremor when his name was mentioned, like tiny shocks under the surface of her skin. Her heart skipped a beat, then raced on again. Everything spun dizzily, the yard, the enormous canopied well, the fussy hens, the tabby cat snoozing on the wall. Sally took a deep breath and the scene righted itself.

'When will he be here?' she said and, to her astonishment, her voice was steady.

William was excited, tossing his hat into the air and catching it as he exclaimed: 'The day after tomorrow! The letter was sent from London yesterday. Lord, won't it be fine to see him again! It's nigh on eight months since he left.'

Eight months. An eternity, thought Sally, but she was used to holding herself rigid, of giving away nothing. 'You did well to find me.' She sounded crisp, efficient. 'There will be beds to air, rooms to clean, food to prepare. Have you instructed Mr Boxer and Miss Potter? Is he coming alone or will he be bringing guests?'

William laughed with sheer joy at the prospect of seeing his brother. 'He did mention one visitor, but you know Guy – if the fancy takes him, he'll bring a dozen.'

Yes, she knew Guy. Inconstant, mobile, never at peace. He might appear in a sombre mood, so dark and tormented that he would storm off to his own apartments and they would see nothing more of him for days. On the other hand, he was quite likely to drive up with a flourish, accompanied by coachloads of raffish companions. Nobly born but undesirable people, calculated to deeply offend Lady Charlotte so that she kept to her own wing, while they drank and gambled and turned night into day with their roistering.

'Did he say who this visitor was?' Sally girded herself for battle. Miss Potter would be most put out by such short notice.

William linked his arm with hers as they walked towards the door, looking down at her with that admiring attentiveness which was a comfort and an embarrassment combined. 'He wrote that he was bringing an important person to meet us, and that we must ensure the very finest of the guestrooms is prepared.'

Chapter 2

The Master is coming! The news spread like a forest fire. Wylde Court shook itself and woke into life. No one had been busier than Sally. She was not quite certain how it had come about but, over the years, more and more responsibility had been put upon her. Now she had to liaise between the steward and the housekeeper, and also keep Lady Charlotte well informed.

On the eve of the expected arrival, she went to the kitchen for a final inspection. It was bustling and alive, ruddy with the glow of the fire roaring in its massive alcove, the pumping heart of the place where the cook and his assistants slaved. A lad was employed to do nothing but ensure that the huge logs were kept burning night and day. A six-foot spit spanned the flames, and there was a side of beef roasting on it, a pan below to catch the fat, a mouth-watering smell arising from the slowly revolving meat. Gleaming copper pans hung on the white-washed walls, and there was an immense dresser on which polished pewter and crockery were displayed. Bunches of herbs and strings of onions were slung from the great gnarled oak beams, and sides of bacon wearing netting shrouds were dimly visible in the mystery of the smoke-blackened ceiling.

Her Ladyship was at dinner with her sons, and those waiting at table hurried in and out, bearing loaded trays of delicacies or staggering under the burden of empty platters. Boxer kept a sternly critical eye on them, sparing none the lash of his tongue. The men wore blue coats and breeches trimmed with yellow serge; the women dark blue dresses, short enough to be practical with the skirts finishing at the ankle, showing black buckled shoes. Their bodices had three-quarter-length sleeves with white cuffs and wide collars, and they were issued with generous aprons and linen caps.

Scullions fell upon the dirty dishes, humping them to the back where the task of washing-up was in progress. Sally knew that Lady Charlotte would scold her for being late for the meal, but she risked that to satisfy herself that all was in readiness. It was better thus – frenzied activity gave her no opportunity to think.

33

Those given pause from chores sat at a long trestle table, furnished with pewter mugs and plates. There was plenty of new wheaten bread and a steaming bowl of stew with a rich, gamey smell. Meggy was ladling this into dishes, whilst the others hacked off chunks of bread and pushed their mugs towards the man who was pouring from an earthenware jug. The ale frothed out, dark and pungent, and Sally accepted a tankard, sipping at the strong home brew. She found their friendly, unconcerned attitude towards her both flattering and upsetting. It sharply pinpointed the gulf between herself and the rest of the Wyldes.

There was a smaller table set a little apart, lit by candles instead of the humble rush and covered with a white cloth. The table-ware was finer, the food more selective, and Miss Potter presided over it. A lean woman with a stern, unsmiling coun- tenance, neatly dressed in black, the formidable doyen of still- room, pantry and linen-press, commander of the battalion of female servants. Boxer sat with her, along with William's and Denzil's valets. Sally smiled, knowing that these privileged employees considered themselves to be most important. They would not demean their rank by eating with the menials, and were giving her reproving glances as she quaffed her ale.

She was waiting for Boxer to finish his meal and address the assembled staff. He was a tower of strength, managing the entire estate, particularly concerned with the farm-labourers, gardeners and woodsmen. He had served Lord Mark faithfully, and had given his allegiance to his son on the old man's death. Though subservient to William, he was given the authority to engage, dismiss and control all who worked there. He ran the business affairs of the house, paid the wages, bought the liveries, kept the accounts and acted as Guy's deputy. Legal and contract work passed through his hands, and the wine- cellar was his special province.

At last he laid down his knife, rose to his feet and rapped on the table for silence. The chatter died away. Rows of expectant eyes turned to him. 'As you all know, Lord Beaumaris will be here on the morrow,' he began, a just man, upright and dignified, not one to be trifled with. 'We were given scant warning, but I trust that you will do your utmost to ensure that his Lordship will not be displeased.'

'He's bound to find something amiss – he always does,' came a voice from the settle near the fire. Several of the younger girls giggled, and Sally looked across at the owner of that drawling accent, guessing to whom it belonged. He always started dissension, motivated by the sheer love of mischief rather than malice.

He was lounging at his ease, booted feet propped on the andirons, a cocky, handsome rascal who had turned up at Wylde Court a couple of years before, after a long absence. Sally remembered him from childhood, though he had spent most of his time with his mother at Old Scratch Mill. Everyone thought them ideal tenants for the ramshackle, rundown place, for it was common knowledge that Old Scratch was another name for the devil. He had disappeared for a time, then suddenly returned without warning, riding boldly up to the main door of the manor, hammering on it with his whipstock and demanding entrance. No one had been able to find out what had transpired in the meeting between him and Guy Wylde, but it had shortly been announced that he was to be given the post of master of horse. He was put in charge of the stables, horses, carriages, dogs, cocks and hawks. The grooms, coachmen and stable-lads took their orders from him.

'Be quiet, Jack Smithers!' Boxer snapped. 'Get you about your duties, you idle good-for-nothing.'

'I shall take my time, for they'll be doubled once his Lordship arrives,' Jack laughed good-naturedly, sitting up and slipping an arm around the waist of the girl who was lingering in his vicinity.

He was impudent right enough, but Sally could not help liking him. A most attractive man, just under six foot tall and whiplash lean. He had clear grey eyes and auburn hair which coiled in tight rings to the high collar of his flashy jacket. There was a nonchalant air about him which was almost but not quite that of a member of the gentry, and that familiar stamp to his features which gave credence to the story that he was one of Lord Mark's bastards.

His charm did not impress Miss Potter. With skirts swishing and chatelaine rattling, she paced towards him, addressing the black-eyed wench who was imprisoned by his encircling arm. 'Bethany Wicker, get you upstairs to bed!'

'Oh, but, ma'am – 'tis too early,' Bethany protested, while Jack grinned and squeezed her waist. Sally had noticed the girl before. She went about her work well enough but with a total lack of humility, ever ready with a stinging retort if chided. There was something shifty about her eyes, a knowing smirk on her lips, and Sally had privately christened her 'Sly-boots'.

'How dare you argue!' Miss Potter was outraged. 'Off you go! The rest of you too!' Bethany opened her mouth to defy her, emboldened by Jack's attentions, but a sharp clip across the ear sent her running for the stairs with the others scurrying behind her like scared rabbits. Miss Potter dusted her hands together, glaring down at Jack. 'As for you – you'd best watch that saucy tongue!'

Jack cocked an eyebrow at her, then pretended to tremble. 'Oh, Miss Potter, did anyone ever tell you how magnificent you look when you're angry? Such fire, such eloquence! May I dare hope that you'll take your cane to my naked arse and beat me till I spend myself over your skirts in delicious agony!'

'For shame, Jack! To speak thus before a young lady!' Miss Potter's sallow cheeks now bore two crimson spots.

'Miss Anstey?' The grey eyes were watching her humorously, and then he lowered one lid in a wink. 'She don't mind. She's a good sort, not half as straight-laced as she looks, are you, miss? Wasn't it her who delivered Dora of her brat, when the rest of you God-fearing lot turned your bloody backs? Call yourselves Christians! A pox on you!' He spat on the floor to show his contempt, then took out his knife and cut off a thick, dripping slice of meat.

'You're a scoundrel – that you are!' Miss Potter stormed. 'Get your greedy hands off that beef. 'Tis for the Master's table. I wouldn't have you under this roof a minute longer, if it was up to me!'

'Well, it's not, so keep your long nose out of it.' Jack lifted a tankard to his lips, throwing back his head and taking deep swallows, his adam's apple bobbing.

The last thing Sally wanted was strife below stairs, so she said quietly: 'Please, Jack. Don't make trouble. We have still so much to do before he comes.'

Jack wiped the froth from his mouth with the back of his hand. 'Your wish is my command, duchess. You know I'd do anything for you. Hell, but I'm looking forward to seeing the old devil again. It'll liven the place up a bit. Dull as ditchwater when he's away. Perhaps he'll bring a good-looking doxy or two with him.'

She answered his grin with a smile. He had always treated her with a pleasing camaraderie, perhaps in sympathy with her unqualified status. He was as much an outsider as herself. But she could not deny that he was a trouble-maker, tough, resilient, violent-tempered when roused, yet with that charm which had been the undoing of more than one maidservant. He made no attempt to hide his faults and underneath his coarseness there was a streak of kindness. She suspected him of being a law-breaker, in league with his mother and her smuggling friends. He drank far too much and, in his cups, was truculent and aggressive. Though they had never discussed anything so profound, Sally knew that his illegitimacy galled him.

After dinner William Wylde retired to the study. It had once been his father's retreat where he could drink with his cronies undisturbed by annoying womenfolk. There was plentiful evidence of his interests. Hunting trophies adorned the walls, along with sporting paintings, weapons and similar paraphernalia. The room had remained much as it had been in Queen Elizabeth's day, panelled in golden oak, the ceiling edged by intricately carved cornices. There was an impressive fireplace, its huge wooden frame cleverly carved with images of the flora and fauna indigenous to the district. Thus squirrels peered out of tassels of pine-cones and rabbits from fronds of harts' tongues, heather and osmunda. Logs from the Wylde timberyards, cut into manageable lengths at the Wylde saw-mills, crackled between the brass dogs. The great latticed, mullioned windows faced out on velvet lawns bordered by oak and cedar trees. William had ordered the servants to leave the damask curtains drawn back. He went to a window and stared out into the darkness. Surely, there must be a signal soon?

He paced up and down, hands clasped behind his back. He could see the good sense behind Guy's dismissal to Morocco, but the responsibility had lain heavily on himself during his absence. He was determined that Denzil should be let into the secret. Guy must be made to realize that he was a stout-hearted fellow who would be of immense help. He knew that Guy had never had much time for the lad, and this was their mother's fault. The Dowager Lady Charlotte, their revered Mamma! William smiled grimly, alone there in that quiet, candle-shadowed room. Did she realize just how much harm her constant meddling had done? He thought that she probably did, the perverse, wilful martinet.

He took up the decanter and poured himself a glass of brandy, raising it to the candelabrum on the side-table, admiring its colour. The cellar was well stocked thanks to Captain Redvers, that swashbuckling old ex-pirate who livened his retirement by organizing the lawless smugglers of the Dorset coast. Self-appointed commander of these free-traders, he employed military tactics to outwit the customs men. The Wyldes had been aware of this for years, turning a blind eye to something which it was virtually impossible to prevent. The people were poor and smuggling improved their meagre incomes. Popular sympathy was always on their side; the government had difficulty manning the customs boats, for the men were drawn from the same class as the smugglers and indeed were often related to them. The contraband trade also offered much greater reward than the miserable pay on board a revenue cutter. So, without a qualm, the Wyldes had accepted gifts of silk, tobacco, tea and brandy, never questioning their source. But now Redvers and a crew of hand-picked, completely trustworthy men had joined Guy and William in an enterprise far more hazardous than the mere illegal trafficking of smuggled goods into the country.

William had organized it alone, since Guy went away, receiving his orders from a higher quarter. He would have liked to have taken Sally into his confidence, but had been forbidden by his brother who had stated sternly that the least people involved, the better it would be. It had been hard for William to read puzzlement in her brown eyes when he went away sometimes without giving an explanation, for he loved Sally deeply, an unexpressed devotion which had grown with the years.

She had been a shy, defensive little creature when his father had first brought her there, spitting at himself and his teasing brothers like a frightened kitten, claws out, fur fluffed up. William had been at university then, only at home during vacations, but somehow the funny child had turned into a young woman – still shy, still unaware of her own potential – and William had gradually become conscious of a joy in her company, a kind of glow experienced only in her presence. He had waited for some sign that she felt the same, but it never came. She treated him as she might have treated a beloved brother, no more, no less.

The ormolu clock on the overmantle struck a quarter to twelve. The house was silent, everyone in bed, except the watchman. William stood by the window, imagining that he saw a glimmer of light amongst the trees, then deciding that his eyes were deceiving him. He could hear the distant hiss and rumble of the sea, and wondered if the vessel rode at anchor just outside the breakers. Boats, loaded to the gunwales, might be passing to and fro between ship and shore. Men would be there on the beach of the sheltered cove to help with the cargo, passing it from hand to hand into the waiting wagons. There was no moon and this was good. Cool blue night dripped out of the clouds, shrouding their activities.

A sound behind him made him spin round, though he had been expecting it. With tingling nerves he strode to the fireplace, his fingers finding a certain ornamental leaf hidden among its carving. There was a soft click and a narrow door, cunningly contrived in the wall panelling, slid back. Cold damp air funnelled up from the black aperture beyond. Jack stepped out of it, muffled to the nose in a long black cloak with a hood pulled over his head. He carried a lantern in one hand.

'Thank God you've come!' exclaimed William, but keeping his voice down. 'Is he here?'

'Yes. All is well. Put your coat on, sir, it's bloody cold down there.'

William was already thrusting his arms into his greatcoat sleeves as Jack spoke, and they both went through the low doorway, sliding it shut behind them. A flight of steep stone steps wound down into blackness. The lantern light flickered over rough-hewn, greenish walls. The stairs twisted at a perilous angle, slippery with moss, but William knew them of old, aware of the danger. At the bottom an arched passage slanted off into even inkier gloom. What a find this had been, William thought as they hurried along, and how useful now. It seemed to echo with the voices of boys – Guy, Jack and himself in years gone by. Such games they had played there, unbeknown to anyone. It was obviously an escape route from the manor, built in the days of war, rebellion and religious persecution. In later life, William had wondered if his father had used it for clandestine meetings with Jack's mother, though the old man had never mentioned its existence. When they grew up, it had been forgotten, until recently.

The passage ended. They were facing a small wooden door which opened easily at Jack's push and they stepped out into the night, concealed amongst a cluster of huge, bramble-covered boulders, part of a long-barrow which ran alongside Skenkzies Lane.

It was but a matter of moments to cross the wooden plank over the gurgling stream, make through the mill garden and let themselves into the house. It was dim, warm and shabby in the kitchen, filled with Molly Smithers' collection of knick-knacks brought as gifts by seamen from every quarter of the globe. She was standing by the fire, talking to a huge, bearded man. Both looked across as William and Jack came in.

'Well met, your Honour!' bellowed the big man, seizing William's hand in a vice-like grip and pumping his arm up and down.

'Good to see you, Redvers,' William answered, managing not to wince. Captain Redvers seemed to fill the small room, standing spread-legged, a many caped cloak swirling about him, a large three-cornered hat covering his mane of grizzled, unkempt hair. A laughing, audacious ugly-handsome giant, the sort that women love and men take orders from. 'How are matters on the other side of the Channel?'

'Bad – hellish bad,' Redvers rumbled. 'Those Frenchies are as mad as Bedlamites. Never trust a Frenchie, say I. Had trouble with 'em in the Indies when I was in the "sweet-trade" – slippery as conger eels, and as vicious.'

'Has the war hindered your contacts?'

'Dammee, no!' Redvers grunted, laughter lines deeply indenting the weather-beaten skin at the sides of his shrewd eyes. 'Free-traders are only interested in cash and to the devil with their governments. They stick fast to their own brethren, be they black, white or yellow.'

'Did you see him? Have you anything for me?' The lamplight planed deep shadows on William's intent face.

Redvers took a step nearer. He brought with him a whiff of the night sea air, salt spume overlaid with a hint of gunpowder. When he moved, he left a trail of wet imprints on the stone floor. His sea-boots were saturated and the breeches above them. 'I did that, sir, though 'twern't easy. Bloody military swarming all over. He gave me this.' One massive hand disappeared momentarily into the maw of his double-breasted jacket. He brought out an oilskin-wrapped packet.

William took it and tore it open. He went to the table, leaning closer to the light and scanning the letter swiftly. Then he re-read it more thoroughly, committing the contents to memory before casting it into the fire.

'Hurry up with that grog, woman,' Redvers growled, slapping Molly playfully on the rump. 'I must be going.'

Molly ladled it into tankards from a pan steaming over the logs. 'You'll be back, won't you, Tom?' she asked, putting one into his fist. She was a handsome woman in her late forties, wearing a fine new shawl about her broad shoulders, her latest present from the captain. Jack took his colouring from her, that dark red hair which she had swept high and fastened with a jewelled comb, those fearless grey eyes.

' 'Course I'll be back. A man needs a bit of comfort after such a gruelling trip,' Redvers bellowed. 'Don't fret your bowels to fiddle-strings, my lass. Just keep the bed warm for me.'

'I have orders for you, Redvers,' William said, accepting the hot drink Molly offered. 'This time next week, you must have the *Mayfly* waiting outside Havre to take on a cargo.'

'The same as before – ?'

'Yes.'

'And the price?'

'A hundred guineas.'

'Done.' Redvers's broad palm met William's to settle the deal. 'Trust me, sir. My ship will be there. Now I'm off to the beach to hurry the lads on. Not safe to hang about.'

'There's a new coastguard in the neighbourhood,' warned William.

'So Molly tells me,' Redvers's teeth gleamed against his bushy dark beard, his hand coming to rest on the cutlass swinging at his hip. 'I'll wager he thinks he's God Almighty, but he has another think coming. Some of his men are in my pay.'

He clipped Molly around the waist and planted a smacking kiss on her lips, then the door crashed shut behind him. William lingered for a few moments, but there was nothing to keep him now, his work over for the time being. He said goodbye to Molly and Jack and returned to Wylde Court the way he had come, fingers sliding the panelling to let himself into the study. He was careful to remove his boots, lest mud on the carpet should betray the hidden entrance and, in stockinged feet, he stirred the embers of the study fire, fortifying himself with another tot of brandy.

It was lonely there and he envied Jack his mother's cosy hearth. Molly was so unlike his own dam, indeed quite unlike any other woman he had known. He had spent many an evening beneath her roof, drinking grog while she sat, elbows on the knife-dented boards of her kitchen table, listening to the smugglers planning their latest run. Her home, dilapidated though it was, had become a place where men could meet freely, to drink, swear, spit in the fire and drop tobacco ash without question. No, William had never met another like Molly Smithers, except possibly Sally. She shared that same earthy quality, and he instinctively knew that he would be able to rely on her in an emergency.

The embers glowed dully and William sat on. He was fully awake, his mind streaking ahead. There was much to be done before next week. Redvers would play his part, but the Wyldes were expected to carry out the planning required to complete the work. Guy must be told as soon as he arrived. They had so much to discuss, the news of months to exchange.

Sally too slept little that night, but for a reason entirely different to William's. She rose early and joined the servants in the routine service in the chapel close to the house. Prior to this, they had been lined up for inspection by herself, Boxer and Miss Potter. Every hair had to be in place, uniforms pressed, linen spotless, buttons and shoes polished to a fault. It was hard to pass muster on that important day. As usual, Jack had arrived late, causing a stir which upset the chaplain. Such laxity infuriated the steward but there was nothing he could do. Jack hobnobbed with his superiors, his knowledge of game-cocks and horses making him quite indispensable.

The children were breakfasting in the day-nursery when Sally returned, and Dora was seated in the low, nursing chair, suckling her baby. 'Good morning, miss,' she said cheerfully, and it was hard to believe that she was the same person as the slattern whom Sally had rescued.

Because of Sally's insistence, Lady Charlotte had given her permission for Dora to reside in the nursery wing. She acted as Sally's assistant but was on strict parole. Accepting full responsibility for Dora's behaviour, Sally had given her to understand that if she defaulted, she would have to leave. So far there had been no cause for concern. Dora was a devoted mother, and proved to be a staunch ally, helpful and astute. She had changed dramatically in appearance, clean, tidy and modest as becomes a young matron. The rest of the staff grumbled, out of earshot of Sally, but Dora ignored their spite, keeping to herself, loyal and loving to her benefactress.

Sally lay her cloak over the back of a chair and went to the mirror to take off her hat. Excitement quivered along her nerves. She would see Guy today. There was the question of his guest, of course, and she had been brooding about this during the dark smallhours. Supposing it was a woman? He had said an 'important guest', and this was unusual. Tossing and turning, her imagination had been peopled with vague vision-

42

ary beauties, fascinating sirens who had smiled at her mocking-ly. Burying her face in her pillow, her tears wetting the linen, she had tried to believe that it was probably some young man whom Guy had befriended in London, but if this was so, why had he stressed the importance of the visit? It was a bothersome conundrum which would be answered in a few hours.

With an effort she put it to the back of her mind, looking at his children with a sense of pride and achievement. He would be pleased with their development, surely? Perhaps she might receive a few words of praise.

Cecily was going to be a beauty: nine now, graceful as a young gazelle, her dark ringlets held back by a bow of red ribbon, sedate and ladylike in her frilled, long white dress. She had all the fine pride of her race. More than once Sally had had to reprove her for giving orders to the servants. She and Barbara were going through that stage of sibling rivalry, tedious to behold. They were close in age, extremely jealous of one another and, to make matters worse, Barbara was plain. She had inherited that aquiline Beaumaris nose which was striking on a man, but too large for a woman. Cecily lost no opportunity to jeer at her about this.

Fond though she was of the elder girls, it was Miranda who held a special place in Sally's affections. Standing in the cosy nursery with the light drizzle blowing against the window-panes, Sally vividly recalled the morning when Miranda had been born. Guy had brought the child to her, placing her in her arms, his face gaunt, his dark-ringed eyes filled with angry pain.

''Tis another girl,' he had said, his voice curt. 'She is alive and well, but Celeste died after giving birth. You must look to her, Sally.'

The baby had flourished, happy and placid, strong in body. But as time went by, the goodwives of the village shook their heads over her. She was a fey elf of a thing, pixy-led, so they said, one of 'God's babies' who would never grow up in her mind.

Five years had passed, and now Miranda left the table and came to Sally, pressing her face against her skirt. Sally drew her close. 'Oh dear, Miranda – you've been outside, haven't you? I did ask you not to dirty your clean dress. Papa is coming home today.'

Miranda's eyes sparkled up at her, half hidden by curls which shone like floss silk. 'Papa! I want to see Papa. You want to see him too, don't you Sally?' There was an unnerving clarity in the wide, greenish-grey eyes.

Sally side-stepped this question, saying: 'Where did you go this time, you naughty thing?' But it was not her intention to scold and she ran a gentle hand over the child's head.

'Went to the stables. Firebird has a baby foal. Went to see it – didn't mean to get dirty.' Miranda cast a rueful glance at the mud smearing her dress.

'Never you mind, Miss Miranda,' called Dora, holding the baby against her shoulder and patting his tiny back. 'Come here and nurse Danny for me while I go to get him a clean nappy.'

Miranda danced over, rejoicing in small, helpless creatures. She sat on a stool and Dora placed the baby on her lap, telling her to be sure to support his head. Miranda's freckled face was radiant as Danny cooed at her and waved his fists. She held him tightly, carefully, and there was an immediate rapport between them. Sally and Dora exchanged a smile, while Sally shook her head in a loving, puzzled way which her friend understood at once.

Miranda was like a wild thing, impossible to cage. More than once the household had been thrown into panic when she had vanished. Sally always succeeded in tracking her down, knowing her affinity with the woodlands and heaths. She loved visiting spots distrusted by the locals, those mysterious barrows built by the pagans and thought to be haunted. She would be found, curled up on a tumulus, in a half-waking, half-dreaming trance, speaking of things which she saw but Sally did not. It was chilling to listen to her, for she was incapable of learning and there was no way in which she could have read of such matters. She described crowds, weapons and garments of a prehistoric age, and scenes too bloody and awful to have sprung from a child's tender imagination. Sally's heart would contract with dread as she wondered if the peasants were right and Miranda possessed supernatural powers.

'You must be good today,' she said softly, reaching out to touch the baby's petalled cheek. 'No running off. Nanny shall find you another frock, then you must play here quietly. I'll fetch you as soon as Papa's carriage is sighted.'

'I wanted to wear my new pink dress,' complained Barbara. She too had left the table and was now making the hooped rocking-horse swing. Its squeak grated on the nerves, persistent, irritating, like the child herself.

'As well you did not,' scoffed Cecily, arching her foot and admiring her white kid pump. 'Pink looks quite hideous on you – your skin is so pasty – just like the dough before cook bakes it.'

'It doesn't! It doesn't!' Barbara started to stamp and yell, her eyes swimming with tears, drawing Sally into the quarrel. 'Tell her she's a liar! The perfectly horrid pig!'

Cecily's malicious remark had, alas, been rather too apt. Yes, thought Sally with a sigh, I'm afraid Barbara's face does look rather like an uncooked bun. Aloud, she said tactfully: 'It was my idea that the three of you should wear identical white, but with differing shades of ribbon. You can have pink, if you wish, Barbara. Papa will be so proud of his lovely daughters.'

Dora had reclaimed Danny, and Miranda climbed on to Sally's knee. Her eyes were abstracted yet penetrating as she stared beyond her sisters, beyond the limits of the room. 'Papa will not notice.' Her voice was clear, rather scornful.

Sally tightened her arms about the little, rounded form. She attempted a carefree laugh which rang hollow. 'Oh, come now, silly – you know that Papa loves each of you most dearly.'

Miranda did not appear to have heard her, speaking in a flat monotone. 'He'll see no one except his visitor.'

She became quiet, her breathing shallow, her head nestled into Sally's shoulder. Sally shivered suddenly. Someone has just walked over my grave, she thought. There was nothing she could put her finger on, simply a sense of foreboding. How could Miranda have known that he was not coming alone? Common sense reasserted itself. The servants must have spoken of it in her hearing. Miranda was forever running down to the kitchen, a great favourite of the cook who, with his blood-stained, flour-dusted apron girding his portly middle, would sweep her up on to the table, encouraging her to dip her hand into crocks of raisins, sugared almonds or crystallized fruits, filling her head with nonsensical tales the while.

Moving slowly, so as not to disturb her, Sally lay Miranda down on the padded window-seat and tucked a rug around her. Cecily and Barbara were still exchanging barbed retorts but in a subdued manner. They knew Sally could be firm, quite likely to send them to bed without any supper and withdraw the privilege of greeting Papa if they did not behave.

'Why not go out for a bit, miss?' suggested Dora, busy with her knitting whilst keeping the hooded rocking-cradle moving with one foot. It had last been used for Miranda, then stored away in the attic until Sally had ordered a manservant to hump it down. It was very old, carved with the Beaumaris crest, and had been occupied by a succession of Wylde infants time out of mind. Thoughts tormented Sally, flowing fast, crowded with memories. Poor little Miranda. Guy chose to ignore her existence, as if by so doing he could forget Celeste's untimely death. After Barbara's birth, the physicians had warned him that there must be no more pregnancies. Guy had dismissed this advice. He had wanted a son.

Now Dora's boy lay within it. Perhaps, in some odd way, he had every right to do so. Sally was still not certain. Friends though they were, Dora had not told her who had sired him. She glanced anxiously at the sleeping Miranda, but Dora smiled and waved her away.

'I'll watch over her, never fear. You're looking pale and peaky, miss. You must be at your best when the company comes. Out you go!'

Chapter 3

The great black, shiny coach rattled along the country road at a brisk rate. Its sides were picked out with yellow lines, and the Beaumaris escutcheon was emblazoned on the doors. The coachman, perched high on the box in front, urged on his four-horse team. He wore a voluminous triple-caped cloak over the deep blue, gold-frogged Wylde livery, and a tricorne hat rammed on firmly.

The beasts were sweating after the long climb from Bath, and that city of crescents, fashion and health-giving spa waters lay beneath them in its hollow, shrouded by early morning mist. The driver eased his animals when they came to level ground and glanced back over his shoulder. The other vehicles were keeping up, elegant carriages bearing the gentry, and sturdy, strong ones carrying luggage and ladies' maids, while the valets shivered on the open seats on top. There was a long haul ahead if they were to reach Beaumaris Combe by dusk, and it was as well if they kept together. He cast a stern eye at the man seated beside him with a musket across his knees, making sure that he did not nod off.

Guy Wylde sat in a corner of his fine coach, the collar of his redingote turned up about his ears, his curly-brimmed oval-crowned beaver hat tipped over his eyes. The other occupants of this well-sprung conveyance thought that he was asleep. He was not asleep but chose to foster this illusion, unwilling to engage himself in idle conversation. Between narrowed lids, he stared morosely at the passing landscape. He had drunk too much wine last night, and lost money at faro. As a gambling man he accepted the latter, but the former had improved neither his health nor his temper. Wylde Court was wearisome hours away. They should be there by nightfall, unless there was some mishap – a wheel broken by the potholes of the dirt road – an attempt at highway robbery. He almost prayed for the last contingency, welcoming the chance to punch a few heads and send a couple of ruffians packing with lead shot in their impudent backsides. He'd give 'em Goddamned highwaymen!

He could feel the stirring of energy within him, itching to

47

hold a sword, to handle a pistol again, to pit his wits against a cunning foe. He had been out of action too long, idling in Morocco, awaiting orders. It was high time he was back in the thick of it.

At his snort of amusement at the thought of walloping brigands, the woman at his side perked up. She nudged her velvet-clad arm against his. He ignored her, but Lady Aurora Mortmorcy was of a persistent nature and accustomed to his snubs. When first setting eyes on Guy almost a year before, she had made up her mind to marry him. Nothing he had done since had altered this resolution, so making light of his rudeness, she drawled: 'La, sir, but I'm mighty weary this morning.' She stifled a yawn behind her gloved hand. 'Did we have to depart at this fiendish hour? The ball was quite exhausting. D'you know, my dear, the gentlemen absolutely refused to allow me to sit out a single dance?'

'How terribly ungallant,' he commented acidly.

'You were abed later than I, were you not?' she murmured, painted lips pouting, eyes sparkling coquettishly from the depths of her elaborately trimmed bonnet. 'I waited and waited, but could not keep my poor tired eyes open past three o'clock, not even for you. Did you come to my room?'

'No,' he growled, his handsome features set in severe lines. Aurora shivered pleasurably, tempted to touch the large, strong, sun-browned hand which rested on his knee. She did not quite dare.

She caught a smile quirking the lips of the man seated opposite. Their companion on the trip abroad, or rather one of them, for there had been several others. He was Sir Sidney Templeton, a gay young spark, something of a wit. Beyond his facility for writing frivolous verse, his only real talent appeared to be that of getting through money with alarming speed. He had staked a hundred guineas that Aurora would not be able to persuade the most eligible widower in the country to marry again.

'Confound it all, sweetheart,' Sidney had exclaimed when she had confided her hopes at the start of her affair with Guy. 'I can appreciate his appeal. He's a quite magnificent savage and has, moreover, such a deuced bad reputation! Makes him doubly fascinating. But, though you play Hell's Delight with the hearts of the rest of we poor, susceptible males, I'll wager he'll not fall for your charms.'

This shrewd observation had, unhappily, proved to be true.

No man had made such devastating inroads into her emotions before, though she had fancied herself in love many times, an incurable romantic who had learned the hard way that it was better to keep one's feelings hidden behind a mask of flippancy. Aurora was the daughter of an earl, the only girl amongst a family of lively brothers. She could only dimly remember her mother who had died young, and had been alternately spoiled and bullied by both brothers and doting father. She had grown to be so wayward and high-spirited that he had eventually married her off to an elderly nobleman. Her romantic illusions had taken a nasty knock. Her husband had been impotent, raking crudely at the fires of her desire but unable to fulfil it. He had died of a heart attack shortly after the honeymoon, leaving her extremely wealthy. She had rejoiced in her freedom from dominating males, determined to remain heart-whole. 'By keeping men off, you keep them on,' had been her motto, culled from a line in John Gay's popular play *The Beggar's Opera*.

This was all very well until the day she met Guy Wylde. Stunned by the impact of his almost flagrant masculinity, piqued and intrigued by his air of aloof hauteur, she had fallen deeply in love, vowing to have him, by fair means or foul. Highborn lady though she was, there were inconsistent traits in her character, a streak of healthy commonness, an uninhibited carnality which suggested cross-mating somewhere along the line. This had made her a rebel at the fearfully expensive and snobbish young ladies' seminary to which she had been dispatched by her despairing parent when she reached thirteen. Its atmosphere of cloistered gentility had driven her nearly mad. With a clear-sightedness unusual in girls of her class, she had seen through the hypocrisy where, under cover of the utmost refinement, these pampered daughters of titled gentry were trained for nothing more than offering themselves to the highest bidder in the matrimonial stakes. There had been violent scenes and arguments when she had been introduced to her prospective bridegroom, the alliance arranged by her father, her feelings and opinions on the matter totally ignored.

Baffled, disgusted and frustrated, Aurora had been over-joyed at her husband's sudden death, delighting in her wealth and lack of restrictions, until Guy came into her life. It had been a tempestuous mating and, for her, it had contained more pain than pleasure. She was a woman of fierce emotions, jealous, possessive, yearning for the security of his wedding-ring on her finger, whilst he, though sexually excited by her, had no intention of agreeing to permanence, telling her this with brutal frankness. Her tendency towards the dramatic, her temper and outspokenness offended Guy. They were continually at cross-purposes and, sick at heart, Aurora realized that she was fast losing control in this morass of misunderstandings and lack of communication. But how could one communicate with such a man? He was so arrogant and unbending, never wanting of his will in all things.

Depression settled over her as the coach journeyed onwards. Guy came to her bed infrequently of late. She had been casual in her conversation with him just now, but in reality had cried herself to sleep in that lonely bedchamber in Bath last night.

She knew only too well that it was pointless trying to attract his attention in his present mood, so she gave up, but was unable to drag her eyes away from his handsome, brooding profile. His skin was still deeply bronzed by the Mediterranean sun, a sharp reminder of how he had set aside European dress when there, adopting the flowing robes of an Arab chief. Gazing through the coach window-glass she saw not damp green England, but the decadent luxury of El Skala. Her breath shortened and she half closed her eyes, experiencing again that heady feeling which had possessed her then, a sensation borne on the hot winds from the desert. Those dreamy days and languid nights, the distances glittering with the glory of minarets and mosques, the sand whispering, the sense of timelessness. She had bedecked herself as a *houri*, with Guy playing the sultan to her concubine, though with that cynicism which prevented him from believing it, whilst she had very nearly managed to convince herself that he loved her at last and that they would remain in this fairy-tale castle for all time.

Aurora had never been so happy and, caution fled, had confessed that she adored him, brushing aside his acid comments, reality as hazy as a mirage under the magic spell of desire, wine and distillations of opium. Perhaps she might have succeeded in wearing him down – perhaps she might even now have been returning to England to prepare for a summer wedding, had something not happened which had damned her chances for ever.

Pain lanced her. Her blue eyes hardened and her generous mouth thinned as she thought of that fatal morning which had signalled the death of hope. She had awakened to find herself alone in that great, shell-shaped divan where, the previous night, she and Guy had explored each other's bodies and followed various avenues of sophisticated pleasure. Just for an instant, whilst coming awake, she had been filled with contentment, stretching sensuously, smiling to recall every delicious moment. She had reached out a lazy arm, eyes still closed, expecting to contact his smooth-skinned, hard-muscled bare body beside her, even anticipating a repetition of passionate indulgence. Her hand met empty space. The sheet was cold, though the pillow had carried the indentation of his head.

Aurora had cursed and flung aside the coverlet, running naked to the balcony which overlooked the bay. Thunderclouds, their inky rims frilled with gold, were fleeing from the huge, amorphous bulk of the sun whose rays were dribbling, spreading over the sky. It had stopped raining and the wet earth steamed in the heat. With frantic, anxious eyes she had scanned the view, seeing a curious little procession coming up the track from the shore. Guy had been in the lead, unmistakable even from that distance, carrying what appeared to be a body slung over one shoulder. Even now, bowling along the king's highway, Aurora felt an echo of the raw apprehension which had shaken her at that moment. He had brought his burden into the palace, striding into the bedchamber and dumping it at her feet. A boy, he had said, a boy whom he had saved from drowning.

In a way it had been flattering, though she had not thought of that at the time. Big-hearted, generous to a fault, he had known that she could care for any stray, be it animal or human. 'The child is half dead – has been cruelly flogged – in need of tender care if he is to survive,' he had said gruffly, and in his eyes she had read his unwillingness to indebt himself by asking her a favour.

By this time, Aurora had covered her nakedness with a silken *djellaba*. A chill had seemed to emanate from the limp, saturated form lying so close to her bare foot, and she had clasped her robe closely around her, giving a shudder. She conquered her revulsion and bent over, staring at the creature. Though its pathetic appearance had appealed to her warmth and sympathy, she had found that her hand would not obey her, refusing to reach out to it. But Guy's stern eyes had been on her and she longed to please him, so she had pulled aside his cloak which wrapped the slight figure. The stripling had moaned and stirred-sooty lashes had lifted and Aurora had found herself looking into slanting eyes which were the colour of sun-filled sherry.

51

People had been crowding in the arched doorway, servants with alarmed faces, murmuring, frightened. Then Sidney had made an appearance, yawning and sleepy, roused by the fuss. Aurora, conscious of her audience, aware that something was expected of her, had assisted the waif into a sitting position on the marble-tiled floor. As she had done so, the existing wrappings had fallen away completely. A gasp had arisen from the onlookers.

Aurora had swung round to Guy, catching a look of astonishment on his face. 'Well, my Lord, is your eyesight playing tricks this morning?' she had mocked, though every nerve in her body had screamed out a warning. 'You thought it to be a stripling? Some stripling, by God!'

Now she laughed silently, mirthlessly at the memory. A boy indeed! Wearing torn baggy pantaloons, and remnants of a bloody embroidered shirt, Guy's find had been a thin, narrow-hipped girl, whose back was striped with the terrible imprint of the lash, and whose hair had been shorn close to her skull.

Of course such a dramatic situation had had instant appeal. Guy's male friends, holidaying with him at El Skala, had found it fascinating. Despite extensive inquiries, nothing came to light about the girl's past. It was as if the shock of near-drowning had obliterated from her mind everything which had happened before. She told them her name, and could speak and understand a smattering of English, but apart from that she was like a piece of blank paper or a newborn child learning to live in the world. Even Aurora had to admit that she was exceptionally beautiful; more than this, her silence, her air of frigid apathy was a challenge. She resembled a statue which every man who entered her presence longed to warm into life. They wooed her, but to no avail. She showed neither aversion nor liking for their company, accepting with chilly politeness the clothing, jewels and rare perfumes which they offered.

Anger, jealousy and resentment boiled in Aurora's breast as she looked across the coach. The girl was seated by Sidney. How demure she was, clad in a simple dress of pink and white striped cotton, the hem peeping from beneath her fur-trimmed pelisse. Her eyes were cast down in contemplation of the big sable muff in which her hands were buried. Her hair had grown a little, no longer a stubbly brush, now clustering in springy black curls on her forehead. A little hat adorned with a circlet of ribbons and artificial flowers gave colour to her olive complexion.

Christ, she certainly is beautiful, thought Aurora grudgingly. That heart-shaped face, broad brow, high cheekbones and those enormous eyes, shaded by lashes so long, black and curly that I'd swear they were false if I didn't know better! Those damned eyes of hers are certainly not virginal. I'd stake my life on it! Nor is her body in spite of her slimness. Yet there she sits, as prissy-faced as a schoolgirl!

Sourly she noted the modest way in which the girl's buttoned boots were crossed at the ankles. It would have been amusing had it not been so galling and tormentingly hurtful. Guy Wylde, that libertine, gamester and rake, rumoured to be a member of a club where sacrilegious rites were carried out before a naked statue of Venus, had been unable to add this chit to his list of conquests. Aurora was certain of it, and it made her gorge rise to know that she had her to thank for Guy's continued, though spasmodic, attentions.

Baffled as always by the girl's passivity, Aurora eyed her rancorously and said in an edgy voice: 'And what do you think of your new land, Lalage?'

The amber eyes lifted to meet hers. 'I cannot tell yet, madame,' she replied in carefully pronounced English. 'It is too soon. I found London amusing. The playhouses were most enjoyable, and the countryside is so green, unlike the desert.'

They had stayed in London for nearly two weeks whilst Guy, to keep abreast of the rapidly changing fashions, had waited on his tailor. To Aurora's chagrin, she had found Lalage included at every function they had been called upon to attend.

His mermaid has turned into a bloody wax doll! She fumed, grinding her teeth in fury as she felt Guy stir into life at the sound of that lisping, foreign intonation.

He smiled at Lalage. 'I'm confident that you'll like Wylde Court. There is so much I want to show you.'

'Thank you, sir,' Lalage murmured, a faint, answering smile lighting her face. It faded quickly, as it always did, and once more there was that aura of stillness about her which suggested a Sphinx-like inscrutability.

The coaches reached Dorchester, crossing the bridge over the Frome river and driving down the wide central street. The sturdy stone houses were a relief after the bleak heath and bare, whale-backed downs. It was market-day, the square milling with farm-wagons filled with vegetables, and cattle-pens and hawkers' booths. The taverns were overflowing with customers, but soon the Beaumaris cavalcade was swinging under

53

an arch and clattering over the cobbled courtyard of a large hostelry.

When the leading carriage rocked to a halt, one of the footmen leapt down, opening the door and unfolding the iron step. Guy held out a crooked arm to Lalage who rested the tips of her fingers on it, the other lifting up her skirt. She looked around, head erect, with a kind of childish disdain, well-dressed, perfectly groomed, tiny rounds of silver bracelets over her gloved wrists, the luxurious muff dangling on its ribbon.

Once, at the start of our affair, Guy would have treated me with such consideration, thought Aurora sadly, accepting Sidney's assistance. Concealing the pain caused by his thoughtlessness, she tossed up her head and called greetings to the friends emerging from the other vehicles. They minced between the rain puddles, the ladies complaining shrilly, the gentlemen smoothing creases from their breeches and twisting their coats straight. All eyes were turned longingly towards the diamond-paned windows of the taproom, fogged by the heat of fire and people, a warm refuge with the good smell of roast meat drifting out into the rainy noon.

A log fire crackled and popped in the wide hearth, and the gentry were ushered to a table near it. Having made certain that Lalage was comfortably seated, Guy went off to consult with his coachmen about a change of horses. Every bench, stool or chair was in use in that noisy, smoky room. Ruddy-cheeked farmers in smocks and Sunday-best hats leaned on the long, polished counter, impatiently demanding the services of the pot-boy. Unemployed servants who had come seeking jobs, stood in one corner. There were a few gypsies, shifty-eyed horse dealers and bold-faced women with black plaits and hooped earrings, hefting baskets of clothes-pegs and paper flowers.

The landlord sweated behind the bar, bullying his staff of flustered lads and serving wenches. Sidney dispatched his servant to fetch wine, kerchief raised to his fastidious nose. The reek of ale, cider and closely packed humans was almost visible in the air. At the other tables sat an assortment of men, drinking, playing cards or rattling dice-boxes. It was obvious that the newcomers were of the nobility, so forelocks were tugged and hats removed, though they were eyed suspiciously. There had been so many foreigners flooding into the country since the revolution in France, and the natives did not take kindly to such an invasion. However, the host singled them out for special attention, recognizing Guy who had stopped often as this was a reliable posting-house. The landlord was proud of his stable which consisted of many good, strong animals necessary for the frequent changes required on a long journey.

He bowed and swept off the dirty mugs and spread a clean white cloth on the table before presenting Aurora with a rather dog-eared bill of fare. She struggled to put aside the disturbed, worrying thoughts which filled her mind, pretending to be amused by this rustic scene. In a defiant mood, she let her mantle fall open. She was wearing one of the new, skimpy, diaphanous gowns which had taken the fashionable world by storm. The upheaval taking place across the Channel had changed not only political ideas but those of dress as well. Out had gone hoops, high white wigs, powder, patches and stilt-heeled shoes. Aurora, delighting in this lack of restraint which gave her carte-blanche to display her charms publicly, had gleefully thrown away her stays. She embraced this neo-classical image wholeheartedly. It could have been designed especially for her. Lovely, semi-transparent silks and cottons, cut on simple lines into floating gowns beneath which she wore nothing. She was travelling in one made of lilac muslin sprigged with tiny gold flowers. The armpit-high waistline emphasized her breasts where a diamond pendant gleamed at the revealing neckline.

With a false vivacity she conversed with her companions, laughing immoderately at their witticisms, causing raised eye-brows among the more sober diners, but most of the men present were goggling at her admiringly. One in particular could not tear his eyes away, a large fellow with a thick-set body and heavy jaw, better dressed than the rest. After several glasses of wine, Aurora became even more outrageous, spurred on by the talk buzzing round their table. There were three smart young men, as well as Sidney, each accompanied by a lady, and they gossiped waspishly, while Aurora declared that she was woefully out of touch with the latest scandals. Yet, at the same time, her nerves were stretched unbearably as she waited for Guy to come back.

'But, my dear thing, have you no tales of your adventures in Morocco?' gushed one agreeable fop, immaculately attired in skin-tight breeches, a silk cut-away coat with wide lapels, a stiff high collar and a mass of lacy cravat wound around his throat.

'La, let me think,' Aurora prevaricated, perfectly aware of his drift. 'Humm, little of note, as I recall.'

'What of that ravishing vision at your side?' he admonished, wagging a beringed finger at her. 'She's the talk of the town, strike me dumb if she ain't.'

'Really?' Aurora's plucked brows lifted a shade. She gave a cool smile. 'You surprise me, sir. I was not conscious of it.'

'I beg to differ,' he persisted annoyingly. 'The story of Guy's discovery of her on some barbarous foreign shore has already gone about. Can you not enlighten us further, my sweet? Gad's life, I've not yet had the honour of being presented to her.' Aurora shrugged and hid a yawn, then made the introduction in a casual, deliberately insulting manner.

The fop sprang to his feet, seized Lalage's hand and conveyed it to his lips. 'Your servant, Miss Lalage. What a delightful name! Just like its owner. Greek, is it not?'

She looked at him expressionlessly, removing the hand which he had retained a fraction too long. 'It may be. I don't know, sir. I have lost my memory, recalling nothing save the coldness of the sea – and my name.'

'A woman of mystery. She may be highborn – or very low.' Aurora's sarcastic voice coiled round the group. 'She was wearing eastern clothing, her hair was cropped, she had fresh weals on her back, and owned nothing but that ring from which she refuses to be parted. Who knows, she may have been a slave? And, would you believe it? Guy thought he had fished out a lad!'

Brittle laughter, astounded disbelief greeted this. Everyone thought it an enormous joke, particularly the fop who was so overcome that he had to rest against the table, dabbing at the mirth-tears with his cuff. 'Zounds! I've never heard the like! I'll be damned if I have!' he cried. 'Guy mistaking her for a boy! I can't wait to tell 'em at White's club.' Then he sobered, collecting himself. 'May I see your ring, Miss Lalage? You must forgive me for I do not laugh at you, dear lady.'

Lalage held out her right hand where silver glinted on her third finger. 'I cannot tell you how I came by it.'

'You most likely stole it from your master and that's why you were beaten,' sneered Aurora, snapping open her painted fan and waving it vigorously.

The fop was examining the ring with interest. 'So? An unusual ornament, and made by a consummate artist, or I'll be hanged as a Dutchman. A strange device. Let me see – yes, it is of a horned moon, is it not?' Lalage withdrew her hand, replacing it in her lap. 'Can't you remember anything else?'

'No, sir,' she answered.

Guy entered at that moment, striding across to the fire, giving a brusque command to the landlord en route. Every eye swivelled to him. He was quite impossible to ignore with his unusual height, his build, the width of his shoulders exaggerated by the caped coat which was slung across them. He leaned an elbow on the overmantel and removed his hat, handing it to his manservant who had followed dutifully in his wake. Beneath this outer garment, he wore a claret broadcloth jacket, cream breeches which hugged his thighs, black topboots, a damask waistcoat and a cravat knotted high under his firm jaw.

He was still feeling his liquor from the hard drinking of last night. What he had already consumed that morning had added to it. He took in the situation at the table in one glance, frowning and saying: 'If you seek further information regarding the young lady, ask me, sir.'

The fop expressed pained surprise at his tone and resumed his chair. 'My apologies, your Lordship – didn't realize that you had such a confounded proprietorial interest in her, sink me if I did,' he muttered, taking out his snuff-box, flipping back the lid, and applying a pinch to his nostrils. He was watching every movement of the dark man staring down at him with such hostility.

Aurora broke in, if only to make Guy look at her. 'I suppose that you do consider her to be your property, Guy, for 'twas you who saved her life.' She arched her slim throat and laughed provokingly, waiting for his reaction, nervous but made reckless by wine.

'I do not,' he retorted sharply. 'Lalage is free to come and go as she wishes.'

'What are you then, sir? Her guardian? D'you regard her as your ward, perchance?' put in Sidney who had been listening quietly throughout, knowing Aurora's inflammable temper, on the alert for storm-signals. 'I must admit that such selfless devotion is an entirely new facet of your character. It astounds me, my dear fellow.'

Guy's lips tightened and his eyes were like steel. He ran a scornful glance over these so-called friends, knowing their vices, their glib tongues which delighted in tearing reputations into shreds. 'Is it so odd that I have taken charge of her?' His voice held a warning. 'As you well know, Sidney, I made every attempt to find her kinfolk, but she was a stranger in Al Hoceima.'

'That is true. It was as if she had appeared by magic.' Aurora was determined not to be outdone, finding a measure of comfort in the effect she was having on the burly man at the next table. He had never once taken his eyes off her. She hoped that Guy had seen him, prayed that this might ignite a spark of jealousy. 'The natives were terrified, babbling about the evil eye, convinced that she was an enchantress.' Her overloud laughter rang out, and she turned to Lalage with a taunting smile. 'Is it so? Faith, it seems that you've cast a spell over the gentlemen.'

Lalage knitted her wing-shaped brows, and her narrow eyes, like golden agates, concentrated on her. This gave Aurora a most unpleasant sensation, and it angered her further. It was quite ridiculous that a woman such as herself, rich, beautiful and popular, could be intimidated by a waif living on Guy's charity. They had judged her to be about eighteen, possibly even younger, and yet those terrible eyes were old, an armour that none could see behind. No one could read her thoughts, disarmed, almost blighted by that wide, black-pupilled stare of worldliness coupled with childish innocence.

'I have told you, again and again – I don't know who I am.' Lalage's voice trembled and she glanced up at Guy. 'You believe me, don't you, sir?'

'Yes,' he said slowly, looking searchingly into her face. 'Yes, I think I believe you.' His hand came to rest on her shoulder protectively, and he faced the others. 'This is no one else's business. I'll thank you to let the matter drop.'

To see him touch the girl tortured Aurora unbearably. She turned her shoulder towards them, a fixed smile on her face. An uneasy silence followed, broken only by the arrival of lunch. The landlord was smiling and serving them, his stout form outlined against the dancing flames, carrying a huge trencher of steaming meat. An underling followed with a roast chicken, four pigeons and a pie which was nearly as big around as the top of a salad bowl. Guy took a chair by Lalage and he ate little, his hooded eyes resting broodingly on the company. The fops were struggling to lighten the atmosphere with quips, but though the others laughed, Guy failed to find them amusing. He had deemed it necessary to invite them to Wylde Court at this juncture because it suited his present purpose if the world at large continued to view him as a debauched rake. Whilst in London, he had given the impression to all and sundry that his stay in Morocco had been one of the utmost depravity, hinting at unspeakable orgies. But now he had no stomach for the charade. These men were dilettantes, their women over-painted and under-dressed, nothing more than courtesans. He wanted no more of them.

'A penny for your thoughts, Guy! You're letting your beef grow cold.' Aurora's strident voice broke across his thoughts. She was staring at him insolently, chin cupped in her hand.

Guy drank up his wine, placed the glass down and then looked her over, coldly, ruthlessly, deliberately. Oh, she was handsome – flamboyant and sensual, rich in an almost barbaric splendour of figure and countenance. There was no denying that he had enjoyed her body, but he could see that at twenty-three, she was no longer in the flower of youth, seeming overblown to him. The soft ripeness of her mouth had taken on a hard line; there was a calculating glitter in her eyes; a twist of temper about her nostrils. She had sworn that she loved him, but Guy chose to disbelieve her. He did not want love – not now, perhaps not ever. The responsibility was too demanding. He might have to marry again one day, but did not intend to bind himself to an aristocratic harpy, apt to stamp her foot and scream with rage when thwarted. He was anxious to be shot of Aurora, closing his mind to her kindliness, her effervescent gaiety which he had once found entertaining.

'It can't be more cold than the feeling I now have for you, madame,' he said.

He spoke loudly and quite clearly, drawing all eyes in the room towards them. Aurora's temper had always been difficult to check, and now rage at this public insult sent the colour flooding to her cheeks. Inside her churned sick nervousness, deep pain and a horrible fear. 'Shame on you, Guy,' she murmured. ''Tis not the time nor the place for a quarrel.'

'Aurora.' His voice was icy. 'It is over. You'll come no more to Wylde Court.'

This can't be really happening! she thought frantically. It must be a terrible nightmare. He can't mean it, not after all we have meant to one another. But she had to brazen it out. Everyone was watching. 'How will you stop me?' she cried. 'You have invited me. I am your guest. I have no carriage here, no way of returning home.' She gave a harsh laugh. 'Oh, no – I'm not one of your whores whom you can buy and then cast off. You didn't pay me, sir.'

'Did I not?' he answered smoothly. 'And what of the diamonds you wear at your throat? Weren't they a gift from me?'

'A gift, yes. That's different. Heavens, man – I'm rich – I can buy as many diamonds as I want. These were a present.' Her hand went to them, those gems which had been doubly precious because he had presented them to her. She would have worn them, valued, treasured them had they been paste.

He shrugged. 'Call it what you will. I looked upon them as fair exchange for your services.'

Aurora rose, the colour deepening in her face. Everyone was still. The whole taproom was listening. 'Very well, then. You bought me.'

If she had hoped to shame him, she was cruelly mistaken. He smiled. 'Aye, so I did.' His mocking, down-sweeping glance reduced her to the meanest drab whom he had desired, used and then rejected as worthless. 'So, madame, I can sell you again.'

A murmur went through the spectators. One of the women tittered and then quietened. Several of the men had drawn closer, eyeing the deep oval of Aurora's bodice. She threw up her head, and drew her cloak about her like a regal mantle. The beefy man who had been studying her so intently moved into the fray, elbowing the locals aside. 'Who would not be glad to buy such a fine lady?' he demanded, glaring around him. 'Were it to cost him everything he owned – his house – his farm – even his dogs and horses!'

Neither Guy nor Aurora heeded him. It was as if they were alone on a bare mountain top, continuing a deathly conflict of wills which had existed between them through eternity. 'How can you say such a wicked thing?' she breathed through the fog of agony, her hand pressed so hard on the table that the blue veins stood out. 'I'm sorry, Guy – I shouldn't have spoken to you thus.'

Guy went on talking as if there had been no interruption. 'You've said it. I bought you and now the matter is ended. I shall sell you again.' He stabbed a glance at the fat man. 'You, sir. You want her? How much will you give me?'

The crowd were in an uproar. There was laughter and drunken ribaldry, these shocking antics of the gentry giving them enormous satisfaction. Tongues would wag of it for weeks to come, those who had been present scoring a point off more temperate neighbours.

'Sir, you're insulting this noble woman!' yelled the man, his heavily-jowled face flushing. He looked like a bull in a field, ready to charge at anything which moved. 'I should call you out!'

Guy, as was his way when he was drunk, had become more

haughty than ever. He stared down his fine nose at his challenger. 'Do as you damn please. My seconds will be only too happy to accommodate you. What will you? Swords or pistols? I am an expert with both.'

'You're mighty high-handed, sir,' the man blustered, regretting his chivalrous gesture when he looked into those flinty eyes. 'I'm no common dung-spreader, you know. I own most of the land in these parts. Squire Copleston of Copleston Rise, at your service!'

'Indeed.' Guy gave an ironic bow. The lines on either side of his mouth were as if chiselled in granite. 'Then you'll be well able to pay a handsome price for her. You are wise not to fight me, squire, for I'd have spit you like a capon.'

'Let there be an end to this!' Aurora could stand no more. 'I'll give you the money for the damned necklace!' She made to brush past Guy but his hand shot out and gripped her arm.

'Not so fast.' He was smiling sardonically, unforgiving. Harsh words had been exchanged between them in the past. 'You're for sale to the man who bids the highest. Nothing else will satisfy me.'

'The jest has gone far enough, Guy.' Sidney stood up, kicking back the chair he had been lolling on, sobered by the serious turn of events. 'You're doing Aurora a monstrous wrong, damme! If you no longer want her as your guest, then let her travel with me to Lyme Regis. I'll hire a carriage.'

The rest of the party agreed, highly embarrassed. It would have been acceptable had this happened within their own select, unprincipled circle, a fine bit of gossip, but it was unsporting of Guy to make such a scene in a tavern, exposing them to the ridicule of the peasants.

Guy refused to listen, as immovable as a rock. 'No. We are weary of each other and wish to part. Come, Squire Copleston – what do you offer?'

The squire, befuddled but resolute, yelled: 'You're an unmannerly blackguard! I'd like to horse-whip you –' but he could not take his bulging eyes from Aurora. Magnetized, his corpulent body leaned in towards her, his coarse, blunt-fingered hands reaching out to touch, to fondle this prize which exceeded his wildest dreams.

'To hell with your threats, sir. How much?' Guy demanded. 'What d'you say to three hundred guineas? The necklace alone is worth far more.'

Something seemed to snap in the squire. With a frenzied

gesture, he plunged a hand into his coat pocket and flung a heap of gold coins on the table, then stretched forward, deep-set eyes glaring into Guy's. 'All right – I'll take her! I'll take her, and damn you for a cold-hearted villain! She shall come with me – if she's willing. I'll care for her!' He swung round to Aurora who stood frozen to the spot. 'Will you come, madame?' he begged, almost implored. 'Stay with me – live with me! I'll treat you like a queen.'

Guy stared at the shiny heap on the cloth. 'You've just struck a bargain, sir,' he said levelly. 'She is yours. I renounce further claim on her. May you have joy of the bitch. I'll drink to that!'

He did not bother to rise, refilling his glass and lifting it to his lips. Aurora's hand flashed up, open-palmed, knocking it from his grasp. Scarlet droplets stained his cheek and dribbled down his ruffled shirt-front like blood. 'You despicable bastard!' she hissed, in awesome, white-hot fury. 'I'll be revenged on you if it takes me all the days of my life!'

She shot Lalage a look which should have blasted her into stone, then stalked out, head held high, glancing neither right nor left. The crowd parted to let her pass, shrinking back, fear on every face lest she should curse them too. Squire Copleston hurried after her, stunned by this incredible stroke of good fortune.

Guy flicked out his white kerchief and dried the wine from his face carefully, before replacing it in his cuff. He picked up the gold pieces, studied them thoughtfully for a moment, then thrust them into his pocket. He looked across at Lalage, but she was staring into the distance as if unaware of the recent furore. In contrast to Aurora's fiery blasts, her tranquillity resembled a calm, crystalline lake, infinitely desirable.

'Let us leave this place, my child,' he said, his eyes bleak, a wry smile curving his mouth. 'I want to take you to my home.'

Chapter 4

It was not hard to understand why Denzil Wylde was his mother's favourite. Quite apart from the fact that he had been her last-born, thus assuring him a unique corner in her heart, he was exceptionally handsome. His features were classical, like those of a knight sculptured on a tomb, his eyes soft and dark with a lustre about them, eyes which could change, when he was angry, to the colour of burning peat. Before returning for his last year at university, he had worn his chestnut hair long, tied back in a queue, but Lady Charlotte had been considerably shocked when he came home this time. His locks were now short, dishevelled, and even his laughing assurance that this was the very latest 'Brutus' style did nothing to mollify her. His height was somewhere between that of William and Guy and his body was still boyishly immature, but his shoulders were broad, his waist and hips slim.

On the morning of the day in which Guy was expected, he had dressed himself for the outdoors, hoping to escape before Mamma caught him. He grinned as he recalled her performance when he had arrived on the stage-coach yesterday, going straight to the Red drawing-room where she was ensconced, to be greeted with cries of horror. In vain he had tried to explain that his sloppy, untidy appearance was that adopted by most students nowadays. She deplored his plain brown suit, the lack of lace at wrists and neck, the scuffed boots and sober, wide-brimmed black hat.

'What the blazes d'you think you look like?' she had ranted. 'A labourer! A coalman! Thank God your Papa is not alive to see you! I blame the revolution! Everything has turned topsy-turvy, with members of the nobility striving to ape the working classes! It is most uncivilized. Pray heaven that you will reform now that you've left Oxford for good!'

There had been a great deal more in a similar vein and Denzil had conformed when he changed for dinner, but now he wore comfortable garb, a touch of defiance in his carriage. Lord, she'd have a fit of apoplexy if she knew he'd bought a pair of trousers, those functional, utilitarian garments frowned upon by the conservative but beginning to be worn by daring young intellectuals who wished to identify themselves with the oppressed. He'd have to conceal them in his luggage until she had cooled down.

Having had breakfast in his room, Denzil passed along the thickly carpeted corridors and ran down the staircase to the Great Hall. He was acutely conscious of the succession of flunkies busy about their duties. They were an ever-present background to his life and, until recently, he had taken them for granted, but during his final year at Oxford, he had taken part in debates where his fellow-students had been of a radical turn of mind. He had listened to their fiery oratory, somewhat alarmed and bewildered. Some were secretly of the Jacobin view, imbibing the heady wine of anarchy, their brains set on fire by the strife in France.

Till that time, Denzil had gleefully romped through the rough and tumble of university life, drinking a lot and chasing women, cramming at the last minute and scraping through his examinations. But his erstwhile carefree friends had changed of late, serious and earnest, maintaining that every man was born equal, ranting on about human dignity, wanting to better the lot of the common man. This was dangerous talk, for the execution of King Louis XVI on the twenty-first of January of that year had tipped an uneasy alliance and England was now at war with the revolutionaries. Denzil had remained unconvinced that rebellion was the answer and had been quite relieved to come home, yet he wanted to do something heroic, filled with confused and vaguely splendid thoughts.

He walked out through the imposing front door and crunched over the gravel of the drive. It had been raining earlier, but now a breeze was drying out the wet foliage, and the sunless sky was tinted with pearl-like clouds. He looked around with pride and affection. The heated talk of levelling wealth had been all very fine in student lodgings, but coming back to Wylde Court had put it in perspective. He had broached the subject with William over port last night and had received short shrift. And brother Guy? What would he make of it? Denzil was unsure of Guy, hardly knowing him. He was a distant, authoritative figure, yet Denzil had heard strange tales about him. Some looked upon him as a libertine.

He crossed a lawn and took a path through the woods in the direction of the village and, as he walked, he continued to speculate about Guy, wondering if he might be bringing any women with him. Aurora Mortmorcy, perhaps. Denzil had met her last summer and had been bowled over. He remembered Celeste, that kindly, simple woman who had been his sister-in-law. Guy had shown little patience with her, but this was his way with women. Denzil, on the other hand, adored them, never happier than when in their company. He had had his fair share of amorous adventures, undergraduate escapades of a scandalous nature which had earned sharp reproval from the dean.

Maybe he should marry. Mamma would arrange it, find him a pleasant girl with a generous dowry, set him up in one of the estate houses where he could breed horses and raise children. Not that he would abandon his little *cocottes*, those low-born women with loose morals and accommodating thighs in whom he gloried. He reached the edge of the wood and turned into a lane, dwelling on them with fondness though they had mostly been drawn, through his own choice, from unsavoury sources. It added to his excitement to know that Mamma would disapprove if she found out.

Presently he came to the churchyard, so peaceful and filled with bird-song, half of it still a field behind the church. There were rows of tombs and monuments where respected members of the community were buried, the rest partially filled with grassy mounds and an odd assortment of headstones. His choice of destination had been deliberate for he was hoping that one of the village girls would walk by. The prospect was exhilarating.

He had not been there long when two women passed him. Both glanced in his direction and their pace slowed a little. They were fine girls, strappingly built and rather grubby. Thick, hobnailed boots showed below their petticoats, brown cotton dresses clung to their big haunches and straw hats were cocked on top of their straggling hair. Girls who worked in the open, agricultural labourers or fishermen's wives. They strode out strongly, their bodies balanced from the hips as if they were used to heavy work. It was easy to imagine them carrying large baskets of fruit on their heads, on the way to market. They walked as confidently as soldiers.

Denzil followed them, tingling with remembrances of domestic servants, shop-girls and prostitutes of varying degrees of expensiveness. There was fun to be had in their rough company and he viewed them in no other light than that of immediate gratification, wanting no entanglements, having no intention of ever falling in love.

The women went towards one of the large monuments which stood among the yews. They had their heads together, whispering and smiling, glancing back over their shoulders at him. He quickened his pace, catching up with them. They were easy to talk with. He had found that class distinctions vanished once bawdy banter had been established. They were a couple of bold hussies who knew very well what he wanted. Their eyes sparkled and they laughed a lot, returning his chaffing. Soon he was offering them money.

'You're a fine young man an' no mistake,' said the older of the two. 'P'raps I'd 'ave 'ad a tumble wi' you wi'out payment, but seein' as 'ow you've bin so generous. You go first, Mary, an' if 'ee serves you well, I'll be 'ot for 'im arter.'

Without further preamble, Denzil took her to a grassy spot, made a bundle of his cloak and put it beneath her head. She made no resistance. He saw the flash of heavy white thighs and belly, a triangle of black hair, and in an instant he was taking his fill of her. He felt her wriggle and sigh, and they lay there replete with the dead all around. Denzil chuckled inwardly. It was the first time he had made love in a graveyard. That would be something to tell his friends.

The other woman had been watching. ''Ave you done?' she said, leaning over them. Denzil turned his head and squinted up at her. She loomed large, featureless, black against the sky.

He sat up so that she swung into perspective. Her skin was good, her eyes blue, and she had splendid breasts which she bared for his inspection. The white flesh gleamed, traced with faint, blue veins, the nipples dark and prominent. The first girl was primly pulling down her ragged skirt and buttoning her blouse.

''Ee ain't bad at it, Peg – not fer a gen'leman, an' 'ees mighty pretty, ain't 'ee?' she remarked casually.

She stood up, combing her fingers through her tangled hair and replacing her hat. Her companion sprawled on the grass, arms held out to Denzil. He experienced a moment of doubt at his ability to oblige her, but she took charge, her large, rough hands working on his body. She was breathing hard, a glassy look in her eyes, her lips drawn back over strong white teeth. Denzil closed his eyes, sinking on to that mouth which seemed to swallow him, his nostrils responding to that peculiar odour which he associated with such women – the smell of sweat, greasy hair and unclean linen. He felt his body swelling, rising again, fragmented images clouding his mind.

In his early youth, his mother had commanded him to stop conversing with the maidservants, and to all appearances he had obeyed her, but his curiosity about them had been insatiable. He had spent time lingering in the hall to catch a glimpse of their legs as they went upstairs, listening at their doors, following them into empty rooms, undeterred in his pursuit of such tempting game. They had accepted his demands and never once peached on him, seeming to enjoy it as much as he did.

The woman beneath him was moaning and arching her hips, murmuring vulgar words. These inflamed him and, once more, he was lost in that eternal circle of seeking. She was superb, taking him to the limits of voluptuous pleasure, yet as soon as it was over and their bodies separated, he found her rather repulsive.

He paid them both handsomely and watched them go away along the path between the headstones, walking with that same swinging gait. No one would have suspected by their looks and manner what they had been doing. Denzil rested for a while, musing on the mystery of women. It seemed scarcely possible that the sweet, demure, softly-spoken females of his own class followed the same course as those two wenches. He had always found it astonishing, as if the whole business of copulation was a dream fashioned by his own fevered imagination.

He stood up, knocked some dead leaves from his cloak, swung it over one shoulder, and resumed his stroll. He went out through the lych-gate and there almost collided with a maid from Wylde Court. He had noticed her last night for she was comely, with small breasts and a trim waist. There was nothing deferential in her stance and she was neatly dressed.

She stopped dead, then stood aside so that he might pass her. Denzil was tempted to engage her in conversation but something about her tilted chin and steady eyes stopped him. 'Good morning, your Honour,' she said, and he wondered if he fancied the amusement in her voice.

He nodded and sauntered off, but had he looked back, he would have seen Bethany Wicker staring after him with a contemplative smile.

Guy reached over to tuck the lap-robe more securely round Lalage's knees. 'You'll find England cold after the Mediterranean climate,' he remarked with a smile before withdrawing to his own corner.

There was an intimacy about the interior of the coach. It travelled smoothly, slung on giant leather springs. The light was dim as it filtered through the windows, and the seats big enough to serve as beds, if need arose. It was panelled in walnut inlaid with rosewood, and there were smooth-sliding doors which opened to reveal small cabinets where drink, provisions and personal possessions could be stored. The tension was leaving Guy now that they were alone after a further distressing scene outside the tavern, with Aurora continuing to swear eternal vengeance as she was helped in to Squire Copleston's gig.

Guy had never seen before such fury on a face, it had turned her beauty into a grotesque mask, convincing him that he had done well to be rid of her. Her friends had been outraged. Brisk words had passed between Guy and them as they stoutly averred that they would not desert Aurora. As the Beaumaris coaches had left the courtyard, they had been bullying the landlord into renting out vehicles.

Guy smiled grimly, chin buried in his jabot, speaking aloud as he pursued this train of thought. 'The worthy squire will find that he's taken on more than he bargained for. Those dandies and their gaudy ladybirds will most certainly outstay their welcome. They'll empty his larder and drain his cellar. Devil take 'em! I've done with providing 'em with free board and entertainment. Let someone else do it.'

Lalage watched him without expression, then she said: 'You have acted for the best, no doubt,' before looking out of the window again, absorbed in her baffling, inner concentration.

The miles sped away beneath the iron-bound wheels and it was some time before either spoke. At last Guy stirred himself and threw back the lid of the large wicker hamper resting on the opposite seat. The landlord had provided it for the road – a salad, cold meat, a venison pie, and several bottles of wine to temper the tedium of the journey.

'Are you hungry, Lalage?' he asked.

'No, sir.'

'A glass of wine, perhaps?' He was pulling the cork, the bottle gripped between his knees. He filled two glasses and handed her one. It glowed like fire in her hand. He settled back, savouring the wine and pronouncing it to be passable. He was studying her with a musing smile, wondering what she was thinking about with those dreamy eyes turned inwards. 'You won't lack company at Wylde Court,' he commented.

She moved her head to look at him, dark lashes making a fringed shadow on her cheeks. 'How so?'

'My brothers will be there, and half the county too, in a while. Mamma will have let people know that I'm expected. Then there are my daughters, and Sally –'

'Who is Sally?' she asked politely.

'She's a distant cousin, she lives there and helps with the children.'

'She is a – how d'you say? A governess?' Her difficulty with English was another charming trait, that slight hesitation, that puzzled frown as she sought the right word.

'Yes, in a manner of speaking.'

'And she is young, this Sally? And pleasing?' There was a disconcerting spark of mischief in her eyes.

For the life of him, Guy could not clearly remember what Sally looked like. 'Well, yes, she's youngish, I suppose – in her twenties.' The picture became clearer and he saw Sally as small, with regular features and fair hair. He shrugged, much more aware of Lalage's slight movement as she leaned over to replace her glass in the hamper. 'She's just Sally – that's all.'

One dark, arched brow lifted and Lalage laughed. 'And you think that they will like me?'

His face expressed surprise, faint anger. 'How could they not?'

She sighed wistfully. 'Ah, but my dear friend, perhaps everyone is not so full of goodness as yourself. What will they make of me, your so-noble family? I think that I shall die if you are ashamed of me.' Her lips trembled, and she twisted aside, but not before he saw the hurt in her eyes, the droop of her mouth.

He slipped a hand up on to her shoulder and drew her back, ignoring her resistance. 'What do you mean?'

'They may presume that I am your mistress,' she whispered. 'Like Aurora.'

His hard, experienced eyes scrutinized her face, and he gave a sceptical smile. 'They will be mistaken, won't they?'

Lalage shrank into her corner. 'I must have great care of my reputation – homeless – parentless.'

He made no response, focusing his attention on the swiftly passing scene, the small, straggling villages, then the moorland where the yellow gorse stood out against the varying shades of green. They were deep into Dorset. In an hour, they would glimpse the sea from the downs and then roll gently down into the port of Beaumaris Combe. He knew the way so well, visualizing the village nestled amidst surrounding hills, where fishermen sat on the quay mending their nets, and donkeys plodded up the cobbled streets burdened by projecting loads balanced on their backs. It would be gay with flags and bunting, filled with cheering people. Through the narrow street they would go, up the steep incline, following the road lined by lofty beech trees. There would be the walls of his manor, thick with blue-grey lichens and that peculiar rusty tint of stone, blending in perfect harmony. Soon he would see his house in all its stately grandeur, welcomed by faithful old Boxer and sedate Miss Potter and the rest of his servants who had tended him for the better part of his life.

Lalage left her secluded corner, moving over to sit close to him, her fingers coming to rest on his hand. He turned his head slowly, his masked green eyes boring into hers, and then his gaze lowered, coming to rest on her lips. 'It is so difficult for me, sir,' she said, very low. 'I must be circumspect in every way.' A flame leaped in her eyes, then dwindled, leaving them appealing and frightened.

He put his arm about her, drawing her close, and she gave a contented sigh, her head on his shoulder. 'Don't fret, my dear,' he said with a thread of humour in his voice. 'Mamma is a stickler for protocol but I know how to handle her.'

'Dear Guy,' she murmured. 'I know that you will look after me.'

He remained still, holding her gently. When he looked down, he saw that she had fallen asleep and he envied her. He had noticed before that she had a capacity for taking refuge in the safe world of slumber, dropping into it easily, like an animal or a child.

Sally climbed the corkscrew staircase which led to one of the four towers of Wylde Court. She stood under the timbers of the conical roof and gazed down at Guy's domain. The wind lifted her hair and beat at her gown, a strong wind blowing in from the sea. Anticipation raced through her. The atmosphere of the house had been charged with it; footmen hurrying, maids polishing, Miss Potter fussing as she selected the finest bedlinen for the main guestroom. Now for the torture; that agonized waiting when every second dragged. Sally had braved those precipitous stairs so that she might be the first to see the carriages lumbering up the hill.

They had played there as children, a spot made doubly attractive because it was forbidden. A former lookout where sentinels had scanned the road for enemies. A couple of rusty swords lay half buried amongst the debris of dead leaves and untenanted birds' nests. Sally picked one up, and in instant, flashing memory, saw William whirling it over his head in hot pursuit of Denzil, then Guy's tall figure appearing at the head of the stairs, furiously angry, clouting his brothers and ordering them below. She remembered the sharp pain of his alarm and anger. He had said it was dangerous and no place for a girl. Tears of humiliation had stung her eyes then, and they did so now.

The gulls wheeled and screamed around the tower, like echoes of the past. She leaned on the stone parapet. The western sky was shot with colour, flame, great bands of peach, a hint of green and eggshell blue where pink clouds trailed. Against that immeasurably distant luminosity, the near branches and clustering foliage looked black. From this vantage point the whole panorama was spread out, an enormous patchwork quilt of fields and purple moors on one side, the sea glittering on the other.

The tangy air mingled with the smoke billowing from the chimneypots on the roof below. Rooks were circling the elms, settling to roost, noisy, quarrelsome. Sally could see the numerous outbuildings stretching in a straggling line from the high walls which enclosed Wylde Court. Like most large country houses, it was very nearly a self-supporting unit. Its flocks, herds and piggery supplied the meat; its fields and gardens gave flour for the bakery, fodder for the horses, hemp and flax for spinning, fruit and vegetables for the kitchen and stillroom. At the rear lay the farm houses, the blacksmiths' forge, the poultry pens and slaughter-house. There was a carpenter's shop, aromatic with the sharp reek of sawdust, carpeted with wafer-thin, curly shavings.

Sally had visited each that day. The genial brewer had lured her into his cellar where he made ale, beer and cider. The maids had been busy in the steamy laundry, boiling, scrubbing and starching, then spreading the clothing on bushes or lines to dry out in the sun. The coolness of the dairy had been a relief after the hot, soapy washroom, a place in which to linger. The girls had been hard at work making butter and cheese, tongues

71

wagging in time to the revolving of the barrel-churns and the clacking of the cheese-press. There was a wholesome scent there, and glasses of buttermilk to drink. Charms were nailed over the doors and tied to the churns. Everyone implicitly believed that witches could badly affect the milk. So the girls muttered incantations as the plungers went up and down, and threw a silver sixpence into the vat to stop it being witched, though some held that three white hairs from a black cat's tail would do as well.

'Charms and witches indeed!' Sally muttered, half convinced, half sceptical, her eyes searching the road which wound like a silver thread into the distance. Meggy was convinced of their powers, and so was Dora. Supposing I brewed a love-potion and gave it to Guy, she mused, would he want to marry me?

It was foolish to even consider it, more foolish still to feel sick with excitement and riven with dread. His important guest could be a woman. Try as she might to drive away the thought, it kept returning like a cloud of whining, persistent gnats. Stop this at once! You'll drive yourself demented! she lectured her wayward mind, but the pain continued until she longed for the courage to throw herself over the rail and end her misery.

The clouds had finally won their day-long battle with the sun and the view was sinking in the evening light. A veil of smoke from cottage fires was drawing a pewter curtain across the sky. Sally shivered and pulled her shawl closer. She walked to the other side of the tower. The front of the house was just visible at an angle below. There were statues of deities in niches between the windows and over the central door. They stared with blind eyes on the trim terrace, walled in by balustraded and pinnacled enclosures with Moorish pavilions at the corners. Were they waiting too? A hush had settled over all, a still, breathless hush. Sally's premonitions, kept at bay during the frenzied activity of the day, now gathered ominously.

She suddenly stiffened, hands colder than the stone on which they were clenched. There was a stirring far off along the road. She stared until her eyes watered, then spun round and flew down the rickety stairs.

'Lalage! Wake up! We have arrived!' said Guy, shaking her. She opened her eyes, yawned and stretched and then joined him at the open window. There were mounted guards riding on each side of the carriage, holding smoky flares aloft, following the tradition of escorting their lord to his ancestral seat.

They crossed the bridge over the murky waters of the moat and came to the house, black and solid in the dusk, fantastic towers and twirling chimneypots silhouetted against the sky. The light of the sinking sun shone like blood on the great bayed windows, making the gargoyles on the gable ends stand out, while the terrace was wrapped in gloom.

Guy did not wait for the door to be opened for him when the carriage stopped. He flung it wide, vaulted out and reached up his arms for Lalage, setting her down beside him. Footmen with lanterns lined the flight of wide, shallow steps which led up to the terrace. Sally stood at the top of them with William, Denzil, the children and members of the staff.

She saw Guy coming, her awareness flickering, the scene slipping in and out of focus. Even from the distance between them, he looked different to any other man. She had forgotten how tall he was. Her heart was beating so violently that she was stifled. I'm going to faint! she thought desperately. I'm going to do something terrible and make a fool of myself! But habit dies hard, and she did neither, calmly meeting his eyes when he reached the terrace, hearing his voice, dipping into a curtsey.

It was only then that she registered the person at his side and in that nightmarish moment, was forced to accept the truth. Guy's so-important visitor *was* a woman, after all. She had the terrible feeling that she was going to fall apart, collapse in little pieces from head to toe.

'Good to see you, Guy,' William shouted, clasping his brother round the shoulders. 'How the devil are you?'

Guy was smiling widely, shaking hands with Denzil who had stepped forward. 'I'm well – very well, and glad to be home. Let me introduce my guest. This is Miss Lalage.'

She curtseyed, they bowed, and she made some murmured response. Sally could not hear what she said, but knew that her voice was low, melodious, heavily-accented. Then William's hand was on her elbow, leading her into the circle where Guy presented her to his beautiful friend. Their responses were most polite, icily correct, but Sally was devouring her with her eyes. Beautiful she certainly was – beautiful beyond the dreams of men. The dark, rich velvet of her crimson pelisse set off her dark, rich colouring to perfection. There was something unearthly about her stance, her stillness. Tall for a woman, slender and graceful; when she moved she seemed to glide, like a dancer. Her head was very upright on her neck, poised, proud, but it was her eyes which struck Sally most, the strange power of her eyes.

'Where is Mamma?' Guy asked.

'She awaits you in the Red drawing-room,' William replied, and they exchanged an expressive grimace. 'May I speak with you when you've done your filial duty?'

'In the study in an hour?'

'Yes.'

The children were waiting and Sally led them forward. The two elder ones dutifully kissed Guy's cheek when he bent down, but Miranda hung back, peeping out from behind Sally's skirt.

'Miranda,' Guy turned to her, smiling encouragingly. 'Come here, child.'

She backed away, her thumb in her mouth. Sally put an arm round her, embarrassed by her reluctance for Guy was looking none too pleased. 'Don't be frightened – come along.'

'Haven't you a kiss for me?' Guy sank down on his heels, holding out a hand, but still the child dragged back, her eyes fixed on Lalage. Huge eyes, unwavering in their intent scrutiny. Guy frowned, straightened up and said: 'Lord, but you're a funny little thing. Aren't you pleased to see me? Tell you what – I've presents in my luggage for good girls. Don't you want to see what I've brought you?'

Miranda removed her thumb. 'No,' she said, and popped it back in her mouth.

William and Denzil laughed at this failed attempt at bribery, but there was a stern look on Guy's face as he upbraided Sally. 'The minx has not improved her manners. I told you to be firm with her.'

'She is shy, sir,' Sally answered, controlling her anger. 'Give her time. A child's memory is short and you have been away for some months.'

'You are too lenient. Dammit, I'll not tolerate her rudeness.' He seized Miranda, hauling her towards him. 'Don't be wilful. I want you to meet my guest.'

Miranda did not flinch or struggle. Though quite capable of kicking and biting if provoked, she was limp in his hands, gazing up at Lalage. Her face looked suddenly old beyond her years. 'Tell her to go away,' she said, her clear treble ringing over the terrace.

'Bah!' snorted Guy, giving her a push in Sally's direction. 'I can see that you need a much firmer hand. I'll speak to you later about this gross misconduct, Sally.'

He turned on his heel, giving brisk orders to his valet about the disposal of the baggage and instructing Miss Potter to conduct his guest to her room. Then without stopping to change his travelling costume, he went directly to the Red drawing-room. Though his step was brisk, his mind lagged. He would far rather have been meeting William for there was much to talk over.

A footman was on duty, bowing and pushing open the high double doors when Guy appeared. He paused for an instant on the threshold, the magnificent proportions of the room striking him afresh. It lived up to its name, the vibrant warmth of various shades of red complementing one another. Deep scarlet drapes, held back by thick golden cords, hung at the long windows which opened out on to a paved walk. Lady Charlotte often took the air there for it was a secluded spot where a black marble dolphin sported in a fountain, while stone urns and naked statues added a distinctly foreign touch, reminding her of trips to Italy in her hey-day. The walls of the room were covered in crimson watered silk, and there were four-branched candle-holders set here and there against its surface. The ceiling was ornamented with a wealth of elaborate plaster festoons, and richly painted with scenes depicting the journeys of Ulysses.

Lady Charlotte had brought the furnishings back from Europe many years before when they had been the height of fashion – delicate walnut chairs upholstered in rose damask, Venetian mirrors in vast gilded frames, side-tables and escritoires inlaid with mother-of-pearl and marquetry. These pieces contrasted with yet complemented the oriental cabinets, lacquered in black and red, supported on squat legs round which golden dragons writhed. A spinet stood near one of the windows, and a large harp, its frame curved like the proud figurehead of a ship.

His mother sat by the fire in a winged armchair. He crossed the wide expanse of parqueted floor. It shone like water and he remembered how, as a boy, he had imagined the bright Persian rugs to be islands on a brown sea. He could almost hear her scolding voice: 'Don't leap about like a frog, Guy! Is that how you enter your Mamma's presence?'

Now there was no greeting. She did not speak or move until his shadow loomed over her. Then she opened her eyes, saying: 'My God, how tall you are. I had forgotten that I bred a giant.'

She spoke sharply, looking up at him without blinking, asserting herself at once, giving him no chance to gain the upper hand. 'It was the dazzle of the firelight. I was not asleep.' Had it been Denzil creeping up on her, he would have mocked her teasingly, lovingly, but Guy said nothing. 'Not quite asleep,' she continued, as if in the hope of attracting some reaction from him. 'I was thinking of your father and of the things that happened long before you were born. I suppose you find it surprising to realize that anything of importance occurred before you strode the earth?'

Guy shrugged, his face shuttered, experiencing that irritation which his mother always provoked. 'I've not thought about it, any more than speculating on what will happen when I'm dead.'

'Death!' she shifted impatiently. 'We don't want to talk about that. A morbid subject too often on people's minds these days. It's the fault of those damned peasants in France, and now the war. Most disturbing. Folk are wasting time wondering and questioning life, death, monarchy and religion, and where does it lead them? Doubting their government and uncertain of their faith. I never doubt mine.'

Guy's lips twitched in a smile. Mamma never doubted. She was always right. This was not a state of mind brought about by advancing years. As far back as he could recall, she had been convinced of her supremacy, conducting her life on broad, simple principles, hating anything vulgar or low, and quite uninterested in the problems of human nature.

She had not risen to welcome him for, though once a keen horsewoman, a fall had damaged her right leg and she now walked with an ebony cane when indoors, and an elegant stick fitted with a chamois-horn handle and a spiked ferrule for outside. This handicap annoyed her profoundly, preventing her from keeping a finger on the pulse of Wylde Court. She was obliged to depend on her companion, the long-suffering Chalmers, or Sally to find out exactly what was happening in and around its walls.

Guy kissed her extended fingers. Their tips were icy despite the lace mittens she wore and her position close to the fire, yet she was indomitable, splendidly attired in black silk, a deeply fringed, brightly patterned shawl covering her shoulders. Her hair still retained its fiery hue, though there were silver strands mingled with it now, beneath the jaunty feathered turban which she wore at an angle. He grudgingly saluted her courage

76

and her good looks, knowing how rigorously she fought the appearance, mind and habits of the elderly. She did not make herself ridiculous, as some women might. It was not part of her attitude to conceal her real age, in fact she was rather proud of it and of the little mark the years had left on her.

Her energetic face was watchful. 'So, home at last, eh? What have you to say for yourself?' she challenged, adding: 'Sit down for goodness' sake! Standing there like some infernal tiger lashing its tail at me!'

He took the chair beside her, his mind full of their quarrels in the past. They had always argued and fought, too alike to be friends for long. She had not mellowed much, autocratic as ever, possessed of a fierce, independent spirit. This fire displayed itself in every movement of her hands, animated each expression of her still-beautiful face. It looked out at Guy from green, vivacious eyes, and spoke in her ringing voice, bestowing on her an unfailing lust for living.

'I am thirty-four years old, Mamma,' he reminded, laying back in the chair, hands locked behind his head as he gazed at the ceiling, long legs in close-fitting breeches stretched out towards the hearth. 'I don't have to answer to you for my comings and goings.'

'You'll give me the respect which is my due,' she retaliated hotly. 'Stop slouching, you rude oaf!' With a grin, Guy obeyed, sitting up and resting his hands on his knees. 'That's better. Now, tell me, why did you not write to me? I've not received a single line all the months you have been abroad.'

'Nor I from you,' he countered in a dry tone.

'Phsaw! That is not the point,' she sparked back at him. 'Denzil writes every day when he is absent – whereas you! Lord, what a fine example of a dutiful son!'

'Denzil, always Denzil,' he snarled. 'The way you dote on him is laughable.'

'At least he cares for me – spends time with me – does not go wandering off God knows where!' She was envious of Guy's freedom, caged in the house with only that stout, tittle-tattle Chalmers for company. 'Much you care!' she added tartly.

'Of course I care!' He ran an exasperated hand through his hair. 'Denzil has been away too, at university, and 'tis high time he pulled his weight around here.'

There was something troubling her and although it was unlike her to speak ill of her favourite, she now said slowly: 'High time he left Oxford, you mean. You must talk to him,

Guy. I cannot think what has come over him. He used to be so careful of his appearance, but when he arrived yesterday he was positively slovenly. At dinner last night, his conversation was most upsetting – so hot in his criticism of King George and the Prime Minister – saying that the rich should give their money away to the poor – even suggesting that we should do likewise!' Her voice rose an octave at such a preposterous idea.

'Denzil was ever the victim of some freakish sentiment wildly at variance with the rest of ours,' Guy laughed without humour. 'He needs something to occupy his mind. I'll see to it, Mamma.'

She leaned forward, her eyes sharp. 'He should have his own property, then he'll know what ownership means. I've been discussing it with him. He wants you to give him Highfield Lodge.'

'The devil he does!' Guy exploded and got to his feet, pacing up and down, his face dark with anger. 'And what, madame, does he intend doing with it?'

'Raise thoroughbred horses.' There was satisfaction in her reply. Horses and racing had always been her passion.

'On my money, I suppose.'

'He has his allowance, his share of the estates. If he needs more, then I shall supply it.'

'It won't be enough to run Highfield. To hell with him! Horses be damned! He'll more likely turn it into a bawdy-house!'

'I don't know what you mean,' she said coldly.

'Oh, come, my dear mother, when will you admit that your sweet, baby-faced boy is a womanizer?' he scoffed unpleasant-ly. 'Why, you've probably a score of grandchildren scattered up and down the country, though I'll wager you would not allow their dams to cross your doorstep.'

'How dare you!' She was white and shaking. 'You of all people! Ha! A fine one to preach morality! I have long sus-pected that it was your profligacy which drove poor Celeste to an early grave.' Charlotte had never shown any compunction at hitting below the belt.

The barb went home and the pain was as clear as a thumb-print on window-glass, but: 'I need Highfield for my own use,' he said frigidly.

'What nonsense! You are hardly ever here. What possible use is it to you?'

'I hunt over that way. It is convenient, somewhere to pass the night if need be. That's what it was built for.' A retreat from you, he wanted to add, but this was only partially true. He had other plans for Highfield just now, a secluded place, hidden deep in the woods.

'So, to satisfy a whim you would deny your own brother,' she shouted, those green eyes which matched his own, that red hair a key to her impetuous temper.

'I shall do as I please. Damn Denzil,' he grated, glaring at her. The years rolled away. He was as he had been in the nursery, red-faced and roaring, pitting his will against hers.

'How can you damn your brother, you unnatural monster?'

'Very easily, Mamma – and I can damn you too!'

'You devil! Oh, if only your father were here, he'd beat some sense into you. Get out of here before I curse you myself!'

He rounded on her, white to the lips. Those aching feelings of tenderness and pity, as he had watched her asleep, reared up and goaded him. Once more she had cheated him, robbed him of the ability to show his affection, his need for her approval. He had thought himself past caring, but found the hurt as raw as ever.

'You've always cursed me! Was it because father favoured me as his first-born son? Were you so eaten out with jealousy that you loathed me from the cradle?' he demanded.

'How wicked you are! Heavens, what a rage you are in! I would never have dared speak thus to my mother, and neither would you if your father was alive! Age has not improved you,' she said with a kind of satisfaction at having made him lose his temper, but his words had been unerringly true.

She remembered her simmering resentment when hunting had been forbidden because he was in her womb. Mark would not countenance any risk to his expected heir. And the birth. She had never dreamed it would be so agonizing – that tearing, racking sensation when she had screamed and writhed like the lowest trollop. How could she not dislike the large, bawling, wrinkled object torn from her protesting body? How share her husband's delight and pride in him?

Guy's hands were knotted as if he longed to take her by the throat and strangle her. Instead, he went to the window, scowling out into the darkness. The moon was full, rising above the black ridge of the east tower. He wanted to turn his back on her, to leap on his horse and ride along the level sand edging the complaining sea, where the starlight gleamed on the slow-turning waves and the moon made a glittering path luring one to adventure. He smiled at his own absurdity. Jesus, he'd have his fill of adventure before long.

Forcing a semblance of calm, he said over his shoulder: 'Perhaps I am being unfair to Denzil. Truth to tell, I don't know him very well. Our paths have crossed seldom of late. William will be the better judge of his character.'

'Yes, you should converse with William.' Her mind had skipped two or three paces and she was launched into a new topic. 'He too is behaving most oddly.'

Guy turned, never able to follow the bewildering convolutions of her thoughts, and he was wary, praying that William had followed orders and been discreet. 'How so?'

Her hands spread in a confused gesture. 'Nothing dramatic, but he seems secretive, preoccupied – quite unlike his usual frank and open self.'

'Perhaps he is courting, Mamma – some young lady must be at the root of this.' Guy was anxious to divert her from the true cause. William must be warned. Mamma was far too cunning at wheedling secrets from the unsuspecting.

She shook her head. 'I think this unlikely. But now, tell me about this guest of yours.' Again, that disconcerting jump of subject. 'Someone pleasant, I trust – a gentleman of good breeding who will prove entertaining, unlike the riffraff with whom you usually waste your time.'

Guy smiled sourly. 'Quite unlike, Mamma. It is a young lady.'

'Oh, God!' She raised expressive hands and eyes to the ceiling. 'I might have guessed! Not like that Mortmorcy creature who visited here last year! Lady Hollingbrook was telling me about that scandalous masked-ball you gave at the town house before you went abroad, and how that woman appeared stark naked!'

'Not at the beginning of the evening,' Guy put in drily.

'Oh, so you admit it? How dreadful! Well, if this is another of your giddy fly-by-nights, I do not intend sitting at table with her,' she said contemptuously, very upright in her chair, hand clenched over the silver knob of her cane.

'So, you are already prepared to dislike her, knowing nothing whatever about her.' He was angry again.

'You've told me nothing. How can I know?'

'Why the hell should I? This is my house. I'll entertain Old Nick himself, if I wish! If you don't approve, then go and live in

the Dower House, and take that confounded Denzil with you.'
Guy could stand no more.

'You'd like that, would you not? So eager to be rid of me. I
only came back after Celeste died because I felt it to be my duty,
and this is the thanks I get!' She was blazing away at him, but
she was trembling.

'You came because you're a bloody busybody who can't keep
out of anyone's affairs!'

'Get out of here!' She rose, bracing herself on the arms of her
chair. 'Such ingratitude. I shall remain as long as it suits me,
and certainly until you marry again.'

'Thank you for being so forthright, Mamma.' He bowed
from the doorway. 'I might even be forced to endure the
shackles of matrimony once more, to enable you to keep that
vow.'

'Go away – go – go!' she cried.

The door slammed behind him and the sudden silence hit
her. She sank back, exhausted. No one else in the world had the
power to upset her so much. His temper had always distressed
her, but now he was terrifying. She had never feared a man
before, not even Mark, though he had been headstrong and
masterful. Yet, when she had awakened and seen him there, she
had surprised something else, a touch of compassion, even
love. Her heart had leapt and she had been thankful that
he was home. But their quarrel had swept this good feeling
away, leaving nothing but the old anger, the life-long misunderstandings.

She reached for the silver bell on the low, round table and
rang it vigorously. Chalmers entered promptly, that plain,
dumpy, annoying woman who was, nevertheless, unswerving
in her devotion. She bustled up, filled with such an air of
importance and hinted indignation that Charlotte knew she
had been eavesdropping. Her impotency, her dependence on
such a woman was like fire on the oil of her wrath.

Chapter 5

Sally took the children back to the nursery, left Dora to put them to bed, and then traversed the corridors to the wing where Lalage had been given a room. She found Miss Potter there, most correct in manner but hardly able to contain her curiosity.

'Shall I send up your maid, miss?' she was saying as Sally entered the magnificent chamber.

'I have no maid,' Lalage answered with a cool look which effectively dammed further questions.

'I will order one of the servants to assist you,' Sally interposed.

'Thank you,' Lalage replied, while Miss Potter curtseyed, gave Sally an annoyed glance at the loss of this opportunity to pry, and went out.

'Is there anything else you require?' Sally stood watching the foreign woman whom Guy had brought home.

Lalage gave a fleeting smile. 'I would like to bathe,' she murmured and she was looking, not at Sally, but at the furnishings. Her inspection was very close, uncomfortably reminiscent of a creditor making an inventory.

There was no doubt that it was extremely luxurious, redecorated when the vogue for chinoiserie held sway, the walls covered with a wealth of hand-painted pagodas, chrysanthemums and brilliantly plumaged birds. These exotic motifs were echoed in the curtains of the four-poster bed whose slender columns supported a domed tester. Lalage crossed to the marble fireplace with its tumbling array of fruit and vines, carved by a master. She spread her hands to the glowing coals.

'Are you cold?' Sally inquired, as befits a hostess concerned for the comfort of her guest.

'England has a chill which seems to eat into my bones.'

'Is this your first visit?' Sally was conscious that it was she who was making the overtures. Lalage was disinclined to talk.

'Yes.' She nodded and silence yawned between them.

Lalage left the fire and began to prowl round the room, feeling it out, easing herself into this new situation, as a cat would. Where on earth had Guy found her? Sally wondered.

Was she some French refugee who had fled from Paris? She seemed refined, unlike that bitch Aurora Mortmorcy whom he had entertained last summer. Everything about her had put Sally's hackles up yet, in some ways, she had been easier to deal with. At least one knew what to expect from Aurora.

'I hope that you will be comfortable here,' Sally said in an almost desperate attempt to be friendly. 'This room has a lovely view and is, I think, one of the most beautiful in the whole house.'

As her lips formed the trite words, she was suddenly dissatisfied with her own modest apartment, a part of the nursery wing. It was little better than the housekeeper's.

'It is very nice,' murmured Lalage in an abstracted fashion.

Still struggling for communication with this odd female, Sally opened the doors of the highly decorative armoire. 'The maid will unpack for you when she comes,' she said brightly, glancing at the bags which had already been brought up. 'Have you many dresses? There should be ample room for everything.'

Lalage was lingering by the dressing-table where the mirror was on an adjustable stand, lit by candles whose sconces were an integral part of the frame. Her fingers were lightly caressing a lacquered toilet-box which stood on its polished surface, then moving slowly to the cut-glass perfume bottles and the pretty cosmetic jars. She raised her eyes and stared at Sally in the mirror. 'I did do some necessary shopping in London,' she replied, her mouth moving like that of an automaton which spoke pat phrases when wound up. She raised her arms and took off her hat, ruffling her fingers through her crisp black curls.

'What of your jewels? You will be able to keep them here if you wish. The servants are trustworthy, but if you have anything of great value, then I'm sure Lord Beaumaris will put it in safe-keeping,' Sally blundered on, acutely aware that this was the most difficult encounter of her life. Making contact with Lalage was like trying to push a great boulder up a hill.

'You're most considerate, and I will follow your advice,' Lalage answered, 'but I possess only one piece which I would be distressed to lose, this ring which I always wear.' There was a musing, secretive smile about her lips as her fingers touched the heavy silver band on her right hand.

There came a knock on the door and Sally welcomed the interruption though she was rather surprised when Bethany

Wicker tripped pertly into the room. Bethany was no longer in a servant's uniform – Miss Potter had decked her out in a brown taffeta gown, lace-edged pinafore and frilled cap. She bobbed a curtsey to Sally and was then presented to her new mistress. After carefully instructing her as to her duties and promising to send up hot water, Sally was relieved to leave them together.

She went directly to the day-nursery, intending to assure herself that the children were asleep before going to prepare for dinner. Her mind was whirling with confused, distressing thoughts as she pushed open the door. Looking across the candle-lit room, she saw someone leaning against the mantel. Her heart gave a great bound and she paused, taking time to control herself.

'You've been an infernal long while, Sally,' barked Guy, raising his head, his eyes meeting hers.

'I'm sorry, sir, but I had no idea that you were seeking me. I'm not a mind-reader, you know.' Her voice was sharp, but it was the only way she could speak at that moment. Her knees felt as if they had turned to jelly.

'God, don't you start!' he snapped. 'What in hell's name ails the women in this damned house? Fine welcome indeed! First my mother, and now you.'

Puzzled and annoyed by this attack, her emotions were in a turmoil. He was in an aggravating mood and his sneer fired her anger. 'What can I do for you?' she asked, very cold and formal.

'You can perform your duties correctly, for a start. That disgraceful scene when I arrived. Miranda should be soundly whipped.'

Sally gasped at this. She stepped towards him with a fierceness which took him aback. 'No one shall lay a finger on her.'

'And if I command it?'

'Then you will be disobeyed, sir.'

She stared up at him defiantly, appalled by his lack of sensitivity yet terribly aware of his nearness. He dominated the room, looking out of place midst the toys and childish accoutrements. So tall, making her conscious of her lack of inches. The top of her head did not reach the pit of his throat yet she stubbornly held her ground, trying to ignore his fatally attractive combination of aristocratic birth and good looks. He had changed for the evening, was magnificently attired. His London tailor had surpassed himself, producing a mulberry silk coat with bold silver stripes, double-breasted, cut very short in front but with tails which reached his knees at the back.

It had large lapels, wide cuffs, a collar up to the ears, and was worn over a waistcoat of wider, sparkling stripes. The white of his high stock contrasted with his swarthy skin, and he wore cream satin breeches which were smoothly form-hugging from waist to mid-calf, the ensemble completed by white stockings and flat, unadorned pumps. Sally was only too conscious that she was still in her practical day-dress, wishing for the thousandth time that she was devastatingly beautiful.

His moods were like quick-silver and now his face softened. He smiled and she felt her will to oppose him weakening. 'Still the spitfire, eh, my dear? I'm glad that you have reminded me for I'd quite forgotten that you had a will and temper all of your own.'

'How else d'you imagine that I survive, here in this house where I'm neither servant nor lady?' Anger was a fine defence, strengthening her resolve, enabling her to resist the powerful pull of his charm.

A new expression crept into the eyes which were regarding her thoughtfully, hypnotic eyes under black brows which soared like wings – a hint of regret, a glimmer of interest, the beginning of respect. Sally held herself erect, hands loosely at her sides, her head thrown back, awaiting his next move.

He was restless, unsure, taking a few irate strides, then whirling round and coming back to her, driving his fist into his palm. 'But that child, Sally – so strange – unnatural! Is she no better?'

'She has not been ill,' she parried, trying to gain time, to think coherently.

'Don't play games! You know what I mean!' He was furious, struggling against the impulse to strike her in his bitter frustration at his daughter's affliction, but in her eyes he saw no fear, only a calm, deliberate look which quietly questioned. He groaned and sank his head in his hands. 'Can nothing be done? Has the doctor visited her of late?'

'She needs no doctor.' Sally felt herself to be a shield between Miranda and blind ignorance.

'We must face the truth, Sally.' He dropped his hands. 'She's not as other children. All the money in the world won't cure her.'

His unhappiness was terrible to see. Impulsively, she touched his shoulder. 'Don't distress yourself, Guy. I honestly believe her to be happy in her own way. We must accept her for what she is and do our best for her. But she must *not* be frightened, and punishment is out of the question. I've spoken to her and told her that she must be polite to your guest. Perhaps it will be wisest to keep them apart during her visit.'

He looked down at her gravely and, taking both her hands in his, he conveyed them to his lips. 'My dear Sally. Whatever should I do without you? You keep this family on an even keel. But it will be nigh impossible to prevent them meeting, for Lalage will be remaining here. She is homeless, destitute yet, I believe, worthy of care. I plan that she shall be educated, taking lessons with Cecily and Barbara, perhaps attending a finishing-school for young ladies later. Will you help me in this design, Sally?'

He was bringing all his charm to bear in order to win her over. Sally knew this but was powerless to refuse, her hand burning with the imprint of his lips. 'I will perform everything you desire, Guy,' she said, and marvelled at the steadiness of her response.

His gratitude was rewarding. His face lost some of its tension and he smiled widely. 'God knows what Mamma will say.'

'Doubtless she will have a great deal to say,' Sally answered, but she knew that Guy did not give a damn for anyone's opinion, ruthlessly ignoring the consternation he often caused. Time and again his actions had caused enmities and estrangements, but she had never once heard him say: 'I wish I had not done that.' He seemed never to question the wisdom of strong measures he had taken or to have a moment's regret at bitterness evoked, a law unto himself.

He was in a fine mood when he left her, as if a burden had been lifted from him. The encounter had been bitter-sweet, but any scrap of happiness Sally had gained now seemed to depart with him. The task he had allotted her weighed like lead in her heart. With dragging steps she went to her room to prepare for the dinner-party.

The dining-room, on the ground floor, was certainly impressive. There were two fireplaces opposite one another, both identical in pattern and of a pinkish marble veined with cream. On each hearth stood a shining brass basket between ornate dogs, filled with coals and logs. Crystal chandeliers sparkled overhead, their faceted drops multi-hued, the candles winking on the polished walnut of chiffoniers, shield-backed chairs and the long oval table supported on lyre pedestals. Ebony figures of blackamoors, picked out in gilt, red and emerald, held flambeaux aloft.

Charlotte presided there. Despite her hot words with Guy, curiosity had prevailed, reaching fever pitch. Besides which, she had already invited several friends from neighbouring manors to celebrate Guy's return. She was like an empress, seated at one end of the table, wearing purple sarcenet and a gauze turban, very bejewelled, with a necklace, earrings and brooch of rubies, while bracelets glittered on both arms over her long white kid gloves. A regal figure, calculated to intimidate any young upstart who might fancy her chances at Wylde Court.

The older guests had not bowed to current fashions, stubbornly clinging to wide skirts and tightly corseted bodices, coats of an out-dated cut and powdered hair, but the younger element excelled themselves in the latest finery. The women drifted along in Grecian draperies, while among the young men there was a predominance of velvet tail-coats with collars high and stiff enough to cut off their ears at a careless movement, frilled jabots, splendid waistcoats and dangling gold fobs.

Guy cast a cynical eye round the table, keeping them waiting, knowing that beneath the brittle smalltalk they were agog to learn the identity of the girl seated at his side. A gasp had arisen at her entry for she was wearing a delicate rose-pink gown girded by a sash of deeper red tied just below her breasts. It was charmingly girlish, the skirt fuller at the back, gathered into tiny pleats and falling into a small train. A gold bandeau with a single, pink ostrich plume bound her hair, and she had gold sandals on her bare feet.

He kept them in suspense as the many courses were served by a fleet of silent footmen with bland, expressionless faces. This amused him too. The staff, no doubt, knew all about it, little escaped their notice, the behaviour of their masters providing an endless stream of speculation below stairs.

Dinner proceeded at a leisurely pace and the conversation was light, weighty matters left until the gentlemen were alone over their port. William chatted of trivial events in the village, and the younger women attempted to cajole Guy into talking of London. Was he looking forward to the season there? Had he seen the Prince of Wales recently? And how was Bath – such a delightful resort, was it not? Guy declined to be drawn, drinking steadily, but only the glitter of his eyes and the hardening of his mouth betrayed it. Without appearing to do so, he was studying Denzil.

Earlier in the evening he had met William in the study and there pretence had been dropped. Guy had listened intently whilst William recounted his meeting with Captain Redvers and important matters pertaining to it. Then William had urged him to approach Denzil with a view to enlisting his aid. Guy had been dubious, but William had insisted that the boy was to be trusted, a brave fellow who badly needed a definite purpose, something in which to channel his energies lest they be directed towards the wrong political party. Guy had promised to sound him out, though still hesitant. But the truth remained; they needed every reliable man they could muster.

In a spirit of devilment, Denzil had gone to the opposite extreme in dress that night. He was garbed like a dandy. Lilac gloves lay near his plate; he wore gold fobs and a quizzing-glass, an extravagant suit and striped hose, yet his manner was not foppish. His face was alive, his bright eyes and open smile inspiring confidence.

Guy chose that moment to test him a little. 'When are you going to join the army, Denzil?' he said clearly, cutting across the laughter and chatter.

There was a shocked silence. Charlotte glared at him over the Waterford glass, the sparkling silver and porcelain dishes. Denzil, unperturbed, turned to him with a smile. 'I've no plans to do so, sir. I don't exactly know if I want to fight the revolutionaries. Maybe Mr Pitt was right and we should have kept out of it.'

Guy toyed with the slender stem of his wineglass, his smile taut, eyes tigerish. 'This was an impossibility, surely, after they had sent King Louis to the guillotine? In any case, it was taken out of his hands when they declared war on England and Holland.'

Denzil was reluctant to argue. Later, he would be happy to discuss politics with Guy, but now there were far more interesting things to do, the most important of which was getting to know his brother's fascinating lady-friend. His mind had done a crazy somersault when they had been introduced, the sight of her dark beauty infusing through his system a delicious sensation like nothing on earth or in heaven.

'Can't we forget troublesome Europe tonight, my Lord?' he answered lightly.

'Well spoken, Denzil.' Charlotte beamed her approval, but

flashed an angry glance at Guy. How dare he suggest sending Denzil into danger? I'll get even with him, she thought, let him give account for that gypsy-looking female simpering beside him.

Guy settled back in his chair, his thin smile betokening compliance, but he could not resist adding: 'I still think it would do Denzil a monstrous deal of good to face gunfire on the battle-field.'

Charlotte ignored this gratuitous thrust. 'I pray that you will excuse my unmannerly sons.' She looked at Lalage who sat, quiet and composed, gazing down at her plate. 'You are a foreigner, are you not? From whence do you come? Are you, perchance, an aristocrat fleeing the vengence of the mob?'

Lalage raised her eyes and met Charlotte's challenging ones. 'I don't know, madame,' she said.

'Don't know? What mean you, child? Speak up. I shan't bite you!'

'She speaks the truth, Mamma,' Guy drawled, but there was a coiled-spring alertness beneath his lazy pose. 'She really does not know where she was born or to whom. She has lost her memory.'

Charlotte found this incomprehensible. Unthinkable! 'Lost her memory! Then how did she come here? And, more to the point, how did *you* become involved in such an irregular affair?'

Guy regarded his mother with unkind enjoyment. 'I found her,' he replied.

The guests murmured in astonishment, fans fluttered like miniature banners and the gentlemen fidgeted with their snuff-boxes. One or two lorgnettes were raised. Charlotte was not amused. 'I fail to understand you, Guy. One can find a lost kerchief, a homeless dog, even an infant abandoned at one's door, but not a young woman. Make yourself plain, sir.'

So Guy told the story of how the sea had delivered her into his hands. He was brief and to the point and no one uttered a syllable until he had finished, then: 'I've never heard such a tale,' exclaimed Charlotte, giving him a suspicious stare. 'It sounds too much like something from a romance.'

'It is true, nevertheless,' Guy commented, finding her reaction more entertaining than a stage-play.

'I don't doubt your word, Guy,' put in William, a veiled expression in his eyes as he looked at Lalage. 'But it is devilish strange.'

'How very unpleasant to be unable to remember one's

background,' said Charlotte. 'One might be mistaken for a servant – or even something far worse. What a nightmare!'

'Oh, it is – you can have no idea, madame.' Tears tangled Lalage's long lashes. 'Perhaps I have no right to be sitting here in distinguished company.' She lay down her napkin and half-rose. 'You have been so kind but, with your permission, I'd best retire. It will be more fitting if I dine in the kitchen rather than embarrass you further.'

A chorus of voices protested, and Denzil's was louder than the rest. 'We know nothing about her,' he declared, 'therefore we must accept her for her charming self, be she princess or peasant.'

Guy placed a hand on her arm. 'What tomfoolery is this? You – a servant? I'll not hear of it.'

Charlotte silenced him. 'The girl is right. She has a deal of sense, it seems. It would be prudent to wait until we can learn her real history.'

'I have tried, Mamma. I sent messengers searching high and low in Morocco. Nothing came to light.'

'But is she a lady?' Charlotte was unconvinced, too worldly to be impressed by meek manners and the looks of a sultry Mona Lisa. 'How do we know that she isn't an adventuress?'

'We don't, Mamma, and that is the joy of it,' Guy answered crisply, his eyes filled with wicked glee.

The lackeys were clearing the table. Boxer walked in, solemn as a judge, bearing a salver set with glasses and decanters of port. At this cue, Charlotte swept up the ladies and bore them off to the Red drawing-room where, uninterrupted by Guy, she could continue her interrogation of Lalage.

Sally went with them, her thoughts too complex to unravel. She was ashamed of the jealousy which was clawing at her vitals. All through dinner she had watched Guy, his movements, his facial expressions, loving him so deeply that she knew what he was feeling before he was even aware of it himself. She had seen women come and go in his life, but sensed something different here. Certainly, there were odd ripples in the ether. Even Lady Charlotte was behaving strangely and as for herself, no one had asked her opinion or taken the slightest notice of her. She felt that she had become invisible and, with this sense of unreality, seated herself in a corner by the fireplace.

Charlotte took up her position in her wing-chair. 'Well, my child,' she remarked to Lalage. 'This is a peculiar tale indeed.'

Her companion attempted to arrange a shawl about her, but she jerked away petulantly. 'I don't need that, Chalmers. God above, I'm not in my dotage yet, though there are some who might wish it. Fetch me a glass of Madeira and be quick about it!'

She had no intention of playing the ailing matron tonight, though doing so without scruple when it suited her. Now she exercised a gracious, queenly and rather theatrical hospitality towards the young foreigner.

'Lord Beaumaris has been kindness itself to me,' said Lalage, gracefully sinking into a chair. 'I think of him as my knight-errant.'

'Do you indeed. How very naïve,' Charlotte rejoined, a touch acidly. 'I have never regarded him in that light. I am not certain that a halo suits him, though he does have the face of a fallen angel.' She leaned forward, staring directly into Lalage's eyes which were as expressionless as if made of velvet. She lowered her voice. 'Are you his mistress?'

This direct question did not upset Lalage's composure; she neither blushed nor dropped her eyes. 'Oh no, madame,' she answered. 'It would not be proper. Though I can't remember my past, I'm sure that it would be wicked to give myself to a man who was not my husband.'

Charlotte found it hard to believe Guy capable of chivalrous motives towards a girl as desirable as this one. 'Then what does he intend to do with you?'

'He has said that I should study, both books and etiquette. I think that he hoped you might arrange this for me, madame. He has great respect for your judgement.'

A crack appeared in Charlotte's armour. 'My son respecting me? You jest, my dear,' she said, though not unkindly, and her eyes twinkled.

'It is true, madame,' Lalage nodded earnestly, the dancing firelight bathing her gown in a deeper rose and glinting on her short curls. 'He has often spoken of you. In Morocco, he talked of little else but his home.' Her hands were restless in the lap of her silk gown. 'Oh, please – my Lady. I am so alone. I have no mother to guide me, or if I have, she is lost to me for ever.'

'I will discuss it with Lord Beaumaris,' Charlotte promised cautiously and her eyes encountered Sally's. 'This young lady will advise us, will you not, Sally?'

'He has already mentioned it,' Sally replied from her

shadowy corner, always out of place when Charlotte was entertaining, and never more so than now.

This led to further conversation, the other ladies clustering round. Sally tried to thrust away the uncharitable thought that Lalage was talking for talking's sake, as they asked her many questions concerning her discovery and stay at El Skala. She noticed that sometimes she seemed to sheer away from a subject or adroitly turn the flow by saying that she did not understand. Yet, on the whole, she answered with convincing frankness.

The gentlemen joined them later and an infectious gaiety prevailed. Each person there seemed quite determined to put the foreigner at her ease, vying with each other in an attempt to coax a smile from her red lips. The men settled down to cards and the ladies to gossip and backgammon. Lalage declined, saying that she could not play so, to amuse her, Denzil sat on the floor and built elaborate card-castles with a spare pack, rewarded by a dazzling smile and the approval of her amber eyes, before a careless movement sent them tumbling to the carpet.

'I'll find you a docile mare, if you want to ride.' He lolled on his elbows at her feet, watching the play of light over her features. 'You do ride, I presume?'

'I can't tell you. I've not done so since being with Lord Beaumaris.'

He sat up, his face eager beneath his rumpled curls. 'We'll soon find out. You simply must ride. We all do.'

Lady Charlotte had persuaded one of the ladies to perform on the spinet. Despite modest protestations of incompetence, she proved to be quite accomplished and soon sweet, lilting tunes tinkled through the room. Everyone was so busy being entertained that Sally could watch Guy unobserved. She could not help doing so, though pain was like a red-hot knife within her as she saw him speak to Lalage. There was an attentive interest, an intimate tone in his voice, totally unlike him.

William too was staring at the girl with an intent expression, and Sally felt betrayed for he usually paid scant heed to women and she had thought that he, above all people, would be her ally. He was basically a countryman, happier with his animals and the members of the simple farming community than with the social set. Both he and Sally knew everyone in the circle which revolved around Charlotte but never quite as intimates, always from the other side of an impalpable barrier. These people now seemed to be enchanted with the lovely foreigner, seeing her as a pleasant diversion. Providing that she continued to entertain without infringing on their rigid code of behaviour, they were happy in her company, but William's absorption in her was a bitter blow.

The dance tunes faded, replaced by notes which were slow, melancholy and beautiful. They gave Sally a feeling of acute isolation, so sharp that it was as if her heart was breaking in two.

It was late at night when the final carriage rolled away down the drive after the guests had said farewell, effusive in their thanks for a truly remarkable evening. It was only then that Guy could retire to the study with his brothers.

They had brought bottles and glasses with them and settled down by the fire. Guy took up a commanding position before the hearth, cravat loosened, jacket flung aside, in his shirt-sleeves and waistcoat. He held a glass in one hand and a long-stemmed pipe in the other. He frowned down at Denzil.

'What is this Mamma tells me about Highfield Lodge?' he asked sternly.

Denzil lay full-length upon the couch, hands locked behind his head. ''Tis her idea. I think she wants to give me an occupation.'

'She's right.' Guy placed his glass on the mantel-shelf and took a spill to the flames before applying it to his pipe. The fragrant smell of illegally imported tobacco filled the air. 'Idleness breeds vices as the sun breeds snakes. However, I can't let you have it. I need it myself.'

Denzil gave a shrug and a laugh. 'So be it, brother. I can't say that I mind. The place is falling to pieces, it needs time and money spent on it. But please don't assume that as an alternative I shall join King George's troopers.'

'Why not?' Guy asked coolly. 'Don't you wish to protect your homeland from its enemies?'

'Is France really our enemy?' Denzil was not in the least repentant, giving an impudent grin.

'The revolutionary government is.' Guy shot William a keen glance, very dubious about his suggestion that they should make Denzil a party to their secret.

'I'm not so sure.' There was a set about Denzil's jaw which added to his resemblance to the powerful elder brother.

'Are you saying that anarchy is the way?' He stared at Denzil from beneath scornful eyelids and, as he had expected, Denzil took the bait.

'That self-same anarchy was the best thing that ever happened to the down-trodden French peasants.' Denzil sat up, swinging his legs to the floor. 'It's bringing about a new, just society which we might do well to emulate.'

'A bloodbath? A Reign of Terror? To lop off our king's head, as the rebels did after the Civil War here, in the last century?' Guy almost purred, still and quiet. Denzil's courage faltered. He knew that when Guy was quiet, he was at his most deadly.

But he clung stubbornly to the ideals of which the other students had spoken so eloquently. 'If that is necessary, yes. If a king is a tyrant, grinding his heel into the necks of his people, then he deserves to die!' he cried.

'High words indeed, Denzil,' murmured William. 'But there is, after all, nothing more natural than a king, with his parallel in every pride of lions.'

Denzil refused to be browbeaten. He had feared yet desired this confrontation. 'Why should one man have so much?' His voice was firm. 'And why should we?' He swept an arm over the opulence of the room, the wine, the warm fire. 'What do either of you really know of the barbarous beggary, the suffering and squalor in which most of the population live? I've visited the London slums, seen their bestial existence. They are milled into money, and starved and sweated until they die. Don't you see that, but for luck, you might have been born in a foul lodging-house in a dingy street, with no other pleasure save visits to some liquor-shop?'

'So you believe that the French revolution is a blessing? The birth of a model society which we should copy,' William said, concerned as he looked from one angry brother to the other. 'And who, pray, is to bring this about?'

'I'll tell you who want to bring the old order down.' Guy's voice cut like a whiplash. While not disputing some of the arguments put forth by rational thinkers, he was experienced enough to know that there were elements at work with nothing in mind but wanton destruction. 'It is the agitators, smooth, glib and educated, out for political advancement, or agents from France whose aim is chaos and pillage.'

'If fighting is the only way, then we'll fight!' Denzil smashed his fist down on the table, making the decanter rattle.

Guy drank another glass of wine and studied Denzil with the

94

clarity brought about by a certain early stage of intoxication. Denzil was a dreamer who with the inexperience and fire of youth visualized a bright future which could never be. Even as he had argued with him, he had been filled with a kind of compassionate rage, remembering his own hot-blooded student days when he had hankered after a similar philosophy far removed from gross reality. He wanted to punch the heads of those who had been influencing his brother, rabble-rousers whose ambitions were complicated by passions, prejudices, intrigue and sheer ignorance of the facts.

With a great effort, he controlled his temper, saying quietly: 'Don't you realize that if the anarchists succeeded, there would be no more Wylde Court – no riches? If you destroy society, you'll destroy this too.'

'It wasn't destroyed when the Parliament cut off King Charles's head. Cromwell was right.'

'Cromwell was a traitor.'

'If he was a traitor, then so am I.'

Guy's eyes resembled the sea in winter. 'Denzil, listen to me. Do you know what is happening in France at this very moment? Have you any notion of the enormity of the crimes being committed against innocent people? Believe me when I say that I am not unsympathetic to the idea of bettering the conditions of the common folk, but men of violent, evil passions always work their way to the fore in times of trouble, staining their cause with their own selfish ambitions. The struggle for freedom in France has spread brutality and bloodshed throughout the land.'

'I'm not an ignorant fool,' protested Denzil, but Guy held up a hand, silencing him.

'Ah, brother, I'm not saying that you are a fool, only that you have not seen, cannot know how terrible it is there. The peasants have over-run the chateaux, smashing, burning, looting – murdering any who try to prevent them. Children have been butchered, men tortured for no other crime than that of being born aristocrats. Have you ever seen an infant torn from its mother's arms, swung by the heels and its brains dashed out against a wall? Have you ever heard delicately-reared girls screaming for mercy as they were grabbed by a gang of ruffians, flung to the ground and brutally raped? Have you stood amongst a mob of savages filled with the lust for vengeance, yelling for blood while the tumbrils come carrying their victims, and the guillotine does its ghastly work? I have.'

Denzil's face was pale and he had lost his defiance. 'You have been there?' he faltered.

'Yes, and William too,' Guy answered grimly. 'France, once so beautiful, is now a living nightmare, hell itself – where they have slaughtered their king, imprisoned his wife and children, and will kill them too ere long.'

'How do you know this? I've heard rumours of atrocities but scarce credited them. So much hearsay, surely? A ploy to recruit men for the army.' The change in Denzil was remarkable. He had lost his swagger, now bewildered, his certainties wavering.

'I have seen these things with my own eyes.'

'You? In France? Not recently – how could this be when we are at war?'

Guy came over to sit beside him, reluctant to resurrect horror but having no choice. Denzil must face the truth. 'I was there until late summer last year. War had not been declared then, so it was easier to get in. Things were very bad. I had work to do, dangerous work in which William was also involved. Then, after one particularly hazardous operation had been completed, it was deemed prudent if I absented myself for a while. I went to Morocco. In January, King Louis went to the scaffold and our government could prevaricate no longer. As soon as the news reached me, I came home, obeying instructions. We know that things have gone from bad to worse. The Carmelite monastery in Paris was taken over, a hundred and fifteen priests hacked to pieces. Now it is a terrible prison where aristocrats are herded together, awaiting trials which are mockeries, after which they go to the guillotine. This is only one of many such prisons where the cells are damp, dark and vermin-infested. They are overcrowded, filthy, appalling. There is no justice. All await death at the hands of the mob. Queen Marie Antoinette herself languishes in just such a place.'

Denzil's face expressed disgust and confusion, his bright ideals crumbling bit by bit. 'But, Guy – I didn't know – I thought the tales were exaggerated.'

William gave a grunt of bitter laughter. 'Nothing could be an exaggeration of the terrible truth.'

'But innocent women and children –' Denzil muttered, shaking his head, not fully convinced. 'What could it profit the rebel cause to murder them?'

'No profit, just blind fury whipped up by agitators, as they would do here if we allowed it to happen.' Guy stood up and

Denzil had never seen him so grave. He could hardly recognize him as the careless, fashionable gamester whom he had thought he knew, a man interested only in money and pleasure.

'What's being done to help these unfortunates?' Denzil demanded. 'Can't they escape before they're captured?'

'Many have, getting out when the trouble started, but others have left it too late.' William was looking at Guy, awaiting his word.

Guy gave Denzil a piercing stare, as if he would read his very soul. 'Would you help them, if you could?' he asked. 'Remember that it could be happening to us. Would you see Sally and our mother ravished, our servants killed if they tried to prevent it?'

Denzil was on his feet, looking as if he was about to swim the Channel and take the Carmelite prison single-handed. 'Of course I'll help! By Christ – lovely young girls, you say? Children and noble ladies? I swear that I'd give my life to save them!'

'And your anarchist friends?' Guy placed a hand on his shoulder, his grip like iron as he stared intently into his face.

'I'd tell 'em to go to hell if I thought that they intended to make mass murder commonplace in England!'

'I'm glad to hear it.' His brother retained his grip, large, menacing, icily determined. 'Your friends have a part of the truth, but only a part. Radical changes will take place here, but it will proceed slowly and, pray God, without a bloody revolution.'

'But what can I do? How can I help?'

'I will tell you,' said Guy, letting him go and taking his place by the fire again.

Time was of no matter then. The logs burned low, the level of the decanter sank, and the three men talked as if they would never stop.

Chapter 6

The face of life had changed at Wylde Court. Sally was aware of it, without knowing exactly how it had come about. Lalage's presence was an important factor, but there was something else, an air about the Wylde brothers which she was unable to diagnose but could sense, as one can be made uneasy by the inexplicable uneasiness of a roomful of people.

Much progress had been made in a week; Lalage was studying under Miss Stanmore, the vicar's daughter who taught Barbara and Cecily. She proved to be an apt pupil, quick and intelligent. It seemed that before very long she would be accomplished in the graces essential for a young lady. She had also proved herself in outdoor activities. Denzil was most impressed when they returned from their first canter.

'Rides that mare as if she was born in the saddle,' he declared, clumping in from the courtyard, muddy and dishevelled.

Lalage followed him, cheeks glowing, eyes bright, wearing a modish habit of tobacco-coloured velvet frogged with black, the skirt hitched up at one side over red leather boots, the jacket cut just like a man's. A round hat with a tall crown and small rolled brim, held in place by a veil, completed this stylish outfit, the effect in no way diminished by a ride in the rain.

'A regular Diana of the Chase, eh?' Guy said, strolling to meet them, having spent the morning closeted with Boxer, working on the accounts.

'You never spoke a truer word, sir,' agreed Jack, whacking the side of his breeches with his crop. 'We must arrange a hunt. Catch a spry little fox for you, milady.' He gave her an impudent wink, his manner affable and easy, never quite according her the respect which others did.

'I would like that.' Her eyes held his for an instant as she slipped an arm through Guy's. They walked into the Great Hall where refreshments were laid out on the refectory table. 'And what of these cockfights which Jack tells me are so exciting? May I see one?'

'A trifle blood-thirsty, my dear,' Guy demurred, smiling

indulgently as he handed her a glass of wine. 'Young ladies don't usually attend mains.'

'But you enjoy them, don't you?' She threw back her veil, eyes coolly regarding him. 'Whatever you enjoy is my pleasure also.'

'Really? Not everything, I think,' he murmured significantly.

Her body stiffened and she drew away. 'Be careful of my glass, Guy,' she warned, then finished her drink and added: 'If you will excuse me, I shall change from these damp garments.'

Without a backward glance, she walked up the staircase, leaving the three men staring after her. Denzil whistled soundlessly, exclaiming: 'What a stunner!'

Jack glanced at him, one eyebrow cocked quizzically. 'She's a dasher and no mistake.' Then he looked at Guy with those impudent eyes which missed little. 'You're a lucky dog, sir – but Gad's life – women! If I live to be a hundred, I'll never understand 'em!'

Guy's expression was thoughtful as his eyes followed Lalage's retreating back but he made no reply to their comments. Denzil, after a discreet pause, said that he too must take off his wet clothing and made for the stairs. Guy's face was stern, accent clipped as he reminded: 'I hope that pleasant dalliance will not put out of your head the important work that's afoot tonight.'

'All is ready, sir,' Jack's voice was low. 'Each man knows his part.'

Guy turned on his heel, picked up his cloak and swung it over his shoulders. 'Walk with me to the cliffs,' he replied. 'I would look at the cove again.'

Jack clapped on his hat and accompanied him into the damp garden. There was nothing servile about his approach to Guy. They had an understanding. There had been no hesitation on his half-brother's part when Jack had turned up at the house like the proverbial bad penny. Their association went back years. As boys, they had met in the woods near Old Scratch Mill, though Guy had been forbidden to mix with him. This only served to add to the adventure. They had snared rabbits, cooked them over open fires, dreamed of running away, of joining the gypsies, of becoming pirates. As they grew older, their sport became less innocent; they lured the local belles to secret nooks in the forest, seducing them, sharing them, using force sometimes, though this was hardly ever necessary. Then Guy had gone to university and Jack went to London where he was soon involved in the nefarious criminal activities of Whitefriars. Caught and thrown into Newgate, he had escaped and returned to Wylde Court. Despite Miss Potter's opinion of him, he was good at his job, a fine horseman and an experienced handler of fighting cocks, but it was not only this which allowed him to get away with casual behaviour. Over the past eighteen months he and his mother's smuggling associates had been of great value to Guy in another way. He needed Jack and kept him well paid.

Jack was not too easy in his mind about Denzil's inclusion in the business, and it was not the young man's extremist views which bothered him. Jack knew of his weakness for women, and whilst he too spent most of his free time indulging in love affairs, his was a hard approach. They never wound their cunning little fingers around his heart and he was way ahead of any tricks they might try. Denzil was too soft, he had decided, putty in their hands.

Guy did not speak as they walked and Jack respected his silence. A glance at the sky told him the weather was on the change, but would not be settled for a day or two. It had been raining almost constantly since Guy's arrival, only at rare intervals had the sun broken through the wet, rolling mists which came in from the sea. Fog was the last thing they wanted that night, and no moon. A dark, starlit run would be a godsend.

Guy too was taking note of the weather as they walked beneath the dripping birch trees. It was good to walk, easing the tension which was always there when they were anticipating the arrival of Redvers. Much better to be with him, finding release in action. He hated kicking his heels, waiting, curbing that huge concentration of energy which burned in him. Next time, he promised himself, next time I'll be there.

Lalage had been a diversion, of course, but this was a mixed blessing. She was an enigma. Her great eyes encouraged, but her frigidity repelled advances. Because of the bad weather, excursions had been hurried, drenched affairs, and they had been confined to the house. They had played carpet bowls, shuttlecock and battledore in the Long Gallery, with Sally and his brothers acting as chaperones. But Guy was a pastmaster at avoiding such inconveniences. No starchy duenna had ever stood between him and the object of his desires. It was Lalage herself who was the stumbling-block.

They reached a low, dry-stone wall, vaulted it and continued across the short springy turf towards the cliffs. The sheltering trees were left behind and the wind was strong. Guy's hair streamed back from his face as he headed into it, welcoming that wild buffeting which swept cobwebs from the mind. The great expanse of ocean came into view as they took a narrow path where the cloven feet of sheep had cut through the sward. The roar of the wind increased, thrashing against them as they stood on the cliff's edge, resting their backs against a boulder.

''Tis a good wind, sir,' shouted Jack, pointing over into the next bay. 'I can almost see old Redvers's ship creeping in there tonight.'

Six hundred feet below, the waves boomed as they pounded the rocks in a great fountain of spray, the white spume flying, the sun gleaming on the fragmented waves. They flooded into the cove, covering the pebbled beach which, from that height, mingled in a faint blue tint, as if ground by distance into coloured sand. The headland, the whole rib of the promontory was wind-lashed. Guy welcomed the biting sting of brine, filling his lungs with it. How different it was to Morocco, that lotus-eating enchantment where he had almost forgotten what was taking place beyond its shores, the bloody strife fading into a dream, blurred and remote, yet not quite. He had been marking time, keeping out of the way, as instructed, but leaving at once when the call came.

The gulls screamed overhead, their crooked wings beating the air. Some swooped in hurtling flight towards the water, then settled on the surface, bobbing like ducks. As if sawn straight down from the chalky turf to the beach, the cliff shut out the world. 'Has it ever occurred to you, Jack, that it is impossible to tell what century one is in just by looking at the sea?' asked Guy.

'That's true, sir,' Jack answered, his eyes on the horizon. 'We could be Saxons waiting the dreaded arrival of a Viking ship, I suppose, instead of our pirate friend. D'you know, I sometimes think about time – it's a funny thing, isn't it? I can remember things we did when we were lads as clearly as if it was yesterday, but I'll be damned if I can recall what happened half an hour ago, sometimes. I've talked to Ma about it – she knows a lot, that one. A wise old girl.'

They both stared down into the cove below, and Guy's mind was slipping notches. Lalage had done this to him, once the most unintrospective man alive. She had the power to stir up destructive memories, lost hopes, lost illusions. He had been sharply conscious of it the first time he had looked into her eyes

– deep pools in which he had felt himself disintegrating. 'Ah, memories, Jack – 'tis as well some stay buried,' he said grimly.

Jack shot him a strange look, charged with a mixture of liking, wariness and a tinge of resentment. 'Not so easy to do, sir. There are some things impossible to bury, some people who haunt one for ever.'

'Such as?' Guy asked, though he knew the answer, gazing at the heaving sea yet seeing the Mediterranean and the wet, oily bundle which had contained Lalage. With this uncomfortable, newly acquired sensitivity which she had aroused, he was aware that Jack was thinking of their father. Had this bastard son had much contact with the old man? he wondered. Had he admired him – loved him – wanted desperately to be acknowledged? Guy had tried to make recompense, to employ his half-brother, even to become his friend, but the gulf remained.

'I was thinking of the wenches, sir.' Jack turned it into a joke. 'We had some sport with 'em, didn't we? Most took it in good part, though there were at least a couple who got the wrong end of the stick, imagining that you were serious – even falling in love with you, silly bitches! D'you remember?' He kicked at the turf on the perilous edge, watching a chalky flake detach itself and begin to fall.

Guy scowled, vague pictures of various pretty girls drifting across his vision. He had paid them off handsomely, annoyed by their tears and lamentations. How dared they presume that he sought more than sexual gratification? They should have understood that to tumble the local lasses was the perquisite of the Master. Women! Another face blotted out the rest. That of his wife, Celeste. What a tiresome creature she had been – cloying, devoted, utterly boring. Though she had adored him, she had proved a most reluctant, shrinking bride. Whenever he had shared her bed, she had lain there, poker-stiff, enduring and dutiful. God, what a paradox! His mistresses were eager wantons, lascivious, demanding, but his wife – the one person with the right to bear him a legal heir, had found coition repulsive.

He shook himself, pushing the past back where it belonged. He had no time for repining, what was done was done and there was no retracing one's steps. 'You must be Denzil's guide tonight, Jack,' he said as they turned their backs to the sea, running down a slope where the grass was as slippery as silk. 'Is your mother prepared?'

'Aye, sir, ready and waiting.'

The land stretched into infinity, rolling purplish downs, hollows and ridges, with sheep and stubble and low hedges, hayricks and farmsteads. Guy owned every stick and stone of it, but now in company with many another man of title and wealth, he was willing to give his money, time, even his life for the cause to which they had dedicated themselves.

He glanced back at the sea, their greatest ally. It appeared to be solid, a boundless plain levelled by distance. It was as if one could walk to France and back. The wind helped him forward as he finished the slope at a run, shading his eyes, looking at the tumulus on the next rise. Butterflies hovered over its low dome. He made for it, Jack not far behind, and reached the top, careless of the pagan bones which might lie beneath his feet. He stood there, hands on his hips, surveying his domain. The fishing-boats were sculling in, heavy with their catch which would mean more money to pay for arms, for men, to grease palms and save lives.

His attention was drawn to a slight movement on the leeward side of the mound. A child was curled there, the tussocky grass forming a snug nest. ''Tis Miss Miranda,' observed Jack.

Guy scowled and bounded towards her. 'What are you doing here?' Concern sharpened his voice, but as his shadow covered her, she did not seem to notice him. 'Confound Sally,' he muttered. 'Such carelessness is not to be endured,' and he swept Miranda up in his arms, making for the house, so fearful that he almost ran.

'She's all right, sir,' Jack panted at his heels. 'She often comes out here.'

'I'll not have her wandering about alone,' Guy snapped, without slowing his long stride. She was as light as thistledown, her flaxen hair spread over his chest. He caught her peering up at him and slowed down. 'Why have you come here?' he asked.

'I wanted to ask the elders about the lady.' There was a faraway quality in her voice which made him stop, puzzled by her strangeness.

'But you are by yourself. There is no one else.'

'Oh, yes – they are here. They always come when I call them,' she answered solemnly.

'It is some sort of game you play, I suppose,' he said with adult condescension.

'I don't play games,' she said, dignified and serious. Over his shoulder, she smiled at Jack. 'Hello,' she nodded her head at him. 'Will you greet your mother for me? Tell her that I've been talking to the elders. She'll understand.'

'Right you are, miss,' Jack answered matter-of-factly. 'You must go and see her soon. She'll bake a cake for you.'

'Put me down, Papa,' she commanded, and walked along, holding his hand.

Guy was moved by the touch of those fingers clinging to his. She was so small, so trusting, this little creature whom he had never bothered to know. 'And what do they tell you, these friends of yours?' he asked gruffly.

She gave him a quick smile, but her reply was disturbing. 'It's a secret. I'm not allowed to speak of it – not yet.'

With that, she tugged her hand free and was away, darting towards the woods which bordered the garden. Guy was filled with dismay. For her, this was no childish invention, no fanciful imagining. She seriously believed that she saw and heard invisible beings.

Denzil was in a ferment of impatience. Lord, the night was a long time coming. Rising early, he had gone riding with Jack and Lalage and, on his return, had a final confab with William, infuriated by Guy who was acting as if nothing of importance was in the offing, working on dull book-keeping with an equally dull Boxer. He had changed out of his riding-clothes, checked his pistols a dozen times and drawn his rapier from its sheath, taking a few practice swipes. Lady Charlotte had summoned him and he had spent a fidgety hour in her company before escaping back to his room.

There diversion had awaited in the comely shape of the maid who was making his bed. They had unmade it together and used it for the purpose for which Denzil was convinced beds were invented, after which she had gone away about her work and Denzil felt better, for a short while.

He still found it hard to believe the tale his brothers had related. Stuffy old William who plodded round like a farmer, and that dashing rakehell Guy, implicated in such a business! It was incredible. Denzil had been moved by the story and very proud because they considered him man enough to assist them. He was determined to prove himself worthy that night. Guy was a dark horse, throwing up smoke-screens all over the place. Who knew what went on under that elegant exterior? And that female he had brought home from abroad, another intriguing thing. She was so young, almost a child with her air of nunlike purity and those sensual eyes. Denzil longed to try her out, to bend her to his will, to project thoughts, emotions, even love into her.

Restlessly he paced his room, then made up his mind and went to look for her. He did not believe that she was Guy's mistress, indeed Guy treated her as his ward, but even if she had been this would not have stopped Denzil. He had had other men's mistresses before. He found her in the deserted Long Gallery, that narrow, lovely room on the first floor, running the length of the building. It had bay windows at both ends and along one side, the glass ornamented by coloured heraldic devices which threw warm patterns on the polished wooden floor. Lalage was kneeling on the padded seat by one of the casements, staring towards the stable block, as if looking for someone. Denzil preened himself, hoping that it was he whom she sought.

The sunlight slanted through the diamond panes, forming a dusky halo round her head, and the pale oval of her face glimmered, as rapt and absorbed as a saint's, her fingers gripping the stone sill. She was wearing a pale peach afternoon dress embroidered with small clusters of flowers, and Denzil silently applauded these new fashions, they were so wonderfully revealing. Her back, turned towards him, was very straight, the head beautifully shaped, that strange air of chilly quietude absolutely spellbinding.

Some sense must have warned her that she was no longer alone. She gave him a sideways glance from her almond eyes. 'Pardon me for disturbing you, Lalage,' Denzil stammered, at a loss, for once, in a woman's presence. 'I was looking for Sally,' he lied.

'She is in the nursery,' she replied with a restrained smile.

Denzil hardly heard the words, only the cadences of her voice, with that enticing, foreign pronunciation. He stabbed about for something devastatingly witty to say. Nothing came. She did not move, poised there, neither encouraging nor dismissive, yet he feared that she was about to fly out of his reach. 'Did you enjoy the ride?' he managed at last.

'Yes, thank you, Denzil,' she answered.

At that moment, he regretted the time he had spent with sluts. This girl was different and he was not certain in which category to place her. He wondered what she would do if he tried to make love to her. He raised his hand, tempted to touch her hair where the sunshine rippled over it, to run his fingers down her long neck and unbutton the tiny seed-pearls at the back of her gown. The scent of her body was in his nostrils, and she seemed to be flowing out towards him, into him. There was nothing in this quiet room, in the whole world but her.

'Oh, Lalage,' he whispered, hardly aware that he spoke her name aloud.

'Yes, Denzil?' Those great velvety eyes were regarding him questioningly.

Denzil shook off the spell, smiled broadly and flicked at an imaginary speck on his cuff. 'Oh, nothing – I was just wondering how your dancing lessons were progressing.'

She slipped from the seat, standing beside him, and a smile curved her glistening lips which were the colour of wild strawberries. 'I've had but two.'

Denzil was on more familiar ground now, sensing a hint of flirtatiousness in her manner. He bowed over her hand, saying: 'Would you care to show me?'

She laughed then, gay laughter which surprised him. 'How can we dance? There is no music.'

He seized her by the wrist before she could move out of his reach. 'I shall whistle the tune.'

Her eyes were veiled, lips smiling. 'Shall I have to pay the piper?'

His arm was about her waist. 'That is entirely up to you, my dear Lalage,' he said meaningfully.

The polished boards made an excellent dance floor, and the great arched windows poured light over the couple. Lalage floated through the intricate steps like a butterfly. First he whistled the loure, an old, slow court dance in 6/4 time, then a gigue, with light, springy steps which gave him ample opportunity to clasp her and swing her off the ground, then followed the stately gavotte, two steps and a hold, with delicate wrist-play inspired by classical fencing movements.

They stopped at length, out of breath, but Denzil continued to hold her. She put up her hands and pressed against his chest, keeping a space between them. Her eyes were shining, her breasts rising and falling swiftly under the thin material of her gown.

'Lalage,' Denzil gave her a shake and pulled her closer, feeling her legs moulding into his thighs, desire rising hot in him. His lips were against her cheek, his fingers smoothing the satin skin of her bare shoulder. 'Lalage – who are you? What are you?'

She pulled free, staring at him angrily. 'Why do you ask? You've heard my story. Do you doubt it? This distresses me, for I had hoped we might become friends.'

'So we are,' he protested, running a hand through his hair, completely at a loss. 'Don't be offended. I'm sorry if I have upset you.' He could not understand the emotions surging in him, having the absurd notion of going down on his knees and kissing the hem of her skirt.

'Ah, would that all men were so understanding,' she sighed, her expression troubled. 'Most of them think of nothing but storming a lady's virtue.'

Denzil conveniently forgot his own peccadilloes. 'Who does this? Tell me, and I'll tear his heart out!' he shouted angrily.

'Hush, you must not speak so wildly.' She laid perfumed fingers lightly over his lips.

'Is it Guy?' he ground out, then when she did not answer, he turned her hand over, kissing the soft palm.

'I'll not tell his name,' she said, speaking very low. 'I refuse to provoke quarrels in a family who have shown me nothing but kindness.'

'If anyone troubles you further, you must promise to tell me. I'll defend you, Lalage, no matter who he is,' he whispered, kissing her wrist, her naked arm, his mind swimming.

She released herself, pushing him away gently. 'Thank you. I know that I can rely on you.' She gave him a dazzling smile, then added hesitantly: 'I have a small favour to ask.'

'What is it? Command me, dearest Lalage.' Standing there with frustrated lust knotting his gut, Denzil would have done anything for her.

'When we next ride, would you take me to the shore? Galloping on sand must be so exciting.' She stopped and one hand flew to her mouth. 'Oh, dear – you will think me too forward in asking.'

Denzil's head felt light. All he wanted was the feel of her in his arms again. 'Never! We'll ride there, if it is your desire.' He took her hand again, bearing it to his lips, pressing it to his flushed face.

She permitted this for an instant and then stepped back. 'Let us go tomorrow. And tonight, you have promised to teach me backgammon.'

He struck himself on the brow. 'Oh, Lord – so I did. I fear that I'll be unable to do so.'

She watched him from beneath her lashes, pouting slightly,

her fingers stroking the ivory sticks of her fan. 'How vexing. I was looking forward to it. You're meeting a sweetheart, perhaps?' She conveyed displeasure.

'No – nothing like that.' Denzil bit his lip, torn between loyalty to his brothers and this longing to please her. 'Guy has some business he wants me to perform.'

'I see. He is so masterful, is he not? He must be obeyed at all times.' Her voice was ever so slightly scornful. 'You don't have to lie, if indeed you are keeping a tryst. My maid, Bethany, tells me that you have quite a reputation for gallantry.'

Denzil flushed to the roots of his hair. That damned jade had seen him in the churchyard. Uncomfortably he wondered just how much she *had* seen. 'I swear that I'm not meeting a woman!'

She was unconcernedly rearranging her shawl. 'No such assurance is necessary. Your dalliances are of no importance to me.'

'We'll ride together on the morrow.' His face was eager. He wanted to detain her.

'I don't wish to trouble you – if you are otherwise engaged.' She drifted to the door, composed, completely indifferent, looking back over her shoulder when her hand came to rest on the brass handle. 'I'm quite sure that Jack Smithers will accompany me, should you be too busy.'

She nodded and went out, a faint, enticing perfume trailing on the air behind her.

Highfield Lodge was deserted when Denzil reached there, shuttered and dismal. By nightfall the bad weather had returned but the rain no longer floated down in delicate strands; it fell like an enormous waterfall hurtling over a cliff of black clouds. It had drenched him to the skin in seconds as he rode from Wylde Court.

He had not visited the lodge for years and, on viewing it, wondered why his mother had been so anxious for him to have it. He dismounted, tethered his animal, and walked up to the front door. In the gathering dusk, he could just make out the inscription carved over the lintel: 'Through this wide opening gate, none come too early, none return too late.'

The atmosphere was so gloomy that he doubted if anyone would wish to return. It was a Tudor house, built solely for the convenience of huntsmen in the days when not only deer but wild boar abounded. Now it had fallen into disuse. There was an acre of garden which had been allowed to run wild, a tangle of ivy swarming the walls, stone-flagged courtyard half smothered in weeds, and an air of dust, muddle and decay hanging over everything.

Inside, it was warren-like, confusing. A main staircase led to the upper rooms and corridors spread away from the hall, which was lit only by fanlights over the doors. Alterations had brought about a bewildering labyrinth of nooks and cranies. Following orders, Denzil found his way to the drawing-room, took some candles from his pack, dusted off a couple of holders and set them on the oak table. The flames flickered in the draught, the tapestries rustled against the walls like dead leaves falling. Denzil wished he had a companion in the eerie place. He found some kindling near the stone hearth and a heap of dry logs, struck a spark with his tinder-box and soon had a fire blazing. The cheery glow made the shadows retreat to the far corners.

He knocked the rain from his hat and took off his coat, spreading it over a chair near the fire, then unpacked his bag, placing food on the table in readiness. After doing this, he took up a lantern, went through the echoing hall and mounted the stairs. The light cast fantastic patterns on the walls, mingling with the patches of damp. His own shadow loomed, grotesque, gigantic, and he was glad when his task was over, dragging dusty quilts and blankets from the four-poster of the first bedroom he entered and carrying them downstairs. They had a mouldy smell and he pulled more chairs close to the fire to act as a clothes-horse on which to air them.

His coat was not dry, and the damp heat penetrated his shoulders as he put it on again and took up his hat. His sword felt strange, banging against his left thigh. Although he had learned to fence as part of his education, gentlemen no longer wore swords as an everyday accessory. His pistols were in leather holsters on each side of his saddle, bullets and powder-horn in the capacious pockets of his greatcoat. He remembered to place the flint and tinder-box on a ledge by the fireplace, carefully checked the bedding to ensure that no spark should ignite it, blew out the candles and felt his way to the front door.

The rain had not abated, gusting in when he opened it. In the dilapidated stables he found three horses, and after he had saddled them he mounted his own beast, keeping the leading reins of the others in one hand. He headed down the muddy track which would take him through the wet, windy forest to the shore. It was a wild night, the entire sky obliterated by thick, racing clouds. The gulley ran on, seeming never-ending, leading him deeper and deeper into the woods. He could see no more than a few inches ahead. Cursing, he groped blindly along, entombed in the thick blackness of cloud and rain and dripping foliage. At last the way widened and he struggled into a hollow at the end of the track. He halted. Jack was supposed to meet him there, but he could hear nothing above the continual rush of rain and the gurgling noises of innumerable runnels.

His heart nearly stopped when a dark shape emerged from the deeper gloom beyond. He dashed away the water which dripped into his eyes from the brim of his hat, recognizing Jack's voice. He was shouting above the tumult of nature. 'Hello there, sir. Follow me.'

Jack was on foot, just ahead. Through the tangle of branches Denzil could discern a dim light. The clamour of the rain was joined by that of the mill-race. Within minutes he was sliding from his saddle, entering a door which was cautiously opened by Molly Smithers, and standing in her warm kitchen, shivering and dripping.

William occupied a chair close to the flames, smoking a long church-warden pipe. He nodded across to Denzil. 'So far, so good,' he remarked, taking the stem from between his teeth.

'Where is Guy?' Denzil searched the shabby room for his formidable brother in vain.

'Someone has to remain and show his face at the dinner-table. Wouldn't do if we were all three absent at once,' William replied placidly, and Denzil envied his calm for his own nerves were jangling.

He spread his chilled hands to the flames. 'What now?' he asked.

'I'll stay here, for there is an outside chance that Redvers may take the next cove, if the coastguards are too thick in the first. You and Jack can reconnoitre the cliffs. If all is clear, you can go down and meet Redvers.'

'I don't think you'll encounter many excisemen tonight – too bloody wet,' commented Molly, taking a wooden ladle to the cooking-pot hanging on its crane over the flames. 'But your particular business, sirs – that be different. Watch out for spies.'

'We have a most effective way of dealing with spies, Molly,' William answered grimly.

'The best in the world,' agreed her son, throwing back his head and making a slicing gesture across his throat with one finger, pulling a gruesome face. He had been perched on a corner of the table, one booted foot on the floor, now he stood upright. 'Come, young sir, let's be gone.'

Jack, sure-footed as a chamois, knew the way, but Denzil, blinded by darkness and rain, had difficulty in keeping up with him. He slipped on mud and shale, groping along behind that darting, shadowy figure. The mill light dropped back, then was no longer visible. They were climbing steadily, no shelter now. The wind lashed his face as he crawled up the cliff path in Jack's wake. Cold sweat was trickling down his back and he could do nothing but go on, trusting that Jack knew what he was about. His fingers encountered rock on one side, and heard the sea roaring two hundred feet below on the other, its breath steaming up from the abyss. He could distinguish nothing, feeling his way with his feet. His hands touched grass and earth as he stole upwards, then the way dipped, widened, and he was clinging to rain-whipped fangs of rock.

He half-sobbed, half-cursed with relief, conscious that he stood on more level ground, a rocky terrace the width of which he could not ascertain. There was danger still, that was inevitable, but it was nothing to what it had been. His heart was pounding with exertion, his eyes smarting with sweat and rain and the effort of trying to penetrate the blackness. Then a figure suddenly materialized beside him and a hand was clapped over his mouth.

'Hush!' hissed Jack. 'Stay where you are!'

He was released, staggering against a solid wall of cliff. His ears were full of the booming surge far below and the noisy throb of the blood in his pulse. He squinted up and saw through the half-translucent vapours. Two black figures were struggling on the brink of a higher rise. Almost instantaneously, a body crashed on to the shelf at his side, rolled over the edge and plunged into the gulf below.

Jack was back again. 'Come on, sir. Down to the shore.'

By this time, Denzil had passed beyond fear. As if Jack's recklessness was infectious, he scrambled after him, slipping, falling to his knees, then up again as they descended. Never had firm ground felt so good as when they reached the cove, sheltering behind a huge, seaweed-covered boulder. They were not alone. His eyes, used by now to the gloom, made out the hunched figures of men in the lee, and there were more where the surf rolled across the sand, and boats bobbing in the dip and swell of the waves.

'The *Mayfly* is in, then,' said Jack to a squat, bulky man who was eyeing them suspiciously, weapons jostling about his person.

''Tis you, Jack, is it?' He lowered his cocked pistol. 'Aye, that's her sure enough. And look, here come the first of the boats. God, what a night for it! Blowing a gale and pissing down with rain! It'll confuse the bloody coastguards, with a bit of luck.'

'I've just dealt with one of 'em,' growled Jack. 'Went over the cliff, sweet as a nut.'

'May he rot in hell,' commented the man.

Jack made off towards the water's edge and Denzil ran after him. The men were wading out, waist-deep, battered by the waves but keeping their feet, seizing the first boat, hauling it to the shore. A silent, orderly operation, considering the difficulties. Denzil could see little, only knowing that Jack was splashing through the shallows, carrying something in his arms. Above the crash of water and wind, a child's voice was wailing, weary, terrified, and there were other people too struggling towards dry land.

Jack led them across the beach, away from the smugglers who were still intent on their own work. He paused in the shelter of an overhanging rock, gathering the party together. Denzil heard women's voices, and they were crying, then the deeper tones of their male companions. He could not understand what was said, but sensed that they spoke encouraging words. Jack delayed but a moment, and then began the steep ascent which led up the cliff and through the woods to Old Scratch Mill.

William's face swam towards Denzil out of the light, warmth and confusion of the kitchen. He stood there dazed, soaked to the buff, bruised and aching, aware of the salt water stinging the cuts on his knees and hands. Molly was taking the child from Jack, standing it on the hearth-rug, pulling off the saturated cloak and swiftly wrapping a blanket round the shivering form. An elderly man was wringing William's hand, his haggard face running with tears. A gaunt, scarecrow figure, dressed in rags, though his mien suggested that he was anything but a beggar. Another, similarly clad, was supporting an elderly woman, while a pretty girl was sobbing and clinging to his arm.

Soon Molly had them seated by the fire with warm blankets over their wet clothes. They could speak a little English and William was making himself understood. Tankards of grog and bowls of good, nourishing stew were to hand, but they ate sparingly. Seasickness had added to their miseries. The wretched refugees seemed stunned, incoherent, unable to believe that they were safe at last. The child, hardly more than an infant, had fallen asleep on Molly's broad, comfortable lap.

William glanced at him, compassion in his eyes. 'A pity to disturb him, but you cannot remain here, *Monsieur le Comte*. There is a place of safety where you can pass the night. I have arranged for a carriage to take you to your friends on the morrow.'

'We are in your hands, monsieur,' replied the elderly gentleman in a strong foreign accent. His lined face was carved with fatigue and sorrow, yet there was a calm dignity about him which told of terrible suffering nobly endured. 'Words cannot express our gratitude to you and your valiant friends. *Madame la Comtesse* and I will remember you in our prayers – my son and his wife also.'

The young man had recovered sufficiently to add his thanks to those of his father, but the women could not speak, starting up at the slightest sound, haunted eyes darting about the room, unable to believe that they would no longer be hunted like wild beasts, fleeing for their lives. Molly was the only one to whom they could turn with anything like trust. She talked to them quietly, never heeding whether they could understand her – her soothing tone was enough. At last, the younger one held out her arms and Molly gave her the child. She snatched him to her breast fiercely, then huddled by the fire, rocking him and murmuring soft phrases.

The whole scene was dreamlike to Denzil, a horrible dream in which these once-wealthy, titled people had been reduced to such a state of degradation. He was sickened by it, chilled to the core, bitterly realizing how blind he and his student friends had been, and that Guy was right. He wanted to go home and creep into his warm bed, but in the face of such suffering, was prepared to accompany them if commanded.

William was putting on his coat and arming himself. He turned to Denzil. 'Go home,' he said, clapping him on the shoulder. 'You've done well in this. I'll make certain that the count and his family are made comfortable at the lodge. I'll return to Wylde Court tomorrow, when they are on their way to

London. Tell Guy that another mission has been successfully accomplished.'

Beaumaris Combe sweltered under an early heatwave. It was too hot to do a stroke of work after ten in the morning, too hot to do anything but idle along the shore, cooling the feet in rock pools.

Sally was sitting in the shade on the terrace, in the company of Lady Charlotte who was languidly stirring the air with a lace fan. In the distance, Cecily, Barbara and Lalage were playing on the swing which hung beneath a spreading oak. Their laughter drifted on the warm breeze. She could see Miranda too, but she was not joining in. She lay on the grass, gazing up at the sky which was laced with milky-white clouds. Lalage's cream muslin dress was moulded against her limbs as she swung high, impelled by Denzil's vigorous push. Barbara hopped about impatiently below, protesting that it was her turn.

'How well Lalage has settled down here,' Charlotte remarked. 'I swear that I've grown quite fond of her. She is always so considerate, eager to be of help yet showing a commendable firmness when necessary. Do you not agree, Chalmers?'

Her companion deeply resented anyone who captured her mistress's interest, considering that she alone had the right to protect her from the minor irritations of life. 'Who am I to disagree with your Ladyship?' she sniffed, and to prove that she was no light-minded, foreign flibbertigibbet, took out her crochet from her bead-bag and commenced working like a fury.

'And what do you think, Sally?' Charlotte's eyes were twinkling. She enjoyed tormenting Chalmers.

'Lalage is becoming quite the model young lady,' Sally answered steadily. This was perfectly true, and she was unable to explain just why she disliked her so much. Jealousy was the obvious reason, but there was something more. It was an instinct, an awareness of trouble fermenting which she had been relieved to find that Dora also felt. Dora had no time for Lalage, nor for Bethany who, since her promotion to lady's maid, had gone around giving herself airs.

Friendship between Sally and Lalage had proved an impossibility, though this should not have been the case. Sally had tried hard for she should have been overjoyed to have another young lady in the house, someone with whom she could have exchanged confidences, enjoyed shopping expeditions and the many other occupations which are enhanced by a pleasant companion. She had given up the attempt. Lalage was so cold, so unreachable.

'What a charming picture,' someone said behind them, and Sally started, recognizing those deep, cultured tones. She looked round, heart fluttering.

Guy was staring fixedly at the group on the lawn. He was scowling, eyes glittering green slits, a hard slant to his mouth. Without his jacket, his hair uncombed, the neck of his shirt unfastened over his brown throat, he resembled a brigand rather than a lord.

'Yes, isn't it delightful,' Charlotte agreed, expressing no surprise. 'Quite, quite perfect.'

'And dear brother Denzil acting the courtier,' he added.

His mother turned her head slightly and scrutinized him. 'I'm glad to find that you're still in the land of the living.' Her voice was acid. 'We've not seen hide nor hair of you for well over a week. What have you been doing, shut up in your apartment?'

'The company was boring me,' he answered ungraciously, hands on his hips. 'It seems to suit you, Mamma, you are looking well.'

'And you,' she returned promptly, 'are looking really awful! Get married, Guy.'

'Ha! You jest! I'll not make that mistake again!' As he demolished her suggestion with this chilling reply, he was wondering what her reaction would be if she knew the truth. He had no intention of telling her. Let her go on believing that he had withdrawn to his rooms in a black mood, sinking his sorrows in drink. In reality, he had been to Paris in the company of his leader, but only William knew this. If he looked ill and haggard, it was not due to seeking solace at the bottom of a bottle, but because the undertaking had been dangerous and desperate and he had narrowly escaped with his life.

'There are several nice girls in the neighbourhood who would make most suitable wives,' continued Charlotte, outwardly unruffled. 'Biddable girls, who would not object in the very least to having a helpful mother-in-law residing with them. Perhaps you will meet one fitting your requirements at the ball I'm planning to give shortly.'

'Leave me out of your machinations, Mamma,' he drawled, resting against the stone balustrade. 'Marriage is not for me.'

115

'Speaking of which,' she went on, ignoring his rudeness, 'Denzil and Lalage seem fond of one another. I'm toying with the notion of encouraging this.'

Guy lifted one dark eyebrow. 'Would you let your darling boy marry this nobody, this foreigner?' He sounded suitably surprised, fostering her belief that he still hated his brother.

'I'm seriously considering it. She appears to be a refined child, and after all, the alliance of a younger son is of little consequence, compared with your own. He might settle down if he had a dutiful wife, and a home of his own.'

Guy rested one booted foot on the low wall and leaned his elbow on his knee. 'At Highfield Lodge?'

'Quite so.'

A smile crossed his lips and his eyes shone wickedly. 'Well, Mamma, I suppose it might stop him whoring around the countryside.'

Charlotte shut her fan with a snap. 'Really, Guy! What a thing to say! And with Sally and Chalmers here too!'

'I trust that their maidenly innocence will protect them. They'll not know my meaning.' His eyes met Sally's and she was struck by their magnetic glint and changing lights, remarkable though dark-ringed. Anxiety stabbed her. He looked so very tired.

'It is a great pity that you did not stay shut up in your Bluebeard's Castle,' said his mother. 'You are anything but pleasant company.'

Guy bowed ironically. 'Poor Mamma, denied the fun of arranging a wedding. Why don't you find a husband for Sally? She is one of the family too, you know.'

Sally could feel herself blushing. Had they been alone, she would have given Guy a piece of her mind. Unfortunately, it was true that his mother seemed to forget that she was a relative. To her, she was simply a pleasant soul who would run errands, read to her, play cards with her, make sure that the nursery staff were diligent. Sally was sick and tired of coping with Lady Charlotte's uncertain temper.

'I don't wish to marry,' she said curtly, her hands clenched together in her lap. 'I am perfectly content, thank you.' Her voice was low and taut, a wealth of bewildered hurt in its stiffness.

Her wide-spaced eyes met Guy's again and something flickered in his expression. She could not tell if it was amusement or reluctant admiration. It was too fleeting. She was unaware of how the sunlight turned her neatly-dressed hair to smooth, shiny gold and emphasized the fine bone-structure of her face which would make her lovely still, even when she was old.

'Naturally, I will do everything I can for our dear Sally,' said Charlotte, watching both of them shrewdly. 'I should hate to lose her, but if some respectable man came acourting her, then no one would be more delighted than I.'

It was too much to bear, listening to them calmly discussing her future as if she had no say in it. Sally stood up, made some excuse connected with her duties, and escaped indoors.

It was dim and cool in the stable, a pleasant retreat from the heat of late afternoon. This part of the manor, once needed for housing cattle during siege, was now used for storing wagons, harness and coaches, whilst a further section had stalls for the horses. Rays of light, grainy with dust and flecked with circling flies, slanted from the high, narrow windows which had once been slits for bowmen, and touched sparks from brass and polished leather hanging from the stone walls.

There was a small cluster of men in a far corner, formed into a rough circle. In their midst, two cocks were sparring. The air was rent by their crows which were strong and deep, making the chorus of the domestic rooster sound thin and puny in comparison. The men were cheering them on, encouraging their violence, far too occupied to notice Lalage when she slipped in quietly. Only a couple of hounds, at ease on the straw, looked up and rumbled as she paused and stared through a gap between two liveried footmen. The birds fluttered high, meeting in a frenzied flurry of wings, bright drops of blood and loosened feathers flying in all directions. Someone was keeping a book and money would be exchanged on the outcome of this bout, the winner going on to be pitted against the next, the stakes rising.

Guy and Jack stamped in, full of vitality and brag and not a little brandy. They had been hawking and successfully; half a dozen rabbits dangled, limp and bloody, from the saddles of their mounts who stepped wearily behind them, coats flecked with foam. The dogs bounded excitedly to greet them, tails lashing, leaping high, sniffing at the kill, as if indignant that they had been denied the sport. Laughing, Guy controlled them, patting each before tersely ordering them back to their places. Then he saw Lalage and handed the falcon on his wrist to Jack. Lalage and Jack exchanged a glance, then he took the bird to the mews before joining in the cocking.

'To what do I owe the honour of this visit? An unlikely venue for a young lady at this hour of the day.' Guy's tone was faintly sarcastic as he stood facing her, legs spread to balance his weight, bare-headed and wearing a shirt and buckskin breeches. The shirt was blood-stained and dirty, dark patches of sweat spreading up from the waist and round the armpits.

'I came to see the horses,' she replied, cool as ice in her cream lawn dress, out of place midst such masculine surroundings. 'I brought apples for my mare.'

'Not lingering in the hope of seeing me? How disappointing.' He was watching her closely as a groom took his horse to one of the stalls and commenced rubbing it down. 'I thought for a moment that you might have seen me with my mother this morning.'

'I did see you.' Her gaze travelled slowly over his face. 'I've been wondering where you have been hiding for the past days.'

'Did they not tell you? Surely Mamma relished recounting that I fly into devilish moods and retire to my apartment, getting drunk. Or were you too preoccupied to listen?'

'I don't know what you mean.'

He grunted with laughter, taking up a towel and wiping his face, his chest and the muscled brown arms beneath the rolled-back sleeves. 'I'll wager that you do. Denzil is in love with you. It's obvious by the way he runs to obey your slightest whim.'

A frown creased her brow under the curling black fringe. 'You have been drinking, sir, to indulge in such flights of fancy.'

His eyes were guarded. 'What is it to you if I drink?'

'It grieves me,' she said softly. 'I would not see you destroy yourself.'

'Then prevent it.' He put down the towel and stepped closer. 'Who knows? You may hold the key to my salvation.'

He felt the warmth of her breath on his face as she answered. 'I'll not speak of it until you are sober.'

He had her boxed in a corner near the stalls, his wide shoulders blocking out the rest of the stable. His face was amused, but there was a hard light in the eyes which looked down at her. 'Come to my rooms tonight. We need to talk, you and I.'

He had not ruffled her cool serenity. 'I'll think about it,' she said calmly.

'You will be there.' His voice held that firmness which even the bravest of his followers feared.

He stood aside with a bow. Lalage subjected him to a long look from her slanting amber eyes, and then walked past him to the door.

When Guy was rumoured to be in the grip of a dirty, evil mood, none of the servants would enter his chambers. Walford, his valet of long standing, attended to his needs. It was he who conducted Lalage there late that night, a thin, stooped, rather sinister-looking man.

It was her first visit to that part of the house. The room into which she was ushered was all dark colours, muted by candle-light, and exotically furnished. Incense burned in oriental holders with serpents coiling round their bases, giving off a warm, sweet odour, like damp gardens on a midsummer morning, exciting the nostrils and reviving long-forgotten dreams and memories.

Guy was not alone. Lalage sank into a curtsey when he presented her to his companion, one Robert Burgess, whom he said was a friend breaking a tedious journey to Cornwall. He was cultured, witty, quick of speech and temperament. A small, sallow-skinned gentleman with restless eyes, narrow lips, dark, receding hair and garments both elegant and practical.

'This is the young person you've been telling me about?' His eyes twinkled and he bowed over her hand with mock gravity. 'How the devil could you have mistaken her for a lad, Guy? You must have been blind – stock-blind! She is quite enchanting. Will you take her to London for the autumn season?'

Guy shrugged, giving a noncommital answer, and they returned to the card game which her appearance had interrupted. Guy waved her into a chair and she sank down gracefully, watching the play. Guy's coat was over the back of his seat, and he was in his belled shirt-sleeves. Hats and whips lay on the top of an oaken coffer, along with a pair of rapiers. He told her that they had not been in long and had spent the evening in the meadow, engaged in an energetic fencing-bout.

'Duelling is against the law, of course, but no gentleman of spirit heeds the edict,' he continued, pushing the cards towards his opponent. 'Robert is never tardy in accepting a fight. He's a fiery old rogue.'

'Not a word of truth in it,' protested Robert, smiling at Lalage. He was shuffling the cards with miraculous precision, fountaining and arching them through the air, without once taking his attention from her. 'Don't believe him, dearest lady. I'm the most amiable fellow on earth.'

Candles burned in silver sconces, their reflections blurred in a waxed, inlaid chessboard on the table. There was a crumpled handkerchief with an embroidered crest, a half-eaten orange with the peel and pips stuck to the wood, game chips and money strewn everywhere. A half-filled bottle stood at Robert's elbow, and the wineglasses before each man made sticky rings on the polished surface. Guy was not drinking now.

Lalage spoke only when one of them addressed some remark to her. This was not often for they were totally absorbed in the game, but at last Robert pushed back his chair and rose, stretching and giving a wide-mouthed yawn. 'Egad, what deuced infernal luck you're having. I can't afford to lose more to you tonight. I bid you adieu, till tomorrow. Sleep well.' He gave Lalage a final bow and left the room.

Silence pervaded the quiet, shadowed chamber. Lalage did not move and Guy was slumped low on his spine, his head resting back against the carved chair. 'I too must leave,' she murmured. 'It is very late, and I should not be here alone with you.'

For answer, Guy reached out and placed a hand on her arm. 'How so, my dear? You spend hours alone with Denzil.'

His fingers bit into her flesh under the tight silk sleeve. She would carry their imprint for days and this pleased him, but when, without struggling, she looked at him and said: 'You are hurting me,' he let her go.

She walked to the flower-filled hearth, one hand clasped around her arm, tall and beautiful in her thin gown, a shawl of silver tissue half covering her shoulders. He watched her balefully, his fist clenched on the table. 'Are you in love with Denzil?'

'No,' she answered.

'What then? If you don't want to marry Denzil and you won't be my mistress, what else is there? You can't intend to remain a virgin all your life. Not a woman like you.'

She sighed, giving a little shake of her head. 'Oh, Guy, why don't you understand?'

'I'm doing my best.' His face was intent, eyes wary, a puzzled smile playing about his mouth. 'Truth to tell, I find the female mind devilish incomprehensible.'

She took a step towards him, skirts whispering on the boards. 'I can't give myself to you like a common harlot. It would be sordid, worthless. Let me go away, Guy. Forget me. Find me a post as a governess – a companion – anything, but just let me go.'

She was no longer an ice-maiden but suddenly impassioned, vibrant. He had never seen her so moved, gazing into that peerless face which held such pride. She wanted to leave him, and her coolness, her resistance added fuel to the fire already building within him.

'What the devil do you want of me?' he asked at last.

'Marriage,' she said.

'Marriage!'

The word exploded through the room, followed by silence. After his disastrous union with Celeste, Guy had vowed never to repeat it. Yet now he asked himself, why not? Lalage was unique. Convention? To hell with it. His mother's disapproval? To hell with that also, he'd lived with it for years. He would do exactly as he pleased. Now he realized that in some unaccountable way he had known this would happen – from the beginning, when her ragged wet clothing had been removed and he had seen not a boy but a slim, lovely girl, beaten, ill-treated, with shorn hair, yet retaining such arrogance, stressed by the heavy lids of her compelling eyes. She had told him her name. Lalage. It had rung through his being and it was as if he had always heard it, born with it on his lips and carved into his heart.

He gave a sudden laugh, leaped up and took her in his arms while she looked at him. 'So be it! Marriage you want, and marriage you shall have!'

She was ramrod stiff, her hands pressed against the hard wall of his chest. 'Is this a proposal, sir?'

'It is. What d'you expect me to do? Go down on bended knee? That is not my way. You'll have to take me as I am. Keep your part of the bargain and never question my actions. Do you agree?'

'Yes, Guy, I agree.' She relaxed in his arms and his mouth closed over hers. It was a chaste kiss, no more than the meeting of closed lips, but it excited him more than the abandoned thrusting of tongues. There was warmth there, and promise. Her arms came up, winding around his neck, fingers caressing the thick hair which curled at the back of his neck.

He took his lips from hers and his hands cupped her head as he stared down into her face. 'We'll keep this secret for a while. I shall make the announcement at the ball my mother is planning.' He was delighted with the idea, imagining the uproar it would cause. A peer marrying a girl of unknown origin! A fine red herring indeed, diverting attention from his other activities.

'It shall be as you wish, Guy,' she answered obediently, submissive in his embrace. The last of his doubts slipped away. It seemed that he had found the perfect mate, someone warm and desirable who accepted his word as law, a beautiful adjunct who would demand nothing from him.

His dissolute London cronies, who had known and shared in his hectic amatory exploits, would have marvelled at the control he now exercised. He did not take Lalage to his bed, consummating the alliance before the ceremony. He disengaged her arms, put his coat over her shoulders for warmth and led her out into the garden. The sun was just rising, sending long pallid rays shimmering through the mist which clung at the base of the wooded hills. A pale blue film stretched over the sky, turning to lemon in the east. In the barnyard, a cock gave voice. A blackbird echoed this imperious summons, waking a chorus of others. It was as if Guy and Lalage were alone in an Eden paradise before the advent of the serpent.

She clung to his hand as they took a path leading away from the manor grounds, following a stream which meandered over dark boulders and gleaming white stones. A flight of steps, cut deep into the rocks, gave access to the beach. Guy kept an arm about her until she found her footing on the firm, damp sand. The tide had gone out, leaving the tang of salt and seaweed, everything washed clean.

'This is my heritage,' he said, drawing her into the shelter of the age-old cliffs. 'It shall be yours too, and our children's. We shall have sons, Lalage, I know it. You'll give me fine, strong sons.'

'I will try,' she murmured, but there was a trace of withdrawal in her eyes. 'Who can tell what the future holds?'

His face was serious in the steadily growing dawn. 'I need a son, now more than ever, so that if I die, I shall leave a male heir.'

She ran her fingers over his face, tracing the black brows, the straight nose, his lips, the line of his jaw. 'Why do you speak of death?'

That sombre bitterness which lurked in his features at all times was more pronounced now. 'These are dangerous days, my dear.' Then the cloud lifted and he laughed. 'Marriages!

Births! What the hell! You belong to me. We live in thoughts and feelings of the moment, not in days and years and looking into the future.'

He began to run towards the sea, dragging her along with him. He did not stop until they reached the edge where wavelets lapped his boots. His head was up, facing that omnipotent power, the wind wrenching at his hair. Lalage pulled back, her gown beaten flat against her limbs. 'Not so near – please, Guy.' Her eyes were wide, terrified as she gazed at the heaving surf.

'Are you afraid? Don't be. You're a mermaid, remember? That'll be something for our sons to tell their children, eh? Grandmother was a mermaid!' There was something wild and dangerous about Guy. He was laughing boisterously, raising his arm, shaking his fist at the sea. 'Do you hear me, you ancient gods of the water?' he shouted defiantly. 'I am Guy Wylde, Lord Beaumaris! I stole this woman from you. She is mine, this creature of flesh and blood, quickened by an immortal soul!'

'Don't, Guy!' Lalage begged, tearing her hand from his and running from the waves which seemed to pursue her. 'Don't provoke the vengeance of the gods!'

Guy started after her, catching her, lifting her in his arms, kissing her cold cheek, her cold lips, carrying her up the beach, as he had once done in Morocco.

BOOK TWO

The Keeper

This lady never slept, but lay in trance
All night within the fountain – as in sleep.
Its emerald crags glowed in her beauty's glance:
Through the green splendour of the water deep
She saw the constellations reel and dance
Like fireflies – and withal did keep
The tenour of her contemplations calm,
With open eyes, closed feet and folded palm.

The Witch of Atlas. XXVIII SHELLEY

Chapter 1

The chapel belonging to the manor was small but ornate, with
frescoed walls and oaken pews. There was a carved gallery by
which the ringers reached the bell-tower. They were already at
their posts, nervously awaiting the signal from the curate to
begin the wedding-peal. The nave was filled to capacity. Men
were standing at the back, close to the pillars, and those
villagers who had been unable to squeeze in hung around the
entrance, watching the arrival of the guests, jostling and
pushing, peering over one another's shoulders. A great shout
had disturbed the birds when Guy arrived, walking the short
distance from the house, and a further cheer when the carriage
rolled up and Lady Charlotte emerged to be assisted inside.
Now anticipation had reached fever-pitch. The bride would be
coming at any moment.

I shall never forget this, thought Sally, taking her place
with the Dowager. Whatever happens to me in the future, in a
recess of my mind, I shall always sit here shivering; I shall
remember it in the throbbing of my heart, the pricking of my
scalp.

She had been thankful not to have been present at Guy's
marriage to Celeste which had taken place at the Marquis of
Rotherly's estate in Norfolk. This time there was no avoiding it.
With wicked deliberation, Guy had dropped the bombshell a
month ago, announcing his intended union with Lalage at the
height of the midsummer ball. The guests had been dumb-
founded, but too polite to voice their real opinion of such
unprecedented behaviour, but his mother had forcefully expressed her outrage. Sally had been seized by a kind of paralysis
which had mercifully persisted. She recalled little, save Guy's
face, amused and arrogant, and Lalage's – pale and expressionless.

Once she had recovered from the shock and accepted defeat,
Charlotte had attempted to interfere, wanting to organize
arrangements. Guy had offended her again by forbidding her to
meddle, but he had given her permission to help Lalage to shop
for her trousseau, suggesting that Sally accompany them,

magnanimously adding that she must also buy a new outfit for the wedding and put it on his account.

With misery her constant companion, Sally had endured this, and when they returned the footmen had been burdened with large cardboard dress-boxes tied up with ribbon bows. Lalage's many purchases were delivered into the care of Bethany; Charlotte's assigned to her companion; Sally carried her own modest box to her room herself, taking no delight in its acquisition. She might have been clothed in sack-cloth for all she cared. Fortunately for the sake of her sanity, there had been so much to do that she dropped, exhausted, into bed at night, the awful reality kept at bay. Lord Beaumaris's wedding was an important event and many notables had been invited. So Sally worked while Lalage was groomed and garnished for the Great Day. In a little while it would be over, She would be Guy's wife, and something small and woeful was dying in Sally's breast.

In vain, she sought comfort in the beauty of the chapel, but prayer was useless; God had deserted her. Guy stood near the oak and gilt of the altar where the vicar waited in his white surplice. The organ played quietly, the well-dressed congregation shuffled and coughed, and Sally looked at him through a haze. He was faultlessly attired in a claret velvet jacket, the frilled jabot, the silk knee-breeches, the dress-sword at his hip, the sparkling order across his chest, marking this ceremonial occasion. He seemed very calm, flanked by William and Denzil who were his groomsmen. The sunlight streaming through the stained-glass windows fell on their faces, white and bright with a halo around them.

There came a stirring near the arched doorway, followed by a gasp as Lalage entered on the arm of the family lawyer, the Honourable Augustus Sanderman. Cecily and Barbara followed, solemnly important little bride's-maids. Miranda had refused, point-blank, and she had been left in Dora's care. Sick and cold inside, Sally did not turn her head to look. The music swelled; the rustle and slither of silk came nearer, passing her, going on and then pausing at the altar.

A sigh rippled through the congregation, promptly hushed as the vicar commenced the ritual which would bind Guy and Lalage inexorably together. Each word pressed on Sally's eardrums like a roll of doom and when he gravely asked if anyone knew a reason why the marriage should not take place, she longed for the courage to leap to her feet. And say what? she asked herself despairingly. There was no impediment to the union. Both were free. How could she shout – I want him? How express this terrible feeling of something dire in the offing when she could not explain it, even to herself? She did not move or speak, and the service drew to its conclusion with the exchanging of vows and gold rings.

The couple turned, now husband and wife, and the organist came into his own. The white-robed choirboys with rosy, shiny faces, raised their voices in an anthem. Sally drew on a reserve of strength she was unaware of possessing and stared at Lalage. She was radiantly lovely in a long white batiste gown which fell into a flowing train. Her elbow-length gloves, the front panel of the dress, sparkled with gold thread and pearls, her black curls were partly covered by a lace veil, held in place by a pearl circlet. She carried a great sheaf of roses, and her other hand was tucked into the crook of Guy's elbow. Just for an instant, her eyes met Sally's, then the couple moved on down the aisle. There was a timely diversion, caused by the Dowager who had decided to be overcome, though more out of pique than sentiment, loudly demanding her handkerchief and her vinaigrette, declaring that she was about to faint.

Wylde Court could have been designed purely for state occasions. The Great Hall had been stripped of its carpets, ready for dancing later. Buffet tables were set up in the dining-room, spread with a cold collation and dominated by the enormous bride-cake, with pillars between each tier and decorated with silver slippers and leaves. The wedding presents, which had been arriving daily, were on display in the salon. It was a regal setting for the older nobility in their silks and powder, dignified and serene. The younger women, gay as butterflies, favoured flimsy, pastel gowns appropriate for the warm weather, accompanied by handsome, cultivated men talking easily and lightly of harmless things, as befitted such a happy gathering. In the minstrels' gallery a small orchestra played carefree tunes, and further guests continued to arrive, leaving their splendid vehicles in the drive attended by grooms.

No one took any notice of Sally, but she was used to this, passing among the throng, her eyes searching for one face alone among so many. She spied him at last, his tall head rising above the laughing, congratulatory group around him and his bride. A shower of paper petals and confetti had rained on them as they left the church. Little colourful flakes lay on his dark hair and the lapels of his coat.

'It goes according to plan, I think, but I'll wager this circus is no more to your liking than mine,' said William, materializing at her side, unusually smart in dove-grey, giving her a droll look to mask the affection in his eyes. 'Lord help me, I've to make a speech later.' His hand was at her elbow, warm, supportive. 'And you, my dear? You have borne yourself remarkably well, but you are very pale. We'll get through this mob and find a glass of wine, shall we?'

William was far too astute not to have scented long ago that Guy was the object of her love. Sally had unwittingly given more than one indication of her feelings. She felt the blood mount to her temples, her heart so full that a touch, a kind word seemed to bruise it. On every side they were blocked by perfumed ladies, feathered headgear, brittle laughter. Greetings were being exchanged with bows and curtseys; snuff-boxes were being tapped; the flash of eyes behind fans vied with the glitter of mirrors. William edged his way through, delayed at every step by someone engaging him in conversation. As bestman he was almost as important as the groom. The voices swelled and dipped, like surf advancing and retreating:

'Such a beautiful wedding! So moving. I'll admit to a tear or two!'

'She's a gorgeous creature, rat me if she ain't!'

'Not one of us, of course.'

'Who did you say she was?'

'I didn't say, dear heart. No one knows. Some little thing Guy picked up abroad. You know what he's like.'

Sally grew dizzy. The glittering throng reeled and the room swam. Out of the mist, William's voice, unnaturally loud, and her brain cleared slowly. He guided her through the Great Hall to the dining-room. She could see the tables, the linen white as freshly fallen snow, scintillating facets of cut glass reflecting all the colours of the rainbow, the shining silver domes of dishes, the gleam of porcelain picked out in gold, each containing the most tempting delicacies. By a kind of mutual consent, she and William paused at the open double doors. On one side of them lay this refreshment room where Lady Charlotte held court, and on the other the packed Hall where knights had once feasted with their vassals.

Sally felt like a sleep-walker, her mind skipping time and space. What use my dreams now? she asked herself. What lies ahead of me? She was engulfed in a whirl of illusions, unsure what was real and what imaginary, staring at the smiling people in a kind of vacuum of ephemerality, an odd air-pocket

130

in her consciousness which was deeply disturbing. Was this sense of apprehension emanating from herself or from the atmosphere?

William placed a glass of wine in her hand and her fingers closed automatically around it. This was better. It gave her something to hold. She tested the solidity of her body against the wall, feeling her weight in relation to it, the tendency of an arm or a leg to relax. Pressures, stresses and strains, all functioning, governed by the persistent beating of her heart.

William was regarding her with a touch of anxiety in his hazel eyes. 'You are looking so pretty today, Sally,' he said softly, encouraging and kind.

'Thank you, William,' she smiled up at him, blushing at the compliment, a heartening flood of actuality rushing through her.

It had been important to her that she look well; like waving a banner defiantly in the face of an enemy. The pale muslin gown was becoming, she knew, the pink silk shawl giving her complexion a delicate cameo tint. Dora had dressed her hair, and it shone like golden satin, swept back and away from her features, coiled into a coronet on the crown of her head, the severity softened by a curling fringe and ringlets covering her ears.

It was a fine, strong wine and acted like a sponge, soaking up pain, but it also made her curiously receptive to the feelings of others and she found herself staring at Denzil. He was hovering near the bridal pair, a dark, sulky expression on his boyish face. Sally wanted to say something to him but, somehow, the words would not come. He must be as anguished as she, for he had made no secret of his admiration of Lalage. Like Sally, he was drinking, almost without being aware of it. A change had come over him since the announcement of the engagement, a disappointing change. Since his return from Oxford he had become a much more pleasant person, spending time with his brothers, seeming to have at last controlled the devils of arrogance, obstinacy and rebellion against authority which Sally had seen rule his development from youth to manhood.

The author of his faulty character was totally blind to the damage she had done, seated in her throne-like chair, graciously accepting the flattering attentions of Augustus Sanderman. Lady Charlotte had spoilt Denzil, giving in to his every caprice. Now he had discovered that he could not get his own way in everything, and his brooding eyes returned constantly to

Lalage, who was receiving the congratulations and praise with calm dignity. He had been shaken, disbelieving when he had learnt that she was to marry Guy. For the first time in his life he had met a woman whom he could view not just as a physical toy but a spiritual ideal. To see her with his brother reduced her to human status. She was not a goddess after all. It was torture.

With his usual impulsiveness, he had asked her why she had encouraged him, leading him to think that she cared. Lalage had repudiated everything, declaring that what she felt for him was sisterly affection. He was plunged into the black pit of despair. Watching her cut the bride-cake, handing pieces to her guests, he still found her irresistibly angelic. It was something beyond mere romantic puppy-love. He had longed to project his own ardour into her, to form a harmonious union on all levels, instead of which he had become her victim. Bitterly envious of Guy, he was filled with sick longing and a woeful sense of the unattainable.

William stood up and made his speech. There was laughter, cheers, and another followed as Guy's friend, Robert Burgess, added his word, shocking the older generation with his frequent illusions to happy nights and plentiful progeny. He was rather drunk and fell off the chair which he had used for his oration. Denzil writhed as he listened. In a few hours, Lalage would lie in Guy's arms and he would know the perfection of her body. His jealousy did not strike him as incongruous, nor did the fact that he had relieved his baser instincts with common women frequently during the time he was courting Lalage. The two feelings of lust and love were divorced in his mind. His eyes burned in his drawn face as he watched Guy giving an answering speech of thanks. His limbs trembled and his hand clenched on his glass so tightly that the slender stem snapped. Blood ran down his hand on to his lace cuff.

There was a lull in the proceedings when the bride and groom went to change into travelling costumes. The guests ate and drank, strolled through the rooms and out on to the terrace. The ladies collected in little, cliquish groups, chattering of fashion, marriages, births and the genius of their offspring with the avidity of females the world over. Their menfolk smiled carelessly, swung their canes and saluted one another, now and then exchanging a pinch of snuff or a racing tip.

William advanced towards his mother to pay his respects, and kissed the hand which, without breaking off her conversation with the lawyer, she extended to him. 'A remarkable young lady,' Sanderman was saying to her. 'I feel confident that your Ladyship has shown your customary wisdom in consenting to the match.'

She compressed her lips, eyes gimlet-sharp as she looked at him, though she replied in dulcet tones: 'I am so glad that it meets with your approval, Mr Sanderman.'

He bowed slightly, his hand on his damask-covered paunch. 'You were too kind in suggesting that I act as a surrogate father to her.' He gave a pompous little laugh. 'A strange role indeed for an old bachelor.'

'You performed it satisfactorily.' She dismissed him with a queenly nod, and he stood aside so that she might converse with William, his eyes missing nothing beneath their yellowish, crêpey lids, small red mouth pursed thoughtfully.

He knew perfectly well the reason why he was allowed intimacy with the family. It was not because he was their legal adviser, but owing to the fact that his father had been a viscount, thus giving him the right to be an 'Honourable'. Had this not been so, the Dowager would have received him at garden-parties but, in company with their physicians, he would never have been invited to luncheon or dinner.

He was fastidious, greedy and snobbish, setting great store on that title which had opened so many wealthy doors. Always faultlessly dressed, he favoured the fashions of a former era. Thus his small portly body was clad in a curved-fronted coat of embroidered black satin, his bony thighs covered in fabric of a twin, sombre hue, black silk stockings outlining his thin shanks and black shoes with diamond buckles on his neat feet. His hair, of which he was inordinately proud, was grey but showed no tendency to baldness. It was lightly powdered and tied back in a queue. Fine Mechlin lace frothed at his throat and wrists. He was one of London's most sought-after lawyers, with a small, high-ranking clientele. Thanks to that title which, though sounding so well, had found him almost penniless at the start of his career, no man could humiliate him, and he had done well out of the nobility whom he served punctiliously.

He tended to strut like a barnyard bantam, but at sixty was still a pleasing personage, with his fine patrician nose, his high forehead. Perhaps his eyes were a little too close together to be trustworthy, his features a shade too florid, his attitude over self-assertive, but his manners were above reproach. He had managed to convince himself that Lady Charlotte looked upon him as rather more than an adviser, possibly even more than a friend. He was wrong in this assumption.

William gave him a cursory nod and said quietly to his mother: 'I trust that you've recovered from the vapours.'

'It was a trifle,' she responded grandly, smiling across at several acquaintances who were bowing to her. 'The emotion of the moment – a mother has a right to weep.'

'Quite so, dear lady – it displays a sensitive soul,' murmured Sanderman, playing with his gold-rimmed pince-nez suspended on a black satin ribbon, 'and I beg to remind you, you are gaining a daughter.'

'I had not viewed it in that light, sir,' she replied with that same grand air which she had adopted since daybreak. 'In truth, I'll freely admit that I have had grave reservations.'

'Indeed?' His peaked eyebrows lifted in polite surprise. 'May I be permitted to inquire your reason?'

'My dear man, don't stand there simpering and pretending that you've not heard the gossip?' Her voice was cutting and querulous. Several heads turned.

Sanderman raised his lawn kerchief to his nostrils, pausing a moment, and then going on suavely: 'I've heard rumours, madame, but alas, times are achanging. England has an influx of foreigners now. I naturally assumed her to be one of these, a member of the *noblesse* of France. I find her charming and most refined. It has been my pleasure to speak with her often, as we rehearsed for the marriage ceremony. I'm certain that Lord Beaumaris has chosen wisely.' He was supple as an eel, wriggling skilfully out of this awkward situation.

Charlotte harrumphed, but permitted herself to be soothed, though her eagle eye had come to rest on Denzil. He had been behaving badly throughout, drinking too much and extremely sullen-looking. She noticed that instead of mingling with the company, he had fallen, half-slumped, on the broad padded seat in the window embrasure, his head resting heavily against the cushions, his long legs extended, eyes closed.

'Rouse your brother, William,' she commanded imperiously. 'What the devil ails him?'

'I did warn him that he'd be rather up in the world if he toped on at that rate,' William answered, bowing and going about the thankless task of trying to get some sense into him.

It was announced that Guy and Lalage were ready to leave and everyone crowded into the Hall. The newly-weds stood for a moment at the head of the wide, magnificent staircase and then slowly began to descend. They were extremely well matched. Guy had changed into a royal blue jacket and fawn breeches, with gold tassels on his boots and his black felt, feather-edged *chapeau bras* under one arm. Lalage seemed to glide down, pausing on the fourth step but last. The afternoon sunlight poured over her flowing silk manteau, turning it to flame. Tall above average, with the presence of a prophetess possessed by power, she commanded rather than attracted attention. The large hat with its undulating plumes threw a shadow across her forehead, but the light touched the straight chiselled nose, the crimson mouth, and slim throat. The scarlet gown she wore beneath the travelling robe moulded the graceful contours of her figure. She held her bouquet in one hand, raising it high as if it were a magic symbol.

In ı froth of silks and lace, the younger women rushed forward, giving excited little yelps and shrieks, while the men stood back, smiling indulgently. Sally was apart from the others, near the carved newel post at the bottom of the stairs. Lalage smiled as she teased the eager virgins who, arms waving above their heads, begged for her favour. She made one or two feints with the flowers which evoked louder squeals, then she turned her head and looked down at Sally. Something flared in those golden, almond eyes which locked with hers and, laughing, she tossed the bouquet at her. It struck her full in the face, then dropped to the floor. Someone retrieved it before it was trammelled underfoot, handing it back to her amidst a chorus of disappointed wails, laughter and amused quips.

'You will be the next to wed,' they shouted. 'It's traditional. Whichever maiden catches the bride's bouquet shall walk down the aisle herself ere long.'

Sally's cheeks were as red as the roses in her hands, their scent overpowering, cloying. She wanted to fling them away. Lalage, still smiling, had her arm through Guy's. He was smiling too. Everyone seemed to be laughing, as if the very idea of someone like her finding a suitor was absolutely absurd. Sally was fettered by the voices and sly glances that hemmed her in, growing more self-conscious by the second, longing to escape yet shrinking from moving. The release from her torment came from a totally unexpectd quarter.

Lalage and Guy had reached the Hall, the guests parting to give them access. Cecily and Barbara, seraphs in their organdy frocks, were chasing after them, throwing handfuls of rice. They had almost reached the door, laughing and ducking, heads bowed under that fertility-bringing rain, when they suddenly stopped abruptly.

Miranda stood in their path, wild-eyed and grubby as a street-urchin. She stared up at her father and his new wife. A hush fell over the gathering and the child's voice rang out.

'Why do you wear red?' she addressed Lalage, standing squarely in front of her, head upraised, completely fearless and unaware of the astonished guests. 'It's the colour of blood. You've seen blood flowing like a river. I know it too. My mother bled her life away when I was born.'

A horrified gasp followed this statement. The laughter had gone from Guy's face, replaced by black rage. He made a grab at Miranda but she backed away, her small form silhouetted against the orange light flooding through the open doorway. 'How dare you!' he thundered.

'Why did you marry her?' the child cried in anguished tones. 'I don't want her to be my mother. Blood! There is blood everywhere!' She was wringing her hands in a despairing, washing motion, gazing at them in revulsion as if they too were covered in blood.

Lalage stood like a stone, her face ashen, eyes resting on Miranda. No one moved or spoke and, thinking of it later, Sally realized that the moment had passed in a flash, though it had seemed to drag on into eternity.

Guy found his voice. 'Be silent!' he shouted.

Miranda lifted her right hand, the fingers spread in a strange gesture, held before her face. '*El ain!*' she cried loudly. '*El ain!*'

Guy started, an expression of angry bewilderment flashing across his countenance. 'The evil eye? Who has been teaching you Arabic?'

Sally pushed through the line of people and was in time to catch Miranda as she fell unconscious. Pandemonium broke out, with Guy raging and cursing, looming over Sally as she crouched with the child limp in her arms. 'She meant no harm!' she said, fiercely protecting Miranda from his wrath. 'These trances come upon her without warning.'

'The little demon.' His voice was low-pitched, ominous. 'Her behaviour is barbarous! It is high time she was committed to an asylum!'

'Even you could not be so heartless,' she answered defiantly.

'Could I not?' He said it slowly, smoothly, but the expression in his eyes was terrifying. 'And you shall not remain here, once she's gone, after this treachery.'

'What mean you?'

'Your treachery,' he reiterated with deliberate emphasis, a cold contemptuous smile curving his lips. 'Someone has been poisoning her mind against my wife, and you are closest to her.'

'What has happened? Out of my way. Guy, what is going on?' Charlotte was glaring at them, offended and quivering with indignation on Sanderman's arm. 'How shocking! The naughty child! Sally, take her to the nursery immediately!'

Sally withdrew to the terrace, lingering there, half hidden by a pillar. The sun, though low, still gave off heat, but nothing could warm the chill which shook her. Order was being restored within, the health of the couple drunk once more before they left, everyone trying to put the unpleasant scene behind them. Only Sally, holding the sleeping child, felt the electric undercurrents.

Soon the crowd poured out, with shouts, more laughter and good wishes. Lalage and Guy were swept along by them, down the stone steps to where the carriages waited. More gay waves, more farewells, as he handed her into the leading vehicle, then climbed in himself. A footman closed the door. Bethany and Walford occupied another one, along with the luggage, while Jack, carefully guarding the bags which contained his Lordship's prize gamecocks, drove a hooded chaise. There were coachmen and half a dozen postillions, but other servants had been sent on ahead to prepare the London house.

Sally heard the crack of whips, the jingle of harness, the snorting of horses and, finally, the rumble of wheels. She looked up, seeing the straight drive running between the trees, the coaches lurching and jolting as they gathered speed, the faces of the solemn lackeys staring back at her through the clear, sunlit air. It formed a vivid, distinct picture in her mind, all else fading into nothingness.

The first stop of the journey was at the Old Green Dragon inn, situated in the tiny village of Micklemarsh. It lay at the foot of great heather-clad hills and on its central green stood a walnut tree with twisted limbs and roots, once used to hang malcontents.

It was already dark when the Beaumaris cavalcade rumbled into the tavern yard. The moon hung on its side in the star-flecked sky, dogs barked, ostlers came running, and the building burst into light and life. Riders had been dispatched earlier to prepare the host for the arrival of his distinguished visitors. Bowing almost to the ground, he ushered them inside. A few locals left their pints and their cards, making obeisance to the gentry before settling back to drink and gamble. The Dragon was a post-house on the London road where the stage-coaches changed horses. Word had spread among travellers that the food was excellent, the rooms clean and the beds kept aired. Guy had chosen this place for his wedding-night. Bethany and Walford went up to inspect the rooms and unpack essentials whilst Guy accepted a bumper of sack and chatted easily with the host, a grave individual who took pride in his reputation as a paragon of courtesy. Lalage went straight to the ingle-nook fireplace, holding her gloved hands to the crackling logs.

'I want a fire lit in the bedchamber,' Guy ordered crisply.

'But the day has been warm, your Honour,' the landlord demurred.

'Light it. My wife feels the cold.'

'Certainly – at once,' said the man, and bustled away.

'Lalage, my dear, I have ordered supper to be served in our room.' Guy joined her, hatless now, his hair shining blue-black in the shadows. He wore his cape around his shoulders over his well-cut jacket. 'Go up now, and I will join you shortly.'

The glance which rested on her was difficult to define. It was good-humoured, compassionate, slightly sarcastic. He did not require an answer, so she nodded and turned to mount the stairs, her manteau rustling on the stone flags. Guy stared reflectively into the flames, then took a position on the high-backed settle, opposite a white-haired old man sitting in a rocking chair and smoking. The taproom was hushed, and Guy correctly guessed that his presence had brought this about. Here a man of his class was still respected, unlike France where one hid the fact that one was of the nobility. Peasants ruled the roost there, strutting, arrogant ploughmen and blacksmiths raised to positions of power, although their leaders were intellectuals, lawyers, doctors, democrats who had appeared on the revolutionary stage mouthing quotations from Rousseau's *Contract Social*. Guy had seen trouble coming years before during his visits there, staying at the chateaux of aristocratic friends.

The terrible winter of 1789, when the trees had blackened and withered, vines were stricken, rye killed, the land fallow and unsown, had been the final spark which had ignited the fire of revolt against those who had ruled for centuries. Guy had tried to warn his French counterparts, but they had coolly dismissed the unrest as something which could easily be stamped out. Even when riding with them, passing groups of ragged, ominously quiet men huddled on bridges and at cross-roads, they would not listen. Guy had recognized danger in those glowering glances and the way in which their hungry eyes had gazed at the towers of the chateaux. The *noblesse* had laughed confidently, shutting their eyes to the bald facts. When the holocaust came, many of them were unprepared and defenceless against the fury of the peasantry.

Guy knew far more about the revolution, its driving force, its protagonists, than Denzil realized. He sympathized with his brother's enthusiasm, having been a student, of wide-ranging ideas, growing up in London and at university where various strands crossed and recrossed. He knew that the French uprising had set off a wave of political excitement in England and considered that Pitt had been wise to enter into war with the Revolutionary Government. The average 'John Bullish' sort of Englishman hated foreigners, proud of his roistering, beer-swilling, roast-beef-eating reputation. French 'dogs', above all, were jostled in the streets. So a wave of patriotism now ruled, silencing the dogma of free-thinking, and holding off revolt while there was a common foe to hate.

These thoughts passed through Guy's mind as he sat drink-ing and smoking by the fire of this typically English inn, while upstairs his bride prepared herself for him. Other things too crowded fast on one another, foremost of which was his rage at Miranda's behaviour. He blamed Sally for it and was dis-appointed in her, fond of this woman who had cared for his motherless daughters. He had decided that stricter measure must be enforced when he returned, though the thought of an asylum for the insane was repugnant to him.

Walford was in the small alcove which served as a dressing-room. He had unpacked a valise, taking out his master's requirements for the overnight stay. He took Guy's garments as he removed them, placing the jacket over a chairback, the breeches on a hanger whilst shirt, hose and cravat were thrust into a laundry-bag. Guy put on an East India robe of rich, dark-patterned brocade, girding the sash round his narrow waist. The valet, never a man for idle conversation, bowed himself out, Guy's boots in one hand. Guy ran a comb through his hair and then went to the adjoining door. He knocked, and with no more than a token pause, went in.

The bedroom was well appointed, though its panelling was nearly black with age and it had sloping floors and a low ceiling. He had to duck his head to avoid hitting the gnarled beams. Darkness, richness and warmth surrounded him, the furniture of that heavy, baroque design so popular in the 1660s. The chairs and stools were covered in thick plush of a ruby-red colour, mellow with antiquity. An immense four-poster bed, hung with the same faded velvet, overshadowed the quiet chamber, where only the soft crackle of logs disturbed the peace. Lalage knelt by the fire, wearing a white cambric nightgown and a lace peignoir. The ruddy glow sketched shadows and hollows over her face.

Guy padded towards her, his bare feet making no sound, and she did not turn her head, rubbing her hands up and down her arms as if to absorb the heat of the flames. There was something childish, infinitely moving about her stance, the dark fronds at the nape of her bowed neck, the simplicity of her attire, giving an instant impression of shyness and innocence. He told himself to be patient. He must not hurry or alarm her. Let her set the pace, at least in the beginning. She turned her head, and her great eyes glowed. Guy lifted her to her feet. His hand was on her arm, exerting gentle pressure, and they came wordlessly together in close, silent scrutiny.

'Lalage,' he said, very low. 'Say that you trust me?'

Her eyes were cloudy, unreadable. 'Yes, Guy, I trust you,' she whispered. The ghost of a smile flickered over her lips. 'Why do you ask?'

He held her away from him, his hands in her hair, the pull on her scalp giving her an oblique, strange look. 'You are a virgin,' he replied seriously. 'What I am about to do may hurt you?'

Her smile deepened and she freed herself, moving a few paces. 'I'm not afraid,' she replied slowly. 'I shall not mind, if we can make-believe that I'm not Lalage.'

So, he had guessed rightly, she was tentative and hesitant. This thought was comforting, stilling the desire which had begun to knot in him when he touched her. Patience, patience, he told himself sternly, go slowly, give her breathing space. This is a child, a lovely child, don't frighten her like you did Celeste.

'And who do you want to be?' he asked, marvelling at her witchery, watching her as she drifted out of reach. 'Sleeping Beauty, perhaps, waiting to be awakened by a Prince's tender kiss?'

'Oh, no – nothing from a fairy-tale,' she answered gaily. 'Let's pretend that I'm one of your ladybirds!'

Guy was shocked into stillness, hardly able to believe his own ears. This was the last thing he had expected. Then reason asserted itself – in her youth and purity, she had determined to please him, but her natural reticence urged her to assume a mask. She had heard that he was a man of experience and imagined that by acting a part she could cover her lack. It was heart-warming, endearing, and he could not disappoint her.

'Are you sure, my dear?' he asked, treading warily.

'Of course, Guy. Come, play my game.' Her eyes were shining, her red lips parted a little with excitement.

'Very well,' he gave her an answering smile, the thought of teaching her amatory pleasure sending a thrill through him. Till now, he had always seen her groomed and bejewelled, a perfect, untouchable picture. Tonight, in her flimsy negligée, she invited touching. The wine he had drunk, the intimacy of the bedroom, the challenge of his young bride, sent heat coursing through his blood. He stood, hands on hips, staring at her. 'What price d'you ask for a night's entertainment, my charming little whore?' he said, making his voice harsh, mocking, contemptuous.

'Everything you own, sir,' she answered brazenly, walking towards him with swaying hips, transformed into a taunting street-walker. 'I'll take your money, your property – even your soul!'

She leaned forward, snapping her fingers in his face and her eyes held his. Before he could speak or move, she had coiled against him, slipping her hand into the front of his robe, brushing lightly across the dark hair of his bare chest. 'You know about harlots, don't you, my Lord? You've had many, I'll wager – but none who will delight you as much as I.'

She withdrew her hand, circling him, considering and appraising, before moving out of sight behind him. He waited, puzzled, amused yet oddly disturbed by her unexpected behaviour. The suspense stretched out almost unbearably and: 'What are you doing, slut?' he called at last, without turning his head. 'Have you looked your fill? Am I man enough for you?'

Silence and stillness. What the devil was the matter? Had she lost her nerve? This was the weirdest bridal-night, far beyond his wildest imaginings. He had anticipated tears, even a refusal, prepared to woo her gently. Her initial reaction had knocked

141

him off balance, its very strangeness a powerful aphrodisiac. He could sense her close at his back, his skin tingling in anticipation, lust hardening in his groin. Suddenly her slim arms came about his waist, white hands visible, sliding into his robe, smoothing, caressing, moving over him as if she was seeing with her fingertips. Her touch was experienced, so was the way in which she moulded her body against his spine. And her hands – trained hands, surely? Deftly exploring his arousal.

'Christ!' he exclaimed, catching his breath. 'What a skilled courtesan!'

She shook with silent laughter and released him swiftly. He turned to see her teeth gleaming, eyes like fire reflecting the glowing embers. His hands hovered. He wanted to seize her, to complete the act, to yield to the turbulence of emotion which she had conjured, but, once again, she had put space between them. With her eyes never leaving his face, she slid out of her peignoir, holding it at arm's length, then letting it drop in billowing folds to the floor. As if swaying to mystic music, she raised her arms over her head, taking a few slow, languorous steps, the fluid lines of her body displayed through the thin material of her nightgown. Leisurely, sensually, she cupped her breasts before beginning to untie the ribbon-bows which fastened the bodice. It fell loosely to her waist, her olive skin accentuating its whiteness. The gown whispered down, and she stepped out of it.

'How do I compare with your other women?' she asked huskily.

'You outshine every one,' he grated.

It was true. Her beauty was incomparable – enough to make the impotent virile and to rouse desire in a dead man. Since he was fourteen, Guy had sampled many gorgeous women, but never one as breathtaking as Lalage. The warm hue of her skin, narrow shoulders sloping down from the shapely neck, perfectly formed small breasts with dark, jutting nipples, tapering waist and boyish hips. Her belly was flat and taut, the dark mound at the apex of her thighs magnetic, hinting provocatively at that part of her which he could not see. Her legs were sleek, long, ending in small-boned ankles and beautifully arched dancer's feet.

Desire throbbed in him. Controlled though he had been, Guy could no longer just stand there and look. He stooped and lifted her, carrying her to the bed where he laid her down, then threw off his robe and stretched flat on his back at her side. All the women whom he had had before had known what was going to happen, with the exception of Celeste. Lalage was a virgin, though trying so hard to pretend otherwise. He did not want to use the position of domination in this their first encounter. Amidst the roaring of his blood, he managed to retain this concept, his hand behind her head, turning her face towards him, his lips meeting hers, intending the kiss to be tender but astounded by the ferocity of her open mouth.

He struggled to curb his impatience. It was impossible with those eager lips devouring him, his hands seized by hers and placed on her breasts, her lithe body writhing into his. She broke from him, resting on her elbow, and her eyes fed on him. It was a predatory look. With a quick, lithe movement, she was up and straddling him, and the first sensation of those fierce thighs parting over him made him groan and fling back his head.

What followed was a revelation. Never in the whole of his long and varied career as a lover had Guy met such sheer animalism. Nothing he performed, it seemed, shocked or dismayed Lalage, her body serpent-like, mouth greedy and feeding, using her hands, her lips, with consummate artistry. She allowed him no respite, and he was lost in a chaos of spangled, fiery darkness where pain and pleasure mingled. His bride was the embodiment of sensual delights.

Much later, when she lay relaxed at last, Guy looked down at her. Moonlight bathed the contours of her face, the lids closed, the raven hair contrasting with the pillow. He caressed her throat, the trembling tingle of a sleepless night slipping from his fingertips. The purity was upon her again. She was as unsullied as a sleeping babe. But was she? With the raw, clear clarity of the aftermath, he wondered about this, happiness fading. She opened her eyes. They had a glazed, drugged look. Her lips parted in a satisfied, feline smile.

'Lalage –' he said, his voice distinct in the gloom. 'You were not a virgin.'

A spark flared in her pupils and she became still and contained. 'Did I tell you that I was?' she countered.

Guy withdrew his hand. Her body was still joined to his, but she had gone a thousand miles away. 'No, but I presumed – I thought by your attitude before we were married – I believed you to be.'

'How do I know?' she said lightly. 'I can't remember.'

He sat up abruptly and drove his fingers through his hair,

angry and perplexed. 'Is it possible that a woman would not know – would not be aware?'

The room was dark, lit only by the pale moon; even the fire had died to dull ashes. He could not read her expression, only seeing her eyes, focused on him unblinkingly. 'Does it matter? I am yours now.'

It did matter. Licentious though he might be, Guy had expected his bride to be pure. Now he would never know for certain if she had been possessed before, by whom or how many. Doubts crowded in, tormenting, obscene. She had been so wanton, so abandoned in her taking. Yes, he admitted it to himself, it was she who had taken him, hungry for pleasure. As he sat there, struggling to correlate his confused emotions, her hand began to wander familiarly over his arm, testing the hard muscles beneath the skin. It glided over his shoulder and down across his chest, inching towards that part of him for which she craved. He pulled back, looking sternly at her.

'Are you really mine?' he asked. 'Will you be faithful? I must have your promise – I'll not be a cuckold.'

'Of course I'm yours, Guy.' Her coaxing voice would have enchanted the deaf. 'You have honoured me – made me your wife. More than this, you are my virile, wonderful lover.'

He moved impatiently, unconvinced, holding her head between his hands, cursing the darkness because he wanted to look deep into her eyes and tear out the truth. 'It has to be so. I won't countenance deceit. D'you understand?'

Lalage ground her body against him, saying in a dusky purr: 'Oh, Guy – Guy – I adore you when you're angry. Hold me. Hurt me. Never let me go.'

He had intended to say more, alarmed and vaguely disillusioned, but it was impossible. Her hand was softly stroking him, and even in the duress of that moment, desire was returning. He rolled over on to her, angling his body as her legs clamped about his waist. Her nails tore at his back, scratching, smarting, while her head thrashed from side to side. For a fleeting, horrible instant, he felt himself caught in the embrace of a succubus, nightmarish demon-consort, then promptly forgot it as, feverishly, they toppled into the consuming abyss once again.

Chapter 2

'Madame! Please! Can you not remain still for a moment? How can I be expected to dress your hair if you insist on fidgeting?' This agonized plea came from the rouged lips of Julian, one of the most sought-after young hairdressers in London. It had been quite a coup, Aurora Mortmorcy remembered with a smile, luring him away from other beauties to attend to her hair first thing every morning.

As was the habit among the élite, she was receiving visitors in her bedroom, reclining between the satin sheets of her ostentatious bed. Never one to do anything by halves, she had spent lavishly of her dead husband's money, modernizing the lovely red-brick Queen Anne house not far from Park Lane. It had been part of her inheritance from him. This chamber, with its atmosphere of oriental decadence, openly attested to one aspect of her diverse personality – that of extravagance.

The whole house was furnished with delightful exuberance, a romantic fantasy in the theatrical sense, carried out with intense gusto. Thus, in her boudoir, the pillars upholding the painted ceiling were designed as palm trees, and she had spent much time in the warehouses at Wapping Stairs, choosing the purple silk imported from China which formed the hangings of her bed, and inspecting the inlaid panels from Italy which covered the walls. Immense mirrors in rococo frames reflected the scene over and over – the polished parquet floor strewn with vivid rugs, the great brass torchères with their rings of perfumed candles, the gaudy barbarity of emerald and gold. In common with the Prince of Wales, that elegant leader of fashion, Aurora shared an enthusiasm for the exotic.

A monkey in a red felt bolero and fez was tormenting the ugly little pug dog curled into a disgruntled ball at the foot of the bed. Its shrill chatter was punctuated by raucous squawks, maniacal laughter and uncannily human remarks from a large green parrot who glared malevolently around with mad eyes, bright as polished pebbles. Sometimes it swung upside down with a flash of its pure yellow crest, flaunting the crimson flight-feathers of its wings and tail, then up again to walk sedately along its gilded perch, its toes turned in.

The centre-piece of this extraordinary room was undoubtedly the bed. This was deliberate. It was the cornerstone of Aurora's life. Within it she spent her happiest hours, wielded the greatest power and plotted the deepest mischief. It was a full six feet across, with three shallow steps leading on either side, and its curtains were of that deep, royal purple with which her astrologer advised she surround herself to encourage the planet Jupiter, who strongly aspected her chart. The head was of beaten silver, chased and embossed and set with mirrors, while the towering, domed tester resembled the canopied tent of some Eastern empress, with bunches of stucco ostrich feathers at the four corners. The sheets and pillow cases were of black satin, and the coverlet was made of matched jaguar pelts. The gilt which tumbled in profusion over every other article of furniture offset the somewhat funereal aspect of the bed, and the hangings at the tall casements were of bronze damask, held back by thick gold cords with fringed tassels inches long.

Aurora held court there, her mind busy with the affairs of the day. She was by nature an active person, and this was the only idle hour she permitted herself. There was so much to do, what with ridottos and balls, dinner-parties and firework displays, and being seen in a box at the opera. All had to be entered into with zest, and she was also one of the most celebrated hostesses in town. Now she sat with a quill, inkhorn, paper and sander on her knees, making a list of details for the supper-party which she was giving that evening, planning it with her housekeeper with military thoroughness. The invitations had gone out days before.

There were several other persons present: a jeweller who had brought along earrings which he had made to order; a man with a box of gloves for her inspection; her maid, Tilly, bustling about laying out the gown she had selected for the morning's wear. Her tiny black page, Zuba, came in at the door, bearing a salver on which was a fragile eggshell-thin cup, a wisp of steam twirling up from it, carrying the rich odour of chocolate. He placed the tray on the bedside table and then sat, cross-legged, on the top step, his face like polished ebony, the whites of his eyes and his teeth gleaming as he gave Aurora a broad, ingratiating grin. He wore a splendid suit of blue satin, a turban of silver tissue on his kinky hair. A saucy, privileged pet for his mistress who treated him in much the same way as the other occupants of her private zoo.

Julian continued his barbed gossip, throwing off bejewelled witicisms as he arranged her blonde hair, sweeping it into a crest at the back, finicky in the precise placing of the kiss-curls on her brow, the loose ringlets coiling over each ear. He stood back to view his creation, head on one side. He was talking about Mrs Maria Fitzherbert, the Prince's mistress, though some said she was his wife. It was rumoured that she had gone through a form of marriage service with him years before.

'As I said to her, only the other evening, "Egad! I never thought I'd see a head of hair like this again!" You should have seen it, my dear lady – Armand had been practising on it and you know what *he's* like when he gets a pair of curling-tongs in his hands. Thinks he knows everything, just because he's French and claims to have been Queen Marie Antoinette's coiffeur. Ha! Perhaps that's why the rebels clapped her in prison – they couldn't stand the sight of her hair! I told Mrs Fitzherbert, bold as brass – "Mrs Fitz," I said, "you might as well have taken the garden-rake to it!"'

'Did you work your usual magic?' Aurora smiled, knowing the spiteful rivalry which existed between Julian and Armand.

'I did my humble best, but she can be so tight-fisted over trifles. Quite odd when you consider the vast amounts she loses at cards,' he replied, still tweaking at her curls. 'She positively refused the almond oil which I recommended. Wouldn't pay for it. So I said: "Very well, madame, go to dinner at Carlton House looking a fright! See if I care!" She could have used that lotion on her face too, and it might have smoothed away the lines. She's five years older than the Prince, you know. And I hear that he's in debt up to his ears. King George won't bail him out unless he agrees to make a proper marriage with a wealthy princess.'

The Prince's extravagance was well known. He had poured money into the alterations at Carlton House, creating a breath-taking palace which reflected his taste, his love of pleasure and splendour. Aurora had attended functions there on many a glittering occasion, and had driven to Sussex where the little village of Brightelmstone had been dramatically thrown into prominence by his Highness's interest in it.

Whilst Julian worked, Aurora creamed her skin to save time. It seemed that he could be as rude as he liked to his customers, no matter how lofty their station. The ladies revelled in his brazen cheek which would have merited a severe reprimand had it been anyone else. He amused Aurora. No matter what mood she might be in on waking, her good humour returned as soon as he minced into the room. Of course, he was a dreadful gossip. This was part of his charm, keeping her well informed as to the state of things at Court and around the town. She had no illusions; without a doubt, he carried tales of her *ménage* on to his next appointment, airing his biting wit at her expense, yet she sensed that he liked her.

He twirled round on the heels of his hessian boots. 'D'you like my hair?' he asked. 'The very latest thing, I assure you. So much nicer than that messy powder, though I must admit to suffering a pang at having my beautiful locks shorn so short. But I much admire the colour, don't you? A shade or two fairer than usual.'

He snatched up the hand-mirror, prinking into it, giving a twist to his curls which were carefully arranged in the wind-swept style. He was wearing an extreme cut of jacket, and pantaloons which fitted his flanks closely, buttoning at the side well below the knee. A casually tied cravat floated round his throat in contrived negligence, and his collar brushed his sideburns. He wafted gusts of jasmine perfume as he moved gracefully, using his flashy snuff-box when pausing in his labours, whisking out a lacy kerchief and applying it daintily to his thin nostrils.

'Conceited jackanapes,' laughed Aurora. 'Don't venture into Vauxhall Gardens, my friend, unless you want to be dragged behind a bush and raped by some lusty hussar!'

'Oh, what a delightful notion!' he squealed. 'Lend me your chaise, so that I may get there double-quick!'

'Have you done with me?' she asked with a yawn. 'I must hurry. There is much to do if tonight's party is to be a success.'

He appeared to be satisfied with her head. 'It will do, for the moment. I suppose you will now ruin it with some monstrous hat – a melon-cap – a Persian calash – a cottage-bonnet or some such nonsense. I'll call this evening, and what do you fancy then? How shall we dress your hair? À la Victime? À la Ninon? Will you be a gypsy or an Arabian *houri*?' He was packing the tools of his trade into a small case before handing it to his assistant. 'By the by,' he added, with a smile and a shrewd glance. 'Have you heard? Lord Beaumaris is in town. On his honeymoon, so they say.'

'I know.' Aurora snapped her fingers at Tilly who held out a silk dressing-robe. 'I have invited them to supper tonight.' She swung her legs over the side of the bed and slipped the robe over her black silk nightgown.

'Who else is coming?' Julian asked nosily. 'Not *Le Fantom*, by chance? That would be a stroke of genius, if you could net him for your entertainment. Everyone is talking about him – his miraculous exploits, springing those poor *aristos* from the very gates of hell! It must be quite, too terribly ghastly in France!' He gave an affected shudder. 'Even I have not yet discovered his true identity, though 'tis rumoured that he is a gentleman.'

'Sorry to disappoint you, Julian, but I haven't a notion who he is. In truth, I'm not convinced that he really exists. It is probably the work of several men who use that name as a blind. And, if I did know, you would be the last person I'd tell,' she said loftily.

Julian was offended. 'Why? D'you think I'd tattle? Not a word of anything you divulge passes my lips when I leave here. I am as silent as the grave.'

Aurora contented herself with giving him a sceptical smile, before dismissing the tradesmen and sweeping the pug into her arms, saying to Zuba: 'Take Didi for a walk, and mind that you go to the park, you lazy little tyke – I don't want to find dog-turds on the lawn.'

'I've heard much talk of Lord Beaumaris,' Julian said, ignoring her remark about his lack of discretion. 'And this girl he has married, a surprise to every one. I know at least three hopeful females who've had their noses put out of joint. I hear that she's the daughter of a sultan – a princess no less, and ravishingly lovely. My dear, everyone is agog to meet her.'

'Princess my arse!' Aurora replied grittily. 'Don't be tiresome, Julian. You know damned well that I was in Morocco when he found the jade.'

'Ah, so this is the same lady!' Julian smiled impishly, with one eye on his handsome image mirrored in the pier-glass. He adjusted his cravat and patted his hair. 'Pardon me if I'm mistaken, but was it not Lord Beaumaris whom I sometimes met when he was leaving here, early in the mornings?'

'You know it was.' Aurora gathered her robe about her with a regal gesture. 'And you know about our quarrel in Dorchester, I'll warrant. One of my dear, sweet lady friends will have informed you of it with the greatest possible relish.'

'Madame, I *never* listen to gossip!' he protested.

'D'you take me for a crack-brained fool!' she cried scornfully.

'It is the stuff of life to you!' Her eyes narrowed, and Julian was alarmed by the emotions which flashed like lightning over her expressive face. 'Here's a tasty morsel for you. I've another interest now, and don't give a tinker's curse about Guy Wylde and his slant-eyed bride!'

Julian stopped admiring himself. He stepped closer to her, eyes eager. 'A new lover? Who is it? Oh, *do* tell! I won't breathe a word!'

Aurora smiled mysteriously and flicked him impudently on the nose. 'That's for me to know and you to find out!' Then she turned her back on him and swept into her dressing-room.

Let Julian fret and fume, she thought triumphantly. He'd know soon enough. Aurora was of a resilient mould and could now forgive Guy, though Lalage would always be her deadly enemy. Happy with her latest conquest, she could look back and laugh at the days she had spent in Squire Copleston's company. Poor little man, she mused as Tilly attired her, he had been most kind and, when he realized who she was, had kept his distance, awed and admiring. Sidney had sent for a carriage from his house at Lyme Regis and the party had stayed with him, enjoying a sea-side holiday before returning to London. Aurora was looking forward to the challenge of meeting the new Lady Beaumaris. Her head went up as she anticipated the evening ahead, nostrils flaring like a war-horse scenting battle.

Julian left the house through the servants' entrance; confidant he might be, but there was no escaping the caste system. His assistant, a pretty youth learning the trade, followed close behind, carrying the case. Julian sauntered jauntily along, tingling at the thought of passing on the information he had just gleaned from Aurora. He reached the imposing double gates set in the high brick wall which surrounded the house and its gardens. They stood open and he passed through, starting to walk along the wide pavement, head buzzing, an incorrigible scandalmonger about to issue a fresh bulletin.

Suddenly a vehicle swung round the corner from a side street. It was travelling at reckless speed, scattering pedestrians with supreme disregard. Julian leapt back to avoid being trampled. It was a phaeton, that dashing, sporting carriage much favoured by the young bloods, undoubtedly dangerous and therefore wickedly attractive. The small seat was suspended perilously from leather straps over the high front wheels, with longer springs arching to the larger, rear ones. Two spirited prancers tossed their flowing coal-black manes as their hooves rang on the road. The driver, swaying on his lofty perch, skilfully avoided collision with a passing cabriolet, wheeled sharply and careered through Aurora's gates.

Julian stared after him, comprehension dawning in his wide eyes. He had recognized him in that fleeting glimpse. That shaggy white-blond hair, startling against the darkly tanned skin of the thin, handsome features, the extravagantly large bicorne hat cocked at an angle, the outrageous cut of the garments. The American was visiting Lady Aurora, and at a shockingly early hour too! Julian sped away, hot with this news, almost running in his eagerness to pour it into the ear of his next client. By noon it would be the talk of every club and coffee-house in town. Mr Ambrose Alington of Charleston, South Carolina, was Aurora Mortmorcy's latest lover!

The Beaumarises had been in London for two weeks. During this time they had kept to themselves, neither calling on nor receiving visitors. This had been accepted for the couple were, after all, but recently wed. Doric House was situated near Hyde Park, gracious and magnificent, eminently suitable for enter-taining on a grand scale. Guy intended to put it to full use once Lalage had found her feet. For the first few days after their arrival, he had driven abroad with her then, bored by her obsession with shopping, he advised that she went with Bethany, and took himself off to his club.

His black brows had taken a downward swoop when the invitation to Aurora's supper-party had been delivered. Had Lalage not been there in the morning-room, he would most probably have sent a coldly polite refusal. He had gone there directly after breakfast, as was his habit, dealing with bother-some correspondence early. It was a finely proportioned room, facing out on to lawns at the rear, and the writing-table at which he seated himself was no mere pretty toy. Though superbly stylish, with its gilt edgings and delicate legs, it had sensible drawers and pigeon-holes for storing addresses, bills and receipts. Paper was neatly stacked on its green leather surface, along with sharpened quills, a sander and a squat brass inkstand.

Guy frowned at the printed invitation-card with Aurora's bold, scrawling signature at the bottom. Her hand-writing was only too familiar and the sight of it irritated him, a reminder of the fulsome love-letters with which she had once barraged him.

Aurora – well perhaps he had treated her rather shabbily. He'd neither seen nor heard from her since that disgraceful scene in Dorchester. She was an uncomfortable part of his past which he wished to forget.

He was roused from his reflections by the awareness of a presence. Two soft, scented arms slipped round his neck as Lalage read the card over his shoulder. 'Can we go?' she murmured, her breath tickling his ear. 'I've not yet graced the scene as Lady Beaumaris. I suspect that you've been deliberately keeping me locked away – you ogre!'

'That's a foolish thought, my dear,' he said evenly, though very conscious of the press of her breasts on his back and the warm breath gently stirring the hair on his temples. 'I'm not convinced that one of Aurora's notorious parties is the most suitable venue for your first public appearance.'

'Why not? D'you think I will be shocked? Or is it that you still harbour a secret desire for her?' Her voice was cool, but her body spoke otherwise.

'Don't mock me, minx – you know bloody well that I don't!' His face wore a shut-in expression as he swivelled around in his chair, eyes hard and inimical as he stared up at her.

Deep in the core of his being, he had never quite recovered from his surprise at her lack of virginity. Sensualist he might be, but he had that inborn male conviction that there was something not quite right about a wife behaving like a mistress. He recognized this in himself, despised it, tried to shrug it off, plagued by its contrariness. Celeste had been exactly the opposite, and he would never forget the reproach in her eyes on the morning after their wedding-night, her fear and distress every time she became pregnant, but in an odd, irrational way, it would have been more to his taste had Lalage been less bold. He should have been the teacher, gradually awakening her to the joys of sexual congress. Though he would have fiercely denied it Guy was, at heart, a conventional man. To see Lalage by day, so cool and aloof, made him strangely uneasy, knowing the transformation which took place when they were alone. He was confused, blowing hot and cold, pleased one moment and vexed the next – unsure of himself and disliking this feeling immensely.

'Oh, Guy,' she pouted, meeting his gaze without flinching. 'Surely you want the world to see how divinely happy we are?'

'Hell, it's none of their damned business!' He started to twist away, but she held him fast, twining her arms about him.

'Are you afraid that I shall make some terrible *faux pas* – commit a clumsy social blunder?' Not in the least intimidated by his scowl, her fingers were tracing over his firm lips. 'I shan't, Guy. You've given me so much confidence in myself. It's your love-making that has done it, turning me from a silly child into a woman.'

He ran a worried hand through his black hair. 'I'm sure that you will behave perfectly, though I'll admit I've been hesitant to expose you. You may be received frostily by some of the older hostesses. A public snub can be a devastating experience.' Then he added somewhat wrily: 'I imagine that there will be no such censure amongst Aurora's raffish set.'

Her shoulders drooped and she looked like an infant denied a treat. 'You know best, Guy. I shall abide by your decision.'

There was a suggestion of reproach in her tone and he relented, half turning, one long arm clipping her round the waist. She was enchanting in her sprigged morning-gown, a red rose tucked into the cleft between her breasts, another in the high sash.

'Very well, my love, we'll go to the party,' he said, half-laughing at himself and his vain desire to show her off.

What an ironic jest it was. He had sneered at love, mocked at others who had become some woman's fool, even denied that such an emotion existed, but here he was, the victim of a chit of a girl who weakened him with her innocent air and bewitched him with her body. Cynically, he supposed that he should think himself lucky because she had every attribute that a man looks for in a harlot but seldom finds in the partner selected by the dictates of society. Already club-members of Brook's and White's had been twitting him about his bride, nudging and winking, having heard how he came across her. There had been envy in their glances, a hint of malice in their coarse remarks. Admire her they might, though as yet most had only glimpsed her from his carriage, yet Guy had carelessly trampled on six hundred years of birth and breeding in making her his lady.

Lalage's eyes danced with delight, then she was on his knee, her mouth finding his with its customary ardour. She removed her lips long enough to whisper: 'I must reward you for your kindness. Lock the door, dearest. You don't have to rush off yet, do you?'

Guy had an appointment in an hour and she knew it, but hers was a challenge to his manhood which he could not refuse. He put her from him, took two strides across the room and turned

153

the key. He could hear the servants moving about in the hall; someone might come knocking for him at any moment. Walking back to Lalage where she had positioned herself on the couch, he could tell that the thought of possible discovery was exciting her. She was insatiable. Scarcely an hour had passed since he had taken her on waking. It was most flattering, of course, as were the feverishly hasty hands which fumbled to unbutton his waistcoat and disappear inside his shirt. Her fingers were like flames, caressing the hard wall of his chest. It went to his head like potent wine so that he forgot his doubts, yielding to that tantalizing touch.

'Oh, Lalage,' he growled, reaching out to embrace her. 'You're an enchantress in very truth – a pagan goddess who has snared me –'

Lalage arched her throat and laughed under the kisses which he trailed over her skin. She was bathed in the strong sunshine which poured across them, her bodice giving up its golden secrets, her long honey-hued legs bared as her skirt rode up under his searching hands. The petals of the crushed roses drifted to the carpet, crimson as blood, breathing out their dying fragrance.

It was rather late when they reached the Mortmorcy establishment on the arranged night. This was a deliberate move, for Guy hated the scramble of coaches jostling for place in the driveway, disgorging their chattering passengers. Let them be settled in the card-room or already dancing so that he might command an unhurried entrance. The house was brightly welcoming, lights glowing in every window, the sound of a string orchestra swelling out into the night. Everywhere there was ample evidence of luxury, with liveried servants performing their duties like a well-drilled regiment. A bowing footman took Guy's hat, and a waiting-maid relieved Lalage of her wrap. They crossed the mosaic-tiled floor under the hundreds of candles burning in the glass chandeliers.

London society was rather thin at that time of the year. Many had retired to their country seats during the summer months, and would return only at the start of the glittering autumn season. Even so, Aurora's house was crowded, her parties notorious for frivolity, licence and wit. There was a fair sprinkling of uniforms, scarlet and blue and gold-frogged, mingling with gentlemen in satin suits and ladies in a startling variety of costumes and colours. Jewels flashed, feathers nodded in time to the music, and light sparked off the steel sword-hilts of the swashbuckling military men.

Not all of the company were English. In spite of the high feeling due to the war, French aristocrats who had escaped the revolution early on, had already carved niches for themselves. They were notable by the chic of the women and the dignified mien of the men, deposed *viscomtes* and *comtes*, even a *duc* or two, people who had found a haven among sympathetic friends, cannily realizing their assets, either from colonial connections or investments in British banks. It was a sedate gathering, but would not remain so for long, once the wine and champagne started to flow.

The salon was alive and ablaze with fantastic hues. The orchestra played and a quadrille was in progress, but when Guy and Lalage walked in, every head turned and there was that split second cessation of talk which is the hallmark of a successful entry. Then those ladies seated on little gilt chairs circling the room began to whisper behind their fans, and the gentlemen stared, forgetting to pass round their snuff-boxes.

Aurora, hovering between the salon and the folding doors of the card-room beyond, sensed the excitement and looked across. She experienced a sharp pang of annoyance. Till that moment, she had dominated the scene. Famed for her daring amongst the dashing and extreme, she wore a tube of white satin, the bodice cut low enough to reveal her nipples, though they were fetchingly veiled by the overdress of nearly transparent gold-spangled tissue. Now she had been eclipsed.

Lalage stood with her arm linked with Guy's, a faint smile touching her lips. It was not only her striking beauty which had startled the crowd, but also her costume which, though discreet, suggested the exotic East. The gown was simplicity itself, white and silver-spangled, but over it she wore an embroidered waistcoat, and on her short curls was perched a little round hat, sequin-covered, set at an angle. It had a gold tassel which spread itself over the crown and down one side.

'Stap me! You might have told me this was to be a masquerade ball,' murmured a smooth voice in Aurora's ear. It belonged to Sidney Templeton, quizzing-glass aloft. 'La, how very Turkish! Every lady present will be hot-footing to her dressmaker tomorrow to order the very same. You'll have to look to your laurels, my dear. She will set the *ton*.'

In answer, Aurora ground her heel down on his toe and, pasting a bright smile on her face, swept across to greet the

155

newcomers. The dancing continued, but she was sensitive to her guests' eagerness to draw Guy and his wife into conversation. She knew her circle only too well; hidden behind a screen of empty courtesies and meaningless formalities lay a medley of contrasting hopes, ambitions and fears. Very well – if the Beaumarises were to be the stars of the moment, then Aurora was going to make certain that she was a prominent member of that shining firmament.

'Guy! Lalage! How delightful!' she exclaimed, pushing her way to the front of the crowd surrounding them, monopolizing the talk, taking charge, radiating benevolence and seeming good-will. 'So nice of you to come, and quite unusual for a gentleman to bring his wife to one of my little soirées. More often than not they're accompanied by their whores! May I congratulate you on your nuptial? But I'm a trifle vexed that I was not invited to the wedding.' She tapped Guy playfully on the chest with her closed fan, over the moon to find that she was now completely indifferent to him.

He looked down into her mischief-inspired face, giving a restrained smile, tall and powerful, his breeding showing in every angle of his face. He bowed over her hand and touched it to his lips. 'Your pardon, madame, but I had the distinct impression that you were never going to speak to me again.'

Aurora held his stare and said: 'I was mighty cross with you, 'tis true, but you know me – inconstant as the English weather. I have forgiven, if not forgotten the incident. I'll not be petty and churlish, and now offer my services in aiding Lady Beaumaris with her first season in town.' She turned to Lalage, adding patronizingly: 'I'm sure that you will be glad of assistance, will you not, your Ladyship?'

Lynx-eyed, Lalage regarded her silently, and Aurora was filled with an intense dislike which she covered with the skill born of long practice. 'Thank you, Aurora,' Guy rejoined, 'but my wife is proving more than capable.'

Aurora took no notice of his chilling tone, rushing on regardless: 'May I call on you, madame? Tomorrow morning, perchance? Have you been shopping yet? Permit me to drive you to the arcades in Piccadilly. It is delightful there, so many shops offering a variety of novelties.'

'If you wish, Lady Mortmorcy. You're most kind.' Lalage inclined her head.

The circle had grown larger for the dancing had ceased while supper was being served. Guy's friends were clamouring to be introduced to Lalage; some remembered her from their brief visit in the spring; others wanted to be presented for the first time. Aurora found Sidney at her elbow and he said: 'How the devil did she manage it?'

'God only knows why he allowed himself to be led by the nose!' she answered pithily as they strolled towards the buffet tables. 'Scheming bitch!'

'You never quite believed her story, did you?' he observed, taking two glasses of iced champagne from the tray of a passing flunkey.

Aurora's eyes were thoughtful as she sipped her drink, her attention on him and yet aware of everything taking place around her, listening to the chatter, the frothy conversations which rose from each corner of the room. Guy's name and that of his wife were constantly repeated. 'I don't know, Sidney,' she said. 'I've an odd feeling which I can't explain.' Her eyes sharpened at his knowing smile. 'Don't look at me in that damned superior way. It is not jealousy, I assure you, not now – not since Ambrose entered my life.'

'Ah, the fascinating colonial,' murmured Sidney with a shake of his head, watching her framed against the opulent setting which suited her so well. She constantly amazed him, seeming to be filled with limitless yearnings – an uncharted sea of violent and capricious emotions. 'And where is he at this precise moment?'

'Where do you suppose? At the gaming-tables, my dear.'

'Shall we join him?' Sidney offered her his arm, mentally saluting her courage in inviting Guy, knowing how much his brutality in Dorchester had wounded her.

The gaming-room was a small, intimate apartment, decorated in russet tints, soft, subdued; nothing must disturb the concentration of the players. Light radiated down from a beautiful lustre of cut glass, designed like a pagoda, whilst on a chiffonier stood a silver-gilt candelabrum of seven lights, its branches chased with lions' masks and birds' heads. Men sat around the green baize tables where the clinking gold pieces exercised a glittering fascination, tempers fraying as play intensified. The most noise and the wittiest comments were coming from a table near the marble fireplace, empty of coal now, its recess filled with a great spray of flowers.

The laughter centred on a lean, good-looking man, clad in that foppish attire imported recently from France and known as 'la incroyable'. His hair was raggedly cut and so fair that it suggested long exposure to the bleaching rays of a hot, foreign sun. His cravat and collar were very large, and high enough to encroach on chin and cheeks, whilst his gentian-violet coat had excessive revers. His breeches were beige, so tight that it looked as if he had been poured into them, and he wore striped stockings and flat, chisel-toed pumps. An enormous *chapeau bras*, trimmed with yellow braid tied in a huge, central bow, had been tenderly placed upright on a vacant chair. A cane with a silver knob, garnished with ribbons, was propped beside it, and he was handling the cards expertly with his long, thin sun-browned fingers.

'Oh, Ambrose, you promised to dance with me,' chided the lady who was leaning on the back of his chair.

Aurora heard this as she came in, darting her a venomous glance. If not exactly pretty, the girl was piquant and agreeable enough to amuse him fleetingly. He smiled up at her, his eyes lingering on the deep valley between her breasts, provocatively displayed as she bent forward.

His voice was a cool, low-pitched drawl, common to the gentry from the Deep South. 'You'll think me a confounded ass, but I'd clean forgot, my dear.'

'You're promised to me first, sir,' Aurora cut in, walking straight to his side and cold-shouldering the girl. 'If you don't keep your vow, I'll consider you to be not only an ass, but a most ungallant one too!'

Ambrose fetched a languid sigh and glanced from one lady to the other with eyes which were of an intense blue, masked by heavy, lazy lids. 'Ladies, please – your attentions are deuced flattering, but I'm engaged in cards with this gentleman.'

The dark-haired youth seated opposite was gathering up the pack. 'Can we not proceed, Alington?' he asked coldly, in an accented voice. 'Or is this some contrived diversion by which you hope to prevent me winning back some of my money? You've had the most prodigious luck!'

Ambrose was still smiling, but only with his lips. 'I am as wax in your hands, *viscomte*. You do seem to be in rather a sad way.'

'And shall soon be in a sadder,' grumbled the *viscomte*, shuffling the pack, turning to remark to a further man who was watching the game. 'Remind me, your Lordship, that in future I choose you as my partner.' He dealt the cards, adding acidly to Ambrose: 'Methinks you have brought your own rules from Carolina, monsieur.'

Curbing his desire to call the quarrelsome French whelp out

and give him something worthwhile to complain about, Ambrose had just picked up his cards when Guy entered the room. He paused, cards in mid-air, his eyes on the woman with his old friend, instantly registering that he had seen her somewhere before. Where? When? He did not know. His experiences had been legion – an adventurer – a world traveller – a fabulously rich man, but he never forgot a face.

He lifted his lorgnette and continued to stare through it as Guy came on, bowing slightly to some chance acquaintance but not stopping until he reached Ambrose's table. The gentlemen rose. They made a leg and were introduced, but still the American did not take his eyes from Lalage's face. Indeed, he stared so hard that she stared back. He could not detect a single emotion in the cold calm of her eyes. Guy took her arm protectively, puzzled by that strange, intense look being exchanged between his wife and his greatest friend.

'Sweetheart, you'll find that Alington is an entertaining chap,' he said to ease the sudden tension. 'You should get to know one another. Make him tell you about his country. Faith, when he speaks of the wide, limitless plains, the rich grasslands and forests filled with game, I could almost abandon England in favour of America.'

'I wouldn't go there,' broke in the Frenchman with a sneer. 'I understand that it is peopled by black slaves, redskins and gaolbirds whom no other country will tolerate.'

Ambrose turned his head and eyed him steadily, seated once more, legs stretched out beneath the table, wineglass in one hand, the cards in a fan facedown on the green surface. ''Tis far more civilized than that, monsieur. True, there are still unexplored regions, but the towns are large and grow ever more prosperous. We have a modicum of culture – concerts and plays – libraries and theatres are sprouting everywhere. It's a land of great opportunity, supplying every need.'

'Then why don't you return there?' snapped the *viscomte*.

'Oh, I shall, one day,' Ambrose answered with his slow smile, studying him over the rim of his glass. 'Why not come with me? I make no promises, but it might even turn the likes of you into a proper man.'

The French youth half rose in his seat with rage, then subsided amidst the laughter. Inconsequential talk followed, with Aurora much to the fore. She had seen Ambrose looking at Lalage, a hot wave of jealousy choking her, determined to stop him from straying in that direction, but had yet to learn how stubborn her new lover could be. Before long, he stood up, rising to his full height and waving Guy into his vacated chair.

'Take my place, there's a good fellow. Give the *viscomte* a thorough trouncing. You can use my stake. Permit me to escort your lovely bride for a spell.' He extended his arm to Lalage, giving his lazy smile.

Whilst not so tall as Guy, he was an impressive figure with his tanned skin, fair hair and easy manner. Aurora was bristling under her fixed smile, and he was aware of it. She amused him, this fiery English lady, so jealous and touchy, cool one moment and a termagant the next. Her temper, her appetites, her streak of commonness appealed to him. Without them, she would not have been such a splendid animal. He gave her his other arm and walked off with two of the most beautiful women in the house.

The Frenchman watched him go with a baleful expression, as he and Guy commenced play. 'Your wife is *ravissante*, monsieur. How can you permit that *canaille* to escort her? *Ma foi*, were she mine, I'd keep her under lock and key. *Absolument!*'

Guy drew out his jewelled snuff-box and presented it. 'You don't like him, de Belcourt?'

The young man gave an expressive shrug. He could have been called handsome but for the look of obstinacy coupled with weakness which lurked in his black eyes, accentuated by the effeminate curve of his lips. 'I distrust him. A damned upstart who makes pretentious claims to aristocracy in your country, even hinting that he's descended from the French *noblesse* on his mother's side. I can't reconcile his soft voice and the swordstick he habitually carries. And that silky deference he show to ladies! Ha, how can he be such a hypocrite when the plantation-owners' habits with negro wenches are a scandal?'

'My friend, you are somewhat biased, I think,' Guy re-marked smoothly. 'I've met more than one from his part of the globe, and believe that Southern gentlemen are a genuine, high-bred, chivalric lot. To my knowledge, Alington has never behaved otherwise.'

'*Pardieu!*' snarled the *viscomte*, a bad-tempered scowl spoiling his looks. 'We shall never agree. I think them to be a race of coarse, sensual, swaggering bullies who terrorize white men and breed little niggers for sale!'

Good God, what has Ambrose been up to! thought Guy, a hundred possibilities flashing through his mind. He's certainly ruffled the feathers of this gamecock. He knew de Belcourt slightly, one of those people who always lurked somewhere on the periphery of popular gatherings. It appeared that he had come to England after the fall of the Bastille, getting out while the going was good. He never spoke of his homeland, hanging around with the dissipated younger sons of the English gentry, wasters and spendthrifts, always drunk, always womanizing, forever short of money, obsessed with gambling.

Zuba materialized at his elbow, proffering a tray, dispatched on this errand by their considerate hostess. Guy turned and picking up the decanter, slowly poured out a glassful and handed it to de Belcourt. He filled another for himself, then dismissed the boy.

'Shall we continue, monsieur?' he asked calmly.

De Belcourt laid his cards, backs upturned, on the table and looked angrily into that handsome, shuttered countenance. 'I still maintain that you are foolish to trust Alington with your wife.'

The green eyes widened, then narrowed again. 'That's my concern, not yours, *mon ami.*'

'*Dieu*, I thank heaven for it! She is too beautiful and he is too bold. I offer my services as your second, should you need to challenge him,' he retorted as he picked up his cards again.

'I'll remember that,' Guy said curtly. 'My play, I believe.'

The subject of their conjectures was, meanwhile, gracefully stepping through the intricacies of a gavotte with Lalage. He had dutifully executed the previous dance, partnering Aurora who had been alarmed by the alacrity with which he had handed her over to Sidney when it was finished.

'You come from abroad, I understand, Lady Beaumaris?' he began as they postured and twirled, dipped and paced, finger-tips touching.

'That is correct, Mr Alington.' She was gazing up at him and there was something quite disturbing about her topaz eyes. He found that he could not read them, but in the next moment the set pattern of the gavotte brought them very close together, her breasts brushing his chest, hands clasping firmly. Her eyes widened, holding his, the faintest suspicion of a flirtatious smile trembling at the corners of her full red mouth.

It lasted for a heart-beat, no more, then she had moved away, leaving him wondering if he had imagined it. So, not as wide-eyed and innocent as she appears, he mused, saying aloud: 'And are you happy in England?'

161

'Oh, yes, most happy – what woman could not be with Guy?' she replied, gaze abstracted as if absorbed in the music.

'A fine man indeed, and do you love him?' he inquired blandly.

Again, the force of those eyes, though veiled by the curling lashes. 'I married him, did I not?'

He chuckled. 'Come, come – there are a host of reasons for a woman accepting a proposal, and usually love doesn't come into it. I'm sure that you know this, Lady Beaumaris.'

The music swelled and they paced forward to its rhythm, hand in hand. 'Do I, Mr Alington?' she murmured.

She's either incredibly clever or extremely stupid, he thought, out of his depth as his further attempts at conversation failed. I was almost reaching her, but she's taken fright, pulled up the draw-bridge and locked herself away. Perhaps I misjudged her just now and she is really shy. I'd better take her back to Guy.

The gavotte ended and he bowed to her deep curtsey, but before he could carry out his intention, a young guardsman, all epaulettes and braid, with a face as shiny as his buttons, was clicking his heels and begging her for the honour of the next dance. Lalage came to life, whirling away with him. Ambrose grimaced and retired to lean against a pillar and watch. He was there for some time, for the men were practically queuing to dance with her and he noted how animated she had become. When at last he went to reclaim her during a lull, he found her drinking champagne with a portly elderly man. It appeared that they knew each other rather well, and she introduced him as Augustus Sanderman, the family lawyer.

'Who the devil is she?' said Ambrose much later that night.

Aurora stirred in the shelter of his arm, turning her cheek into the moist hollow of his bare shoulder. 'Darling, I've told you all I know,' she answered sleepily. 'You'll make me quite jealous if you harp on about it. Lalage is a mystery. Can't you forget her, even when in bed with me?'

His rangy, loose-limbed frame was stretched out lazily under the quilt, his fingers playing idly with her hair as he rested among the satin pillows. 'Aurora, I sense a distinct note of spite in your voice whenever you speak her name,' he teased, a thread of amusement in his voice. 'Don't you approve of her?'

Aurora bounced up, wide awake and cross, her tangled blonde

locks streaming over her naked breasts. 'Approve of her? I hate her!' she shouted.

He reached for the glass of wine standing on the top step of the bed, his every movement reflected in the small, gleaming mirrors of the head-board. 'That's coming it a bit strong.'

She was angry, unwillingly roused from the warm, sleepy glow engendered by his love-making by talk of that damned woman! So much attention had been showered on her during the evening. By Ambrose. By everyone. It was infuriating. Fortunately Guy, so careful of his wife's sensibilities, had taken her home before the party really got out of hand. It had, of course. Fragments stood out, though she had viewed it through an incandescent haze – mad dances, greeted by shouts of merriment like exploding fireworks – gentlemen expounding with drunken rhetoric – the disordered rooms strewn with entwined couples. Everything was coming back to her now. There had been a silly incident when not only had one young gentleman insisted on drinking champagne out of her slipper, but had eaten it, fried in butter, to win a wager. She had taken off the other one and run around barefoot. The high spot of the evening had been a special show which she had hired from a brothel in Pall Mall – a Tahitian Love Feast, performed by naked girls and youths who had danced and postured obscenely to the delight of her hooting, cheering, wildly bawdy guests.

All in all, it had been most successful, though tomorrow would bring to light how much damage had been sustained by her property. She vaguely remembered a mock duel fought up and down the staircase by a couple of quarrelsome guardsmen, and there had been a furore in the gaming-room with that fool de Belcourt, slapping down his cards, ready to fly at Ambrose's throat, not only angry because he had been losing heavily, but shouting insults to the effect that Lalage's virtue was being threatened by the American.

'Even though Guy had conducted her home, she still managed to cause an upset.' Aurora spoke her thoughts aloud. 'That scene with the Frenchman!'

Ambrose yawned, listening to this tirade with amusement. She was such a fine woman, resembling a tigress when in the throes of rage or passion. 'He was foxed!'

'So were we all.' She calmed down, soothed by his large hand which was caressing her breasts, and sank back beside him, taking a sip from his glass. 'He acted like an enraged boor. The gaming-room is a shambles.'

Amidst the confused memory of whirling happenings, she retained a vivid picture of the uproar when the Frenchman had seized the table, tipping it up, money, cards and game chips cascading to the floor – the crash of breaking glass – the other gamesters leaping to their feet, bellowing. Then Ambrose had towered over him, using the full force of his shoulder and arm to fetch him a blow like the flat of an axe. He had swooped, picked him up bodily and hurled him through the door.

The bed shook with Ambrose's full-chested laugh. 'You'll have no more trouble with that poltroon. Silly young fool. I should've kicked his noble backside!'

Aurora shivered pleasurably. Ambrose was so strong, muscles rippling smoothly under his golden-brown skin, marked here and there with old scars which told of a tough training. In public he appeared to be a dilettantish dandy, indolent, self-indulgent, a wealthy planter amusing himself by returning to the old country to trace his ancestry. In many ways he resembled Guy, with that same steely quality, but tempered by genuine kindliness and good humour.

She distrusted this trembling, knee-weakening emotion which shook her whenever he was near, wondering why on earth she had not taken immediate notice of him when he had first arrived in England, bursting like a comet on the social scene. Her husband had been alive then, and after his death her affair with Guy had closely followed. When she had come back from Lyme Regis, heart-sore and angry, she had met Ambrose again and been swept off her feet. When she was alone, she found herself daydreaming of going to America with him. He had told her a great deal about his life there; his big house on his plantation up river where he owned acres of timber, rice and tobacco fields; his friendships with local Indians and fur-traders, his adventures in their company. The fine life-style of the 'Quality', as descendants of early English settlers like to call themselves, was another intriguing aspect. Apparently his town house in Charleston was every bit as grand as any found in London.

He was the subject of much speculation. Several ladies in her circle of friends had boasted openly that he had been their lover, most put out when he abandoned them for Aurora. She was worried, starting to miss him too much on the occasions that he disappeared into the depths of rural Wiltshire to visit his manor house. He was reputed to be fabulously rich, and had poured money into the restoration of this ancient seat, Holt Hall, finding it in a sad state of disrepair. Parts of it had been used by generations of farmers for stabling cattle. The Alington family had originally left England after the English Civil War. As Royalists, they had preferred voluntary exile to living in penury under the heel of a vengeful Parliament, sailing to South Carolina where they already owned thousands of acres of wild, uncultivated land. They had worked hard, been astute and businesslike, perhaps a little lucky too, amassing wealth again, and always at the back of the minds of their children and grandchildren had been the intention that one day a member of the family should return and claim the Wiltshire estate.

Thank God for that vow, mused Aurora as she ran her hands over Ambrose's broad chest and muscle-knotted arms. It brought him to me. She was determined not to lose him. Not to Lalage – not to anyone. 'Darling,' she breathed, gazing into his face. 'You won't forget that Lalage is married to Guy, will you? She was flirting with you tonight.'

He cocked one fair eyebrow, his penetrating blue eyes rather disconcerting. 'Honey, don't worry. Guy is my friend, and I value that friendship too much to risk it,' but he could not resist adding teasingly: 'A damned pity for that is the most beautiful – most serene-looking female I've ever seen.'

'Damn you for a rogue,' she hissed, trying to pull away.

He merely hardened his arms slightly, trapping her, making her aware of his superior strength. 'Hold hard, vixen,' he chided gently. 'Stop showing your teeth at me. Talking of flirting, you do your share.'

'It means nothing – you know that – an old habit which dies slowly.' Her eyes were wide, sincere, yet she held something back, wary of giving any man absolute power over her. Such cynicism was born of experience coupled with a streak of strange wisdom, a wistfulness behind her determined gaiety – sometimes fear, and nearly always the haunting memory of a loneliness which hurt her soul.

At the same time, her hand slipped up behind his neck, attesting to her frailty. His mouth came down and he kissed her searchingly, then held her face in his hands and looked at her. There was an intent expression in his eyes, framed by that unruly, shaggy hair.

'Aurora – baby,' he said, in that soft, drawling tone which he had told her most Southern children learn at their black 'mammy's' knee. 'Don't like me too much,' then, as she struggled to tear away so that he would not see the pain in her eyes, he added: 'I'm a rover, an unsettled kind of fellow. Why d'you seek my company?'

She tried to laugh. 'You're made of iron, and power fascinates.'

'That's what the jackrabbit said to the rattlesnake.'

A sudden awful suspicion shot through her. 'You aren't married?'

He chuckled, coiling his long legs round hers, one hand sliding under the sheet to caress her hip. 'No, I'm a free man, or I was till I met you. I'll have to marry one day, I guess, if it's only to keep the Alingtons going, but just at present I'm mighty busy, one way or another. You understand, don't you?'

'Oh yes, I understand right enough,' she replied tartly, fighting the urge to stop talking and make love again. 'You damned men are all the same, be you English, American or citizens of Timbuktu! You look upon women as playthings, forgetting that *you* are the children needing toys!'

Ambrose laughed and kissed her again, but more roughly this time. His eyes were bright between the golden, astonishingly long lashes – he always seemed to be amused, laughter lines crinkling the corners of those eyes and the fine-drawn, narrow mouth. 'Waxing philosophical, eh? My sweet, a woman who has such beautiful breasts should leave that to the pundits.' He rolled over with her till his weight pinned her down, silencing her angry protests with a: 'Shut up! Kiss me!'

She flung her head from side to side, avoiding his mouth. 'If you don't want to listen to what I have to say, why trouble to visit me?'

This riposte delighted him, as did her fruitless struggles. He gripped her wrists and held her arms wide-spread across the bed. 'I come to you for cold nights, and days when there's nothing to do – not to hear you talk.'

'You beast! Heartless blackguard!' she cried, but it was only a token protest.

He shook her playfully. 'Hellcat! We have ways of dealing with your kind back home. A flick of the whip would tame you – but no – Goddammit, you'd enjoy that!'

'Don't dare try it!'

With a light slap, he let her go and she sat up, arms clasped round her hunched knees. She was content. He could be as masterful as he liked with her. For the first time ever, she loved being dominated, having met her match.

He snapped imperious fingers, saying: 'A cheroot!'

'At once, your Highness! Your wish is my command!' She salaamed obsequiously but her ironic smile was not in the least servile. She took one from a small wooden chest stamped with the tobacconist's name, put it between his lips and lit it. An aromatic odour coiled up in the bluish haze as he drew deeply on the thin brown cigar, blowing the smoke back through his nostrils. She gloated on every detail of his handsome face, the eyes heavy-lidded, thoughtful, taking on the colour of that same smoke. Somehow it seemed as if they had been together always – teasing, laughing, talking in the smallhours after loving, so natural, so familiar, so good. Aurora had never dreamed that she could be so totally wholehearted in the giving of herself, nor so selfishly eager to receive all that he gave back.

His next words roused her from this reverie, and the idle, lazy note had gone from his voice. 'Aurora, I want you to do something for me.'

His serious expression startled her. 'What is it?' she asked.

'Make a friend of Lady Beaumaris.' As she began to protest, he held up a finger, silencing her. 'This may be important. I've an odd feeling that I know her. Can't remember where I've met her before, but I'm sure that I have. I don't think she's French, but can't place her accent. I know this goes against the grain, honey – but you can do it.'

She pulled a face, mouth turned down dubiously. 'If you really consider it necessary –'

'I do,' he said, stubbed out his cigar and drew her into his arms.

His kiss was sweet and very gentle, tasting of wine and smoke, then he shifted her down so that she lay with her head on his chest, his fingers stroking over her hair.

Chapter 3

Contrary to her expectations, Sally did not run amok through Wylde Court, screaming and tearing out handfuls of her hair. She found it was possible to go on living when all incentive to do so had gone. Suffering had to be borne silently, misery must smile, and despair be cloaked in decorum. The everyday existence rolled remorselessly on.

After the excitement of the wedding, the household settled back into its usual routine. By the following morning one might have imagined that the weeks of hectic preparation, the joys and traumas of the actual day were nothing more than a dream. The servants had cleared away the evidence of jollifications; the musicians had gone; the marquee had vanished from the lawn, leaving only flattened grass to tell tales. The dining-room was restored to dignified solemnity, buffet packed away, rugs re-placed, the table once more in its central position with rows of chairs placed precisely on either side. Sally hung her new gown at the back of the armoire and closed the door. She never wanted to set eyes on it again.

The children were her salvation. Over-stimulated by their moment of glory as Lalage's bride's-maids, Cecily and Barbara did not take kindly to the resumption of lessons. Several days of storms and tears passed before law and order could be restored. Miranda was subdued, wandering no further than the stable, where she sat in a dusty corner with the old tabby cat and her nest of mewling newborn kittens. Dinner was a staid gathering, with Lady Charlotte endlessly reminiscing and William and Denzil rather glum and preoccupied. Every evening Sally repaired to the Red drawing-room to yawn the time away over the backgammon board with the cantankerous Dowager. Chalmers was always there, engaged upon some endless piece of knitting, a patient, loyal soul, but quite unintelligent. She rarely failed to annoy by asking questions to which the answer was obvious and commenting on everything whether her opinion had been asked or not. Bedtime came at last, with nights of anguish until sleep brought peace.

The weather was hot and oppressive, making everyone

irritable. The sun scorched by day, but at night storms threatened but never broke. More often than not, Sally could not sleep, feeling as if an iron band was squeezing ever tighter round her temples. She would get softly out of bed and pad to the window, leaning her arm on the sill, while sheet-lightning flashed, blue-white, across the sky, blasting the breathless garden, for an instant, into crystal-sharp detail.

Early one afternoon, unable to endure the sticky atmosphere a minute longer, Sally suggested a picnic on the beach. Dora went too, carrying Danny, whilst a footman came behind, laden with rugs, towels, a basket of food and drink. They camped in the cool gloom of a cave mouth, and Sally helped the children to change into their bathing-costumes before putting on her own. It was a long, grey flannel robe, fastened by a drawstring at the neck, modestly shrouding her whole body and legs, her feet encased in pumps like a ballet-dancer's, with cross-over ribbons round the ankle. She stuffed her hair into a frilled cap with a pert bow, hurrying over her own preparations, one eye on the children who were already splashing about at the water's edge.

In the distance, a group of fisher-girls was diligently searching for whelks, trugs over their arms, skirts hitched high, their bare, brown legs shiny with salt and sea.

'This is nice, miss,' sighed Dora, seated against a rock, sturdy limbs spread out, ankles bared. 'What a relief! How cool it is here. I'm glad you thought of it. See how Baby loves it, bless his little heart,' and she addressed the child who lay on his back on a colourful shawl, gurgling and blowing bubbles, his dimpled hands trying to grab his toes, fat legs waving. 'Look at the pretty birdies, my lamb.' She pointed to where the seagulls mewed and curved overhead, one or two bolder ones coming to rest close by, on the lookout for scraps.

Sally smiled down at him, tickling his chin till he chortled, but there was a shadow of sadness in her eyes. Was he Guy's son? Was this the boy he had longed for, born ironically on the wrong side of the blanket? Certainly, as the months passed, that Wylde likeness grew ever more apparent, though no one had commented on it. She had watched Denzil and William, even Guy himself, but they had shown no curiosity or undue interest in Dora's infant, accepting him as part of the nursery *ménage*. But then, it was almost *de rigueur* for noblemen to carelessly take their pleasure among the peasant women with no regard for the possible consequences. The girls concerned dared not complain; that would have meant the loss of their livelihoods and a smear on their characters. Dora had been fortunate. She could have been stoned out of the village, driven from place to place until she died of starvation, her bastard with her. It was a hard, cruel, male-dominated world, and the injustice of it rankled Sally.

She tried not to dwell on it, nor to think of Guy seducing Dora, concentrating on making the most of the lovely afternoon. Her spirits rose as she joined Cecily and Miranda who were plunging their miniature fishing nets into rock-pools. The little rills, as the sea advanced and retreated, had made an island of a big, rugged boulder. It was greenish-black with limpets. Sally hunted for the tiny, shy crabs, then built a sandcastle for Miranda after towelling her dry when she fell into one of the larger pools. Next she was called upon to act the peacemaker, for Barbara, who had spent the entire time digging a large hole in the soft, golden sand, refused to share it with Cecily, who was most upset by such selfishness.

'Sally,' she shouted, her voice clear above the gentle hiss of the waves and the quarrelsome clamour of the gulls. 'Barbara won't let me get into her hole!'

Sally looked up from putting the finishing touches to the castle. Small paper flags fluttered on its turrets. Cecily was glaring at Barbara who, her dress primly settled about her knees, squatted within, her black straw hat giving her the aspect of a scrawny raven as she mouthed triumphantly: 'Go and dig your own hole, silly!'

'Oh, Barbara, won't you share it with your sister?' Sally remonstrated, walking towards them, her pumps sinking in the slithery sand. ''Tis such a glorious day. Must you bicker?'

'It is *my* hole,' Barbara announced stubbornly. '*She* can make her own!' and so saying, she unfurled her parasol so that it covered her completely, and sat there like a large, malevolent toadstool.

Sally stood and surveyed them, hands on her hips, irritated by this mulish display of territorial rights. Useless to argue with her, for she was a most pig-headed child, usually the instigator of trouble. 'I'll help you, Cecily,' she offered, and they dug feverishly so that presently each child had her own private lair.

Sally wiped the sweat from her face and went to paddle, thoroughly exasperated, wishing that they had the passivity of Miranda who was playing contentedly with her castle, peopling it with princesses, knights and enchanters from the rich store of her imagination. Selfish little beasts, she thought, frowning at the distant humps which were the two sisters, sitting with their backs to one another, not speaking unless inspired to hurl savage insults. It doesn't occur to either of them that I might wish to enjoy myself too. They take everything for granted, the wretches!

It was with a sense of disappointment that she went to sit by herself on the jumbled heap of rock, drained and depressed, staring out at the limitless space of sea and sky. She wondered glumly if she would still be visiting this beach in twenty years' time, a dried-up old maid who had wasted her life bringing up Guy's children. There would be others then, Lalage's offspring, and this time it would be far worse. She had learned to accept Celeste, that timid, self-effacing lady, knowing that Guy did not love her, but this new match was so unusual, the foreigner's beauty so intensely fascinating that Sally feared he had lost his heart to her. She had tolerated his other women, had painfully learned to live with the fact that he visited, dined with, slept with them. Creatures like Aurora Mortmorcy could be dealt with. It was as if they stood on common ground, and Sally had conquered her anger and jealousy, telling herself firmly that one day these giddy lights-o'-love would grow old, he would become tired, indifferent, and not want them any more. But Lalage would never, never grow old. She would remain the same in his eyes. She was his wife.

Oh, Sally would always have a home and must be grateful for that, but she faced a desolate future. Lady Charlotte would become increasingly demanding and there would be a great deal of sickbed nursing before she eventually passed away. The girls would need skilful guiding through their adolescence, with coming-out balls, seasons in London, engagements and, finally, marriages. Miranda would always be in need of care. Her thoughts winged, annihilating time, and she saw Lalage's children, born with perhaps a two- or three-year gap between each – dark, handsome sons and lovely daughters. People would say, condescendingly: 'What a blessing that dear Sally is there to help. Such a pleasant person, and so reliable. She's been with the family for years, you know. Of course, she does take on a great deal of responsibility for Lord and Lady Beaumaris are rarely in residence. They spend much time abroad, so I hear. Such a popular couple. Why, no soirée in town is complete without them! Fortunately, they have Sally. The children could not be in better hands.'

Sally shivered, though the sun beat hotly on her shoulders. A chill autumn wind touched her spirit, harbinger of old age which lurked just around the corner. What would they do with her then? she wondered bleakly. Wrap her in shawls and set her in an ingle-nook by the fire to keep the ague from her bones? Be patronizingly tolerant of her senile ramblings, whilst she sank ever deeper into the past which held a greater reality than that of aching, feeble limbs and uselessness? And on her tombstone, midst rank yellow grass and long-forgotten bereavements, would be carved: 'Sarah Alice Anstey. Faithful unto death. 1769 —'

'I trust that your thoughts are pleasant ones to absorb you so deeply,' said a voice at her back. Sally jumped, coming to herself, feeling that she had just passed through a nightmare, awakening to the glorious sunshine, the warm breeze of life on her face.

William had scrambled up behind her. His eyes were laughing, questioning, and he came round to sit at her side.

'Lord, you gave me a fright!' she exclaimed, glad of the reality of his sun-tanned face. His wet hair glistened darkly, and he was naked to the waist, a towel knotted round his hips. There was a slight sheen of moisture on his firm, smooth flesh. 'Where did you spring from?'

'I've been swimming in the next cove,' he answered. 'Didn't want to shock you, so kept my distance,' and he laughed with that lovable spontaneity of his, a man innocent of guile, full of generous impulses and warm affection.

'I wish that I could swim naked,' she replied, with rebellion in her eyes. 'This stupid thing gets in the way, tangling round my legs.' She yanked impatiently at her robe, and then shook her head free of the bondage of her cap so that her hair fell to below her waist in an unbroken sweep of gleaming gold.

William did not look at her, his fingers employed in popping the green, slimy pods of seaweed. 'There's nothing to prevent you,' he said quietly. 'I sometimes bathe in the evening, just before it grows dark. The beach is quite deserted then. You know what the villagers are like. They go to bed early – eight or nine o'clock seems wickedly late to them. Why don't you come with me?'

Glancing at him from beneath her lashes, she asked herself, why not? His features were handsome and clear-cut, a firm set to the mouth and jaw proper to a sporting countryman. She knew him to have a keen mind, the temper of an ice-brook, an indomitable will, self-command and tolerance. He had always treated her with great consideration, flattering her self-esteem by talking to her seriously and sensibly. Now, overcast by the menace of a loveless destiny, Sally was at the mercy of every impulse.

'Very well, William. I'll meet you here tonight,' she said, and was rewarded by the delighted smile which spread across his face.

'Good.' He linked his fingers with hers. They were cool and strong. 'I know why you've been in the doldrums lately, Sally, and I admire your control. I'll do anything for you, please believe that.'

She did not reply, and they sat there, hand in hand for a while before being disturbed by the fractious voices of the children. Sally left the rock. Dora was already packing up, and so they dressed and trudged up the path to the house with the girls complaining because they had to carry some of the equipment. Sally turned to look back once. William saw her and waved.

Lady Charlotte expressed displeasure when Sally declined the invitation to the drawing-room that evening, but she remained firm in her refusal, slipping a shawl about her and taking the track to the shore. William had been right. There was not a soul in sight anywhere, indeed the loneliness was rather frightening with the cove no longer calm and sun-filled. The tide was on the turn, and she had to wait for a while on the lower terraces of the cliffs, while the waves pounded and spume ran almost to her feet, gradually retreating. Behind her the distant trees held the delicate tracery of their leaves to the sky, and it was an amazing sunset, shot with palest blue, orange and deep rust, stormy nightclouds rushing across to swallow the flaming orb which was sinking on the horizon.

She was glad when William came. 'We'll leave our clothes up here, on this ledge,' he said. 'When we come out, I'll light a fire.'

He disappeared, undressing behind a rocky screen, then slipping into the turbulent water. Sally hesitated for only a moment, then began to divest herself. It was exciting. There was a strange exhilaration in the night air. She had never realized she had such a wealth of skin, or so much hair to be caught and tossed by the breeze. The water was cold, attacking her with stinging slaps, the rocks slippery with weed. With a gasp, she plunged in and this was better, swimming away from the buffeting surf out to the calm swell beyond. She could see William's head, black, bobbing, then his arms and his streaming chest. He was calling to her and laughing.

It was dusk when they waded back to the beach, too dim for them to see each other plainly and be embarrassed. When they had dried and dressed, he climbed up and found some dry, dead wood, and soon a blazing fire crackled at the base of the cliff. Sally sat, knees drawn up, staring into the flames, feeling the warmth penetrating her chilled skin which was slightly salty, sticky, difficult to dry. William produced a bottle of brandy from his pocket, drinking from it, wiping the neck and passing it to her. It burned her throat and settled in a comforting, fiery circle in her stomach. She curled her bare toes in the sand and, leaning forward, poked a further stick into the fire.

'Shall we not be disturbing the local hellions – the smugglers?' she asked, glancing at his long form, propped up by the elbows.

'They won't be abroad tonight.'

'How do you know?'

'I know.'

He was watching her, seeing the narrow oval of her face in the ruddy glow. The bones looked delicate, thin, making him want to fondle them, to take her head in his hands gently, as one might hold the tight bud of a rose between one's palms, not quite touching the petals for fear of injuring their perfection.

Sally asked no further, half suspecting that he knew far more about the lawless smuggling fraternity than he would admit. This might explain his mysterious absences, and Denzil's too. If they sought adventure and profit bringing in contraband it was no business of hers. The warmth, the tiring swim, the brandy, were combining to relax her. She cautiously allowed her thoughts to stray to Guy and Lalage on their honeymoon, and found that the pain was dulled. She and William sat in companionable silence, and she realized that she was at ease with him. She felt well and curiously happy, aware of a sense of freedom, as if she had no responsibilities at all. It was rather like a holiday when one was a child. No lessons, no study, one could do as one liked. Oddly, though madly in love with him, she would not have felt this if Guy had been there instead of his brother. She would have been anxiously watching him, wondering what he was thinking, feeling that it was her fault if he was not enjoying himself.

'I love this coast,' William said into the peaceful night. 'I never want to leave it. Let Guy have London. It means nothing to me.'

'He loves Dorset too,' she reminded.

William gave a short laugh. 'He's an exceedingly selfish man, filled with dark, destructive energy, hurtful to himself and sometimes fatal to others. Angels and devils both make uneasy bedfellows.'

Sally stared at him sharply. 'But he is your brother. You sound as if you hate him.'

He sat up, arms resting on his knees, an amused smile on his face. 'Hate him? Of course I don't hate him. I've always idolized him, but I'm not blind to his faults. Neither are you.'

She tried to brush this off, but was unable to meet his eyes. 'All this is neither here nor there. He has married Lalage, and is now her concern.'

William shifted closer and she was thankful. There was such a sense of emptiness on the long stretch of sand and, beyond the circle of orange firelight, the night was dark, filled with the eternal murmur of the sea. 'In my opinion, Guy may live to regret it,' he said.

This surprised her. 'Really, William? I thought you admired her. It had even crossed my mind that you wanted to marry her yourself.'

He chuckled and, taking up his cloak, spread it about her shoulders. 'Lord, save me from such a fate! Denzil may have thought of it, but not I.'

'I was under the impression that everyone wanted to marry Lalage.' There was a resentful tinge to her voice.

William was looking at her intently. She seemed to be built of starlight, soft mauve with purple-black shadows. Without giving himself time to reflect, moved by seeing her quivering with hurt, he said earnestly: 'My dear, sweet girl, how wrong you are. I've never wanted her. It is you whom I love with all my heart.' She started to speak, but he stopped her gently: 'Nay, hear me out. I've watched you pining for Guy, but now he is a married man. Why waste your life yearning for the impossible? I would deem it the greatest of honours if you would consent to become my wife.'

'Oh, William,' she answered, distressed and unsure. 'I'm so fond of you – too fond to see you settle for second-best. The woman you marry should love you without reserve. I can't do that.'

'It doesn't matter,' he insisted, reaching over and taking her hands in his. 'Time is a great healer. Let me care for you, give you a home and children of your own. You will forget Guy.'

He was controlling himself with much effort, curbing the desire to take her into his arms. She had drawn away from him, a small, hunched figure, head down, her hair hiding her face. Her hand had come up and she was pressing the knuckles against her mouth. William went to fetch more wood, busying himself with this mundane task in order to leave her alone.

When he returned, he saw that she had not moved. He knelt on the damp sand, adding driftwood to the embers so that the flames licked hungrily around them. Sally raised her head. 'I don't know what to say, William. I am truly fond of you. If Guy had never existed, then I might have been content with you for ever.'

She was putting it clumsily, afraid that whatever she said it would be wounding. William deserved better than this luke-warm reception of his proposal. If was unfair, for in so many ways he transcended his brother, but love is a wayward thing and cannot be commanded.

He stopped playing with the fire, the better to listen, the better to study her wide, anxious eyes. The stillness of the night, the distant hoot of a barn-owl, and the gentleness of her manner moved him deeply. Her face betrayed tenderness of spirit and a nature which was open and utterly without subterfuge. Even her misguided feeling for Guy showed her capable of appreciating permanent, not transitory values. He felt drained, as if his conversation with her had sucked out his strength, and yet he had never felt more alive.

'You don't have to give me an answer at once,' he said. 'Take your time.'

Why do I hesitate? thought Sally sadly. Why not accept him? She was heartily sick of holding no real status, dependent and poor. She recalled that dour picture she had painted of her future only that afternoon. Two paths stretched before her, one easy and smooth, the other arid and toilsome. She was over-flowing with life and the strong need for a close human relationship. Continued spinsterhood could not be endured. There was something else too, another factor for worry. That scene when Guy and Lalage were about to leave on the wedding-day was deeply etched in her memory. She dreaded Guy's action concerning Miranda when he returned.

'There is the child,' she said, and William understood.

'She can come with us, if Guy gives his consent. I've thought about this. Lalage and she can't live under the same roof, and I'll not see her sent to an asylum. The other two will survive. They admire Lalage and will enjoy having her as their step-mother.'

'She indulges them.' Sally voiced a resentment which she had not been conscious of harbouring. 'She buys them everything they ask for. That fuss about their bride's-maids dresses! Why, left in her care, they'll become a pair of silly young hoydens who'll put pleasure before learning.'

'Let them,' he advised. 'You've spent far too much time and energy on their welfare.'

'All that work,' she shook her head mournfully. 'I can't see it go for naught.'

'It won't, my dear. You've had them for their formative years. This will never be forgotten or undermined, stamped indelibly on their characters.'

This was more like their usual talk, direct and to the point. She trusted in his good sense, and knew that if she were to marry him, her existence would be serene, with no uneasy ripples to mar its tranquillity. There would be no sorrow, no grief, only a quiet pleasure in the little, unimportant issues. She visualized it – Miranda safe for ever under William's aegis, and visits from Cecily and Barbara giving her the opportunity to temper Lalage's influence, and babies coming, her own children for which she longed.

After its brief burst of glory, the fire was dying again. The sky had clouded over and Sally shivered. 'It is late,' she said. 'Let us return to the house.'

'Not yet, stay a moment longer,' he entreated, his face dark-hollowed. 'May I dare hope? Will you consider my proposal?'

'William – I'm tired. Weary to death of making decisions.' Her voice broke, and she was obsessed by a feeling of compulsion, of being swept along by the remorseless tide of fate.

'I can't make up your mind for you, much as I may wish to,' he replied with his customary honesty. 'You're not a child, and know the pitfalls as well as I. I offer you my love. I know that you will be faithful and true, if you give me your pledge. I can only pray that your affection for me will grow into something stronger, if we marry. I'll be patient, and will not press you to do anything you don't want. We'll occupy separate bedrooms, if that is your desire. I shall not force myself upon you.'

Sally had risen to her feet and now she reached down her

hand and pulled him up towards her. 'My dear, I would not ask that of you,' she assured him. 'If I marry you, then I'll do everything in my power to return your goodness.'

A sigh shuddered through him, then his arms were around her, drawing her close. Without speaking, they embraced, a spontaneous nearness, his hand pressing her head against his heart, while a tangle of sensations passed through him, a feeling of beatitude, close to tears. 'My darling,' he whispered in a choked voice. 'You'll never regret it, I swear.'

He held her there for a long moment, hardly daring to move, and Sally yielded to the comforting feeling of having found a refuge, of being protected and defended. A little awkwardly his lips found hers, and it was the first time in her entire life that a man had kissed her on the mouth. She closed her eyes and tipped back her head against his arm, waiting for the magic to begin, that shortening of the breath, that tingling under the skin which, so the poets stated, was the presage of love and desire. Nothing happened. William's was a pleasant, warm mouth, but no more exciting than when she kissed one of the children. This encounter was a pale thing compared to the hot passion which she experienced in her secret trysts with Guy's miniature.

He, however, seemed transported, crushing her to his chest, wanting to hold her there for all time, armoured by his love. She could feel his hands trembling, then he groaned and tore his lips away. 'Sally – oh, Sally! There's something I must tell you. I've been a coward. A fool! I thought to persuade you to be my bride without confessing my folly, but I can't do it.'

His distress was touching, making her want to draw his head down to her breast and kiss away that look of anguish. 'What is it, William? You can trust me. There must be no dark secrets between us, if we are to become husband and wife.'

He took her hands, grasping them tightly in his, the pressure hurting her, but she did not try to free them. 'Listen then, and judge me. If, after hearing what I have to say, you turn away in disgust and have nothing further to do with me, I shall under-stand.' He paused for an instant, and then rushed on, the words tumbling out in a torrent. 'It happened last year. On the evening of the midsummer-ball up at the house. D'you remem-ber?' She did. Guy had danced with her. 'After it was over, I went down to the village where the peasants were enjoying their own celebrations. I was drunk, very drunk. That night had been a torment for I had seen you dancing with Guy, read the

178

adoration in your eyes, and knew that I meant nothing to you. It was all for him, and he was so blind – so unaware. I couldn't stand it. You didn't know, did you?'

She was staring at him. 'No, William, I did not know.' If she had, it would not have made a scrap of difference, riven as she had been with jealousy and pain, with Aurora flaunting her triumphant beauty, that bizarre, sensual woman who had captured Guy's fleeting interest.

'There was a huge bonfire on the green,' he went on, pulling away from her, walking up and down on the sand. 'A kind of madness in the air. Everyone had come for miles around, drinking, singing, dancing round the fire where a whole ox roasted. All reservations had long gone and it was a riotous, pagan festival. I can remember drinking a lot more – people kept thrusting pots of cider into my hand. I don't know if they recognized me. It didn't matter. There were girls, giggling, screaming, couples kissing and fondling, disappearing into the bushes. I noticed one wench dancing by herself. I don't know how it came about – so confused. I could see nothing except your face as you looked up at Guy in the ballroom. The girl wouldn't leave me alone, winding her arms round me, urging me to drink.'

He paused before Sally, holding out his hands. She took them, saying: 'Go on, William.'

'You despise me, don't you?' he said. 'How can someone like you understand my shame, my loathing and disgust?'

She did not say that she understood it well, face hot as she recalled her actions when alone with her mementos of Guy. 'I don't despise you, William,' she whispered and held his hands against her breast.

'It was so hazy – she seemed to swim in light, luring me into the woods, and there, in the darkness, we fell to the ground. I pretended it was you – I was very drunk, you see.' His voice was muffled.

'You took her. You made believe that it was myself,' she repeated, and it was wonderful to think that she was not alone in her solitary fantasies.

He nodded miserably. 'Wretch that I am, I sullied your purity with my lustful thoughts while I lay with a village drab. You don't understand. How could you? Someone as sweet and innocent as yourself, what can you know of bodily desires? You find me loathsome now. You want to wipe my kiss from your lips. I can read it in your eyes.'

Sally shook her head. 'No. That isn't true.' She held his hands and nothing he had told her mattered, save to make her feel better and lighten her own load of guilt.

'I've not quite finished,' he went on, each word dragged out of him. 'I must hold nothing back. The girl was Dora.'

'Dora!' she cried. 'Then her child is –'

'My son,' groaned William, his shoulders bowed as if crushed by the weight of remorse.

Sally could not speak, her heart feather-light, caring for one thing only – Guy was not Danny's father. William was standing there with a hang-dog expression, and she had the absurd, hysterical desire to burst into peal upon peal of laughter. 'Oh, William, my dear –' she managed at last, and she laid his hands against her lips and kissed them. 'Thank God I was able to help her.'

He was astonished, bewildered by her calm. 'You don't hate me?'

She knew that he expected her to be solemn, reproving, and fought to control the smile she could feel spreading over her face. 'No. I'm rather vexed with you for not providing for her.'

'I didn't know about the baby until you brought them to Wylde Court, then I wondered if he could be mine. Dora had a bad reputation. How could I be certain?'

'One look at his little face should have convinced you.'

'I know,' he said miserably. 'I realized when I first saw him, but it was too late to make amends. To have meddled then would have done nothing but stir up trouble. I swear that it is the only time I've tampered with a village girl.' He was so earnest, so thoroughly ashamed, that she leaned forward impetuously and kissed his cheek.

'I believe you, William. It makes no difference. I love Dora and Danny. She is happy. They shall live with us and you can watch him grow up.'

William could hardly believe her words, filled with contrition since he had first realized that Dora was at the manor, wondering if she had told Sally the sorry story. 'You can't mean that you are still prepared to consider marrying me?' he declared when he could trust himself to speak.

Her face was uplifted towards him and she was smiling. 'More than that – I *will* marry you, William,' she replied, whilst in her head rang the one phrase, repeated like joy-bells – 'Guy is not Danny's father!'

After this, there followed a long spell of kissing and embracing. Sally was glad to be the giver of so much happiness, listening while he poured out his plans for a rosy future, an entirely new aspect of his personality emerging, the tender, respectful lover who never stepped over the boundaries of propriety. Sally gave him the answers which she knew he wanted, kissed him with feigned warmth, and wondered how quickly the news of their betrothal would reach Guy and if he would be hurt by it.

The fire had gone out and it was pitch-dark. Jagged lightning split the sky and thunder rumbled warningly. William led Sally through the woods towards the house, his arm round her waist. The rain began to fall, a light pattering on the leaves at first, then louder and faster so that they ran the last few yards. William had given orders to the watchman earlier and the front door was unbolted. Quietly they let themselves in and stood dripping in the hall, where William fended off the overtures of the friendly spaniels who rushed up in frenzied delight to greet him. He bade Sally goodnight, giving her small, exploring kisses on the mouth and temples.

She knew that he was watching her from the shadows as she mounted the stairs, turning to kiss her fingertips to him, waiting to see him enter the library, dogs at his heels, before deliberately taking the corridor which led away from her room. You've done it now, my girl, she thought, feeling her way along, the only light coming from the sudden blue glare of the storm which flashed through the long, high windows. The die is cast. You've burned your boats, good and proper! She felt dizzy and quite ridiculously light-hearted, not realizing until the pressure had been lifted just how much she had worried over the question of Danny's paternity. Now she could cuddle him happily without the painful thought that he might be Guy's son.

She could hear the rain beating against the panes, sluicing down from the black sky as she turned into the passage which led to his apartments. Only rarely had she visited this part of the house, and she half expected the door to be locked. The handle turned easily, and she went inside. She tingled with a sense of sin. She had just promised to marry his brother, yet needed to stand in rooms where Guy had lived and slept, to breathe the atmosphere which must still be charged with his vibrant personality. In a strange way William's love had given her the strength to do so, releasing her from inhibitions. She was a person in her own right now, no longer alone.

She got her bearings, finding a candle-stick and matches, and soon had a light, holding it on high and surveying the parlour of this strictly masculine abode, then passing through the door opposite which led to the bedchamber. There was a faint, sweet, musty smell which rooms acquire after being unoccupied for a while, and a strangely expectant air about the furniture, like faithful dogs waiting the return of a beloved master. Only next time he comes, my dears, she whispered to these inanimate objects, he won't be alone – *she* will be with him.

All the personal things were there, as if he had just walked out for a few moments, to see Boxer perhaps or consult with Jack in the stables, but the room was too tidy. There were no whips, books, riding-boots or playing-cards. Sally wandered into the dressing-room with large wardrobes round the walls, the light from the single candle making weird, dancing patterns as she set it down on the shaving-stand. She opened an armoire door. Musky perfume coiled out. His clothes hung there, with bare hangers between where Walford had taken down coats, breeches, waistcoats, folding them neatly, packing them for the honeymoon.

Sally's searching fingers found a crimson robe with a black sable collar. She buried her face in it, imagination running riot, enflaming her. He would reach for it as he got out of bed in the mornings, making some laughing comment to Walford who, perhaps, would be standing by, holding a tray with a coffee cup on it. She rubbed her cheek against the velvet, the sensual softness of the fur. It smelled of Guy, intoxicating her, and she hugged it close, allowing herself to dream, but the dream was shattered by the vision of a pair of slanting, golden eyes looking up at him from the bed, two cups on the tray now, and Walford bowing himself out as Guy turned to smile down at his wife who stretched out her arms invitingly.

With a violent curse, Sally slammed the door, and flew back to the bedroom, staring at the massive four-poster, neatly made up, the pillows showing at the head beneath the turned-down edge of the quilt, smooth unwrinkled pillows of virgin white-ness. Not for long. When they come back the bed will not look like that, she thought wildly. The sheets will be threshed, sweat-drenched from their loving. She ran to the window, flinging one of the casements wide open, the rain rushing in, wetting her face, mingling with her tears. The arched bay faced the sea, and she could hear its roar above the noise of water gushing from the gargoyles above the windows, splashing down on to the stones of the terrace. The thunder had died away, and the air contained the scent of hot stones suddenly cooled, wet earth and the wistful, poignant perfume of drenched blooms.

Sally found herself on her knees by the bed, her head on her outstretched arms, great sobs racking her. She beat on the coverlet in impotent fury, her emotions swinging from one extreme to the other. She cried until she was exhausted and it seemed that there could be no more tears left in her. Then she sat up, running an unsteady hand through her hair, thinking wearily: I shall be safe as William's wife. I'll show Guy that I too can take my place as a gentleman's bride. She would do it for Miranda's sake, and William's and, maybe, a little for her own.

She blew out the candle and left his rooms, closing the door carefully behind her. As she walked to her own chamber, she carried on this monologue in her head, repeating it like a catechism, as if by so doing she could convince herself. I'll make Guy know that I too can be indifferent. I will be! I will be! I'll make myself whole and free from his damnable sorcery!

Chapter 4

The east side of the river Thames belonged to the poor, the west side to the powerful and the affluent. Between these two vastly differing areas of society were shops, warehouses, factories, banks, mercantile and insurance businesses. The rapid spread of growth over the past centuries had made London the pulsating heart of England, causing it to sprawl far beyond its original walls. Like some great, greedy amoebic growth, it sent forth tentacles in every direction, absorbing the outlying villages so that they gradually became a part of it.

One morning, not long after the Wyldes had taken up residence there, Jack Smithers ventured into the parish of St Giles. He was careful to wear his plainest suit and carry a sword-stick. Fortunately, he knew it well and could therefore pass through the dark, ill-paved alleys with a measure of confidence, familiar with the delapidated houses, once magnificent homes of the well-to-do, but now rotting, crumbling into shabby tenements. Because of his former involvement with the criminal class, he was conversant with certain passwords and gestures which saved him from attack. Not even the constables dared go there except in a large squad.

He strolled along, knowing that to hurry would have been an open invitation for trouble, suggesting fear, and he could not help comparing these squalid surroundings with the streets he had left behind. The slums seemed as remote from the palatial houses, broad roads and tree-shaded squares as it was from the busy shops of the tradespeople, and the sober offices of businessmen. He had walked from Doric House, through the Mall where horses and carriages and the occasional sedan-chair carried important dignitaries on pleasure-jaunts or to meetings. Leaving the leisurely environs of Hyde Park, he had soon found himself in the thick of the marketing area, where the narrower streets were jammed with carts, coal-wagons, hackney-coaches and a hurly-burly of activity. The raucous noise of trade deafened his ears on every side, the street vendors crying their wares, and apprentices lounging at the shop-fronts, bawling out a list of things which their masters had on offer inside. Jack had had to keep his eyes peeled for jostling pickpockets, and refuse the bawdy overtures of twelve-year-old prostitutes.

Dodging through an iron turnstile, he had begun to penetrate the maw of St Giles, known as the Rookery, where every kind of vice and crime was carried out in the midst of gin shops, brothels and filthy doss-houses where, for a penny a night, beggars, whores, children and drunken labourers could sleep on lousy, rat-infested straw, with no one asking the whys or wherefores. He knew them well, having spent many a wretched hour in such disgusting lodgings.

It was a violent place where murder was an everyday occurrence, and depravity the order of the day, a refuge for the hardbitten criminal who, once within the sanctuary of its walls, could escape the power of the law, such as it was.

Jack's lips set grimly as he stepped into a mean lane with walls rising cliff-like above him, hemming in the narrow way. Shadowy shapes flitted in the deeper gloom of doorways. He could feel eyes boring into him – a tidy, well-dressed stranger. He knew what was running through their gin-sodden minds. Could he be lured into the yawning mouth of a cellar? Coshed and robbed? Was it worth it? He sauntered on, but his eyes were everywhere, muscles tensed, the thieves' cant on the tip of his tongue, should one of them accost him. The dingy human shadows crept after him, closing in like hungry hyaenas. They would butcher him for his *toge*, his *famstrings*, his *mish*; clothing could be sold to the nearest fence and the money spent on gin.

Underfoot it was slushy with refuse and excrement, a thick, sour smell arising, the hot day making it worse than ever. Women's strident shrieks of pain and anger, the deep, gruff tones of male voices came from every broken window-pane – children's too. One of them was crying and there was the sound of a leather belt whacking down on bare flesh. Babies were wailing fretfully, starved, desperate, mingling with crazy bursts of laughter, drunken shouts, a fiddle being tunelessly scraped. It took a cool nerve, a strong stomach, and a large amount of guts to enter this infernal purgatory of the doomed and damned.

Jack did not actually feel the touch at his back, warned by the prickling of the hairs at his nape, swinging round, hands clenched into hard-knuckled fists. A man cringed away, huddled in his web of rags, arms flung up to ward off the blow. His hair was like grey twists of yarn, his face a network of black seams. One watery eye glared piteously at Jack, the other was filmed over with white, matter oozing from the diseased lid.

'Don't 'it me, gov'ner,' whined this stinking dreg of humanity.

'You were trying to bone my clout!' snarled Jack, pulling a wicked-looking knife from his belt and pressing it hard against the throat of the beggar who crouched in the muck at his feet, while his mates looked on with grim, impassive faces. No one lifted a finger to aid him.

'I only wanted a clank o'bub, ter keep out t'cold, fer me an' me ole' bouser 'ere,' lied the man, trying to enlist pity for the mangy mongrel tethered on a bit of rope, who was barking ferociously, and making savage, strangled lunges at Jack. 'I'd not 'arm yer – I knows a bleedin' friend from a bloody enemy. Gawd bust me if I don't!'

Jack's eyes were as fierce as the cur's. The point of his knife went deeper, puncturing the grey, filthy skin, a line of blood trickling across the dirt. 'Bah! D'you take me for a flat? By Christ, I'd like to scrag you myself – save Ketch a job!'

'I knows yer now – you're one o' us, ain't cher. I seen yer somewheres. What be yer? A queer cull? A bridle cull?'

Jack slackened his hold, but did not once take his eyes from that grotesque face. 'Nay, I'm no forger nor yet a highwayman. Not now, any road. I've come to see Leitchman.'

'That bloody Jewish pimp! What 'cher want w' 'im?'

'That's my business. Out of my way.'

The man and his cronies parted to let him pass, and Jack made his way to a dingy door which had once been the entrance to a fine building, now as tumbledown as its neighbours. A couple of half-naked children were fishing in the open sewer which crawled sluggishly down the side of the alley. A woman lolled on the doorstep, her face covered in scabrous sores, a half-empty bottle in one hand, a baby hanging on to her bare teat like grim death. Another infant, small, wizened as a monkey but with a huge, misshapen head, clung to her tattered skirt. Its slack mouth drooled as it made grunting sounds, dragging itself along, its buttocks bare and raw, plastered with dried-on faeces. Jack flipped a coin into the palm which the woman had thrust towards him, automatically and without hope. She stared at it with lacklustre eyes, then poked it into the depths of her stained bodice, coughing fit to spew up her lungs. The idiot started to wail fitfully. The mother fetched it a backhanded blow which felled it to the ground. She raised the bottle to her lips, and Jack hammered on the door with his cane.

There was silence. He hammered again with greater force, hearing the echoes thundering away inside as if it was a vault. Presently there came a shuffling sound and the door opened a crack. Jack wedged his boot into the gap.

'Leitchman,' he shouted. 'Let me in, you old goat. 'Tis I, Dandy Jack!'

The opening widened just enough for him to slip through, then it was slammed and the bolts thrown. The interior was dark and smelled of stale cooking and bad sanitation. Jack followed the shambling figure of the Jew between the clutter of dusty objects which filled the hall. They mounted a staircase which had once been noble but now creaked dangerously as Leitchman groaned and puffed his way up. The banister rail was loose, and greasy with the fingers of former occupants, the treads slippery and worm-eaten. Jack leaned over and looked into a black drop as steep as a disused well. The walls were sagging, bare to the laths in some places where the plaster had crumbled, and there was an ominous shaking and settling which suggested that the house might fall down at any moment.

'Jesus Christ! Why don't you spend some money on this gaff before it collapses about your dirty ears?' he snapped at the hulking, wheezing figure just ahead.

'My life – I'm a poor man,' complained the fence. 'The taxes – the war – the prigs expecting to be well paid for a night's work. They skin me, my dear! 'Tis as much as I can do to scrape a crust together already.'

They were at the top of the staircase. The air was musty but sweeter. Light filtered sluggishly through the sooted glass of a huge oriel window. 'Lying dog,' muttered Jack. 'Bloody old skinflint. If that's the case, then things have changed since I had the misfortune to thieve for you.'

'Good days, eh, my dear boy?' Leitchman opened a door, bowing in a gesture of welcome. 'Come in – come in. I may have a bottle of diddle somewhere about.'

It was a curious room which Jack remembered of old, when as a green youth he had come to seek his fortune in the capital. He could grin wrily now that he was free of it, for Leitchman and his ilk had fleeced him without a qualm. Gambling and wenching had led him deeply into debt, so that no matter how he twisted and turned, he had been trapped. The operations in which he had to engage to satisfy the fence's demands had

187

become increasingly dangerous, the noose a constant threat. He had escaped at last, fleeing to Dorset whilst he was still able.

'You scarpered, my boy.' The old man hobbled around the room, putting a couple of twigs on the smoky fire in the large fireplace whose carving was chipped and broken. He then went to the oak table and poured out two very small measures of gin. 'Ai-yi-yi,' he murmured sadly, with a dolorous expression, sheep-eyes and a shake of his grizzled head. 'For all your airs and graces, honest you are not!'

Jack took the glass and swallowed the contents in a gulp. 'You crafty old bugger. You'd have seen me swing rather than let me go. I repaid you later, didn't I?'

Leitchman was a fat man with sallow skin, bird-bright eyes under yellowish lids, a pronounced nose and greying beard. He was wearing a shabby gaberdine robe. In their long association, Jack had never seen him in anything else. Now he spread wide his broad hands and raised them heavenwards, as if beseeching aid as he cried: 'Repaid! Repaid! *This* I need yet? Ingrate! A fire should burn out your heart, God forbid!'

Jack snatched up the bottle and poured a generous glassful, casting a scornful eye around the overcrowded room. It was filled with odds and ends of furniture, paintings stacked against the walls, statues and antiques, bedlinen piled anyhow, pots, pans and candle-sticks, books and racks of clothing, mute witnesses to the sorrowful plight to which debt had brought their former owners. 'Hell, what more d'you want?' he demanded. 'You and your bloody pawnshop. No wonder the whole house shakes. One day the floor will cave in and you'll be plunged down into Hades where you belong!'

'To think that I took you in – gave you a home, broke bread with you, even though you are a *goy*! *Feh!*' This last exclamation was a crisp and exact delineation of distaste, and Leitchman wrinkled his nose in visible reinforcement of its meaning. Then he shrugged fatalistically. 'I was a fool to expect more. A Gentile remains a Gentile!'

'Watch your tongue.' Jack was scowling blackly. 'Did you think I'd go on risking my neck for you? Be careful that I don't bring a gang round here for a bit of Jew-bashing! How dare you speak to me like that? I'm a gentleman, and don't you forget it!'

The fence cackled with laughter, his dark eyes ironical and shrewd. 'Oh, so – by *you* you're a gentleman, and by *me* you're a gentleman, but tell me, Jack, by a *gentleman* are you a gentleman?'

Jack spat out a filthy oath, wanting to take him by the throat, knowing, as Leitchman knew, that he was not and never could be of the class he boasted. In revenge, he took another swig of gin, from the bottle this time, while Leitchman watched him closely, sad, wry, self-mocking. 'No Jew-baiting now, *fonfer* – there's a law against it.'

'Say you so?' Jack was seated on a corner of the table, swinging one booted foot, his cane gripped in his fist like a cudgel. 'I'd like to see anyone try to enforce it.'

His loathing of the man made his voice thick as he recalled the humiliations, threats and coercion he had once endured. 'Christ, money is the only thing that speaks to you, isn't it, Leitchman? Words like honour, integrity and friendship are alien to your nature. But you've got your uses. I'm not here on a social call. This is strictly business.'

Anger simmered in Leitchman's eyes, his hands wringing together. '*Momzer!*' he muttered.

Jack was on his feet in a flash. 'Don't you call me bastard! I know enough of your lingo to understand your insults! Keep a civil tongue in your lousy head or I'll tear it out!'

'Now, Jack – don't get so heated,' the fence said placatingly. 'Have you news? When may I expect a further consignment, eh?' Not only was he a receiver of stolen goods, but contraband also. The smugglers had distribution networks deep inland.

'This week. It'll arrive in a cartload of turnips,' replied Jack ungraciously.

'Good – good.' Leitchman rubbed his hands together, then added slyly: 'And how is your Master?'

'My half-brother, d'you mean?' Boiling with annoyance, Jack gave answer. 'He's a bridegroom again, in London on his honeymoon.'

'*Hoo-ha!* A surprise for all, no doubt. Did he marry a pretty girl? Is she rich?' The fence pottered around this dingy, lofty-ceilinged room, where he lived, ate, slept and carried out business transactions. There was a large, bulbous-posted bed in one corner, covered by layers of dirty blankets.

'Pretty, yes. Rich, no. To my mind he has married an armful of trouble,' Jack observed acidly.

Leitchman shook his head dolefully. 'Foolish. A pretty face soon fades, but a wife with a goodly portion, a substantial *nadan* – ah, this will not wither with time. Take my advice, Jack, don't marry for money, but marry where money is. A honeymoon, you say? This would explain your presence here at this time of the year. London is too hot, too noisome for those who can afford to leave it.' He gave a heavy sigh, stirring at some unnamable concoction bubbling in a black pot on the trivet. 'Ah, that I might see the countryside once more before I die.'

Jack was examining a fine pair of duelling pistols which lay in an opened leather case on the table, squinting down the sight of one of them, resting the beautifully worked barrel on his left arm. He trained it on Leitchman, then slung it back to join its fellow. 'You – longing for green fields and fresh air?' He barked incredulously. 'Good God, you've lived in this fleapit the whole of your miserable life! A blast of clean wind would kill you!' He drew a washleather bag from an inner pocket and tossed it over. 'Here! Cast your gimlets over those. Let's get down to business.'

Leitchman caught it expertly, untied the drawstring and tipped the contents on to a small area of the table free from clutter. Jewels cascaded out to lie in a shining puddle of colour, rainbow shards sparkling up from diamonds, rubies glistening like blood, emeralds glowing like cobras' eyes. '*Oy-oy-oy!*' Leitchman sang out happily, other words failing him.

His hands hovered over the hoard, then with delicately tender fingers he picked up a superb necklace, handling the gems as if they were beloved children. 'Beautiful – beautiful,' he crooned. 'How fine this would look round the throat of my Rachel.'

She was his grand-daughter. Jack knew that he worshipped her, that meek, dark, quiet girl who lived in the gloom of the house, caring for the old man, slipping silently in and out like a wraith. 'You'll buy them? Their present owner wants two thousand pounds.'

Leitchman reacted by instinct. He pursed his lips dubiously, still running the jewels through his fingers. 'Made of money I am? Would you break me? One thousand, and that's my last word.'

Jack settled down to haggle having purposely named a high price, prepared to drop considerably to a sum which would still give him a profit margin. He was no philanthropist. 'For Christ's sake, light a candle, you tight-arsed sod! It's as dark as a bloody coal-mine in here!' he shouted. 'How can you see what they're worth?'

'I can see – I can see.' The fence carried the gems to the sooty window. 'One thousand, I say – not a penny more.'

'You can stuff that offer right up your poxy backside!' responded Jack with lofty scorn. 'My client needs the money.'

'They always do, my dear.' The joy of barter made Leitchman almost jolly, his eyes darting from the jewels to Jack's hard face. 'Hard-luck stories they always bring.'

'These people are *aristos*. They've escaped from France and could bring little with them. They've lost everything to the revolutionaries.' Jack brought this out craftily, knowing that Leitchman did not approve of anarchy. It disrupted commerce. Then he added crisply: 'What say you to one thousand and eight hundred guineas?'

The fence did not reply immediately, his face deeply carved in those lines of sombre melancholy typical of a persecuted race. '*Aristos*, you tell me? Was their rescue the work of *Le Fantom*? That saviour who steals prisoners from beneath the very noses of the accursed rabble?'

'Yes,' Jack replied cautiously.

Leitchman thoughtfully replaced the gems in the bag, weighing them in his hand. 'Who is this man? D'you know?'

'No.'

Dark, soulful eyes met Jack's, then they crinkled with disbelief. 'You work with him – you don't know him?'

'I take my orders from others.' Jack did not want to discuss it. He had been warned to avoid the subject. The stuffy room was oppressive, too full of bad memories and he was anxious to leave, but it was a further hour before they finally agreed on a price.

'Robbing me you are!' wailed Leitchman at last, when Jack had beaten him up to a figure acceptable to both. 'One thousand, four hundred guineas – guineas, not pounds – for a *mishmash* of stones that I'll find it hard to sell! With a friend like you who needs enemies?' He retired to a far corner, muttering, shaking his head and evoking the help of the spirits. He burrowed like a mole into the depths of an enormous, monstrously carved desk, and emerged with the money. He handed it over reluctantly. 'This I do for the sake of your *aristos*, and to confound those false prophets who preach anarchy and the destruction of property and wealth.'

'Oh, yes, turned kind and generous of a sudden, have you?' Jack tucked away the cash and picked up his hat and stick. 'Well, there's another little job you can do, and you'll keep the fee moderate. We need more passports.'

Leitchman trailed after him to the door. 'My pleasure any

time, but alas, the price has soared. The forger, a greedy *shmuck*, is asking double. 'Tis the demand, my boy.'

Jack's hand shot out and he grabbed him round the throat, hurling him back against the wall, almost lifting him from his feet. 'You'll get them and the price will stay the same! If not, I'll bloody well throttle you!' he grated, and let him drop to the floor.

'All right –' Leitchman gasped, massaging his neck. 'By the end of the week – you shall have them.'

'Make damned certain that you don't keep me waiting!' Jack gave him a final, warning glare and marched out.

Aurora ordered her coach on the morning following the party and drove to Doric House. She was ushered into the drawing-room where Lalage received her, seeming genuinely pleased to see her.

'What can I offer you, Lady Mortmorcy?' she asked sweetly, her hand on the bell-rope. 'Some chocolate, perhaps?'

'My dear girl, let us not delay for that – my carriage awaits. We must go shopping.' Aurora successfully fended off memories of her visits there in the days when she and Guy were lovers. It was odd to see another woman in command, stranger still to think that it was Lalage. She went over to the large mirror hanging on one wall, twisting a curl into place under her wide-brimmed straw Country Girl hat.

'I haven't told Guy that I was going out,' Lalage demurred, conveying the impression of a young bride fearful of upsetting her husband.

'Is he here?' Aurora knew perfectly well that he was not. Ambrose had told her that they were meeting early.

Lalage shook her head, still hesitant. 'No, but he might return and be angry not to find me.'

'Leave him a little *billet-doux*,' Aurora suggested brightly. 'I'm sure you'll know exactly what to write. Really, you mustn't allow him to become too dictatorial. Husbands have to be skilfully managed. A clever woman can always wheedle round them.'

'What a good idea.' Lalage was already looking for paper in the escritoire. 'Thank you for befriending me, Lady Mortmorcy, I have so much to learn.'

Fiddle-faddle! thought Aurora unkindly, you, my dear, could probably teach me a thing or two, but she smiled and replied: 'I should be a poor creature indeed if I didn't take the wife of an old friend under my wing. By the by, can't we drop this "your Ladyship" business? You used to call me Aurora, not so long ago.'

Lalage looked up from the note she was penning, that smile, which put Aurora in mind of a sleek cat, lifting her mouth. 'If you wish – formality is such a bore, is it not?'

Oh, Ambrose, sighed Aurora inwardly, you've set me a task and a half! Gritting her teeth, she asked: 'Where would you like to go first?'

'Would you take me to your milliner?' Lalage picked up her shawl and reticule, propping the note on the mantelpiece. 'I so much admire that hat.'

It was against Aurora's principles to share either her dress-maker or hatter with anyone. She wanted no other woman aping her style, but she had taken on this job and must make the best of it. 'Certainly – I'll be delighted, though in truth, Lalage, I was going to ask you who made that charming creation you were wearing last night.'

Lalage named a new shop which had only recently opened and Aurora declared her intention of ordering one just like it, as gay and charming as she could possibly be, with Ambrose's approbation firmly in mind. The two women rustled towards the door, talking as lightly and intimately as if they had been inseparable companions for years. This was the start of a close association, with Aurora working diligently on Ambrose's behalf. Soon, Lalage's wardrobe had been doubled by their frequent excursions to the smart, glass-fronted, bow-windowed shops, her education widened by visits to the theatres, magic-lantern shows, the wax-works, tea-parties, balls and masques. With her predilection for low-life, Aurora insisted that they go to the circus with its freaks, midgets and women-gladiators, contortionists, fire-eaters, stunt-riders and mathematical pigs. And, amongst less innocent pastimes, she taught Lalage how to scandalmonger or seduce with the language of the fan.

At first Guy was puzzled and suspicious, not too happy about his ex-mistress's influence, but Ambrose put his mind at rest. In a way, it was a relief to know that Lalage was being entertained, permitting him to settle down into his customary town routine. Every morning, after a light repast of fruit and coffee, he drove his cabriolet to Battling Billy's gymnasia in Bond Street, and there practised the art of fisticuffs. As a patron of 'the fancy', he had financed Billy, for prize-fighting, though very popular, was technically illegal, yet tens of thousands of pounds were staked on big bouts. Successful fighters were now setting up schools and turning mere bruising into the science of pugilism.

Guy was not the only gentleman present in the large, bare sports-room when he arrived one bright sunny morning. Many others were finding such exercise advantageous, a sure cure for a hangover after a heavy night of boozing, gambling and whoring. He watched the formidable Billy putting one man through his paces, then strolled into the changing room to take off his outdoor clothes and put on garments he kept there. He soon emerged, stripped to the waist, wearing light nankeen breeches, white stockings and low pumps. In a while he entered the roped-off area, pitting his strength and skill against the large, red-headed, broken-nosed fighter, who grinned at him in a friendly way, fists bunched, taking up the boxer's stance.

Whack! Whack! The clean blows fell on the iron-muscled bodies of the contestants, Guy practising the catlike steps, back and forth, ducking and weaving, his right fist shooting out to connect with some part of Billy's anatomy. A couple of gentlemen leaned on the ropes, passing the time before going on to their club, and the bout continued to the accompaniment of semi-satirical, semi-affectionate gibes and ejaculations. From the tail of his eye, Guy saw Jack come in and, during a pause, went over to speak to him whilst towelling the sweat from his face and chest. Jack quietly told him that Leitchman had delivered passports and documents. Guy nodded and went back to the ring.

'How do, Wylde!' Someone greeted him, passing through the small gaggle of men who were standing talking. It was Ambrose, cool and exquisitely attired, ambling towards him. 'Zounds, my dear old fellow,' he continued, smothering a yawn, 'did you ever see such a confounded hot day? Damned climate this, either raining or scorching one's hide.'

Guy laughed, swinging out beneath the barrier. 'I swear that it's the English weather that gives us our rather warped sense of humour.'

'Begad! I protest, 'tis marvellous, damned marvellous how you can be so hellish energetic, Guy,' Ambrose drawled, fanning himself with his hat. 'Beats me!'

'You should try it, Alington. Do you good,' Guy advised, taking the glass of wine which Jack had poured for him.

The golden eyebrows shot up till they met the ragged fringe of bleached hair. 'I? What a suggestion! Get my nose bloodied! Not likely! But I've a couple of buck niggers back home who'd win us a fortune if I shipped 'em over. We'd clean up a few thousand dollars between us.'

Billy came over, wide chest heaving, sweat trickling down his face. 'Can those darkies really fight, sir?' he asked.

Quizzing-glass at the ready, Ambrose looked him up and down. 'Fight? You've not witnessed boxing till you've seen a black in action. I'd pit one of my chaps against Daniel Mendoza any day and expect to come out the richer. You should see 'em. Built like deuced warships!'

'Ah, it's not the size what's important, sir,' said Billy earnestly. 'Mendoza's a small bloke, but I've seen him drop a hulking great Irishman with a tremendous right between the eyes. A medium-sized lad who's clever on his feet can always beat a slow-moving slugger.'

'I know all about that, my good man.' Ambrose leaned lazily on his cane. 'My niggers move like dancers, using footwork of a sort previously unknown. They're fast, full of uncommon strength and *bottom*.'

'What about it, Billy?' grinned Guy. 'You're the one for arranging contests.'

'More of this anon.' Ambrose nodded towards the door. 'Here come the ladies.'

As usual, they were not alone. Zuba led the pug along by its gem-studded collar and leash. Sidney was in tow, carrying parcels, followed by two gorgeous young men, painted, powdered and gaudily garbed, swinging their canes, toying with their snuff-boxes. Aurora was wearing the latest rage from Paris. The *Merveilleuse* look consisted of an extravagantly long and full white muslin gown, its high waist and tiny sleeves embroidered with flowers, with strappy sandals, a red silk stole, and an exaggerated, very wide-brimmed hat over wildly flowing hair. It was strange how the English loudly maintained that they hated the French, yet could not wait to copy their fashions.

'Guy!' Aurora shrieked, rushing up to him. 'My dear, what are you doing here half-naked? What magnificent shoulders! What elegant waist and hips! Don't you agree, Charlie? What say you, Nick?'

The beaux simpered, running their eyes over his remarkably fine proportions, but backing off when they saw the hard line of his mouth, the cold steel of his stare. 'Good morning, Aurora,' he said coolly. 'Are you taking good care of my wife?'

'She is exhausting herself in her role of guide,' put in Lalage, more simply but none the less effectively gowned, miraculously keeping her cool appearance even in the blaze of August.

Ambrose was studying Aurora through his quizzing-glass. 'My sweet, what have you got on? Or should I say, very nearly got on?' His sleepy-looking eyes lingered on her exposed bosom.

She was brimming with mischief. 'It matches your *Incroyable* suit. Today, I am a *citoyenne* – a member of the *bourgeoisie*. D'you approve? Ideal for a picnic party, don't you think? We are going to Vauxhall Gardens. Will you come?'

'It would be much cooler at Brook's Club, and I could play faro,' he objected.

'You can play cards there any time. Bring a pack with you, if you must. Get old Sanderman to give you a game. We are meeting him there.'

'The lawyer?' Guy's brows winged together as he took his shirt from Jack, flinging it around his shoulders.

'Oh, yes. Were you not aware that he's our latest escort? I think he fancies himself as a duenna, keeping an eye on us, you know,' she trilled, her voice growing louder.

'Please come, Guy,' said Lalage, her eyes resting on him. Her quiet dignity had a pleasant, astringent quality. Becoming Lady Beaumaris had given her a sense of authority and power which showed in the regal tilt of her head, the set of her chin.

'Later,' he replied, smiling down on her. 'But now I must go up to Maestro Giaconi's studio to study the finer points of fencing.'

'Now, that I *can* appreciate.' Ambrose shifted his shoulders from where he had been lounging against a pillar. 'I'll join you.'

'Oh, men!' Aurora rolled her eyes in exasperation. 'Must you! What are you trying to prove? We are all aware that you're devastatingly virile and masculine! I suppose we shall just have to watch you and utter screams of admiration.'

Walford carried Guy's clothing and Jack walked with him. The little procession went up the stairs to where the fiery, lithe Italian, Mario Giaconi ran his flourishing school. Guy exchanged greetings with him, and then put on a padded, protective jacket and gauntlets, whilst Aurora and her friends took up seats in a window alcove overlooking the busy street. Ambrose handed his coat and waistcoat to Walford with strict instructions not to crease them, and similarly clad as Guy, walked to the centre of the room where Giaconi waited with a pair of foils selected from the many hanging round the walls.

'I must be cracked in the head,' complained Ambrose as he

took up his weapon and bowed to Guy. The tips of their foils touched in a brief salute. '*En garde*, my friend!'

Had this been a duel to the death, Guy would have been a formidable opponent, an accomplished swordsman who had slain more than one rash challenger. Ambrose seemed indolently relaxed in style yet gave Guy no opportunity to pierce his guard, unhurriedly retreating before his first slashing attack, parrying it easily, almost lazily. The air whistled and rang with the clash of expertly wielded steel as he counter-attacked, remarking: 'You handle that blade rather well – for a novice.'

'How would you know? Trained by some hack in a barbaric school in the colonies!' Guy scoffed. They spoke no more, concentrating hard, with Giaconi standing by, giving vent to the voluble expressions of Italy, critical and fussy. They lunged, parried, and employed the graceful *riposte*, faceless in their masks.

Ambrose seemed to slip, almost prone, his left hand on the ground – a thrust upwards and he was under Guy's guard, his point at his throat. Guy leapt back, swiftly parrying this attack, but before Ambrose could recover his footing, Giaconi knocked up his foil.

'Foul play!' he shouted passionately, wiry, fierce and imperious. 'A stroke *dessous*! *Signore*, it is not *en règale*!'

Ambrose stood breathing rapidly, leaning lightly on his flexible rapier. 'Rot!' he said contemptuously. 'Why not, pray?'

The Italian gesticulated wildly. 'I do not permit it! I have my rules – I follow and teach only the ancient laws of fencing.'

'Ha!' Ambrose was laconic, casually derisive. 'D'you think that if we were fighting for real, we'd be worrying about some petty code imposed on us by a dago mountebank!'

Spluttering, indignant, Giaconi stood his ground. 'While you fence in my school, you will abide by my edicts!'

'Let us proceed,' said Guy calmly, bending his supple foil between his gloved hands. 'Shut up, Ambrose. If the stroke was irregular, Giaconi has a right to intervene.'

They fell on guard again, but more fiercely now and with less caution, Ambrose continuing to use a rough, sweeping parry more favoured by professional soldiers than students at fencing schools. This left him open to a *riposte*, the circle too wide, and Guy's blade slipped like a serpent under his. For an instant, the blades locked together, the fighters close as lovers, then they broke apart and once more the blades met with a clash.

Aurora had been idly listening to the fops who were gallivanting from subject to subject, now love, now poetry, now politics, but she kept an eye on the swordsmen. 'Well done!' she cried, clapping her hands as the furious exchange between them caught her attention. 'La, I can't make up my mind who to admire most! Guy looks as if his rapier is an extension of himself, but Ambrose has such style, such vigour! I vow and declare, my fingers itch to hold a blade myself.'

Charlie gave a faint, superior smile, snuff-box out, lifting a pinch to his nose. ''Pon my soul, what a fanciful notion! A female duelling!'

'This astonishes you?' She eyed him mockingly. 'Supposing I were to tell you that I had six brothers, and took my lessons in fencing with them?'

'I, for one, should say that you jest.' Nick lowered his newspaper and glanced at her over the edge.

Their sneering inference that this was a masculine occupation, out of bounds to women, riled Aurora. She knew that these young men sought sexual satisfaction at Mrs Berkeley's flagellant bagnio in Charlotte Street, and belonged to various sodomites' clubs where they indulged their transvestite tendencies to the full.

'Why the devil should I not use a rapier?' she demanded belligerently, her eyes snapping. 'I'd best you any day! D'you want to take a wager on it? You think yourselves superior to a woman, eh? At least I don't spend my nights in "molly houses"!'

Ambrose and Guy caught the last part of the dissension, coming across, removing their masks, their faces drenched in sweat, strong, vital men, one as fair as an archangel, the other dark as the devil. 'Sounding off like a fishwife again, Aurora,' Ambrose chided, pulling at his gauntlets and smiling. 'What the deuce is it this time?'

She explained and they laughed at her fire. 'A veritable she-devil,' observed Guy, taking his street clothes from Walford.

'Best watch your step, young sirs,' advised Ambrose, but the fops chose to take offence at her barbed references to their vices and took their leave, coldly formal.

'Buffoons!' shouted Aurora as they went out of the door. Then she turned on Guy and Ambrose, finding their laughter annoying. 'The patronizing attitude of men – even half-men, like them, towards women is truly infuriating. We have ideas and feelings too!'

Ambrose shrugged his broad shoulders into his light silk coat and stood patiently while Walford tied his cravat. 'Not turning into some dowdy blue-stocking, I hope? In my experience, if one gives a woman a mirror and a box of bonbons, she'll ask for nothing more,' he teased, then his eyes rested on Lalage. 'And what have you to contribute to the debate, Lady Beaumaris?'

By now, he had met her several times but could not fathom her. He tried vainly to read those large amber eyes under the arched brows, appreciating her beauty, admiring the high cheekbones, the thin nose and full mouth, yet she remained a mystery to him. Her manners were above reproach, her sense of dress impeccable, her walk graceful, sensually languid yet vital. With all these attributes, she retained an air of purity which was tantalizing, and kept up barriers impossible to breach.

Aurora was different; he could understand, be amused by and get to grips with her. She was arrogant, rude and delight-fully detestable, aware of her body's glory and power, and proud of it. Guy's wife was an enigma, and Ambrose had spent much time thinking about her. He had even questioned Guy discreetly, adept at playing on weak points and finding the spot in the mind most tender and unprotected, but he had drawn a blank. Guy was not prepared to discuss her, answering curtly that he had chosen to marry her and that was that. So Ambrose remained puzzled, knowing his friend to be a man of good sense and dauntless courage, though admittedly he had a few weak-nesses, among which were personal vanity, stubbornness, and a craving for the exotic and sensational.

He shrugged the problem aside for the moment, listening seriously as Lalage replied to his question. 'Everyone is entitled to their point of view, Mr Alington. If Aurora wishes to fence, I see no reason why she should not do so. Indeed, this morning's exhibition was so exciting, that I'd certainly like to try it myself.'

'Devil take it, my love, you'll be wanting to play cricket next,' Guy said blandly. 'Shall I make you captain of the Beaumaris Combe village team?'

Aurora laughed, refreshed by her skirmish with Charlie and Nick. ''Tis my belief, she'd excel in any sport. My dears, you should see the way she handles the reins! A regular charioteer! She insisted on driving us here in your phaeton, Guy. What a breakneck speed! I very nearly lost my hat and had to cling on for dear life!'

'I hope you didn't mind?' Lalage stood close to him, slim and fragile-looking in pale rose gauze, face shadowed by her full-brimmed bonnet. 'It was so smart, standing there in the stable. I simply couldn't resist taking a turn in it.'

'You must be careful, Lalage,' he said sternly. 'The traffic in the streets is appalling.'

'Damn right!' yawned Ambrose. 'Ale-wagons, complete with a team of shires, farm-carts, hay-wains – driven by an insolent bunch who think they have right of way and resent a gentleman pushing to the fore. I've more than once been insulted by common dray-men – the most cursed brood in existence. I trust you didn't scratch the varnish, dear lady. I should be mightily incommoded if a female drove my own spanking new equipage and it returned looking like a down-at-heel hackney.'

'No fear of that, sir. I am competent,' she answered, levelling him a challenging look.

'The hell you are! I've never yet met a woman who could match up to a man with a pair of skittish thoroughbreds out front.'

'I'd lay money on Lalage any time,' put in Aurora eagerly as a novel idea began to take shape in her mind. 'What say you to a race with her in Hyde Park? We could open a book on it. Or are you afraid of being whopped, Ambrose?'

'What a capital notion!' enthused Sidney, eager to gamble. 'I know any number of game fellows who'll squander their allowances on it.'

'So do I,' affirmed Aurora.

England was in the grip of gambling fever, and nowhere more so than London. Vast fortunes were lost night after night in the clubs or at parties in private houses. They bet on anything and everything – if the sun would shine in five minutes' time or how long it would take for a raindrop to trickle down a window-pane. Money was staked on life and death – on the sex of an unborn child – on political events – on a man drinking a quart of beer in one gulp – on dog-fights, cockfights, human-fights. Until a few years before when public executions were still held at Tyburn, the sporting fraternity would sit, pocket-watches in hand, eagerly betting on how many minutes it would take for the wretch on the gallows to die. Aurora was right in her shrewd assessment that a phaeton race would be a popular event, better even than the Derby.

Lalage was eyeing Ambrose and he was shocked by the intensity there. It was the taut look of a wildcat, such as he had encountered hunting in Carolina, sharply reminiscent of tearing claws and rending teeth. For an instant her calm cover of icy restraint had betrayed itself.

'It might be amusing to accept Lady Beaumaris's challenge,' he said placidly, 'but dash it, Aurora, it seems pretty long odds. I'll be bound to win.'

'Not if I have anything to do with it,' she cried merrily.

'You won't sink to underhand tricks, surely?' he said, pained at the very idea. 'Who'll be engaged in the organization?'

'I can do it,' she declared.

'A thousand pardons, my sweet,' he purred, 'but I would prefer an outsider. Not that I don't trust you, but treason and duplicity are the female's natural element, don't you know. You might be tempted to rig it.'

This drawling condescension made Aurora see red, as he had known it would. 'God damn you for a rogue, Ambrose Alington!' she cried, in a fine temper now, her eyes almost purple, a flush mounting to her cheeks, her indignation underlined by a few, more vigorous swear words.

'May I make so bold as to offer my services in this respect?' inquired Sidney, artfully positioning himself between them, for the protection of both.

Ambrose chose to ignore him, looking over the top of his head at his infuriated mistress. 'Darling, you're at your most fetching when cross,' he observed, without batting an eyelid. He turned to Guy who, dressed now, was waiting with his thumbs hooked in his waistcoat pockets, a smile playing about his lips. 'What about that *tonish* chap whom you employ? He's over there, with your valet.'

'Jack Smithers? Aye, he's mighty capable.'

Ambrose was staring at the door. 'Oh, God – here comes that puppy, de Belcourt,' he said with ill-disguised impatience. 'What a poser! Let's get out of here, before we have to exchange civilities.' Even as he spoke, he was bowing graciously to the Frenchman who returned his salute before engaging Giaconi in conversation.

'The *viscomte!* How delightful!' gushed Aurora with a lightning change of tactics and opinion. 'He's such good company. Lalage and I had a lovely time with him at the Ranelagh ridotto the other night. Our dance-cards had his name scribbled all over them.'

She was chaffing him mercilessly and Ambrose knew it, but he laughed and lifted his brows with an air of sufferance. 'He is, no doubt, attempting to get back into your good books, after wrecking your gaming-room, my love. He's a touch unhinged. Don't be duped. There's nothing in his heart save a deck of cards.'

'Indeed?' She tossed her head impertinently, and by way of revenge, added: 'I think I'll invite him to the picnic.' With that, she picked up her skirts and flew across to the Frenchman, turning on the full benefit of her ravishing smile.

'I think the air would be sweeter in Brook's, don't you?' said Ambrose, giving Guy a significant look.

'Good idea,' answered his friend. 'Let's go.'

Chapter 5

The Wylde residence was one of a crescent of magnificently ornamented town houses with pleasing lines, handsome doors and stone mouldings, complete with basements and attics for the large staff of servants. Built during Mark Beaumaris's lifetime, whilst leaning towards the classical in its style of architecture, it had several modern innovations, including a kitchen range in the subterranean domain of the chef, water-closets and baths fitted into the dressing-rooms adjoining the principal bedchambers. Hot water still had to be lugged upstairs by strong-muscled footmen, but cold was on tap. Despite these new-fangled sanitary arrangements, diehards among gentlemen visitors preferred to use the china pot kept in the sideboard for the relief of nature during lengthy after-dinner drinking sessions.

The green square fronting the houses was private, guarded by iron-spiked railings, and used only by the occupiers. Arches separating each mansion gave access to the rear where the gardens were large and planted out formally with bushes and trees of English extraction, to which various exotica had been added, in the shape of goldfish ponds, fuchsias and pineapple trees. They also led to the mews buildings, housing the horses and carriages.

It was to the stables of Doric House that Lalage found her way on the day of the phaeton race. It was a warm, still morning, and the trees were alive with birds. As Aurora had predicted, the contest had engendered hectic excitement and the stakes had soared. Lalage had been practising daily, getting to know each idiosyncrasy of the spirited greys when they were between the shafts.

Jack was busy inside, giving a final polish to brass and leather. The phaeton gleamed, its dark green varnish mirror-smooth. Thin traceries of gilt accentuated its high, sporting lines. He took one look at Lalage and stopped in his tracks, whistling soundlessly. 'God, are you really going out dressed like that, my Lady?'

His astonishment quickly turned to admiration and his eyes

burned hot with desire. She was wearing a shockingly daring outfit, hips and thighs displayed in an unbroken line from ribcage to calf in white breeches which fitted without a wrinkle. A military-styled jacket over a wide-lapelled waistcoat, a stock, dangling gold fobs, top-boots of black leather, in fact every item of masculine attire adorned her, transforming her into a sleek-flanked, dandyish youth. A low-crowned topper was set rakishly atop her crisp curls, and she was looking extremely pleased with herself.

'Do you approve, Jack?' She asked with an inviting glance from her tip-tilted eyes.

'*I* approve, madame,' he replied with a laughing bow, 'but what will your husband say? I assume that he hasn't yet seen you.'

'Truth to tell, I don't give a brass farthing what he says,' she answered, smiling pensively, looking down at her rings which she was turning around.

'So certain that you can twist him round your finger, eh?' He was staring at her speculatively. 'Don't push your luck too far.'

'I'm the best judge of that.' She was cool, dismissive.

His hand closed on her arm in its red velvet sleeve. 'No need to be frigidly condescending to me, milady,' he warned, with a tight smile. 'It won't work. I recognize a deep little baggage when I see one. I'll wager you haven't a vestige of conscience in the whole of your beautiful body.'

She did not try to shake him off, passive under his grip. 'I'm not much interested in what you think, Jack,' she said, looking at him strangely.

Jack's smile broadened and he dragged her slowly nearer till her breasts touched his chest. 'Aren't you, Lady Beaumaris?'

She was unyielding in his arms, but her eyes were alight, and the tip of her pink tongue showed between her even teeth. 'Let me go, Jack,' she said steadily.

'What will you do if I refuse? Cry rape?' His taunting challenge was brutally direct.

She brought up her heel and kicked him savagely on the shin, hand upraised, claws spread to rake his cheek. Jack was used to St Giles harpies. He ducked, avoiding her nails. She broke free, springing for the door, but his arm snaked out and pulled her back. He crushed her to him, deliberately hurtful, and his mouth clamped down on hers. She fought for a moment more, hands beating at him, then she subsided, body lax, lips opening beneath his assault.

Jack took his time, savouring her mouth, running a hand smoothly under her jacket, sliding it inside her shirt. Her skin was like warm silk. But just when he thought he had conquered, wondering if there would be time to take her before the race, she suddenly opened her eyes wide, latent fierceness in her pupils, huge, unnaturally close. Pain made him yelp as her teeth fastened on his lip, biting deep.

He slapped her hard, once, twice on the side of her face. She let go, smiling, her mouth smeared with his blood. 'Bitch!' he snarled, and flung her off.

Lalage laughed, took out her handkerchief and wiped her lips, picked up her hat, knocked off the dust, and set it on her head. 'You forget your lowly station, Jack,' she said crisply. 'I may have you dismissed. We must go. You can take your place beside me. We mustn't keep the punters waiting.'

Jack was staring at her narrowly, his handsome face bloodied and angry. He gave his cravat an impatient twist, setting it straight. In all his vagabond life of squalor and bravura, no woman had ever got the better of him. Lalage would be no exception. She had betrayed herself in that moment in his arms, displaying an unbridled lust. There could be only one end to the game, but let her wait, the hot-arsed foreign jilt.

He gave a wolfish smile, cruel and jeering. 'Your servant, milady. By all means, let us proceed.'

She swung up on to the seat with agile grace, taking the reins without glancing at Jack as he seated himself. In dead silence they left the mews, rumbling over the cobbled yard and under the arch, sliced across by shadows, into the blinding sunlight of the wide road. Jack settled back against the scarlet leather upholstery, admiring the deft way she handled the high-stepping horses. He pointed to the right-hand one.

'He's a demon,' he warned. 'Use a heavier whip.'

She did not turn her head, but a smile flickered across her lips. 'It could be yourself of whom you speak. Perhaps such an insolent bastard also needs breaking in.'

His laughter had an edge to it, his words a hard ring. 'Try to thrash me if you dare, madame, but it'll be your skin that's marked, not mine. I'd enjoy that, hearing you scream, seeing you bleed. Name the time and place, and we'll put it to the test.'

Hyde Park was the largest of those tree-filled areas of green which astonish the stranger, an unexpected feature of such a vast, complex city as London. It was open to all; rich and poor alike could go there to have tea, listen to the band, stare at the dandies and keep assignations. The resident roe-deer were so tame that they hardly bothered to glance at the holiday-makers or heed the gorgeous equipages which formed one of the principal sights.

Rotten Row was the meeting place of the equestrian-minded, redolent of fashion and pleasure, combined with a certain air of luxurious dissipation. But accustomed though they were to flagrant nonconformity, Lalage's unconventional attire became the talking-point of the day. It was enough that she was racing against Ambrose Alington, but word passed like wildfire among the chaises, hooded curricles and coaches – Lady Beaumaris is wearing breeches!

Her challenger was standing at the heads of his team of ebony prancers, the dark brown phaeton gleaming as sunlight dappled through the walnut trees. His flashing repartee was amusing the group who had arrived with him. He was splendidly turned out, his tall figure shown to full advantage with the coat pared away in front to complement the risen female waistline, his pantaloons cut so high in the rise that they reached almost to his chest, very tight, light in colour, presenting his body as nearly naturally as could be acceptably allowed. He twirled a pair of gloves by the tassels, his curly-brimmed topper under one arm.

Aurora was with him, wearing floating white, parasol aloft to protect her complexion, purring with satisfaction, knowing that the newsmongers were busy tattling about her affair with the handsome American, feeling herself to be the cynosure of every eye. She opened her fan. 'Heavens, what a hot day! I shall burn to a crisp if I'm not careful. Would you still love me if I looked like a gypsy?'

Ambrose pointed to the Wylde phaeton drawing up alongside his own. 'You'll be even hotter in a moment. Look at Lalage.'

Aurora followed his eyes, and her expression hardened, a flinty glitter in her blue eyes. 'Hell and damnation! The strumpet! Why in the name of all that's holy, didn't I think of it first?'

Lalage drew her horses to a standstill. 'Good morning, Mr Alington,' she called across. Jack jumped down but she remained in her seat, the greys throwing up their heads and snorting.

Ambrose regarded her through his raised eye-glass. 'Pardon

me, young sir, but do I have the honour of your acquaintance? This is deuced queer. Why are you driving Lord Beaumaris's rig? Rat me, was I so toped when I accepted the challenge that I misunderstood? I thought I was to race against her Ladyship.'

His eyes widened as he saw Jack's swollen lip. 'What happened to you? Been fighting again?'

'I was mauled by a spiteful cat,' Jack said, grinning. 'You've not made a mistake, Mr Alington. You're looking at Lady Beaumaris.'

Ambrose's eyes raked over him with that stand-offishness which he always reserved for Guy's brash master of horse. 'Don't trifle with me, fellow. I don't believe his wife would appear in public dressed like that.'

'Stop twitting me, Alington,' Lalage's voice rang out clearly. 'Is this a deliberate move to avoid the contest which you know I'm going to win?'

With one booted foot on the front wheel, he swung lithely up, peering into her face. 'Well I'll be damned!' he exclaimed, feigning great surprise. 'I behold a lady beneath these false colours. Why aren't you flying a feminine flag to champion the fair sex?'

He was back on his feet in an instant and making her a leg very elegantly, conscious of the interested spectators around the two vehicles. Guy was at his shoulder, a none-too-pleased expression flashing across his swarthy features before he controlled himself, giving everyone the impression that he not only applauded but had even suggested his wife's brazen attire.

'We thought it a droll notion, Ambrose,' he said coolly. 'You must admit that it adds a certain dash. We're expecting the Prince to arrive for the start, and it will entertain him mightily.'

'Priny will adore such a fine pair of legs,' Ambrose answered airily, glancing down the long avenue. 'Protocol demands that we wait for him. I hope he won't be late.'

The Prince of Wales was a sporting fanatic, and it was not very long before loud cheers welcomed the glittering cavalcade when it entered the Park. Outriders flanked the open carriage, postillions rode the four Cleveland bays who trotted sedately in front, and the Prince lifted a gracious hand to acknowledge the acclaim. He was a good-looking, popular man, pleasing commoner and peer alike by his staunch support of the ring, the race-track, blood-sports and gambling. His lavish balls at Carlton House were already legendary, and this patron of pugilists, the theatre, music and the arts, was also a man of fashion. On that glorious summer morning he was wearing the latest colour which he had popularized, a brilliant blue-grey called Emperor's Eye.

He was not alone. Maria Fitzherbert sat beside him, a woman of exceptional distinction, if not particularly beautiful. The opposite seat was taken by a hussar from a cavalry regiment, resplendent in his plumed kalpak and furred, braided dolman. He was Priny's bodyguard. Ambrose and Guy performed the brief ceremony which greeted this Royal personage, and he strolled round the phaetons with them, while they pointed out the various advantages of the sporting vehicles. Then he retired to his carriage to watch the race from a commanding position.

A roar went up from the crowd as Ambrose took his place on his lofty perch. Grooms gentled the horses. Jack and his assistants checked that the phaetons were precisely placed on the starting line. The atmosphere was electric. Ambrose could feel the tension, stretching like a drawn bowstring. Silence fell, everyone holding their breath, so quiet, so hushed that the carolling of the birds seemed strident. Above, the blue, cloudless sky; around, the sea of faces, expectant, eager, the wealthy in the front, the rabble well back, envious perhaps, yet seeing the protagonists as gods who would achieve a victory, a greatness that they could never hope to know in their drab, ugly lives.

'Don't let 'er beat yer, gov'ner!' A man's voice shouted from the throng. 'Shameless trull!'

Laughter welled up, and Ambrose turned to solemnly salute the owner of the voice, locating him up among the branches of a sycamore tree. This pleased the mob and they shouted and clapped before hushing again as the Master of Ceremonies lifted his white kerchief. The linen glistened in the heat, then fell.

Simultaneously, Lalage and Ambrose shook their reins and the spirited thoroughbreds, freed from restraint, shot ahead like bolts from crossbows. The phaetons rocked and bounced as they gathered speed, yellow gravel flashing under flying hooves and wheels, the trees, the faces, a whirl of abstract colour rushing by. Ambrose's blacks were not yet at full stretch. He controlled them, holding them in reserve and, neck and neck, both teams reached the far end of the avenue, grit spraying up as they wheeled. Lalage's face was a pale blur, dropping slightly behind as they galloped back to complete the first lap.

A sharp turn, the phaetons teetering precariously. Lalage's shot forward in a burst of sudden speed, rearing towards Ambrose, her team plunging wildly. He swerved, quick as a whiplash. She crossed his path. He cursed. That swerve had cost him the lead. He was a fraction behind her, marvelling at her recovery for her greys were a high-strung pair, he could tell. He set his teeth grimly, letting out the blacks, little by little. The thunder of the crowd was like the sea in storm. His horses inched nearer to hers, gained on, passed them and, in passing, Ambrose shot her a glance. She was white, furious, almost on her feet.

Ahead lay the turn and he took it at reckless speed. So did she. Together they tore down the stretch which marked the end of the second lap. Four more to go. They took three without mishap and the punters were dancing with excitement, wagers flying fast and furious. No one could judge the outcome for those two were driving as if possessed, first one, then the other in the lead. Ambrose's steely strength was astounding those who knew him. Who would have thought that lazy American fop would handle horses with the skill of a Derby winner? As for the woman! They couldn't believe their eyes. So lissom a girl to contain such fortitude, such bravery!

The tension had mounted to fever-pitch, every eye trained on the dust-covered phaetons as they commenced the last and final round. Ambrose was half a length ahead, his team full out now. Foam creamed their satin backs, and he shouted encouragement to them so that they gave of their uttermost. Glancing back, he saw the greys pounding in pursuit, ears flat, tails and manes streaming, nostrils dilated, eyes rolling and bloodshot, lips back. Shoulder to shoulder with his own they flew. Lalage's long whip whistled over the sweating animals, drawing blood. In terror, they strained forward, but so did the blacks. He saw her as she veered closer. The spinning wheels grated sickeningly as they locked for a jarring second, breaking free in the sweep of the turn. The four horses were straining every sinew, taking the home-stretch, galloping in formation. Ambrose saw Lalage's eyes fixed on him, blazing like coals. Her whip cracked. Its tip flayed his cheek. Agony struck through his whole body like a red-hot iron. The crowd bawled its disapproval, but during that instant's loss of control, she streaked ahead. Again the blacks sprang forward, almost in flight, but he could not recover the distance in time. Lalage reached the finishing post a hair's breadth in front of him.

They slewed to a halt and the crowd went mad. There was tumultuous applause, though there were some who booed. That blow of the whip did not please the purists, particularly those who had put their money on the American. But the socialites who had taken Lalage to their fickle hearts were praising her to the skies, picking her up and carrying her around on their shoulders, when she leapt nimbly from the phaeton.

When they had set her on her feet, she took off her hat, running her hand through her sweat-plastered curls and Guy did not speak to her. He frowned to see the mob of gaily dressed women and dandies being over-respectful to her, while her eyes glittered with impudent importance. He could not speak to her in this flurry, amidst so many watching eyes. Instead, he went over to Ambrose, who had collected his own knot of sympathizers. Blood stained his cravat, and he was holding a handkerchief to the weal on his cheek. Someone was with him, a doctor by the shape of his hat and the gold-topped cane he carried. Guy heard him saying:

'Let me attend to that at once, sir, or you'll bear the mark to the end of your days.'

'So unfortunate.' Augustus Sanderman was at his elbow. 'A most regrettable accident.'

Ambrose was hot, angry and vexed with himself as he stood impatiently enduring the doctor's ministrations. It was not that he minded losing, but he knew that it was no accident and should have challenged Lalage, but there was Guy to consider. How could Ambrose declare that his wife had cheated? He knew that the blow had been deliberate, the viciousness on her face branded into his mind for ever. So he made light of the incident, clapping Guy round the shoulder.

''Tis nothing, a mere scratch. Lalage is to be congratulated, Wylde. Be proud of her and don't worry about me. I hope you put money on her. I certainly did.'

Aurora was pale with furious indignation. 'You're too generous, Ambrose. I saw what happened. She intended to strike you. I hope you'll take her to task, Guy, for if you don't, then I most certainly shall!'

Anxiously, her eyes went over Ambrose's face, appalled to see the long, raw line which ran from cheekbone to jaw, while she contemplated various unpleasant schemes for getting even with Lalage. It had been hard to keep up a pretence of friendship. Now it would be an impossibility. Guy promised to get to the bottom of the matter, and when he had gone, Ambrose bent his head close to hers, and murmured:

'You'll not let this influence you. Though it be as bitter as gall, you must continue to cultivate her.'

'How the devil can I do that? She has hurt you, and it is unforgivable.' In that fraught moment, she could not mask the love in her eyes. It startled Ambrose, throwing him off kilter. This charming, gay ladybird was sincere. He felt an answering warmth stirring within him, a soft emotion which instinct warned him to reject. He had to be free – no ties, no woman winding her possessive fingers round his heart, even if he wanted it. The secret admission that he *did* want it alarmed him.

He threw her a stern look which commanded obedience, and she bowed her head in assent, face smudged with shadows under the fringed parasol. By now she had realized that his interest in Lalage was not motivated by desire, indeed she sensed a dislike unusual in the affable American. That cruel lashing served to alienate him further. There were mysterious elements in Ambrose's activities which puzzled her. If she tried to probe, he shut up like one of those clams he had told her about, who skulked in the rivers of South Carolina.

Aurora made up her mind to continue her vigilance, her smile letting him know that she would carry out his commands to the letter. She held his arm as he sauntered from group to group, discussing the race, making light of his defeat, evoking laughter with his quips. Something could yet be salvaged from the day; let Lalage be as triumphant as she pleased – Aurora was Ambrose's chosen lady. So she sparkled, charming everyone who swam into their ken, whilst inside she was gauging his reactions. With the insight wrought by her growing love, she sensed something held back about him, suggesting that his pleasant, lazy friendliness was a cloak.

Champagne corks sounded like pop-guns around the Wylde phaeton where Lalage held court. Servants were unpacking hampers and spreading damask cloths on the grass. Rugs and cushions made comfortable lounging places, and several ladies and their escorts had taken up positions under the trees. The hussar came swaggering from the Prince's carriage, setting hearts aflutter, a magnificently handsome figure in his gold braid and frogging, sword swinging at his hip. He wore a moustache, twirled and waxed into sharp points, and tiny plaits over each ear, his long back-hair drawn into a pigtail. Kalpak under one arm, hand on hip, the other resting on his sabre-hilt, he clicked his heels and bowed stiffly, announcing His Royal Highness's request that Lady Beaumaris should be presented to him.

This caused a buzz and raised brows, for he was notoriously interested in attractive women. Some of the dandies started to lay discreet bets on how long it would be before he added her to the Royal seraglio, and also on what Guy Wylde would do about it. Lalage walked to the carriage with her husband and the hussar, answered the Prince's questions and thanked him for his compliments. He was enthralled for she looked like an Amazonian queen, radiant in her excitement, eyes lustrous, red lips glistening where her tongue had moistened them. Before he departed, he issued her with an invitation to attend his next party at Carlton House. Cheat or no, Lalage had made her mark on high society.

Guy contained his anger until he and Lalage returned to Doric House. He drove home in his cabriolet, leaving Jack to bring the phaeton, and did not speak until they were in the bed-chamber. Walford was in the dressing-room and though he expected to indulge in a chat about the day's happenings as his master changed, he took one look at his dark face and swiftly completed his tasks, leaving the room without a backward glance. Guy strode straight to the small table under the window and poured himself a large glass of brandy.

'Get out of those things at once,' he ordered, his back to her.

'Am I not to have a drink also?' she said softly.

'You've had too much champagne as it is.' He swung round, his eyes resting broodingly on her, stabbed with fresh annoyance at the sight of her slim body clothed in those scandalous garments which she wore so casually.

Oh, yes, his lovely bride was a great success, yet he found himself wishing that it were otherwise. His mouth set and he was aware of an unease which had been nibbling at his mind for some time. Having to blame someone, his angry thoughts turned to Aurora. He had had misgivings at the onset of her friendship with Lalage, remembering her behaviour in Morocco and Dorset, but Ambrose had condoned it, and Guy respected his opinions. Yet the suave magnificence of her mansion, furnished with all manner of exotic embellishments, the infinite variety of entertainments which she offered – the eating and drinking, cards and dice, flirting and toying, and the licence of continual *déshabillé*, had infected Lalage, of this he was convinced. All very fine for profligates and ladies of doubtful reputation, but not good enough for Lady Beaumaris. Lalage was still cool, aloof, rather austere, but she had changed in a subtle way on which he couldn't quite put a finger. Hard, perhaps? Somewhat brash?

Two spots of hot colour burned on her olive cheeks as, with a kind of insolent deliberation, she took up the decanter. Her eyes were no longer soft. 'I'm more drunk with success than champagne,' she stated.

Diffuse light filtered through the silk drapes which had been pulled across to keep out the glaring sunshine. The room glowed with it, luxurious, decorated in style, pale colours contrasted with white, and a marble Adam fireplace where brass glinted. It was heavy with the fragrance of flowers arranged in ornate Etruscan vases from the Wedgwood factory. Guy stripped off his coat and stood in his full-sleeved shirt and tight breeches, cravat tossed aside, the neck opened to the waist, bigger, harder, more menacing than ever in his anger.

'Put that bloody thing down!' he snarled, and when she did not do so, he reached her in a couple of lithe strides, snatching it from her hand, banging it on the shiny surface of the rosewood table. 'It's time we had a serious talk, you and I.'

Lalage yawned. 'I don't want to talk. I'm going to take a bath.'

'You are not!' he said grimly. 'You're going to listen to me. There are certain things which you can and cannot do in your position as my wife. Parading about in breeches will stop forthwith! I don't mind you indulging in outrageous feminine apparel, and you can't complain that I am ungenerous regarding your dress-bills, but this I will not tolerate! I'll not be made the laughing-stock of London to satisfy your damned whims. I don't like some of your companions either. That ass de Belcourt hangs around you as if moonstruck, and Sanderman is like your lapdog!'

'How ridiculous!' she retorted. 'The French boy is lonely, and Sanderman is your lawyer. Surely, you cannot object –'

'I *do* object!' he snapped, glowering at her. 'My dear, I don't give a damn what you do in the day, providing that you don't offend too many people, but your nights belong to me. God knows this society is liberal enough, but your manners leave much to be desired.' Now that the words were out, Guy cooled down a little, his anger fading, leaving him feeling absurdly pompous.

'How can I be expected to understand the nuances of the English courtesy? What is permitted and what is not? Do you forget, Guy, that I have no memories on which to base a code of conduct? Every day, I have to learn something new. It's most confusing.' She had abandoned her boyish swagger, was now the defensive, childish creature he had first known.

'I had thought – had hoped, that you might continue your education whilst we were here. Oh, I don't expect you to pore over schoolbooks. There will be time aplenty for that in Dorset, but there are many lending libraries you could join, concerts we could attend together, if you were only interested,' he said, calmer now, though her sudden reversal to meekness was raising another emotion in him, that strange protectiveness coupled with desire. He could feel his body betraying him, hardening uncomfortably even as he walked towards her.

Lalage had a most devastating effect on him, one which he could have well done without. It was a driving, compulsive sexual need which, to his chagrin, he found hard to control. All other women paled in comparison, and he had tried, going on the town with Robert and Jack, drinking and whoring in the lowest boozing-kens, awakening with a sour, stale taste in his mouth, satiated but unsatisfied. What piqued him most was the fact that Lalage showed no jealousy, never once asking where he had been or why he had left her alone for nights on the run, opening her arms whenever he wanted, warm and eager.

'But, Guy, I do read,' she protested. 'Aurora has given me books.'

'And what books!' he commented acidly, eyeing the pile beside the bed. He picked up one of them, flicking over the pages contemptuously. 'Trashy romances filled with melo-drama and sentiment! Fashion magazines, catering for the pleasure of silly fribbles!'

Lalage smiled slowly. 'Not all. Look at these. I'm sure you will like them.' She handed him the well-thumbed volumes. One was *Fanny Hill*, and the other an illustrated sex manual called *Aristotle's Masterpiece*.

He glanced through the latter. It contained many erotic illustrations of couples straining in the last extremity of love. 'I'm sure *you* don't need instructing in this,' he remarked drily.

He was amused, excited and perturbed, seeing the eagerness with which she feasted her eyes on the pictures. 'Can one ever know too much? I read them so that I may give you the greatest pleasure.'

He knew that she wanted him to touch her, to share in this perverted delight. Guy was no prude. He had read similar manuals, joked about them in the clubs, but there was something distasteful in doing so with his wife. She seemed unaware of it, and he admitted to himself that she had no taste. This was patently obvious by the rubbish she bought, surrounding herself with cheap bric-a-brac, toys, trinkets, frivolous ephemera, novelettes and gaudily presented chapbooks. She enjoyed visiting the markets, haggling with cheapjack traders. At first, this immature streak had been endearing, but now his patience with it was wearing perilously thin, as he waited and hoped that she would become more selective, once the novelty of spending had diminished. Her choice of entertainment reflected this lack of discernment. She much preferred burlesque to opera, music-halls to classical concerts, farce to serious plays, and Grand Guignol theatre to Shakespeare.

'I don't want you to become a dull, bookish sort of woman,' he said, trying to forget his disappointment, glancing at her with a smile for she was looking crestfallen. 'Come, I didn't mean to scold. I like you to enjoy yourself while you can. There won't be much to do when we return to Wylde Court.'

Lalage had lain the books on the coverlet, the *Aristotle* open at one particularly explicit drawing. She sighed, turning to him, running her hands down the sleekness of her breech-covered thighs. 'I'm so sorry that you don't think these suit me,' she murmured, her eyes full of voluptuous languor, witchery in the melodious, accented voice.

'They suit you too well. That's the trouble,' he growled. She was lovely, tantalizing, everything he wanted in the world, but she must not know it. Only the strong could tame her; she was too exciting, too potent a drug for weak, unbalanced natures.

She came closer. She smelled of the race, the heat, the thrill – of horse and leather, and her own enticing body odour breathing out from between her breasts. 'Shall I wear them sometimes, when we're alone?' she whispered, with a catch in her voice. 'For your pleasure only? We could make-believe that I'm a boy. There are ways of love which we've not sampled yet – things that would be sinful, were we not man and wife. Nothing we do together is wrong.'

Involuntarily, his hands came to rest on those firm buttocks, smooth beneath the linen. He pressed her close against the hard need of his groin. Her mouth, open, love-drugging, found his, and then she drew him gently, inexorably, down onto the bed. 'Siren,' he said gruffly. 'Irresistible siren!'

Lalage laughed, deep in her throat. Soft fingers touched his face, moist lips sought his till he was blinded, overwhelmed. He felt her clever fingers unfastening his clothes, caressing him, moving over him, and then she squirmed, flexible as a cat, and it was her mouth that held him, tongue and lips working sweetly until he groaned, in spite of himself. She uncoiled, lips against his again. With another supple movement, she rolled over on to her side, back to him, the golden skin of her naked hips contrasting with the white of her shirt, the white of her partially lowered breeches. A pagan hermaphrodite, inviting a new way of taking. It was too tempting to refuse.

A sleepless night brought Guy no solution to the problem of Lalage, but one came with the morning mail. She slipped into the breakfast-room while he was reading the letter from William. He glanced up, entertained by the cool control of her greeting. She was looking exceptionally lovely, a glow highlighting her prominent cheekbones, as serene as a nun. No one would have guessed that they had spent the entire night in the frenzied pursuit of unnatural pleasures.

She had been asleep when he rose early. He remembered the mixed emotions which had tugged at him as he stared down at her. She was like an innocent babe in slumber, peaceful and undisturbed by dreams, curled into a ball beneath the sheet. Something had tightened painfully deep inside him.

Calmly she walked to her usual chair which a footman drew out before pouring her a cup of coffee. Guy waited until they were alone and then said: 'I've just heard from William. Rather astonishing news, my dear. He and Sally are to be married.'

Lalage's attention seemed to be wholly engaged in spreading butter on her toast. He wished he knew what went on behind those black-lashed eyes. 'How nice,' she said.

'We are to go home for the wedding,' he continued. 'It will be at the end of this month.'

She added peach conserve to the butter and her face wore that closed expression which was so perplexing. 'If that is the case, I shall have to shop rather quickly if I'm to look my best for the event,' she replied, very matter-of-factly.

He had expected her to be annoyed at having to leave London, but saw instead a secret, satisfied smile curving her lips. He frowned into his coffee cup. Could he have been mistaken in yesterday's judgement? Was she really content to repair to the country? It suited his plans well. She did not know it yet, but it was his intention to keep her there for as long as possible. The honeymoon was over. He had concluded his business affairs in town and must take up the gauntlet again. Others had been performing feats of daring whilst he introduced his bride to society. It would soon be his turn again. Far better for his peace of mind if Lalage was under the Dowager's eye, rather than running loose in London.

His mood should have been tranquil at this turn of events, but this was far from the truth. He had read William's happily penned missive through without really realizing what his proposed marriage entailed. Sipping his hot, strong coffee, he mulled it over, discovering that he was annoyed, surprised and impatient with himself for being so. Somehow it had never occurred to him that Sally would ever be in a situation other than that which had occupied her for years. He found it nigh impossible to envisage her as his brother's wife – his own sister-in-law. Never having given her much thought before that moment, he was suddenly aware that in some inexplicable way he had assumed that she belonged to him. It was as if a trusted, long-term servant had announced that she was taking up a new post – without a by-your-leave. What about the children? he asked himself, a scowl settling on his brow. How thoughtless of Sally to walk out on them! Somehow he wasn't sure that he wanted Lalage to have too much to do with them. At one time, vague visions of her as a sweet, pure, kindly stepmother had floated in his brain, but not now – not after last night.

Staring grimly at the curve of her breasts visible through the skimpy muslin dress she wore, he was suddenly enraged at how easily she had seduced him into forgetting to be firm with her. She always succeeded in doing this and it terrified him. He felt himself floundering, and at the same time was furious – furious because she awakened emotions in him which he had thought long dead. Lost in her ensorcelled bed, he could never judge accurately whether his feelings were true or false. He wanted most desperately to regain his usual indifference to women and to convince himself that he was master of the situation.

He was dressed for the street, immaculately shaved, his black hair brushed away from his forehead and temples, waving across his head and curling on the high collar of his brown jacket. He intended to find Ambrose, for there had been some talk of them visiting Holt Hall soon. It might be possible to combine this with the journey to Beaumaris Combe. He placed his napkin on the table and pushed back his chair, rising to his feet. It occurred to him that Lalage might be disappointed, thinking that she would now miss the American's famed hospitality.

'You can tell Aurora of our change of plans,' he said, picking up William's letter and putting it in his pocket. 'We may yet be able to visit Alington's estate, but I warn you, you'll find it exhausting.' A smile hovered about his mouth as he continued: 'Of course, he's as rich as Midas, everything he touches turns to profit, and he has spent thousands of pounds on improving Holt Hall, but a stay with him is an extraordinary experience. He lives like an emperor, and entertains on a lavish scale, but when in the country, he becomes a sportsman, through and through. His woods are stocked with pheasants and the fields abound with hares, rabbits and deer. He loves shooting – don't forget that he's been a trapper – and his guests are expected to share his enthusiasm. They may be bitten by gnats, soaked to the buff, the poorest of shots. Nevertheless, they have to join in.'

'If Aurora wants to try her skill, then so shall I.' Lalage took up the Spode coffee-pot and refilled her cup. 'I've already proved that I can beat him at racing.' A pleased little smile lingered at the corners of her lips as she glanced up at him, and he wondered if she was amused because his dark-circled eyes denoted a sleepless night. She knew well what had caused it. His face became stern, for that smile reminded him vividly of the things he had done to her, things he preferred not to dwell on in the cold light of morning.

'You are merry, my love?' he said in a sarcastic tone. 'May I not share the joke? Were you perchance thinking that you could best Ambrose at any time by the use of your whip?'

'No, Guy, my mind was on other, more pleasurable matters,' she answered unblushingly, seeming not in the least startled by his sudden harshness. Her eyes were bold over the edge of her cup, and the tip of her tongue circled it suggestively in an open invitation which he chose to ignore.

He bowed curtly and bade her farewell. She delayed him for a moment to remind him that they were expected at Mr Sanderman's for luncheon and that he had an appointment with his banker at three o'clock. The scene could not have been more cosily domestic, with his wife seated demurely at the table in her delicate white robe, the sunlight streaming in at the sash-windows, illumining the gracious room with its pale green silk walls, white paintwork and Sheraton furniture. In the background were the sounds of the servants going about their work; the sharp, staccato note of hooves striking the road outside, and the voices of Guy's grooms indicating that his chaise awaited. Yet despite this he could not avoid the sensation of dangerous undercurrents swirling through this orderly, well-heeled façade.

As he walked away from Lalage, it occurred to him that William's written suggestion concerning Miranda's living with himself and Sally was a godsend. It would certainly solve the problems caused by the child's aversion to her stepmother. Miss Stanmore and the nanny would cope with Cecily and Barbara until they went away to school. He swung up into the chaise, his eyes thoughtful. Hopefully, Lalage would soon have a young one of her own – that would steady her. The idea of her bearing him a son soothed the uneasy feelings in his breast. He straightened his shoulders and gave a jerk on the reins – action was what he needed. He turned the horses' heads in the direction of Ambrose's house.

Chapter 6

William Wylde's betrothal was the talk of the county. No one had expected him to marry that mousey little governess, Sally Anstey, a girl without a *dot*, and in the general opinion of all, a rather plain creature. Who would have thought she would make such a match! Done very well for herself, for William was popular – so different from that brother of his – an unsociable devil whom one could never invite to dinner unless prepared for sarcastic remarks and unconventional topics. Of course, one had to accord him respect because he was Lord Beaumaris, and one would invite him at least once, now that he was home for the wedding, if only to get a glimpse of that foreign woman he had married. Sally and William were a much more comfortable couple. How wise of the dear Dowager to give her consent, and how pleasant for her to have them residing so close. That poor mad child, Miranda, was going to live with them. How very convenient.

Guy and Lalage had arrived on the eve of the wedding, bringing Ambrose with them. They had broken their journey at Holt Hall and left a disgruntled Aurora to make her own way back to town. There were so many people staying at Wylde Court, such a bustle and so much excitement, that Sally greeted them only fleetingly. By that time she had reached a state of numb exhaustion so that no emotion touched her. Dora, ever watchful, had seen to it that she retired early that night, guarding her fiercely, firmly shutting the bedroom door in the faces of intruders. But in spite of a good strong posset of hot milk and spices laced with brandy, Sally did not sleep peacefully. She kept stirring, enmeshed in strange situations among strange faces, conversing aloud about events which vanished as she surfaced briefly. By degrees, the blank spaces of darkness between flashes grew shorter, and she woke from her dreams with uneasy starts and shivers, then lapsed back again. All the time, whether dreaming or waking, she was conscious that Lalage lay in the Master bedchamber with Guy.

She rose at cockcrow, standing at the open window. The sun was breaking through the light ground mist which shrouded the garden. The villagers had predicted a fine day, eager for their own part in the event. A respite from toil, a plentiful supply of free food and drink, and it was the second time it had happened that year. The tents had sprung up on the lawns like mushrooms, soon to be filled with trestles loaded with delicacies, ale and cider flowing in rivers. No wonder the peasants rejoiced. It was such a pagan ritual, this uniting of a man and woman in holy wedlock, a shameless time when fertility charms, left-overs from pre-Christian days, were given quite openly to the happy pair. Happy? Sally shivered as she thought about it. William was happy, no doubt about that, going about the complicated arrangements in a state of calm joy, surmounting difficulties, levelling opposition, but hers was a troubled happiness. Deep inside, she knew that she was living a lie. I must think only of William, she told herself, he has done so much to bolster my self-esteem, with his love, his tender attentions. A few leaves swirled past the window, in drifting flight from the trees. The wind seemed heavy with sorrow. There was a touch of autumn in the air.

When the time came for the ceremony, Sally moved through it dreamily, completely lost in a numbing reverie. She could hear the vicar speaking, feel the eyes of the congregation, and knew that William was beside her, and yet she kept thinking about other brides, other weddings involving the Wyldes. Her eyes wandered to those grandiose, recumbent effigies of knights, the numerous shields and various quarterings which lined the walls of the chapel. Wylde ancestors laid to rest. In a few, short moments, she too would be a true Wylde. How many other women had stood there as she was now doing? Had they been happy with their dominating menfolk? Celeste had not been happy with Guy.

What was the vicar saying? She had missed her cue, for he had called her 'Sarah' and she was unaccustomed to that name. She stumbled over her responses, afraid of embarrassing William, thoughts passing through her mind like tattered banners fluttering in the wind.

There was no impressive memorial to Celeste. Only the male members of the family received such plaudits. Why, just over there were two stone Cavaliers, protected by iron railings. How selfish of them to lie in state while statues of their wives knelt below, by two little stone cribs containing their infants tucked up in orderly rows like mummified bambinos. William took her hand and slipped a wedding-ring on to her finger. It felt odd, cold and heavy, and she was still thinking about those other Beaumaris ladies. Everyone knew who those Royalist soldiers were, but there was no mention of their wives or dead children. Five painted cherubs reclined on the circular arch above them, and a little coffer was chained to the railings. Were the warriors' hearts inside, she wondered as William kissed her and the organ thundered out a bridal march, or the bones of the five infants? Her heart was chained too – chained to that dark, savagely handsome Wylde who sat in the family pew next to his foreign wife.

She did not look at him, staring straight ahead as she walked down the aisle on William's arm. Her wedding dress felt strange, stiff, certainly not a part of herself. The tug of the long train, the weight of her veil, forced her to hold her head high. The perfume of her bouquet was sickly, strong, reminiscent of graveyards.

She saw the reception through an undulating fog in which faces appeared momentarily – Jack's, sharp and knavish, with laughing eyes – Miranda's, tiny and freckled, she had been Sally's only bride's-maid – Lady Charlotte's, more than a touch condescending – and Lalage's, framed harmoniously by the satin of her hat. A cloud of diaphanous gauze clothed her, part-revealed, part-concealed her iridescent skin, her hair longer, deliberately disordered, suggesting a struggle with a lover, with Guy. Her eyes and her smile were terrible.

Sally played her part, cutting the cake, thanking the donors for gifts, drinking champagne, then the trial was over. She went up to change and met Guy on the stairs. They stopped. She saw his lips move and guessed the content of the trite speech, but the sound of his voice was distorted, then words formed: 'I hope you will be happy,' he said.

He was pale, drawn, looking at her strangely. She saw the strength of his face, the questions in his eyes. It was the worst moment of the nightmare. She loved him so desperately and now the barriers were insurmountable – he was a married man and she was his sister-in-law. Not the least of her misery lay in the reflection that she had done no good, had shown herself to be independent of him, capable of making another life, to no purpose.

Guy was finding it difficult too, making no contact with this stranger in the white satin wedding-gown, finding himself searching in vain for the gentle person he had once known, with that sweet, sunny smile which had always welcomed him. He wanted to break down this invisible wall to talk with her seriously as he had once done, suddenly shockingly aware that he had lost her, perversely interested now that it was too late and she was someone else's wife.

'Thank you, Guy,' he heard her saying, in a high, unnatural voice. 'Are you well? Did you enjoy London?'

'Lalage enjoyed the manifold delights of town,' he replied with cold politeness.

'I'm sure that she did. And you? Did you find it amusing?' Sally was stumbling over the words, rushing on to stop herself uttering things which she must never, never say.

'Not very. Town life can be awfully boring.' A smile touched his lips, that charming, slightly ironic smile which stabbed straight through her.

'You'll be staying here for a while?' She prolonged the agony by asking a further question, hating and despising herself but too weak to move.

'A few days only.' He paused, hesitating while Sally held her breath, something in the intent look he gave her sending crazy hopes chasing through her brain, but he added: 'I'm grateful for your offer to give Miranda a home. You are always so considerate, Sally.'

'She'll be happy with us,' she answered, knowing that her motive was not the selfless one with which he credited her. She wanted to have a part of Guy with her always. 'It will be for the best.'

'Of course, you always act for the best, don't you, Sally?'

A woman's voice rose above the chatter and laughter in the Great Hall. Guy glanced back down the stairs. Lalage was in the doorway, with Denzil and Jack. His mouth hardened, and Sally saw the look of angry pain which glinted in his eyes. She knew that something was wrong, though he covered it well. He had forgotten her, and she ran on up, glancing back once when she reached the top. Guy had not moved, leaning on the banister rail, watching his wife.

Briar Cottage was a rather whimsical name for the spacious house which Guy had given William as a wedding present. It bore no resemblance to the humble, white-washed and thatched cots of the peasants. Lady Charlotte had wanted the couple to live in a wing of the manor, but William had stuck to his guns. Sally must be mistress of her own abode, and he had found the erstwhile tenants alternative accommodation. He had refused to allow her to see it until they drove there after the wedding, and had been very busy during the weeks before, overseeing its repairs and re-decoration. Rooms lay in readiness for Miranda, Dora and Danny, but William and Sally had it to themselves on the bridal-night.

Evening was drawing in when he drove the gig to the cottage, which lay beyond the woods in the direction of the port. The heat of the day lingered as they took the road winding between fat, purring hedges, the peace and quiet almost startling after the festivities. It was like coming to a place which she had always known, though Sally had never been that way before. Somehow, she knew it in advance as they came in sight of a row of elm trees and the grey tiles and gables of the house, glimpsed through a screen of hawthorn bushes, elder and ripening brambles. Fields stretched beyond to the soft rim of blue hills. Her hand went straight to the latch of a door in the low, mellow-stoned wall. Blackbirds were singing as they walked up the path, doves cooed on the roof-ridges, swifts wheeled above the weather-vane twirling on its quaint tower and rooks clamoured in the sentinel poplars. The scent of late-blooming roses was pungent and sweet.

It was a small, old, picturesque house, stone-fronted, with a high-pitched roof, dormer windows under the eaves, and stout, square chimneypots. The stables were in a building a few yards off, rather overrun with creepers, the walls and roof stained by time and lichen to a rich, greyish red. There were lawns in the front, with ornamental bushes and rockeries symmetrically placed, a sort of formal garden which had long thrown off its formality. Part of it was in the open, the rest shaded by a pair of gigantic oaks, a kitchen garden lay at the back, tidy and well-worked, and this led to an overgrown orchard.

Inside, the parlour, music-room and lobby were simply and neatly decorated in pastel shades, and the window curtains were of buff chintz with sage-green leaves and small pink flowers. The furniture was of walnut, light and delicate in structure. Flower-stands of basketwork were placed in angles of the rooms, containing plants of the choicest scents and colours. It was a fairy-tale home to delight the heart of any bride.

Sally's mood lightened, and she insisted on going over it, admiring the kitchen with its range, sensible cupboards and pine dresser. Upstairs were the rooms set aside for Miranda and Dora, and above those were attics where the servants would sleep. Every area was serviceable and well thought out, designed by William, determined that she should want for nothing.

When they returned to the wide landing, where the windows aspected the sea, he opened a further door with a flourish, bowing and saying: 'Our bedchamber, my love.'

Sally drew in a sharp breath for it was as dainty a boudoir as anyone could have desired, decorated in madder-printed cotton, with the woodwork painted in a light blue-green, like a starling's egg. Chattering feverishly so that he would not kiss her, Sally skimmed about the room, examining everything several times over, but at last there was nothing left to talk about. It was growing darker and silence prevailed, almost tangible between them, like a third presence. Each was conscious of the other, and of the enveloping intimacy of the bedroom.

'I'll light the candles,' he said, taking a box of lucifer-matches from his pocket. A pale glow illumined her face.

William was sensitive to her moods and knew that she was uneasy. He would have preferred Guy not to have attended the wedding, but this was impossible. He too had suffered that day, wondering how she felt on seeing his brother, fearing that she regretted her decision. During their short engagement he had kept himself extremely active, hardly ever alone with her, completing unfinished estate work so that he might be free for a few days to learn to know his bride. William was short on experience with women. They were a race apart, and he was frankly frightened of the physical act of love. He had been rehearsing the wedding-night in his head since the day she accepted him, thinking to woo her tenderly with pretty speeches, patient, forbearing, but now that the moment had come, he stood there helplessly.

She was so small and, to him, very beautiful. Her body was firmly moulded, her eyes the gentlest of colours, pansy brown in most lights, but paling in the sun, flecked with gold, modest eyes, yet when the spirit moved her, they sparkled with secret joys. Sadly, he realized that this did not often happen. She was his now, this delectable, mysterious creature. His dream had come to fruition. They were alone on their nuptial-night, and he was afraid to lay a finger on her lest terror flare in those eyes.

In the dim light, Sally could barely discern William's features, only his eyes, the straight nose and firm mouth. He was her husband. She kept repeating this to herself, but it did not make sense. Her husband, who had the full legal right to do whatever he willed with her; he could beat her, mistreat her, her life was in his hands for good or ill. A sigh escaped her and at the sound, William's warm fingers found hers.

'Does it make you so sad – being married to me?' he asked very gently.

'Oh, no – it isn't that. I just wish – I wish that life had dealt the cards differently,' she answered haltingly, choking on a sob as she vainly struggled to keep back the scalding tears held in check all day.

The sound of her grief tore through William like a bullet. Moving blindly, he gathered her into his arms, holding her there like a hurt child, his lips resting on the top of her head till the storm had passed. He wiped the tears from her cheeks with his handkerchief, and his kindness filled her with shame. He was a better man than Guy would ever be, honest and sincere. She had no right to treat him so shabbily.

He withdrew his arms reluctantly, his voice husky as he said: 'Dearest, sleep here alone if you want. I told you in the beginning that I would never force myself on you.'

'No, William. Don't leave me.' She shook her head and smiled through her tears, fighting to forget the hopeless dreams, the might-have-beens. She went to the bed and turned back the covers, while he watched her wonderingly.

Her hands went to her head, and took out the pins which constrained her hair, letting it fall. Slowly, she started to undress.

It was Ambrose's first visit to Wylde Court and he took Lady Charlotte by storm. She had been prepared to dislike him on sight, highly suspicious of Americans, never quite forgiving them for the War of Independence which had happened nearly twenty years before. When she saw him alighting from the carriage and entering the Hall with Guy and Lalage, she had exclaimed to Chalmers:

'Who, in the name of all that's marvellous, is that?'

At first, she had stalked around him with the caution which reflected half a century of experience, but Ambrose was quite accustomed to dealing with autocratic dames. His aunts in Charleston were of the same breed, stiff-necked members of the 'Quality', and he soon won her over, a most attentive cavalier. He was one of those rare men who possessed the eye, subtle sympathy and knowledge of human nature which enabled him to adapt to almost any situation.

During the days following the wedding, he spent hours in her company, playing cards, losing to her sometimes, amusing her with his savage witticisms, uttered in his drawling, languid voice, listening politely to her lengthy anecdotes, and delighting her with tales of South Carolina. She particularly liked hearing about his exploits amongst the Indians, pirates and slave-traders, even confessing that she had a penchant for scallywags. He was a great talker, pouring out an incessant stream of interesting chat. His accounts of the fascinating doings of Charleston society, where architecture, furnishings and fashion were direct copies of those in England, intrigued her. She kept him with her, far into the night, eagerly lapping up his descriptions of the grand houses, the plantations, the cellars full of Madeira, the barbecues and balls, the open-handed hospitality and horse-mindedness of the wealthy colonials.

'It's kind of like England, ma'am,' he would say, holding his snuff-box between thumb and index finger. 'I guess you'd think you were still here. We still call the old country "home", you know.'

'How touching,' she would respond, giving him arch, rather tipsy glances, admiring his style, his clothing, those extra-vagantly short-waisted tail-coats he wore and the tight panta-loons which set off his manly figure to perfection. 'And were you disappointed when you first set foot on our soil?'

'No sir! Begging your pardon, Lady Charlotte, ma'am. It's mighty small, after America, but it sure was a joy to find the manor house of my forebears. I'm crazy about this country. Wessex, to my mind, sums up all the landscapes of England, its prehistoric and medieval past, and its charming present. You've got to come to Holt Hall, I'll be mighty offended if you don't.'

Charlotte willingly agreed, beaming her approval. She liked the way he addressed her as 'ma-am', and his quaint expressions, never guessing that he was over-acting, deliberately stressing his Southern slur and mannerisms for her benefit. Nothing he would do was wrong, apparently, and she even permitted him to smoke his cheroots in her drawing-room.

Even the most pleasant of interludes come to an end, however, and although the departure of the gentlemen for London was not unforeseen, the brisk interchange of words which crackled between her eldest son and his wife surprised Charlotte. Lalage was furious because he refused to take her with him, and his mother found a certain perverse pleasure in seeing Guy's angry face and hearing the rage in his voice. So, he was finding her self-willed was he? Serve him right!

He flung himself on his black stallion and rode off in a fine tear with Walford hard put to it to keep up on his own stocky nag. Ambrose dug in his spurs and gave chase, hallooing like a maniac. They would reach London in record time, too impatient to travel by coach. Lalage stood on the terrace watching them disappear in the distance, and her expression was not that of a young bride who was sorrowful at this enforced separation. She was white with temper.

Charlotte took her indoors, saying cheerfully: 'I shall miss Mr Alington dreadfully. What an entertaining man, and so well-mannered – for an American. Come, my dear, let us be cosy together. I'm agog to hear the latest *bon mots*. What's all this nonsense about you caracoling in that Paradise of the Lost – Rotten Row? Alington told me that you beat him in a phaeton race. He still bears the stripe of your whip, you naughty girl.'

In spite of her efforts, luncheon was a stilted affair. Lalage ate in frozen silence, and Charlotte's attempts at conversation elicited only monosyllables. When the servants quietly took away the dishes, she suggested that they spend the afternoon seated beneath a shady tree in the garden, but instead of dutifully complying with her mother-in-law's request, Lalage rose from her chair.

'I intend to go for a walk, madame,' she said, and with that she left the room.

Charlotte snorted, and then rang for Chalmers. Her mood was irascible by the time she reached the Hall with the aid of her stick and her companion. She missed Sally's calm efficiency, forced to rely entirely on Chalmers now and the woman got on her nerves. She was about to mount the stairs when she saw Lalage coming down, dressed for outdoors in a military coat of amber-coloured velvet which clung to her body. It was fastened across with gold frogging, and had a broad band of white fox fur running round the neck and right the way down the front, circling the hem. A close-fitting hat of matching material was placed squarely on her head, the fur framing her face. A chain of flat cold discs banded her forehead, adding a distinctly Persian touch, and she swung a small, tasselled reticule in one hand, her feet encased in amber kid half-boots.

The three women stopped on seeing one another. 'How

splendid you look,' Charlotte observed crisply. 'But is not your walking-dress more suitable for promenades in the Mall than a stroll in the country? I trust you will enjoy the air. Sensible of you to wrap up well, for there was a slight frost last night.'

It was the golden season of the year when the harvest had been gathered in and the trees delivered of their fruit. The birds had begun their migration. It was time for them to go, for though the days were warm and food abundant, the nights were growing cold. Lalage watched a great flock wheeling and sweeping over her head as she crossed the lawns towards the lake. South – they were flying south!

A bent, wizened gardener was using his rake to clear away the scattered russet leaves. He touched his cap as Lalage passed. The colour of her pelisse echoed that of the beeches. Denzil saw her long before she reached him, from where he sat on the bank beneath a willow, fishing-rod in his hand. He did not wave to her, in fact he contemplated moving, for he was no longer a happy young man. Oh, he kept up a pretence for his mother's sake. She still thought him to be the epitome of boyishness, candid and self-centred as a child, but underneath this display of high spirits there was now a brooding preoccupation. Denzil was in hell, for he loved his brother's wife.

It had been a relief when they were away on their honeymoon. Although he thought about her constantly, he had not been put to the torture of her daily presence. Also, after that first adventure with Jack, he had helped William to ship in further boatloads of refugees, and this had given him something else on which to focus his attention. But now she was back, more alluring than ever, employing those coquettish tricks which she had learned under Aurora's expert guidance. He had watched her keenly, jealous of Guy's American friend, but soon realized from the barbed remarks they tossed at one another that there was no love lost between them.

Too late to run without looking a fool, for Lalage was coming along the path edging the bank. The sunshine turned her gown to flame, and her smooth-flowing walk was a potent incitement to passion. 'Have you caught anything?' she asked him, when she came to rest at his side.

He shook his head, but instead of looking at her, he kept an intent watch on his float bobbing far out, where the water was the colour of old sherry. Dark green bulrushes grew thickly there, making the almost hidden current in the deeps look black. The willow tree dipped its branches in the lake, and a stately cob with his snowy consort sailed across the surface, accompanied by their clutch of large, dark cygnets.

'The fish aren't rising yet,' he said, his voice unsteady. 'Perhaps at dusk, when the gnats swarm.'

'Spread out your coat so that I may sit on it,' and this prosaic request sounded like music to his ears. She smiled, eyes slanting at him. 'We have a long wait.'

Denzil jumped up to obey her, his heart pounding as he sought to read some sign of affection, some hope for him in her expression, but she seemed coolly absorbed in watching the water, and he took up his vigil once more. 'So Guy and Alington have gone?' he asked, unnecessarily, for he had seen them depart, been delighted, ashamed and despairing to know that she had not accompanied them.

'The rogue has left me to rot in the country.' Her eyes were stormy, full lower lip rolled out in childish petulance. She tore up a few marsh-marigolds and began to rip the petals to bits.

'How can he bear to be parted from you?' Denzil was no longer concentrating on fishing. He jammed the rod in its rest and turned to her, the nearness of her body stirring him into a frenzy which he found hard to control. 'God, were you mine, I'd be with you constantly, happy to steep myself in the ecstasy of doing nothing but look at you.'

'Would you, Denzil?' She had a blade of grass between her teeth, biting at it musingly, her lips crimson, moist, driving him mad. 'Ah, but you, dear friend, are of a more gentle mould than your harsh brother.'

Breathlessly he leaned closer, seeking the truth in those topaz, innocent-seeming eyes. 'You really think that? But you married Guy. You love him, don't you?'

She sighed and turned away, her head bowed. The dark fronds of hair curling below the velvet of her hat partly hid the tender nape of her neck. The light played on it. 'He is so cruel, Denzil. He doesn't understand my needs.'

Denzil's eyes were fixed on that enticing area of satiny skin. He wanted to place his lips there, to push down the fur collar and caress her spine, her shoulders. 'I never did imagine him to be over-endowed with sensitivity,' he managed to say, after swallowing and taking a deep breath.

He was feeling wretched, torn in two, lust tugging him in one direction, loyalty to Guy in another. His face grew hot as her eyes met his. She sighed again, filled with sad, gentle charm.

'You're right, I'm afraid. I did not fully appreciate the defects in his character until I married him. He often leaves me at night, when in town. He prefers the company of gamesters and coarse women.'

Denzil was on his knees by now, gazing ardently into her face, hating to see the small, troubled frown marking her smooth brow. 'How dreadful for you!' he exclaimed.

She gave a shrug of her slender shoulders, and the brave way in which she controlled the quiver in her voice impressed him deeply. 'Wives must learn to accept these things, it seems. I'm told that it is the way of the world.'

He was genuinely puzzled and distressed, but he believed her. Guy's reputation where women were concerned was something of which he had boasted at university. 'Dearest Lalage, if I can help you —'

'Oh, you do help me,' she insisted earnestly, taking his hand. 'It's such a relief to unburden myself to someone I can trust.'

'Come to me at any time — I'm only too happy —' he blundered on, gripping her hand tightly.

He felt the touch of her fingers on his cheek, his lips, running caressingly through his hair. Then she withdrew her hand from his, glancing at the sky, shivering. 'It is growing cold. I must go back.'

'Not yet,' he begged and rose to his feet, catching her by the wrist, drawing her gently towards him. 'We will find shelter from the wind and talk further. I know a place.'

He took her to the ruined temple — a folly — a pretty conceit for a rich man's entertainment. Up the marble steps, between mock-Greek pillars and into a small, round room where garden-chairs were stored, cushions and pillows for those who wished to spend an idle hour dreaming of antiquities or love. He made her a comfortable couch of these and they continued to converse for a while, but the pauses between sentences lengthened, and Denzil was acutely conscious of her closeness, losing the battle with his instincts. The musky scent of her perfume tormented him, awakening carnal longing until it was a physical pain. He finally gave up the struggle to maintain any semblance of normality, staring at her, no longer able to hide his need.

She was lying back amongst the brocaded cushions, her flawless skin in contrast to their bright surfaces. Her burning eyes came to rest on the obvious manifestation of desire which

231

even his clothing could not conceal. 'Poor boy,' she murmured, smiling. 'You want me so very much, eh? Come here – let me help you.'

There was something terrifying about her, and he glanced around uneasily, wanting to escape. 'You're married to my brother,' he gasped, speaking his torture aloud. 'It would be a sin!' She did not answer, stretching her arms above her head languorously, and that movement tipped the scales with its energy and grace, its subtle promise of ferocious delights. He kept repeating, over and over, even as he kissed her: 'I love you, Lalage – I love you!' Everything else was wiped from his mind – his honour, his feelings for Guy. Nothing mattered but this compelling urgency. He was driven half insane, bewitched by the responsive body in his arms, the tasting and touching which made his head spin.

The sun sank towards the sea, and the tall trees around the temple caught the level beams, while the pillars shone crimson. The red light gradually faded into purple, and the wind-stirred branches gave off the solemn sound of rolling surf, as the day ended.

It took Sally a while to believe that Briar Cottage was truly hers, but once she grasped that she was really mistress of it, she accepted the responsibility most seriously. Her earlier training at Wylde Court was invaluable, and she knew therefore if her servants carried out their chores to the letter, a thorough housekeeper who kept a sharp eye on the accounts so none could cheat her. Miranda loved living there, bright-eyed as a little sparrow, exploring a wild corner of the grounds, grass-grown, which had once been an orchard, and still had a few gnarled apple and pear trees, nearly past bearing, with good nesting-holes for the tits and starlings in their decayed mossy trunks. Sally did not worry if she disappeared for hours, for she had taken over the small, half ruined outhouse which stood beyond the walled enclosure, ivy-covered and weather-stained, as much in harmony with its surroundings as the cottage itself. In Miranda's imagination this became a palace, a robbers' den, a pirate ship, a tropical island, anything she willed. She never spoke of Lalage, and at the wedding had kept well away from any contact with her. Cecily and Barbara were quite the opposite, forever following her about, hanging on her every word, possessed by girlish hero-worship of their exciting step-mother.

Dora and Sally had had a long talk after she had agreed to marry William. At first Dora had been cagey, rather embarrassed, but when she realized that Sally bore no resentment against her, she came out with her part of the tale, as relieved as if a tremendous burden had been lifted from her soul.

'I never loved him, miss,' she had said, her comely face a mixture of concern and earnestness, almost comically so. ''Twas just a silly, drunken prank, but even when I knew that I was with child, I kept it to myself. He's a fine gentleman, and I didn't want to harm him. I wish you well, deary, I really do. Just you be sensible, count your blessings and be happy with him.'

Though William could not openly acknowledge Danny, he proved to be a devoted father, taking much interest in him. It did Sally's heart good to see them together, with her husband pulling out his gold pocket-watch and dangling it before the wide blue eyes, or carrying the baby round the garden, solemnly telling him the names of the birds and shrubs while Danny gurgled and dribbled and grabbed at his father's hair. He did not understand a word, of course, but was content to hear the deep timbre of a masculine voice. Sally wondered what the servants made of it, certain that they must suspect, though on the surface Dora was there in the capacity of nanny to Miranda. Neither Denzil nor Guy had commented, but she did not expect them to, knowing the tacit agreement which existed among the upper classes regarding such indiscretions. They simply turned a blind eye to this common enough happening.

Dora was courting now; a big, amiable farmer called Josh Appleyard had closed his ears to the advice of the gossipy goodwives and was determined to make Dora his wife. Sally knew that William would be saddened to see his son go, but the four adults had talked it over and agreed that it would be for the best. Maybe I'll have a baby of my own soon, Sally thought, praying that it might happen, for her own sake as much as William's.

He was so good to her, adoring, tolerant, and had proved to be an understanding lover, eager to please, too eager perhaps. Her body had responded to him on the wedding-night, and ever since. She was thankful for the deep reserve of sexuality which he had successfully tapped, that new-found cynisicm which had become hers of late recalling the old saying: 'In the dark, all cats are grey.'

What did it matter if she felt empty afterwards, tears running back across her temples into her hair as she lay awake, staring up into the gloom of the tester, while William slept beside her? His rapture was great enough for two, surely? How foolish of her to yearn, like some silly, romantic schoolgirl, for blissful moments of joy atoned for by misery – for burning passion, a meeting of twin souls, tortured, ecstatic, making one willing to lay down one's life for the beloved – consumed by a sacred flame which would burn bright even when body and spirit fell asunder. I have a wonderful marriage, she kept telling herself, filled with affection and common-sense practicality. It is only in the pages of novelettes, and in the ravings of neurotic poets, that this other, obsessive, mystical love is to be found.

William drove to the manor daily about the estate affairs, and sometimes Sally went with him. Guy's older daughters had been delivered into the safe-keeping of Miss Stanmore, that prim, studious lady-spinster who was rather glad to now have complete authority over them. Sally was flattered, touched and not a little surprised to find that the girls had missed her, begging to be allowed to visit Briar Cottage. When Sally and William went to dinner at Wylde Court one evening not long after the wedding, Guy was still there in the company of Ambrose Alington, whose racy wit and un-English way of speaking Sally found disconcerting, never quite sure whether or no he was making sly fun of her.

Sally was reluctant to attend, but Lady Charlotte had been so insistent that there was no way she could refuse without giving offence. The only means by which she could endure the ordeal was to encase herself in ice, be formal and polite, exchange smalltalk with her mother-in-law, and look anywhere but at Guy. All through the meal she listened to the flow of talk concerning Ambrose's manor, Holt Hall, and his stories of America, and of London where, apparently, the latest fad was to attend public dancing-parties at the Ranelagh Rotunda in Chelsea. Lady Charlotte snorted her disapproval of this mingling with the masses, though Ambrose soothingly assured her that it was terribly *bon ton*. It made Sally feel even more hopelessly rustic and out of touch.

Denzil joined in, showing-off, but Sally sensed a kind of desperation beneath his clowning, and Guy brought the conversation down to earth by mentioning the unrest among the English poor fanned by the chilling gusts from revolutionary France. This led to some unpleasant discussions about the mock trials taking place in Paris, where renegade nobles, flaunting the tricolour cockades and munching chocolates, sat in the public galleries watching the downfall of former associates.

'Those confounded Jacobins have even had the diabolical cheek to bring in a new system of weights and measures,' commented Ambrose, lounging at Lady Charlotte's right hand while, admiringly, she watched him cracking walnuts in his palm. 'Litres instead of pints, metres replacing yards, and money now counted in tens. Most confusing.'

The many main courses had been removed and the company were lingering over fruit, nuts and wine. It was a warm still night and the table had been laid on the terrace outside the Red drawing-room windows which were opened wide. Great, solid floor-standing torchères threw splashes of light, illumining faces, reflected in silver. It was not yet truly dark, great bars of molten gold spreading over the horizon. The footmen were discreetly collecting used dishes and replacing empty decanters. At a signal from the Dowager, the butler went round topping up each glass.

She tut-tutted in response to Ambrose's statement. 'Really they are too dreadful. Pray God our soldiers can stop them.'

Guy eyed her impatiently, in a disturbed black mood, accentuated by drink. 'My dear Mamma, when will you accept that the old order is changing? They've outlawed religion, and I'm not sure that this is such a bad thing.' Ignoring her flustered exclamation of disgust, he went on: 'Churches have been desecrated, used as storehouses, prisons and meeting halls where their leaders preach their dogmas. God no longer exists in France. Statues of the goddess Reason replace those of the Virgin Mary. It is Reason which is worshipped. Devout priests are being slaughtered, and frightened bishops are trading in their mitres for the red cap of the sansculotte.'

'It's shocking – disgraceful!' she averred indignantly, and Sally was angry with Guy for deliberately upsetting her. How could he be so unkind? He was leaning with one elbow on the table, a peculiar expression on his strong face. Lalage was beside him, more lovely than ever, sleek and sophisticated from her stay in town. Now that she knew exactly what took place between a man and woman, Sally could not bear to look at them, quivering with pain, her soul tossed in a restless, never-ending search for peace from the sick longings within her.

235

Guy's eyes met hers and she lowered her head, embarrassed at having looked directly at him. She fell into an examination of her fan, while to the left of her, Denzil shifted restlessly.

'Don't be alarmed, Mamma,' he said, but his intention was not so much to comfort her as to draw attention to himself – Lalage's attention. 'Take heart in the knowledge of the gallant groups of Englishmen who have formed themselves into a secret army, hellbent on saving as many as they possibly can from the guillotine.'

Lady Charlotte was a little calmer, fortified by another glass of Canary, poured by Ambrose. 'Well, yes, my dear – I have heard a whisper of this. D'you know the names of these saintly souls?'

Denzil's eyes were feverishly bright, his face flushed. He leaned forward eagerly. 'I can't tell you that. Few know, but there are several such bodies in existence, with spies and helpers on both sides of the Channel – it's all very hush-hush. The Prince may be in the know, familiar with their leaders, but no one else save those working closest to them.'

Guy's mouth had hardened, eyes narrowed warningly. 'They are rash fools – even traitors!' he snapped, to still his brother's babbling tongue. 'How dare they presume to help Frenchmen, be they never so nobly born, when England is at war with that country?'

'I can't help but agree with you,' said Ambrose, expressing mild surprise at such foolhardiness. 'What the deuce can they hope to achieve?'

'At least they are trying!' exploded Denzil incautiously, aware of Lalage's gaze resting on him, an enticing smile playing about her lips. 'They don't sit on their backsides talking and doing nothing. There is one who is known as *Le Fantom*, a man of mystery who slips in and out of France like a spectre, hated by the Jacobins. They've offered a huge reward for information concerning his identity, and a larger sum for his apprehension. Doesn't such courage inspire even you, Alington?'

Ambrose hid a yawn behind his hand. 'La, it inspires me to keep my nose out of trouble and sleep sound in my bed at night. Don't you agree, ma'am?' He smiled at the Dowager.

'Of course it *is* frightfully brave, but I do hope you're not thinking of joining them, Denzil?' She cast a look of appeal at him, never quite certain what mad scheme her youngest son proposed to engage in next. He did not reply and she immediately seized on the hiatus to change the subject completely. 'Shall we go in and play cards? Or would you prefer backgammon? I fancy bezique, myself.'

Chairs were scraped back as the gentlemen stood when she did. 'I heartily agree that we should not waste such a lovely night talking of boring politics,' said Ambrose, holding out her shawl so that she might drape it over her shoulders. 'But must we go indoors, ma'am? I was kind of hoping that you might fall in with a little plan of my own.'

She paused, clapping her hands, as excited as a child. 'Oh, what is it, Mr Alington? Nothing too daring, I trust.'

'Would I suggest anything that wasn't perfectly innocent, dear lady?' Ambrose smiled, while Sally and Lalage gathered up their wraps and bags, assisted by their husbands. 'Did you know that the nightingale sings fit to burst if someone plays the fiddle in its vicinity? We used to go down to the woods, back home, on such an evening as this, taking one of the slaves who was a genius on the fiddle. I'm sure your trees around here are alive with such birds. Let's go find one.'

'It will be damp. I shall be eaten alive by midges – they attack me in hordes, the horrid creatures. I'm a martyr to them!' she protested, but the idea appealed to her.

'It's your blue blood, Mamma,' said Guy tetchily. 'They find it irresistible.'

'There's one drawback,' put in William, an arm about Sally's waist, giving it a squeeze. 'No one here can play the violin.'

'Old Ned can,' Denzil cut in. Nervous, eager, he saw this as an ideal opportunity for sneaking time alone with Lalage. Amidst the dark, fragrant forest, moon-washed and secretive, he might be able to get her away from Guy for a few, heavenly moments.

'Then let us find this Ned.' Ambrose turned to him with a laugh. 'Is he a servant?'

'He's one of the village eccentrics,' replied William. 'Lives in the inn – does a few odd jobs for a crust and a pint of cider.'

Everyone went in then, the men to dispatch Boxer to the inn, the ladies to collect further wraps and order a hamper to be packed. They might be in for a lengthy wait before a nightingale obliged. Food and wine would help to pass the time. Sally lingered in the doorway, aware that Guy had remained silent. He had no interest, it seemed, in either singing-birds or drunken violinists.

She saw that he had taken off both jacket and waistcoat once he thought himself alone, his shirt opened at the neck. He

237

leaned with one shoulder against an angle of the wall, booted legs crossed at the ankles, a glass in one hand. He was staring out across the garden, watching the moon lift its ghostly white face above the tops of the black trees. There was a quality about him which called her forcefully, like a great summons from lofty heights. Before she knew what she was doing, she found herself standing beside him.

He turned his head and looked at her. 'Aren't you going to join the rest in their frivolous invasion of the forest?'

'I shall go, when they're ready.' She was trembling, knowing that she had no business delaying there with him. William was being helpful, getting things prepared. He trusted her implicitly. It was unfair, making her guilty and joyous at once. 'Aren't you coming?'

'No. When I seek the night woods, I do it alone – or with a chosen companion.'

He is not happy, she thought, and it made her glad. 'Why are you so gloomy?' she ventured.

'I'm foxed. Drink effects me thus sometimes.'

'Then drink no more tonight.' She reached out and took the glass from him, setting it down on the balustrade.

'Oh, nursemaid Sally,' he mocked, teeth and eyes shining in the torchlight. 'That's right – take the nasty stuff away – tell me to be a good boy and pull myself together.'

His pain and anger ran along her nerves, mingling with her own. He did not have to tell her what was troubling him, indeed it would have been unlike him to have done so, but there was no need – she already knew. It was Lalage. At that moment she forgot that she was married to William, haunted by the feeling that in some inexplicable way she belonged to Guy, and by an insidious conviction that she had always been destined to be so.

Time meant nothing then. She could have been standing there for a second, a century, it did not matter. They did not speak, but their minds were touching. He shifted his position and the spell was broken. With a shock which she felt in her very marrow, his hand came to rest on hers. 'Would that I could turn back the clock,' he whispered.'

Sally backed off, fingers folded protectively over the spot where his had been. She resorted to primness as a means of defence. 'We've made our beds, Guy and must needs lie in them.'

His head went up, black hair silvered in the moonlight, and he laughed, harshly, mirthlessly. 'Bravo! I expected some pious

238

platitude.' His face changed, sombre and frightening. 'Beds can be changed, you know.'

'Not ours. There are too many people to hurt – too much at stake.' Go, she was urging her wayward feet, run from here, find dear, safe William. It was as if Guy was daring her to embark on something dangerous – something wild, tumultuous. She was terribly afraid. When he looked at her, when he touched her hand, when she heard the sound of his voice, strange, half-buried memories stirred in her as though she had known him long, long ago in some other existence.

The way he was staring at her showed only too plainly that he saw in her face a shadowy memory reflecting that same feeling in him. 'Sally – Sally, don't lie to me. Would you not do whatever I asked of you?'

Oh, where were the others? Why didn't they come? She was caught in his web and couldn't break free. To struggle was to display her weakness. Useless to argue or protest, so: 'You had your chance. You didn't want me.'

'I do now.'

'No!' She was fighting for her self-respect, and had already turned, running for the drawing-room when she heard William calling her from within.

'That's right – fly to your loving husband – Mrs William Wylde!' jeered Guy, and his words thundered in her ears.

She could see people in the room and William's tall figure was outlined at the glass doors. Sally bit back a sob, the powerful emotions of love and hatred writhing and twisting like poisonous serpents inside her. Just before she reached the safety of her husband's arms, she looked back once. Guy had picked up his glass again and, raising it to his lips, he toasted her silently, mockingly.

She had never been more thankful to see Briar Cottage when they reached there at last, in the small still hours of the morning. Nerves jangling, totally wrung out by that meeting with Guy, she sank gratefully into its tranquillity, so untouched by the world. She did not venture into the stresses of Wylde Court again, glad to hear, a little later, that Guy had left for London.

Everywhere the woods were yellow and the stronger red-gold tints of the beech trees had already vanished. It was misty by day with windy storms after dark. Sally had a fine excuse to stay at home, shutting herself into the cottage, her fortress where she could hold unpleasant things at bay. She heard William returning from the manor one morning, glancing up from her sewing in some surprise for she had not been expecting him till noon.

He came into the parlour, and he had not removed his top coat, his face rather grave. 'I've had a letter from Guy,' he said. 'Denzil and I are to go to him in London at once.' He stood quietly, his eyes fastened on her face, tapping the side of his boot with his crop.

Her first thought was, I shall be able to sleep alone tonight, and then because such disloyalty shamed her, she was over-wifely in her concern, running to him, swept up against his hard, upright frame. 'But why must you go?' she managed to say between hugs and passionate kisses.

'Business, my love – some legal documents which must be signed by each of us,' he replied, wondering whether to tell her the serious news which had been contained in Guy's letter. Queen Marie Antoinette had been beheaded at eleven o'clock on the morning of the sixteenth of October. Soon the newspapers would be full of it so, to spare her, he decided to say nothing.

'Will you be away long? It's been weeks since Guy left,' she said, having counted each hour, each day. They walked into the hall, William's arm around her. Harrison, his valet, was coming down the stairs carrying a portmanteau.

'I don't know, probably not. Sanderman will conclude the transaction speedily, I should imagine.' William felt awkward, unable to cope with the pain of parting, trying to fill his eyes, his mind, with the sight of her. Life was so good now. He almost regretted his involvement in Guy's plans. He had been too canny to write anything incriminating, but William hazarded a shrewd guess that the news of the Queen's execution would galvanize the rescuing leagues into desperate activity.

Sally went with him to the little wicket gate. Denzil was waiting there on a strong brown gelding. He was well wrapped for the long ride, and greeted her with a smile and a salute of his whip. William bent to kiss her. He smelled of cold air and damp mist, but his lips were warm and firm, saying all the things he could not put into words. She watched them ride away. The clouds were thin and a pale gleam of sunshine filtered through the stripped branches. There was even a patch of lucid blue sky, but the light soon faded, leaving a universal greyness of earth and heaven. The bare, dusky woods looked more beautiful than in fine weather, lines clean and sculptured. Sally did not know how long she stayed there, staring at the deserted road, then rain came scudding in with the freshening wind, and she turned and went indoors. Peace had gone, and with it satisfaction in her home. She paced the parlour restlessly, driving her fist into her palm, longing to be with the horsemen, galloping towards London – and Guy.

Denzil was subdued on the journey. Even stops overnight at various coaching inns failed to cheer him. The weather was atrocious. They were frequently soaked to the skin and muddied to the thighs, but William would not delay, grimly determined to reach their destination quickly. At any other time, Denzil would have thrown himself, heart and soul, into such an adventure, for William had warned him that there was serious work afoot, but now every beat of his gelding's hooves took him further and further away from Lalage. They seemed to pound out her name, in his brain, along his nerves – Lalage! Lalage!

What he now felt for her was no longer admiration and desire but a fatal enchantment. He was infatuated, on a seesaw of violent emotions, knowing no peace, happy, unhappy, he was too confused to differentiate between the two. When they were apart, he was tortured by memories, seeing her in seductive poses, how her eyelids would flutter, her features ripple into a slow smile, the crimson of her mouth coming to life, closing or unclosing, that honey-tasting tongue glimpsed briefly, every nuance of her beauty a feast for his eyes. He craved for her kisses as a man dying of thirst in a desert craves for water. Sometimes he dreamed of her at night, and woke in tears.

Obsessed by her as he was, there was still room for self-loathing. Denzil was riven with a guilt which made him fear to look Guy in the eyes. He resented him too, and the fact that Lalage belonged to him, and hated himself for such feelings. There had been a heady, dangerous excitement in their clandestine meetings. Wylde Court was rich in hiding places for adulterous lovers. Outside there were the grotto, the temple and the woods and, within were disused, empty rooms which Lalage's presence had transformed into throbbing jungles of varied sexual experience. Denzil was enslaved, and despised himself for his bondage.

They reached the outskirts of London on a murky afternoon, and the squalor struck them afresh as they clopped through the slums. A miasma of sick misery hung in the air, the streets littered with garbage, rat-infested, the inhabitants rowdy, drunken and vicious, the houses built higgledy-piggledy in packed confusion. Many of them were crowded, airless factories and workshops. It was a relief to leave them for the better-paved, brightly-lit commercial centre, better still to guide their mounts west of the river to the broad streets with elegant shops, palatial residences, finely laid-out squares and solid stone houses. A different strata of society, nearly a different world.

Denzil was stirred out of his sullen trance, registering surprise that they did not go to Doric House. The valets were dispatched there, but William rode on, reining in at last before a tall house in Bedford Row. They climbed stiffly from their saddles. The lights from the street-lamps were reflected in the rain-puddles. Denzil followed his brother up the steps and soon they were ushered into a spacious hall, while a footman took their wet hats and coats. The butler requested that they accompany him, his pompous back ahead of them all the way up the mahogany staircase, its balustrade ornamented with Chinese fretwork.

The sudden warmth and light were dazzling, and Denzil began to wake from his state of lovesick stupidity, pricked by a multitude of painful thoughts, not the least of which was a great reluctance to meet Guy again. He grasped at the notion that he might not be there, but the butler opened the door of a drawing-room, and he was unable to avoid the fateful moment. Guy was standing by the fire, a broad smile of welcome on his face. His brother, the Head of their House, the man whom he had wronged so grievously by having unlawful carnal knowledge of his wife.

Fortunately for Denzil's frenzied state of mind, Guy was concentrating on hurrying the travellers to the fire and thrusting large glasses of brandy into their chilled hands, saying: 'You've made capital time. Well done. Is everyone well at home? Good.'

The butler had withdrawn, and William was thawing out, mopping the moisture from his face. 'What's this about?' he asked, the warmth spreading pleasurably over his wrists. 'I presumed that your urgency was sparked off by the Queen's death.'

Guy sighed, his arm resting on the overmantle, staring down into the glowing peaks and caverns of the burning coals. 'Too late to aid her, poor lady. Our spies report that the regicides show no mercy. Thousands are going to the guillotine. The

Terror is far, far worse than ever before. Robespierre is all-powerful, and extremely popular. He has introduced a Committe of Public Safety. The prisons and Houses of Arrest are crowded to the ridge-tiles, the Committee spreading its net everywhere, gathering their harvest and storing it for trial. A harvest of aristocrats! My God, the soil of France is being purged with a vengeance!'

'It's hard to believe that conditions could become worse,' replied William gravely, and their faces were so similar, cast in the same mould. 'A pity Mirabeau lost control, but happily, Marat is dead. Charlotte Corday struck a blow for freedom when she stabbed that maniac in his bath. God rest her soul, that valiant Royalist lady who forfeited her life for her cause.'

They both fell silent for a moment, while Denzil drank his brandy, wanting to speak to Guy but failing to find words. The momentous events of which they were talking did not move him. Of far greater significance were his own guilt and remorse, his obsessional desire and the dreadful fear that Guy would look at him, and know.

He was so keyed up that he jumped when Guy flung himself down in a chair, booted legs stuck out towards the hearth, his head resting on the cushioned back. 'If what our men there tell us is true, and we've no cause to doubt it, the Convention have now voted a new, terrifying law – the Law of Suspects. D'you understand what this means? Anyone can be denounced as a traitor and imprisoned on some trumped-up charge. A spiteful neighbour, an envious relative, has only to give a hint to one of the committees set up in every town. All it takes is the word that they've dared criticize the régime or imply that they've been in contact with an *aristo*, be it never so long ago, and they face prison, the confiscation of property and a bloody death. Even the placebo of religion has been taken away.'

'So, this is what mass education can do, is it?' said William thoughtfully. 'It strikes me as a grave mistake. The more a ploughboy knows of the world beyond his village, the less fitted it makes him to suffer hardship, rendering him fractious and disloyal.'

Denzil found his voice, political argument providing a fine red-herring. 'I don't entirely agree. It's through education, surely, that the poor become better acquainted with the duty they owe society.'

'Clap-trap!' Guy snarled, sitting up. 'It isn't the poor who've stirred the shit! Danton is a lawyer, and Marat was a doctor.

243

Robespierre is a cultured man, the son of an advocate. It is the Republicans who've tottered a throne, and their supporters, the fanatical Jacobins, are the ones determined to weed out and destroy any who stand in their way.'

William was heavy-hearted and horrified. The situation in France was past hope or remedy, and it did not seem important at that moment to argue about how it had come about. He was thinking of Sally, vividly picturing the last evening they had spent together and of one breathless instant when she had got up to light the candle, the whiteness of her face caught in the glow, the transparency of her hands, the perfection of her profile. It occurred to him that he might never see her again if he was swept up in the maelstrom across the Channel.

'I suppose our work is to be doubled,' he said quietly.

Guy nodded. 'The others will be arriving soon. I've called you here because it's time for you to meet our leader, Denzil.' He was rather amused by the alarm which shot across his young brother's face. 'Don't worry. He won't eat you.' He sobered again, leaning forward, eyes aglow with enthusiasm. 'He's the finest man I've ever come across. A resourceful, exceptionally brave, cool-headed customer whom I'd follow to hell if need be. You'll bear this out, won't you, William?'

With a nod and a smile, William answered: 'Oh, yes – our *condottiere* is one in a million.'

Guy rose and crossed to the door which lay opposite the closely curtained windows, his brothers behind him, but before he opened it he turned and placed a hand on Denzil's shoulder. 'I want your solemn oath that you'll never divulge his identity, even under torture. Do you swear?'

Denzil's knees were unsteady as he was forced to look up into those hard, clear green eyes. His conscience was so painful that he would have promised anything to get away. 'I swear, Guy. I'll not speak,' he stammered, and was released from the pressure of that iron hand.

'Come then,' Guy said as he pushed open the door. 'Come and meet *Le Fantom*.'

The room was a study, intimate, cosy and firelit. There was a faded, yellowish globe on a carved ebony stand, and a table spread with a map. A circular set of steps was conveniently placed for reaching the topmost shelves of the bookcases which lined the walls. Denzil hesitated on the threshold, suddenly afraid of facing this man whom the Jacobins wanted so badly. He must be a giant indeed, a great general perhaps.

The study seemed to be deserted. Silence held sway, broken only by the gentle purr of the fire. Denzil thought, half hoped, that Guy had been mistaken and their elusive commander was not there. Then he saw a movement on the couch close to the hearth. Someone sat up and yawned, saying in a sleepy drawl: 'Dammit, I must have dropped off. Good evening, William, and to you, my young bucko! What a beastly night, but hell, you might be a bit more careful. You're getting mud on my carpet!'

Denzil gaped as the lean, fashionably dressed figure uncoiled to its full height, and he found himself looking into the amused, lazy-lidded blue eyes of Ambrose Alington.

BOOK THREE

The Loser

Two loves I have, of comfort and despair,
Which like two spirits do suggest me still;
The better angel is a man right fair,
The worser spirit a woman colour'd ill.
To win me soon to hell, my female evil
Tempteth my better angel from my side,
And would corrupt my saint to be a devil,
Wooing his purity with her foul pride.

Sonnet 144 SHAKESPEARE

Chapter 1

The collection of gentlemen in the drawing-room of the house in fashionable Bedford Row could have been gathered there for an evening of gaming and drinking. This would have been the impression given to an intruder. Cards were scattered about on the table, bottles and glasses stood on the sideboard. Four men were positioned there, as if about to engage in play, others sat by the fire, smoking and talking. Everyone looked up when Ambrose came in from the study, accompanied by the Wylde brothers.

Just for a moment, Denzil thought that he had been mistaken in imagining that he was about to meet *Le Fantom*'s followers. Not yet recovered from the shock of learning that the American was the spectre, he was rendered even more confused by instantly recognizing one man who was the last person on earth he would have suspected of joining in such enterprises. His eyes met the dark, amused ones of Robert Burgess, seated with two extremely effeminate fops. The party at the table included a tough-looking mercenary and a squat, rather ugly man dressed in black.

Ambrose took the floor, and the transformation in him was astounding. He was brisk, commanding, the façade of the lazy Southern beau completely discarded. His men were eager and excited, hanging on his words, dominated by his tall, powerful form with the broad shoulders and narrow hips, every inch of him emanating energy and purpose.

'I bid you welcome, gentlemen,' he began, finding a perch on the corner of the table. 'Firstly, I want to introduce you to a new member of our band. You know his brothers, Guy and William. This is Denzil Wylde, who has already proved himself.'

Denzil could feel his face growing hot as they scrutinized him. He was aware that he should make some response, trying to gain time, to think. At last he found his tongue, managing to blurt out: 'You do me much honour, sirs, to include me in your company. You'll not find me lacking in courage.'

'Let's hope not,' growled Giffe Barnhart, the stocky man of military aspect, seated bolt upright in a chair next the table, fixing Denzil with fierce eyes set in a rough-hewn face. 'I for one don't intend to play wet-nurse to a bloody fledgling!'

'I'll answer for my brother,' said Guy crisply.

'And I,' added William.

Ambrose's penetrating eyes went over his followers, knowing them to be a touchy lot, suspicious of strangers. They had every right to be, for this was no game, no light-hearted pastime or honourable sport. It was a grim, often dirty, sometimes sordid, always hazardous matter of life and death. Giffe was a crony from slave-running days in the Caribbean. Ambrose had bumped into him in a dockside tavern shortly after arriving in England, his plans for helping the persecuted *aristos* just forming in his mind. A man of many parts, Giffe had been a soldier, a forthright, fearless rogue, devoted to Ambrose, providing a kind of sixth sense in action, protecting him, filtering the dangers through. His dress was plain and serviceable, rather disordered as is often the case with men of intense energy and constant gesture.

Next to him sat Dick Kingston. He was a civil servant, hobnobbing with politicians over brandy after official dinners, privy to many a State secret: a small man, with no distinguishing features, the sort of person one would pass on the street without noticing. He worked behind the scenes, running the complicated espionage service of *Le Fantom*'s league, beavering away arranging rendezvous, obtaining passports, some forged, others purchased from venal officers, or merely stolen. His job was mundane, unglamorous, but it was factor essential to their success.

Ambrose smiled as he considered the two fops who lounged, elbows on the table, as gorgeously attired as if they were attending a function at Carlton House. Aurora would have been amazed to see them there, for they were the young men with whom she had quarrelled at Maestro Giaconi's fencing studio. Charlie Trevellion and Nick Prewitt had unhesitatingly offered their service. At first, Ambrose had entertained doubts, and Giffe had been downright rude, but they had proved to be quick-witted, spoke French like natives, were able actors and masters of disguise. With their easy access to certain clubs denied to those of heterosexual persuasion, they also aided Dick with his spies and informers.

Guy had recommended Robert, and there were half a dozen others present that night, handpicked members of this élite coterie. Ambrose could muster a further twenty freedom-fighters, but some were in France, others on call at various ports along the coast. He liaised closely with other organizations, led by other leaders, men of the intelligensia, tolerant of advanced ideas, not religious in the accepted sense, but with a sincere conviction of duty towards fellow creatures in distress.

'You've heard the news?' Ambrose addressed them collectively.

They nodded and murmured, faces grave, voices angry. 'Poor lady,' Robert lamented, his swarthy face clouded. 'Poor Marie Antoinette. That murdering crew of bastards!'

'She was not very sensible,' opined Dick, steepling his fingers together thoughtfully. 'An Austrian princess who didn't understand the French.'

'She meddled in matters which were not her concern, making herself intensely unpopular in all camps,' observed Guy, his elbow on the mantel-shelf, glass in hand. 'I visited Versailles, years ago. The general opinion there was that she offended the nobility as much as she did the peasants. She detested the stiff, unbending protocol of Court traditions.'

'But she was so beautiful, so gay and carefree,' protested Robert. 'Such dire news gives a man wings! I'll do anything to save her supporters.'

'She was beautiful, I'll grant you that.' Guy stared down into the flames, visions of that sumptuous palace of Versailles flickering across his memory, its luxury of too great a contrast to the misery of the poor. 'But her beauty didn't compensate for her rudeness and lack of dignity. She was too easily deceived by sycophants, and made sentimental friendships, unwise for a woman in her position.'

'The Swede – Axel de Fersen? It's rumoured that he was her lover,' sniffed Dick disapprovingly. 'He certainly tried several attempts at rescuing the Royal family, each of which failed dismally.'

Robert sprang hotly to her defence. 'She was faithful to the King! I'd stake my life on it. And she had cause to be otherwise. Why, they were married for six years before he could fuck her! A snick of the surgeon's knife was necessary first, and he put off having it done because he was a coward!'

'And there are two children still living out of the four born to them. Does anyone know what's happened to the Dauphin, Louis-Charles?' asked one of the other men.

'He was removed from the prison he shared with his mother and sister,' Ambrose answered, drumming softly on the table with his fingers. 'Louis-Charles Capet, as they now call him, was placed in the care of a tutor, selected by the Jacobins. How they'll treat him is anybody's guess. At the Queen's trial, she was accused of having an incestuous relationship with him.'

'Preposterous!' shouted Robert, amidst the uproar brought about by this statement. 'A little boy of eight years old – committing immoral acts with his own mother! It's bloody absurd!'

'Whatever her crimes, there was no need to chop off her head,' grunted Giffe, fists clenched. 'Why didn't they pack her back to Austria? Let her own people deal with her?'

'I guess they didn't dare.' Ambrose was pacing up and down, hands locked behind his coat-tails. 'While she lived, there'd always be the threat of a Royalist uprising.'

'The Dauphin lives,' reminded William.

'Ah, but you see, the Convention will indoctrinate him and raise him as a good Republican, unless they lose their nerve and slit his throat one dark night,' replied Ambrose with a grim smile.

'Can't we rescue him?' Charlie was leaning forward, with Nick backing him up.

'It would be sheer lunacy to attempt it,' barked Giffe, giving him a glare. 'Can't you just picture how he'll be guarded? By God, even *Le Fantom* wouldn't try – would you, sir?' He appealed to Ambrose, hoping that such a scheme was far from his thoughts.

The American sighed; old prejudices stirred in his blood, old traditions, centuries of precedence and privilege awoke in his memory. It was horrible to think of a Prince of the Blood Royal being brought up by some tavern-cook, blacksmith or cobbler, the sort of person typical of those whom the Jacobins had dragged out of obscurity and given positions of authority. But no, Robespierre would ensure that the Dauphin was educated well, and carefully indoctrinated.

'I agree with Giffe.' His tone was firm, his voice slow, letting every word sink in, lest any be foolhardy enough to imagine they could steal the Dauphin away single-handed. 'To try a rescue and to fail might trigger off his certain death. If we leave it alone, but be vigilant, the boy may one day come into his own. Believe me, my friends, we'll have our work cut out springing lowlier members of the *noblesse*. The violence will be intensified now that the mob have seen the heads of both King and Queen roll.'

'Mob-rule is a devilish thing.' Guy's eyes were bleak. 'What happens to human decency when men are gripped by blood-lust? Not only men, alas. It was the women of Paris who stormed Versailles, drunken hags, armed with pitchforks and butchers' knives, vowing their intention to cut out the Queen's entrails and wear them as cockades.'

'They sit around the guillotine in the *Place de la Revolution*, knitting and counting the heads as they drop into the basket, cackling like fiends, and bawling obscenities,' added Ambrose. 'Lord defend us from the "gentle sex".'

'Starvation turns the most placid housewife into a screaming Fury,' put in Dick, even-tempered and reasonable. 'Those women are justified, I fear. They've suffered privation for years. What's worse, they've watched their children die of hunger, seen their men brutalized. 'Tis small wonder they've gone mad and don't know how to handle freedom. I think they're in for a rude awakening shortly, that dream of equality will never be realized. Politicians will promise anything for their own ends, but there will always be the rich, some who lead and some who follow.'

Ambrose called the meeting to order, and gave each man his instructions. Guy was to go to France; William and Denzil were detailed to return home to hire the services of Redvers and his smugglers to ship out a further consignment of refugees.

'What you got there, my lovebird?' asked Molly Smithers when Miranda entered the mill-house one misty afternoon.

She was leading a fat puppy on a length of string. He was not used to this indignity, tugging at the leash, falling backwards, ungainly with his barrel stomach and short, bowed legs. 'This is Rex,' she announced proudly, her big, sea-grey eyes sparkling with happiness. 'He's mine. Old enough to leave his mother now. She's one of Uncle William's spaniels, you know.'

'Rex, is it?' Molly stood, arms akimbo, smiling down at the child fondly. 'Well, ain't that a fine name, to be sure? He's a funny wee chap though, all belly and legs and floppy ears. Let's see if we can find a bit of cake for him, shall we?'

She drew Miranda to the fire and settled her down on a low stool where she gathered her treasure on to her lap, whispering into his silky ear, while Rex looked up with bright, intelligent eyes, his feathery tail wagging. She was perfectly at home in Molly's muddled, cosy kitchen, a capital place for the young, for her easy-going kindliness demanded no perfect manners or clean boots or best clothes.

Molly had a soft spot for Mark Beaumaris's youngest grand-daughter, cherishing fond memories of him, that fine, hand-some man, very like his son Guy, when they had first met twenty-five years before. Then his hair had been black and curling, his body powerful and lusty. He had swept her off her feet when she had come to the village from Plymouth, a comely young widow investing the small amount left her by her husband in buying the mill. Within a week she had become Mark's mistress, and later Jack had been born. A strong woman, well able to stand on her own two feet, she had asked nothing of his Lordship, and their relationship had continued until the day he died. He had grown gaunt with the passing years, she remembered, his skin lined and seamed, though his eyes still flashed like burnished gold. Although his hair had silvered, his bearing had been such that he could still set female hearts beating fast, including Molly's. To her, the title of Lord Beaumaris would always belong to Mark.

It had hurt her because it would not have been seemly for her to attend his funeral. Lady Charlotte must have known about her, the village was small, inbred and gossipy, but her Ladyship had never given the slightest intimation that she was aware of Molly's and Jack's existence. With that wonderful independence given her by the profits of contraband, Molly did not miss Mark's occasional money gifts. It was the man himself whom she mourned. Oh, she hid it well, the good-looking, lively woman, hid her sadness, her loneliness, never confessing to anyone that what she missed most was the honest-to-goodness satisfaction of bodily desires. Mark had never disappointed her in this. Then she had met Tom Redvers. He was coarse, swaggering, ready with the tallest of tall stories; he and Mark were as different as chalk to cheese, and yet they shared one common factor. They were both what she termed proper men.

'Tell about grandpapa,' said Miranda, with her uncanny knack of knowing what was passing in the minds of others.

Molly took up the large brown teapot, pouring the dark, stewed brew into two mugs. She cut Miranda a hunk of fruitcake and took mugs and plates over to where the child sat. Nothing loth to speak of Mark, she recounted some of his hunting exploits while the child listened, eyes wide, mouth full of cake.

Molly glanced at the window and then at Miranda's inadequate clothing. She tried to look stern, unsuccessfully. How can one be severe when one is motherly and ample-bosomed, wearing gay shawls and flouncy petticoats? She had never been able to manage it, even with Jack, though she had walloped him good and hard on many an occasion.

''Tis a raw, cold day outside,' she scolded. 'Why aren't you wearing a hat and coat? You'll get a chill, that you will.' Miranda's head was bare, and she wore only a shawl over her woollen dress, fingertips poking out of her mittens.

'Then you can make me one of your potions, Molly dear,' she answered solemnly. 'Will you show me how to mix them? I know I could. I've helped you gather herbs, and remembered their names. Teach me how to heal people.'

'We'll see,' Molly hedged, 'but you won't be no help to nobody if you gets sick, wandering about all over. What would your Auntie Sally say?'

'She's excited because Uncle William is coming home today.' Miranda shifted the pup into a more comfortable position. 'Denzil's coming too, but not Papa – not till later.' Her gaze was directed towards the glowing logs, but Molly had the feeling that she did not see them. One small hand clenched in the puppy's fur, making him grunt in his sleep. 'Papa isn't in England.'

Molly's eyes alerted. She knew precisely where Guy was, on edge for his safety, and that of her man. Smuggling was one thing, but playing fast and loose with a vengeful crew of bloodthirsty madmen was entirely different. She sympathized with the wretched refugees, but wished that neither the Wyldes nor Redvers were mixed up in it. She thanked God that Jack was too selfish to volunteer for service on French soil, but he was not idle, and at times like these he half redeemed his vices by his native cunning and reckless valour, pitting his wits against the coastguards.

'Who told you that your Pa ain't in England?' Molly said, wondering if her son had let the cat out of the bag in the child's hearing.

'No one told me. I can see it in the fire.' Miranda's voice was dreamy, and Molly felt a chill touch her, having recognized long ago that this infant was gifted or cursed with 'the sight'. 'He's driving a cart, and he doesn't look like Papa at all. He's dressed in funny ragged old trousers and wooden shoes.' She gave a queer little laugh. 'He does look odd – like a farmer. He's very dirty, and his chin is stubbly – his hair's dirty too, and he's wearing a red cap.' She stopped, drawing in a sharp, terrified breath. 'There's something across the road – a kind of gate. There are soldiers guarding it.' She sighed, the tension leaving her. 'It's all right – they've let him pass through.'

Molly's eyes were stinging with the heat from the blaze. She could see nothing except the picture formed in her mind by the child's vivid description. 'Is he alone?' she whispered.

Miranda was drooping, fair lashes hiding her eyes. 'What?' she asked sleepily. 'No, he's not alone. There are two men hiding under the hood of the cart.'

Molly put an arm about her and drew her close so that her head rested on her broad breasts. 'There, there, lovey,' she crooned. 'Don't you fret. Your Pa'll be home soon, quite safe.'

The child was asleep and Molly let her rest, watching the flames playing around the massive oak log. It looked like glistening crimson velvet. Spiky blue flames darted and flickered over the glowing depths of the fire. Molly was a wise woman; many of the villagers braved the woods to consult her, begging love potions or charms for begetting children, perhaps medicines to abort an unwanted one. She did what she could, relying on her life-long study of herbs, but only at rare intervals could she penetrate the veil between dimensions as Miranda did. She did not for a moment doubt that the child had seen something sketched against the background of flaming purple and crimson. It was true that Guy was on the other side of the Channel. Jack had told his mother about their activities, not all, of course, but she had put two and two together and filled in his omissions.

It was growing dark in the mill-house, and the mist hung thickly outside, blown in from the sea, pressing its grey fingers against the windows. Simultaneously with Molly's thought that it was high time for Miranda to leave for Briar Cottage, she opened her eyes, stretched and yawned. 'Had a nice nap, little turtle-dove?' asked Molly. 'I'll walk part of the way with you.'

She put on the splendid fur-lined cloak which Redvers had given her, pulling the hood over her head, and adding another shawl to the one Miranda wore. They set off through the fog which rolled and billowed, the shapes of trees rearing up out of it, every branch dripping. Sounds were muffled, even the brook was reduced to a strange, trickling distance. Molly and Miranda went up Skenkzies Lane. It held no terror for either of them.

'I'll leave you at the top,' said Molly, her breath mingling with the clammy mist. 'You mind and go to the manor. Get Jack to drive you to the cottage. 'Tis too far for you to walk in this pea-souper.'

'I'll be safe, Molly.' Miranda trudged at her side, Rex in her arms. 'I like the fog. It's so pretty and swirly. I feel the touch of the spirits of men lost at sea.'

'The saints defend us!' exclaimed Molly, glancing over her shoulder as the sea-mist wraiths swept by. 'The things you come out with, child!'

'Don't be alarmed, Molly,' Miranda assured her cheerfully as they climbed the steep, muddy lane, walking through a tunnel of darkness towards the glimmer of light at the top. 'The dead are my friends. They bring me news and warnings. I welcome them.'

Molly, brave though she was, heaved a sigh of relief when they reached the clearing. The mist was thinner there and, higher up, she could see the stone gatehouse and gables of Wylde Court with the latticed windows peering over the moss-grown wall. She gave Miranda a quick kiss, hovering over her for a moment, tucking in a fold of shawl, filled with a sense of apprehension. 'Off you run then, pet. Mind and look out for Jack. Tell him from me to harness the gig and get you home, quick as a wink.'

'Kiss Rex too,' Miranda insisted, holding him up. 'He says, to thank you for the cake.'

Molly watched her as she took the path towards the stables, and she sighed wistfully, blessing the purity of childhood when the world is touched with bright magic. Standing beneath the bare, whispering trees, she was overwhelmed by nostalgia, recalling awakening in the days of her own innocence, looking out through the dormer window of her father's cottage by the sea, breathing in the smell of roses and honeysuckle, the countryside ringing with the call of the skylark, the morning mists lit by rosy dawn, sparkling with jewels of dew. How long ago it seemed, and how much water had flowed under the bridge since that time. Molly shivered, the trailing fog resembling black crepe, veiling the beauties of nature, coming between her and life. She gave herself a shake. It was unlike her to indulge in morbid speculations and, resolutely, she turned down Skenkzies Lane, thinking of Tom Redvers and the loving welcome she planned to give him when he stamped in later, bringing with him a whiff of danger, excitement and the tang of the sea.

The long low garret above the stable smelled of hay and apples. It was Jack's domain, warmed by an iron pot-bellied stove with a flue pipe sticking out through the slate tiles. It contained little furniture save a huge, old-fashioned bed hung with faded remnants of tapestry curtains. He lay within it, and he was not alone. Partly dressed, for they had been exercising the horses, he was flat on his back, his arms folded beneath his curly head, laughing up at the woman who rode astride him, naked thighs spread wide, skirts hitched up out of the way. She was moaning, writhing, impaled, head thrown back, hands braced on her black-stockinged knees, heels of her leather boots jabbing into him.

'Go on, Lalage!' he urged, roaring with mirth. 'That's it! Work yourself off on me. I'll let you. Faster, faster!' There was triumph in his voice. He had her, this fine lady, wife of his brother and master. She was powerless to control herself, powerless to do anything but hump away, desperate for release. Her head shot up, an appalling look on her face that he had seen before at the onset of her climax. It was devoid of expression, her eyes disoriented, slightly out of focus.

Her body shuddered, and she gave a strangled cry, then slumped across him, cursing him, her nails ripping into his flesh. Jack continued to chuckle, one hand clenched in her hair, listening to the stream of filthy abuse which poured from between her snarling red lips. It gave him the greatest possible amusement, far exceeding any sexual satisfaction he gained from their savage encounters. A sense of control that was sweeter than gold, sweeter than the embraces of a thousand gorgeous women. She was Guy's property but, like a thief in the night, the despised illegitimate brother took her, had knowledge of this woman, this odd, secretive woman who needed him with a consuming fire whilst he did not give a damn about her.

'Put a padlock on your lips, bitch,' he mocked, tugging at her hair, forcing her to look at him. 'I'm mighty tired of hearing you repeating yourself. I'll have to teach you some new swear words.'

Lalage tore herself free, hammering at his head with her fists, till he caught them and twisted her arms painfully behind her. 'You sod!' she hissed and spat in his face.

Jack bunched his fist and knocked her across the bed. She lay staring at him, eyes wild and dilated, breasts heaving beneath the jacket of her riding-habit. Jack got up, adjusting his breeches, making a lunge for the brandy bottle, eyeing her cautiously as he drank from it. She was likely to renew her attack. 'What's wrong? You wanted it, didn't you? You always want it. Hell, there's so much bother about swiving. How does Wilkes's doggerel go? "Life can little else supply, but a few good fucks and then we die"!'

Lalage began to laugh with him, jumping to her feet, studying his handsome, raffish features, strong and uncaring, the grey eyes like honed steel. 'You're incorrigible,' she said, smoothing the creases from her sable velvet skirt.

'And so, my dear, are you,' he mused, leaning against the oak bedpost, taking another hard pull at the bottle. 'First Guy, then that poor bugger Denzil, and now me. How many others, I wonder, have burrowed between those beautiful, rampant thighs?'

'How do I know?' She smiled, that strangely wicked smile which hinted at such wonders that, despite his cynicism, it caused Jack to catch his breath. 'I can't remember what happened before Guy found me.'

'Bullshit!' snapped Jack.

'Are you calling me a liar?' she sparked back at him, so close that he could smell the heavy perfume of sandalwood, overlaid by the animal odour of their loving.

His eyes widened with injured innocence. 'I? Would I dare to call Lady Beaumaris a liar?' He swept her an elaborate bow. 'Forgive me, your Ladyship. I'm your devoted doormat, like the other simpering boobies who fall into your neat traps.' Then his mouth hardened and he yanked her into his arms, breathing harshly into her ear: 'Of course you're a liar. A cheat. A strumpet. For you, love has to howl in torment, touched with savagery and bloody storms of rage before you can get fulfilment. You're either biting or caressing, using every enticement a woman can offer, except the soft sighs and sincerity of a virgin. You enjoy bursting into a violent rage, tearing yourself and your lover to pieces. The lash excites you, doesn't it?' She struggled but he gave her a hard shake. 'Doesn't it? Tell the truth. You revel in it, whether you are trying to flog me or I wield the whip. You're incapable of love, but I'm telling you, here and now, that what you feel for me is the closest you'll ever get to that emotion.'

'You think I could love a lout like you? Ha! You fancy yourself, Jack Smithers. You stink of the midden!' she sneered.

'And you like it,' he grated, his hand trailing along her spine, watching her reaction, feeling her tense then relax like a cat

259

having its fur stroked. Teasingly, he hoisted her skirt, running his fingers up her thigh, smiling grimly as her legs parted, welcoming his invasion. In a coldly calculating manner, he played with her, looking into her eyes the while, judging the exact moment when she was reaching the peak of sensation. Then, just as her breathing quickened and she started to moan, he roughly withdrew his hand and pushed her away.

'Damn you!' she yelled, in furious frustration. Jack stood, hands on hips, laughing at her.

Lalage changed her tactics, falling on her knees before him. He lounged against the post while she unbuttoned the flap fastening of his breeches, her fingers and mouth fondling and kissing the hot flesh which was beginning to harden. Jack grinned down at her, seeing her dark hair falling forward, accepting her homage, proud of his erect manhood, despising her for her worship of it. She was his creature, eager to obey his every wish. A bitch of the first water, without any doubt, and there were things in her which he disliked intensely, but she was beautiful, available, and Jack was a sensualist. He too, took pleasure in their love-hate relationship.

Not only this – it pleased him to know that this promiscuous doxy, working so diligently to give him lustful gratification, was the wife of Lord Beaumaris. He liked Guy, admired him in many respects, yet at the back of all lay a deep-seated envy and resentment. He laughed, low in his throat, as wave after wave of feeling gathered in his loins. At any moment now, the seed of the bastard brother would spurt into her Ladyship's mouth, bedew her lips, her face, her hair. Long-awaited justice was about to be done.

He was spiralling upwards, straining towards the peak, when he suddenly stopped, his hands clamping round Lalage's head, holding her still, his eyes on the small figure which had appeared at the top of the loft-ladder. 'Christ!' he barked. 'What are you doing here, Miranda?'

The child stood stockstill, her knuckles pressed against her mouth. Lalage sprang to her feet, spinning towards her, while Jack attempted to cover himself with his hands. Miranda stared at her stepmother for an instant, then turned and fled back the way she had come.

The short dark day was dying. The mist swept up in an array of thin cloud which veiled the house, the woods, the road, thickening into a wall of muffling vapour. Miranda made for higher ground, pausing, listening. She could hear nothing. Behind and around there was a dead, dripping stillness. She ran on, peering into that blanketing whiteness. When she reached the crest of the rise, the mist slipped away, lying in a steaming lake at her feet, with rocks and stones poking through it like watery ghosts.

Used to the terrain, she ducked and darted like a hare, heading for the cliffs, Rex held tightly beneath her shawl. She found the path, sure-footed, agile, and now the fog was filled with sounds, rocks falling from a great height, water rising in a whirlwind, voices, animals rustling, the ringing of bells. She glimpsed the edge of the sea, a curdled grey against banks of vapour, and ran on along the track which led towards the tumulus. She was almost there when an apparition loomed right up in front of her. A demon beast, huge, supernatural, eyes glowing red in the weird light, nostrils flaring, smoke pouring out like dragon's breath. He was ridden by a terrible, black giantess, with hair that was alive, swirling up and bursting over her head in writhing, shining snakes.

Before she could run, that awful thing had sprung at her, seizing her in unnaturally strong hands. 'Why were you spying?' she shouted.

Miranda struggled, screaming: 'I wasn't spying. Molly told me to find Jack.'

Pain exploded in her head as Lalage's palm made contact with her cheek. 'You're mad! Wicked! This mist is your work. Devil's work!'

The grey vapour filled Miranda's eyes, her nostrils, her mind. She could not breathe, icy tears crawling down her face. 'Let me go,' she choked. 'I want Sally.'

'Damn Sally and damn you!' Lalage was clothed in black flame, the serpents hissing, coiling as she expanded to even greater size, a creation of mist and fiery darkness. 'Don't try your tricks on me. I've not forgotten my wedding-day and your talk of the evil eye. You are the one who is evil.' Her fingers were eagle's talons, biting deep into Miranda's arm. 'You're a witch. They'll burn you alive. Your skin will blister and bubble from your bones – your eyelids will drop off – you'll die in agony and go straight to hell!'

Miranda's head went down and she bit Lalage's hand, thrashing out with her feet at the same moment. Lalage cursed and the child leapt away, but in the struggle she dropped Rex. Lalage swooped, picked him up by the scruff and dangled him.

Miranda made a grab, but Lalage's arm went higher so that he was out of reach, wriggling and whimpering.

'Give him to me!' Miranda shouted.

'Yours, is he? Perhaps I'll just drop him over the cliff, see if he bounces, eh?'

She was standing close to the edge of the abyss which boiled with fog, the menacing sound of waves pounding the rocks far below drowning the puppy's frantic cries. Behind them the moon appeared over the trees, a finger of pale colour, gathering strength, dissolving the vapour to transparent gauze, but it was still thick over the sea. Lalage's face was whiter than that rolling mass, her mouth black.

'Don't hurt him,' Miranda begged.

Lalage laughed, holding Rex at arm's length over the brink. 'I want your promise to say nothing of what you saw in the loft. Never to speak of it, even were you torn apart by wild horses.'

'I promise.' Bewildered though she was, Miranda meant this. She never lied and never made a vow unless she intended to keep it.

Lalage threw Rex into the child's arms. 'Don't cheat me. I shall be watching and listening. You'll think you are safe, at the cottage with Sally or down at the mill with Molly, but you won't be. I'll creep up on you when you're least expecting me. At night, in bed, you'll hear a sound in the darkness, and it will be me. I can fly on the wind, be anywhere I wish to be. No use locking your door, for I'll transform myself into a mist, just like this one, and slide under it!'

Those slanting, yellow eyes bored into hers, and every nerve in Miranda's body quivered. 'I'll not tell,' she whispered, clutching Rex.

Lalage floated towards her horse. She mounted him, black, tall in the saddle. 'I shall be there – watching – listening.' Her voice was carried on the night wind as, phantomlike, she became part of the darkness and mist.

Looking back in later life, Sally was to remember that night as the longest, most heart-rending she had ever known. She was not at Briar Cottage when William returned from London, instead she was leading a search-party. Miranda had not come back by tea-time and Sally began to worry. She went to the window a dozen times, stood by the door, frustrated by the fog which had grown increasingly dense. She regretted giving the child permission to visit Molly, but she had been so eager to take Rex to meet her old friend. The weather had been singularly mild, that season of wet, soft airs, and Sally had let her go without any misgivings. It was pleasant to be outdoors in such weather. Miranda loved to wander through the woods, listening to the sounds of the resident birds high in the trees, calling to one another in their small, sharp voices.

Sally had been extremely busy, preparing William's favourite dishes, then changing into a pretty new woollen gown. She had spent some time in the bedroom before the cheval-glass, not because she was vain, but wanting to make a good impression on her husband. Her dress was autumnal-hued, with long ruched sleeves fastening at the wrists with tiny gold buttons. During William's absence she had turned herself over to her meditations, enjoying the solitude. She was not a skilful dissembler, living under the constant strain of pretending that her feelings for him had changed through marriage. In reality, they were as still and lifeless as tepid water. To be alone was bliss, an indulgence of which she was feeling terribly guilty. She had already hidden Guy's miniature, trying to forget that she had taken it out as soon as William's back was turned, her desire for Guy so intense that she was no longer mistress of herself.

She stared at her image in the mirror, seeing her marriage-bed reflected in the background, horrified to find that she was dreading sharing it with William, weary of the charade, of faking a love which was not true. All she would want to hear when her husband set foot over the threshold would be about Guy. How was he? What was he doing? She hated the sight of her calm face framed by the golden ringlets, knowing that she would lie, put on that false front, too cowardly to see the pain in William's eyes if he guessed.

Her love for Guy was inextricably woven into her life, colouring it with the grey hues of misery or the flame of occasional bursts of joy. More vivid than hours spent in her husband's arms were memories, fleeting, all too brief, for she had never been much in Guy's company. Nevertheless, she recalled strange nuances of emotion, nothings that meant so much, small remarks he had made in a tone more expressive than the most thrilling of poems, glances that were compelling. With feminine realism, she knew that she had made a grave mistake in accepting William. It was hopeless. Not fair to either of them. William would be home at any moment, and Guy, when he did return, would go to his wife.

Dora came to her, pulling the chintz curtains across the windows, shutting out the night, saying anxiously: 'Miss Miranda should be here by now, shouldn't she, milady?'

That was the beginning. Till that moment when her friend had spoken, Sally had succeeded in pushing worry to the back of her mind. Both women put on their cloaks and went out into the chilly evening, searching the garden, the outhouse in vain. A boy was dispatched to the mill, returning after a short while to say that Molly had sent the child to Wylde Court so that Jack could bring her home before nightfall.

Fears sprang out of the gloom then, wearing hideous faces. The menservants were alerted, some going to the manor to inquire, some combing the woods. They came back with the same answer. Miranda had vanished. Sally struggled to maintain an appearance of calm, but dread weighed heavily upon her. She ordered a horse to be saddled and, leaving Dora in charge at the cottage, set out with some of the men, riding for the cliffs, the long-barrows. The feeble light of their flares sent smoky flickers over the fog, bringing it to life so that it moved like a sluggish serpent, creating an instant impression of impenetrable depth, of darkness, of swamp.

'Miranda!' Sally called. Her voice bounced back, mocking her. 'Miranda, where are you?'

Nothing. The stillness was oppressive, the silence so marked that the bleating of a sheep inland or the barking of a dog down in the port reached her distinctly. Overmastering fear obscured details. They rode along the cliff path and Sally's heart plummeted when one of the men brought a soggy woollen object to her. It was Miranda's shawl. Time and distance seemed endless as they made for the tumulus. Sally was trembling. Her horse's hooves must be made of lead, his limbs rusty for he went so slowly, or so she thought. The wide flat top of the burial mound was free from cloud, the grass smooth, glistening damply under the flares. It was deserted. So were the hollows around its sloping sides.

They went to the village and Sally's sudden appearance in the inn startled the customers away from their pots of cider, their cards and skittles. Lights sprang up in the cottages, women huddling in the doorways whilst their men pushed in to collect coats and boots and lanterns. Miranda was loved by them, with her gentle ways and wise remarks. In such remote areas, the simple-minded were held in awe. The rugged fishermen, the farmers and labourers stood round Sally. The cold fitted like masks on their upturned faces and their breath hung on the air. She recognized some of them, touched by their offers of help. They made crude, kind attempts at comfort.

'Don't you worry, missus – the little 'un be used to them woods, 'ere abouts. She be at one with the wild things, God love 'er.'

The blacksmith held his torch aloft, big, muscular, with sooty face and broken teeth. He was a special friend of Miranda's. She had spent hours in his forge, fascinated by the roaring bellows, the white-hot fire, the smell of singeing horn and sweat as he hammered on the shoes. 'We'll go down to the beach, Mrs Wylde,' he said. 'Come on, lads. Look lively.'

Sally felt an arm about her waist, helping her into the saddle. It was Josh Appleyard, more wholesome looking than the rest, neatly clad, clean white linen taking on the fire of the torches. There was sympathy in his eyes, in his whole attitude. He looked out into the darkness over the harbour, a darkness which seemed more dense beyond the restricted circle of flickering lantern-light. Sally followed his gaze, as if she could wrest the child from that inky blackness. She saw the silhouettes of the houses, the rigging and masts of the fishing-boats vaguely defined in the gloom, reminiscent of gallows. The shadowy buildings on the quay glared with blank windows, the boats bowed and nodded, bumping against the festering timbers of the wharf, while the sea sucked and gurgled around the piles. That sickly white vapour overhung the water, the foul smell of rotting fish wafting up in thick, nauseating puffs.

'Anything I can do?' Jack asked, coming from the tavern, a cut above the others, wearing a beaver hat and warm overcoat, leading his horse.

'We're going to search the coves,' she answered, gazing down into his eyes, smelling whisky on his breath. Was weariness warping her perception or was there really something shifty there? On impulse, she restrained him a moment longer. 'Jack, did you see Miranda this afternoon?'

He was bending over, adjusting his stirrup. She could hardly hear his reply. 'No. I'd have told you.'

The tide had retreated, dragging the mist with it, as a ghost will drag a shroud. The moon had risen in full glory as they reached the first cove. Far out, the sea was glassy, but in-shore the white-crested waves beat up the level sand and rushed upon the shelving cliffs, throwing skywards mighty masses of creamy foam. The men spread out, examining each cave, the lights bobbing like fireflies, their voices echoing amongst the rocks.

Sally galloped along the firm wet shingle, splashing through the shallows, rounding the ridge of tumbled boulders which led to the crescent-shaped bay beyond. She was aware of other drumming hoof-beats. Jack was following. The purple shadows at the base of the cliff face were baffling. She swung down from her saddle, letting the horse idle along behind her. Her skirt was heavy, wet to the knee, her thin shoes saturated, the cold making her legs slow, though she was sweating, heart pumping with effort. The boom of the billows crashing against the ridge was thunderous, followed by a sucking hiss as they drew back. Black rocks, bright moonlight slicing through them. A terrible urgency drove Sally on, but it was like a nightmare when one is pursued by some faceless, nameless horror but can only move at snail's pace.

Jack shouted and she stopped. He was retrieving something from the water's edge, bringing it to her. Her fingers closed on wet fur. She drew in a tortured breath, almost a moan, as she recognized the puppy, limp and lifeless.

The wind was freshening, clouds scudding across the sky, but before they covered the moon, it struck something in a cleft of rock which the sea had been relentlessly pounding before obeying its pull and dragging back. A tiny bundle, snowy white. The coming cloud was too quick for Sally to see much, shadows shut down almost immediately. She did not wait for a second glance, flying up the sand towards the fissure, reaching the weed-slimy rocks, missing her footing, falling to her knees, rising with salt stinging the cuts, the feel of blood trickling. The cloud passed and the moonlight struck again. Sally forced her way into the narrow cleft and bent over Miranda.

Her lips were parted, and she was breathing in long, heavy gasps. Her clothing and hair were soaking wet. Sally braced her feet and hauled her out of the hole, clasping that ice-cold body close. As she did so, a shudder passed through the child. Somehow, Sally scrambled down to the sand, and Jack was there, taking off his coat. Together, they wrapped Miranda in it. He wanted to carry her, but Sally would not let him. Now that she had found her, she must pour her own vitality into her, never let her go lest the frail hold on life should be loosened.

She said, shakily: 'Bring Rex. We can't leave him as food for the gulls and crabs. Miranda wouldn't like that.'

The bay was filling up with men, each carrying his glow-worm light. There were shouts, feet thudding on wet sand. Just for one brief moment, Sally let the gentle giant of a blacksmith take Miranda. Josh held the stirrup while she mounted. When she had gathered up the reins, the smith gave her the child. Josh walked with his hand on the withers of her horse as she rode back to Briar Cottage with the men marching on either side. Miranda did not recover consciousness, a dead weight in her arms, sighing occasionally.

The house loomed out of the darkness; a pale moonmist covered it, outlining its walls and chimneys. It blazed with lights, the front door wide open. In a daze of exhaustion, Sally found herself staggering under the burden of the child. She took a step forward as the tall figure of a man came out of the light, and collapsed into William's arms.

Chapter 2

Sally kept constant vigil at Miranda's bedside. Dora and she had undressed her by the fire in the nursery, horrified at the cuts and abrasions marking the small body, clothing her in a flannel nightgown, packing stone hot-water bottles at her feet and heaping blankets on the bed. Try as they might, they could not rouse her, though she shivered and wept silently. They poured brandy between her blue lips, attempted to spoon in cordial, but nothing penetrated the deep unconscious state which had claimed her.

Sally had hardly spoken to William who, once he had carried the child upstairs, had stood around awkwardly, helplessly, as men do in times of illness, relieved when she asked him to fetch Dr Rowsell. Dora was on one side of the bed, Sally on the other, as the doctor leaned over Miranda, taking her pulse, listening to her chest, while they tried to guess what he was thinking by his gestures or the slightest wrinkle of his brow.

Rowsell was a youngish man whose broad forehead and brisk manner inspired confidence. He still had some belief in his profession, despite the awful odds of ignorance and superstition with which he battled daily. He had taken on the practice at the death of the former physician who had struggled for years to heal the peasants. Though Rowsell had been there for a decade, he was still regarded as a 'foreigner'. He was pleasant featured, wearing smart black, and having the stamp of a gentleman. He had often visited Wylde Court to advise on childish ailments.

He straightened up, but remained studying Miranda with a pensive expression. 'Well?' asked Sally, unable to stand the suspense. 'How do you find her?'

He pursed his lips, and took a bottle of brownish medicine from his bag. 'Well, Mrs Wylde – there is little I can do. You have already carried out the two most important things in a case such as this – warmth and rest. Found on the shore, so your husband told me.'

'Why has she not come to herself?' Sally hung over the child, watching that tiny sleeping face which was almost as white as the pillow.

Rowsell closed the bag with a snap and picked up his tricorne hat. 'She appears to have been half drowned, and is suffering from exposure. The shock, dear lady, will have affected her thus. It is nature's way of ensuring the healing of both mind and body. Let her sleep. Don't be alarmed if she does not stir for days. Try to get her to take some of this medicine. I will ride over tomorrow.'

Dora went down to let him out, and William came into the bedchamber. Sally looked up at him. He was like a stranger. 'Oh, William – what a homecoming. I'm so sorry –' she began.

His arms clasped her in a warm bearhug. 'Sally, my darling – don't think about that. Is the child recovering? Poor little thing. Do you know how it happened?'

This was so typical of him, always so concerned for others. Sally could not tell him much. They would perhaps learn the truth when Miranda came to her senses. Sally would not permit that doomy word 'if' to enter her mind. What had taken place was a tragedy, and yet there was an odd element of relief in it. William and she were prevented from personal talk and intimate actions. They spoke briefly of London, and Sally was most controlled, reacting quite casually when William brought Guy into the conversation.

They were interrupted by a sound from the bed. Miranda's eyes were wide open, glassy. She was moaning, rolling her head from side to side, her fingers plucking at the quilt. Words formed on her lips. 'No! No! Don't come near me!'

Sally winged over to her, cool fingers on her burning forehead. 'Hush, dearest, Sally's here. You're at home, in your own bed.'

Miranda did not recognize her, convulsed with uncontrollable sobs which turned into a fit of coughing, frightening sounding and leaving the child bathed in perspiration. William helped to raise her while Sally lifted a glass of water to her lips, but she would not drink, sinking back as if drained, lids half closed, the whites of her eyes glittering slits between.

Sally was wringing her hands in anguish. 'Bring Molly,' she implored. 'I've no faith in that doctor. Molly will know what to do.'

When Molly arrived she took one look at Miranda and began to brew a cordial of her own in a saucepan set on the trivet over the nursery fire. She had other things in mind too, but would not put these into practice until William had gone. Men were so sceptical of charms and spells, delicate rituals which would not work if an unbeliever was present. She had not been surprised when William appeared at her door. Deep in her bones she had known that something dire was about to happen. Had the child been 'overlooked'? Who could hate her so violently, wishing ill upon her?

Molly pondered on this as she stirred the potion, with Miranda laying on the bed as if already a corpse. She knew what to do, if she could find the witch. The hag's blood must be drawn to counteract the spell. Her plump face was grim; the ladle in her hand felt like a sharp knife. The liquid bubbled and Jack's eyes seemed to be laughing up at her through the steam. Jack. Yes, she would question him, but not tonight. Dear God, the men had work enough under the cover of darkness.

William was wearing his greatcoat. 'I must go out again, Sally,' he said, but gave no explanation. When he kissed her in farewell, his lips were so night-chilled that they made her shiver.

She did not see him again until the smallhours, when the reflection of dawn was high and far over the sea. She had fallen asleep by the bed. Molly was nodding in the rocking-chair near the fire which they had kept stoked. The room was very hot, and Sally opened her heavy eyelids and saw William looking down at her.

'I need your help, Sally,' he said as she came out of her dreams.

It was like a hazy continuation of muddled dreaming. For an instant she thought that Miranda's sickness was part of it, but one glance at the feverish face on the pillow brought her back to grim reality. William looked tired and drawn in the grey light. He was wet and his boots were muddy.

'I can't leave the child,' she replied, but she was already putting on her outdoor clothing.

'Molly will care for her.'

'What's wrong?' Molly was awake and on her feet. 'It's not my Jack or Tom, is it?'

'No.' William ran a worried hand over his hair and sighed. 'They are safe, but there is an injured man who needs urgent attention.'

'I don't understand.' Sally was ready, hooded and cloaked. 'What man is this? Where is he?'

'I'll tell you as we ride,' said William.

Molly helped Sally to pack the medicine chest and William tucked it under his arm. That sense of unreality deepened as they went through the quiet house. A pristine clarity quivered in the air of the garden. William's horse was waiting, and he had already saddled another for Sally. Frost had sculptured a web of crystal over everything, each branch, each cobweb glittered with fairylike strands. It was barely light, though the cocks were crowing, and so still that the twigs cracking beneath the iron-shod hooves gave off the alarm of a pistol shot. A pheasant ran across their path, panicking. A wood-pigeon, disturbed by its cry, fluttered up to roost on a higher branch.

'Where are we going?' asked Sally, huddled in her cloak.

Then William, clopping beside her, so close that his knee bumped hers, placed before her a clear exposé of the situation. He told her everything, but excluded Ambrose Alington's commitment. She was neither shocked nor surprised, as if she had always known, deep in her heart, denying it, laughing it to scorn as absurd, yet aware that it was so. He was taking her to Highfield Lodge. Redvers had brought in two aristocrats last night, and one of them had been badly wounded.

'You want me to tend him?' Sally said as they rode out from the woods and crossed a misty meadow where poised deer watched them before leaping away in startled flight.

William nodded. 'If you will. I daren't call in Rowsell. No one must know of this escape route. In other circumstances I would have asked Molly but, quite frankly, if it's a question of removing a bullet, I would prefer that you did it.'

His faith in her was touching, but Sally squirmed. She had never done such a thing before, but then, she thought soberly, she had not delivered a baby until Dora had lain there helplessly, dependent on her skill. 'I'm no surgeon,' she reminded.

'You will manage, my dear. At least the poor fellow won't die of blood-poisoning, as he might under Molly's ministrations. She'd put a poultice of nettles or deadly nightshade on the wound,' William replied, with a laugh intended to hide an agitation which Sally felt as if it were her own.

Against the black hills behind it the lodge looked desolate, built at a time when houses needed to give shelter and safety, tucked tight in, guarded by thick, sentinel trees. William pushed open the old, grumbling gate and they dismounted, crossing the courtyard. The front door was unbarred and when they entered they were greeted by two rusted suits of armour stationed at the foot of the stairs. The hall was sparsely furnished, a long bare oak table, some stiff-backed chairs, a carved dower-chest, and the portrait of a woman in a blue dress and white ruff. The small heavily-paned windows let in little light.

William led the way upstairs, and they came to a room on the left. It was dark. William pulled back the curtains and Denzil awoke from the armchair by the dying fire. Bleary-eyed, he stared at them and then got up, his clothing crumpled and sea-stained. 'Thank God you've come,' he cried. 'Yon Frenchie's in a bad way.'

He nodded towards the bed in which a man was laid, the curtains of patched purple velvet, the woodwork handsomely carved. More velvet, also torn and shabby, was tacked on to some of the panelled walls, to keep out draughts.

'Where is his companion?' asked William as he set down the medicine-chest on a side-table.

'In the next room, sleeping soundly,' Denzil answered, giving Sally a friendly grin.

She asked him to fetch hot water while she put on her apron and rolled up her sleeves. The Frenchman was young, hardly more than a boy, watching her with hollow, dark eyes in an ashen face. When she pulled back the coverlet, she could not suppress a gasp. He had lost a lot of blood. His shirt was stained with crimson, also the sheet on which he lay. Someone had packed a wad of linen against his shoulder, and this too was soggy. William introduced her. The youth's title was impress-ive. He was Raoul, Duc de Remiville.

'Isn't he rather young to be a *duc*?' she murmured.

'His father was guillotined three months ago. Sons inherit rather early in France these days.' There was a wry twist to William's lips.

She quickly discovered that Raoul could understand little English, whilst her knowledge of French was sketchy. All she could do was smile, and make encouraging, reassuring com-ments while she put him through the considerable pain of probing for the bullet lodged in a muscle of his shoulder. William had added opium to the brandy which they made him drink before the operation. Sally forgot her squeamishness, concentrating on getting the forceps round the stubborn mus-ket ball. At last it was done, the lead shot dropping into the basin which Denzil held. Raoul had fainted, and Sally washed the blood away and dressed the wound, making quite sure that he was as comfortable as possible. It was only then, when the tension was lifted, that she found her legs refusing to obey her.

'You've saved his life, my dear.' William's face swam mistily before her.

Sally made no attempt to hide the forebodings gathering in black, oppressive clouds about her. 'You are fools!' she shouted. 'You'll die, most horribly – every one of you! Leave France to sort out its own problems. You'll be caught, butchered on the guillotine, and then what will become of us?' She was unable to continue, the words choking her throat, and sank into the nearest chair.

She felt William's arm about her, heard him saying something about the strain of Miranda's illness coupled with this extra burden. She sensed that he was not talking to Denzil and looked up, blinking away the tears spiking her lashes. Guy was standing in the doorway, wearing filthy canvas trousers, a broad belt with a brass buckle round his middle, a disgustingly dirty shirt and sabots. He looked as if he had not washed or shaved for a week.

'I snatched a couple of hours' sleep,' he said to William, strolling towards the bed like an idler with time to kill.

'Sally's done a magnificent job of patching up the *duc*. Was it bad over there?'

'Diabolical! We had hell's own trouble getting out. Hence the bullet-hole in this young buck.'

Sally was shocked by his scruffy attire and sudden appearance in the room. Steeling herself to speak to him, she said: 'Do you know that Miranda is ill?'

'Yes. What the deuce has happened?' This was delivered with an ominous, disconcerting change of tone. He scowled, ruffianly in his coarse garb, those flaring nostrils, the lips hard against the even white teeth giving him a vulpine look. Peace was always of such short duration between them, and Sally was aware of an immovable, antagonistic force sparking from him.

'You are not blaming me, surely?' she asked, then repented that she had spoken.

He darted her an unpleasant glare, but William sprang to her defence. 'The child wandered, was cut off by the tide. You must go and see her, Guy. Perhaps your presence may recall her to consciousness.'

'I doubt that.' Guy uttered a short laugh. Stress had marked his face with deep lines.

Sally saw them, nursing her wrath, her thoughts locked in combat within her. She could hate him for his arrogance, yet feel sympathy for him, totally confused by those imperceptible things associated with him which had such an influence on her. There had been a mad scheme for running away nibbling at the corners of her mind during William's absence. Now this evaporated completely at the sight of Guy. More than anything else, greater than his harsh condemnation, his coldness towards his sick child, was that consciousness of the unfinished nature of their relationship.

She stood up, feeling stronger now. 'There is so much to do, this sick boy to tend, and I must go back to Miranda.'

'Change places with Molly,' suggested William. 'Take it in turns.'

'Lalage can help,' Guy interposed in his deep, incisive voice.

'Lalage?' William gave him a sharp stare, wondering if his brother had taken leave of his senses.

'Why not? She can do her share.'

'What will she say about you harbouring a fugitive?' William asked, then fell silent with a questioning look.

Guy gave a shrug. 'I shan't tell her the truth. We'll simply inform her that he's a smuggler, and that his life will not be worth twelve hours' purchase if she peaches on him.'

Guy delayed at the lodge for a while after William and Sally had departed. He walked out into the yard, seeking the old pump. Denzil was leaning against the wall, yawning and staring at the lights of the sky over the hills. Long bands of yellow lay across pale ivory, and the tops of the trees rippled with fire. A robin sang in the poplars, and other birds joined in as they beat their way up through the clear air.

Guy pumped water into a wooden bucket and then stripped, not caring who saw him. 'Come and help me, Denzil, you lazy devil!' he shouted, taking a deep breath, unaware of the cold or the sharp frosty tang, impervious to pain and discomfort, a powerful creature of force and feeling. He stretched widely, proud that he was in such fine shape, surprising indeed considering the life he had led. The wind played on his naked back and thighs.

Denzil advanced unwillingly. It hurt him to see his brother's wide-shouldered, strong body – a man's body, hard muscles, in its prime, possessed of magnificent virility. He was aware that he was not yet fully developed, retaining the slenderness of youth, and he envied Guy's prowess, unable to avoid glancing at his genitals, furious at the thought of Lalage sleeping with him. Lalage. He ached to see her, to hold her, worked up into such a state of infatuation that it was difficult to be discreet. He wanted to drop everything and go rushing off to find her. It was impossible. Guy would get there first. He would burst into the bedchamber and fling her on to the four-poster, taking her fiercely, possessively. She belonged to him, not to Denzil.

'Hey! Stop mooning!' Guy was laughing, thrusting the slopping bucket at him. Denzil seized it and, lifting it high, sent the ice-cold water cascading over his brother. Guy did not flinch, he laughed again and offered to do the same for him. Denzil declined, so Guy took up a rough towel and vigorously rubbed his chest and back, glowing and splendid. Denzil felt sick in the stomach, watching him.

Shrieks of childish merriment greeted Guy when, later that morning, he strolled into his apartment at Wylde Court. He was transformed from a sansculotte, to a superbly dressed English lord. His well-tailored bottle-green jacket was exactly suitable for practical bookwork with Boxer, whilst cream breeches and brown top-boots were ideal for riding round the estate. His hair curled waywardly, as it always did when damp, his square jaw was closely shaven, apart from the sideburns which sharply defined his swarthy cheeks. He had successfully avoided an encounter with his mother, though he could hear her voice resounding in the distance, and the querulous tap, tap of her stick.

Lalage was seated at the dressing-table, hairbrush in her hand, while Cecily and Barbara romped on the bed. They silenced immediately on seeing their father, relapsing into occasional stifled giggles. Guy's mind did an unpleasant backward flip, and he found himself remembering Celeste. What a misalliance that had proved. She had been cheated as vilely as he, no judge of men, poor fool, believing him to be as noble in character as he was presentable in person.

Pretty, in the beginning, before she lost her figure when the children were born. Totally opposite to him in tastes and ambitions, but he was sure that their quarrels and misunderstandings had not been entirely his fault. A sentimental woman, given to overeating and a weak indulgence where Cecily and Barbara were concerned, coupled with an infinite capacity for tears. Unfortunately his bad temper, his faithlessness, had not made her love him less. She had adored him and this, above all, was what had vexed him most. He could see her at that very moment, looking up at him with the nervous smile with which she always greeted his sarcasm, too stupid to know whether he spoke in jest or not. An exasperating female, who had given him an uncomfortable conscience and had not been able to produce a son.

'Guy, darling – I was not expecting you! What a lovely surprise!' It was Lalage's voice which spoke, banishing the sad, shrinking ghost of his first wife. She had turned on the stool, one bare, shapely leg slipping out of her black satin robe, a tiny, feathered, high-heeled mule dangling on the tip of her toe. She gave him a look which would have addled a saint's brain.

'Madame,' he bowed over her hand, smiling down into her eyes. 'Your servant.'

'Indeed, not my *servant*.' She gave the protest a caressing inflection. 'My beloved husband, returned to me after too long an absence.'

'Business, my dear, only pressing business could have kept me from your side,' he replied, raising one dark, peaked eyebrow. 'And now that I'm home, will you show me how much you have missed me?'

She kept her hand in his, and laughed with a light, effortless candour. 'Certainly, my Lord. I am ever mindful of my wifely duty.' She was exquisitely beautiful with her vibrant colouring, the robe open over her breasts, her olive skin gleaming invitingly. 'Children, it is time you went to the schoolroom,' she called in that same, playful voice. 'Miss Stanmore will be waiting.'

They wriggled from the bed, pouting and complaining, and Guy stared at them hard, a frown gathering on his brow. 'What the hell?' he began, and left Lalage, seizing his daughters and dragging them to the window. 'Good God!' he exclaimed, exploding into one of his dark, evil rages. 'You look like a couple of painted jill-flirts! Wash that stuff off your faces at once!'

The two girls began to cry loudly. Lalage sprang up, her voice hard and defiant. 'Guy! For heaven's sake! They've only been playing with my rouge.'

'You should never have permitted it!'

'I helped them. Isn't it better that they learn to use it properly?'

Guy was boiling with anger. The day had started so well. He had been pleased to be back, satisfied at saving the *duc* and his friend, exhilarated by the stiff fight with the militia on the sand dunes of Havre. He had come to Lalage filled with the best of intentions, tingling from that dousing of pump water which was

276

the clearest, sweetest on earth, and now to find this! His daughters learning to use paint, to preen before mirrors, to employ all the silly, vapid, coquettish tricks which he despised. Lalage had no business encouraging them. He shuddered from contemplating what further possible contamination their innocence may have suffered.

They were bawling, terrified. Black tears ran down their cheeks as the kohl melted from their lashes. He controlled himself, an angry pulse throbbing like a cord in the centre of his forehead. 'Begone! Go to your room!' he ordered sternly, and they fled.

'Have you quite finished?' Lalage asked loftily.

He stabbed her with an ice-green stare. 'No!'

She did not retreat or drop her eyes before his fury. Her face was white, masklike and cold under the black, smoke-gleaming hair. 'I think you have left your manners in town, Guy. This is no way to behave in a lady's boudoir.'

'I'll not have my daughters led astray.'

With a toss of the head she seated herself at the mirror once more, carelessly toying with the cosmetic jars. 'How foolish you are. I'm not damaging your precious children. They love spending time in my company. Don't forget they are females, soon to be women. D'you want them thrown on to the marriage market without knowing one end of a man from the other?' She gave a light laugh which he found intensely irritating.

'I want them to preserve their virginity as long as possible,' he barked, face carved into brooding lines. 'Don't rob them of their innocence.'

'Innocence? Ignorance, more like.' Lalage picked up a tiny brush, dipped it in kohl and applied it to her lashes.

'I suppose you'll be giving them *Aristotle's Masterpiece* to read, unless you've already done so.'

'Now you are being quite ridiculous,' she replied dispassionately. 'La, how is it that the greater the whoremaster, the more tiresomely righteous he becomes concerning his own daughters?'

'Christ! I regret having ever taken you to London!' He shouted with a savage energy. 'That's just the sort of remark Aurora would make. I expected you to show a touch more finesse.'

Lalage sighed, seeming to lose interest in enhancing her appearance. Her shoulders drooped, that cloud of hair veiling her face, and she spoke softly, hesitantly, and the hardness had gone out of her voice. 'Oh, dear, I meant no harm, Guy. How sad that we should quarrel at the moment of your return.' She glanced up at him, her eyes shy, almost awed. 'I am truly overjoyed to see you. I've been so lonely, that is the reason why I've sought the friendship of Cecily and Barbara. Selfish of me, I'm afraid, but they are such sweet companions.'

'What of Miranda?' Guardedly, he watched her, resting one hand on the dressing-table. The fluency of his passion was draining away. It vanished into nothing as his attention was caught and held by the poise of her head on that slim, graceful neck.

'Miranda?' Something flickered across her face but was instantly controlled. 'Why, I hardly ever see her. Sally keeps her close at Briar Cottage, and you should reprimand your sister-in-law, Guy. I've only once been invited to visit her. I think that most unfriendly, don't you?'

'I shan't lose any sleep over it,' he answered mockingly. 'Really, my love, I think it hardly likely that Sally and yourself will ever become friends of the bosom.' Then he grew serious, frowning, distressed. 'The child is ill. Did you not know that she was lost yesterday? They found her late at night, hiding in a cave on the beach. There was a high tide and she very nearly drowned.'

'Of course I didn't know! Should I be sitting here in idleness if I had? I'm never told anything! Your mother – Sally – they treat me as a person of no importance!' She half rose, hands on her breasts. He was acutely aware of her by the rustle of her robe, a soft sound filled with seductive sorceries. 'Oh, my poor Guy! How beastly of me to complain, when you are so worried. What can I do? Shall I go to Miranda?'

Guy regretted his anger. After all, his bride was still so young herself, a mere handful of years older than his children. It was her cool, austere mien which made him forget, giving her an illusion of maturity. Time alone would bring this about – time, experience and motherhood. He had been half hoping that she would have good news for him, perhaps a baby had been conceived on their honeymoon, but she said nothing and her body was as slim as ever.

'Leave her in the hands of Dora and Sally,' he said, lifting one of her curling tresses and brushing it across his mouth, inhaling its fragrance, his eyes darkening like a stormy sea. 'But there is something I want you to do.'

'Anything, Guy, simply name it.' Her arms were clasped

about him, fingers smoothing the muscles of his shoulders beneath the fine wool of his coat. She moulded herself into him, with that sensuality which reached out to any promise, any challenge, offering him her lips with teasing languor.

He told her about the injured man at Highfield Lodge, making a joke of it, giving her to understand that the fellow was a smuggler who had been shot escaping from the revenue men. He totally omitted mentioning the labyrinth of adventure and intrigue which was so much a part of his life, heeding that inner voice which warned him to hold back. Lalage laughed delightedly, like a child made privy to some naughty secret, and wanted to leave at once, declaring that she was longing to meet a real live rogue in the flesh.

'I must dress,' she cried excitedly, breaking from him and throwing aside her robe. 'Ring for Bethany, Guy.' She took up the morning-gown which was spread out on a gilt chair.

He made no move towards the red worsted bell-cord, his eyes following her as she glided about the room, completely naked. 'Not yet,' he said, walking towards her. 'I'm going to lock the door. Later, she can attire you.'

A son. That was the main criterion. His brain was on fire with the thought. His life was uncertain now, precarious, and he must waste no opportunity to impregnate her. As he reached for that perfect body he forgot those sensations of disquiet which her behaviour often aroused. Lalage was all woman then – giving, loving, wild, tender and satisfying. A child of nature, without guile or calculation.

Miranda was desperately ill. Dr Rowsell diagnosed pneumonia, but Sally knew instinctively that there was something else contributing to her rapid decline. She lacked the will to live. The days and nights overlapped, flowing into one another. Sally never left the sick-room. Miranda was wasted, a tiny, shrunken figure with deep bluish crescents under the fever-bright eyes. When Sally lifted her to change the sheets or shake up the pillows, it was like holding a doll cut out of paper, fragile, likely to blow away at the least puff of wind.

People came and went; William and Guy, Denzil and Jack, even the Dowager braved the weather, accompanied by Chalmers, Cecily and Barbara. Everyone was awkward, lost for words or if they did speak it was in those hushed, unnatural accents reserved for illness and death. Dora was a comfort and so was Molly, but Sally could not eat or sleep, certain that she must act as a buffer between the child and that unknown thing which was slowly but surely killing her. She dared not relax her vigilance for a second, lest it pounce, bearing Miranda into the dark nether regions for ever. Perhaps it was exhaustion, the feeling of utter helplessness, but seated at the bedside in the long, lonely night hours, she could have sworn that she heard stealthy rustlings, felt rancid breath fanning her cheek – death lurking in the shadows, waiting for Sally's sentinel guard to slip, so that it might wind its bony arms about the child.

Guy called every day, but Sally hardly noticed him, absorbed in bathing Miranda's brow, smoothing salve into her cracked lips or coaxing her to take a sip of water. Most of the time the child lay inert, though occasionally she broke into delirious rambling, heart-rending to hear. Sally tried to make sense of the impressions, recollections and hideous terror, blurred and confused in Miranda's fevered mind.

The doctor had warned her that the crisis was approaching. In a few hours Miranda would recover or die. When he had departed, Molly lifted her in capable arms while Sally spread the bed with fresh sheets and refilled the stone bottles from the kettle constantly bubbling on the trivet. They laid her back tenderly, folding the covers about her. Molly turned and pulled the curtains across the windows. It had been a depressingly dull day, the sky heavy with rain. Shutting it out should have made the nursery a pleasant haven, full of firelight and candleglow, but there was too much sorrow and dread in the atmosphere.

Sally suddenly realized how tired she was, her back ached dully and her bones seemed to be crumbling with fatigue. William tiptoed through the door, coming across to brush her cheek with his lips. She leaned against him briefly, trying to draw strength from his strong body.

'I'll take Molly to the lodge now,' he said gently, his eyes going over her face with worried concern. She looked weary enough to drop, her features gaunt, careless of her appearance, her heavy, corn-bright hair coiled into a loose knot at the back. 'Can you manage alone for a while?'

'How is *Monsieur le Duc*?' she asked listlessly. She had almost forgotten the young man, vaguely remembering that they had told her not to worry as Molly and Lalage were nursing him between them.

'Mending well. He'll soon be fit to travel, thanks to you. He asks after you, my dear, expressing his eternal gratitude. I must say, I'm pleasantly surprised by the resourceful way in which Lalage's behaving. Perhaps she's found her niche at last – needing some purpose.'

It was hard to visualize Lalage dressing wounds and caring for the injured, but after the dramas of the past week, nothing had the power to astonish Sally. Molly was hovering uneasily over Miranda, though she was already dressed for the ride.

'You should've let me try that remedy I suggested, ma'am,' she said with a shake of her head. 'Consumptives are said to be cured by carrying them through a flock of sheep, early in the morning when the animals are first let out of the fold.'

'Miranda is not a consumptive,' Sally replied in a flat, tired voice. They had had this argument several times already.

'Consumption – congestion of the lungs! What's the odds! I've known this cure to work! That doctor ain't doing much good!' Molly did not approve of modern medicine.

Sally imagined Dr Rowsell's face if he called unexpectedly and found them parading his patient through the fields at crack of dawn. Yet there was a great deal to be said for folklore and herbal treatment. Old wives' tales were often proved to be not so far off the mark. She thought about this as she stared into the fire, alone with Miranda. It occurred to her that she should pray, but she had never found solace in religion. From childhood she had hated going to church, shivering every time she passed under the porch. It was so gloomy, steeped in superstition and myth, a means by which the masters and clergy controlled the ignorant. Hellfire. Damnation. Words to frighten them into submission. They had been far happier with their pagan worship of the gods of nature, before Christianity came. A God of love? How could this be if sins were to be punished with eternal fire? That God had not listened to Sally when she begged Him to make Guy love her. Why should He care if Miranda died? One tiny girl among so many countless thousands of children.

Miranda was resting quietly, momentarily free from pain and that hollow, dry cough. Her flaxen curls were plastered damply on her brow under the frilled edge of her night-cap. Sally took one of the hot little hands in hers, caressing the fingers. A tear dripped on to the flesh which looked almost transparent. Sally wiped it off.

'I've come to be with her for a while. I hope you don't mind,' said a voice behind her. Sally had not heard Guy come in.

'It is a wild night. You are wet,' she answered. The capes of his redingote dripped with water and she took it from him, spreading it out near the fire.

He looked so unhappy, so desolate standing there, that her heart ached for him, and the anger which had been gathering through years of his treatment of her, of himself, of those dependent on him, reached a peak at that moment. The time had come for a settlement, and she was glad of it. Yet she held her tongue, waiting for him to speak.

'You are alone?' he asked.

'Yes.'

'And not afraid?'

'No. She needs me.'

They both looked at the child in her small four-poster with its blue curtains. His wealth could not help her now, nor the comforts of this room with its wallpaper of blue and white temples, Chinese bridges and flowers, its carpets, toys and warm fire. It would have made no difference had she lain in some crude hut with the wind whistling through the cracks. The sense of frustrating impotence was the hardest thing to bear.

'I'm sorry, Sally. I spoke to you in anger that night at the lodge. Please forgive me. I was wrong to blame you.' He was so close to her that she could clearly see the new lines, sharp as incisions at the corners of his eyes and around his fine mouth.

She had thought she was beyond surprise, yet could not speak for astonishment. Guy, the lordly and arrogant, was actually apologizing, and to a humble cousin too! She busied herself with the fire, needing something to do while she composed herself. She wished he would leave. He bent down and took the tongs from her, adding further glittering lumps of coal to the red flames, and she looked at him, seeing how the glow defined his hard, handsome features, trying to relate this well-dressed gentleman with the ragged peasant of his dangerous adventures.

There was so much she wanted to ask him concerning this, but she did not quite dare, even now. He would speak of it, when the time was ripe. This was not why he had come; all he wanted to hear was something to soothe his uneasy conscience. 'You do not answer,' he said in a tone of respect and affection which was disarming. 'Am I not pardoned?'

'This is foolish talk.' She could feel herself blushing. 'There's nothing to forgive. You were worried about Miranda, and had just come through a considerable ordeal. I understand.'

'My dear, sweet girl, would that everyone possessed your generous nature,' he countered, with that wonderful charm which he had been able to summon at will ever since he was a boy. Before she knew what was happening, he had bent his tall head and kissed her on the lips.

Sally stepped back, all her hopes, her stern resolutions jarring one another in confusion. 'Please don't praise me,' she faltered, having the absurd desire to weep. 'I only follow the dictates of my heart. I love this family. Every member of it is dear to me, therefore I give what help I can.'

He was looking at her strangely, as if seeing her for the first time. 'Does this love include myself?' he asked softly. 'How odd. I thought that you disliked me.'

Sally took flight at this, moving to the far side of the room, opening a drawer of the tallboy and taking out a completely unnecessary pile of towels. She was petrified; dreaming so often of being alone with him but finding that fate was presenting her with that golden opportunity in a way she had neither wished nor expected.

Silence would be a more damning admission than speech, so: 'I am William's wife. You are kin to me. Naturally, I regard you highly,' she muttered, continuing to rummage among the linen, keeping her back to him.

'How very circumspect and proper.' His voice came from behind her, and there was a trace of irony in it. 'I'm flattered that you can find it in your compassionate heart to tolerate, nay even feel sisterly love for so great a villain as myself.'

She knew that he was standing very near her. His shadow blocked out the light. She could feel his breath on her hair as he spoke. Then his hands were at her waist, and he turned her slowly round to face him. So deep and intent was his scrutiny of her that it was a second before she realized that she was returning that probing gaze.

She was trembling, so tired that the fight had left her, but a vestige of pride remained, somewhere in her being. 'Guy –' she whispered, pleaded yet commanded.

He held her a moment more, then: 'Let me carry those for you.' He took the towels from her arms and she was aware that she was holding the bundle like a buckler before her. He smiled. 'After all, I'm here to assist my loving sister-in-law.'

She winced under the sarcasm, and the mockery in his eyes. 'Perhaps it would be better if you were to leave now,' she murmured unsteadily.

She was shocked by his lightning change of mood. 'Leave?' he cried wrathfully. 'Like hell I will! Miranda is my daughter, not yours. I have a father's right to be here!'

'Aren't you remembering your paternal duty a little late in the day?' she parried, escaping to the bedside.

'Tsha! You think I've been cruel to her, unfeeling? No matter. When the chips are down, she's my own flesh and blood – my child!' he reasserted harshly.

'When it suits you!' she flashed.

'It never suits me,' he replied, in a fresh excess of rage. 'I wanted sons, not a pack of girls!'

Sally's face was white. How dare he come here and feel no humility in the presence of the sick child? Let him hear a few home-truths, the high-handed brute! 'How galling it must have been to find that in such a matter even *you* could not play God! Well, my Lord, you may be relieved of the burden of one of your despised female-children before the night is out.'

A spasm crossed his face, as if a sharp pain had shot through him. 'Oh, Sally – Sally.' His voice broke. He turned and leaned his head on his arms against the fireplace. 'You're right. I have treated Miranda badly. Everything in me turns to evil. Was I the cause of her sickness? If I believed that, I would never forgive myself.'

Miranda began to toss restlessly. Sally forgot Guy, on her knees by the bed, holding her hand, speaking soothingly, using little endearments and pet-names, hardly aware of what she was saying or doing. The fever was at its height, and the child struggled to sit up, a peculiar light in her eyes as she stared through Sally, crying pitifully: 'She's coming! Oh, don't let her burn me!'

Guy was there, his arm going round her shuddering form. 'It's all right, Miranda. No one is going to hurt you.'

Her eyes switched to his face, starting in terror, but she knew him. 'Papa! Papa! Keep her away!'

Her distress was awful to witness. Guy swore under his breath and gathered her up in his arms, wrapped in her warm bedding. He held her tightly against his chest and paced the room, while she sobbed and stared at some invisible apparition which seemed terrifyingly real, not a fever-created image.

'There's no one here, my love,' he kept repeating. 'Only Sally and I, who love you.'

'She's here! She's here! She's everywhere!' the child gasped. 'She's going to take me to hell!'

'Who is it? Who do you see?' Sally stopped Guy, her hands on Miranda's face, striving to capture her wandering attention.

'I can't tell you. She made me promise.' Miranda's strength was failing. Her head lolled back and she was limp in her father's arms.

'Oh, my God!' Sally whispered. 'Guy! Do something. We're going to lose her.'

'Jesus Christ!' he muttered, completely at a loss. 'What can I do?'

The candlelight seemed to have dimmed. Even the fire was sullen, dull. The room grew dark and was filled with a strange thrumming. Sally's scalp pricked and she almost dragged Miranda from Guy's hold. 'Fight it!' she screamed. 'She believes you to be invincible. Show her you can fight it and win!'

A desperate madness had seized them both. Guy picked up the brass poker and using it like a sword, challenged the black nothingness on which Miranda's eyes were fixed. '*En garde!*' he shouted. 'Back! Back, you fiend who dares to frighten my child! Take that! And that!' He lunged savagely. A stool went flying and there was a crash as he knocked over a small table.

Back and forth he stamped, the poker gleaming rapier-like. He was duelling with his own black shadow, huge, misshapen, flung against the wall, using every trick Giaconi had taught him. The room rocked and shook, but whether from the force of his feet or from something beyond their dimension, Sally did not know. In that frenzied moment, everything was insanely confused, and she could not tell what was up and what down.

Miranda lifted her head and watched her father, that glazed, hypnotic look clearing from her eyes. 'Papa is fighting for me.' There was a note of wonder in her feeble whisper, but her grip on Sally was firm, life flooding back into her.

'He loves you, Miranda. He will always defend you.' The words came unbidden to Sally's lips.

With one final lightning-swift lunge, Guy pinned the shadow to the wall. The candles stopped wavering, burning brightly with a strong flame. The atmosphere lifted, clear and calm as a summer morning at daybreak. Guy laid the poker back on the hearth. He was sweating profusely for the fight had been taxing, the enemy strong and cunning. In silence, Sally handed him his daughter, and he sank down into the armchair, cradling her on his lap. She snuggled against his chest, gave a yawn and a sigh and went to sleep.

In a while he stood up and replaced her in the bed. Very delicately for so large a man, he pulled the coverlet over her. She was sleeping normally, head to one side on the pillow, lashes clinging to her cheeks to which the colour had returned, her little ear, wreathed in a wisp of curls, invited the benediction of a kiss. Guy leaned over and placed his lips there. 'Goodnight, my darling,' he whispered.

Sally meanwhile had righted the table and was seated at it, wrapped in the peace of utter exhaustion and relief. Guy moved one of the candles to get a better view of her features, but she still looked down at the surface, fingers fidgeting with the lace cloth. He wiped his face with his kerchief and took a chair.

'Thank God,' he said. 'The crisis has passed and Miranda will live. What happened here in this room? It was most strange. I've scoffed at the notion of the powers of darkness, but Lord – did I imagine it or was I really fighting an invisible opponent?'

'I don't know.' Sally had given up trying to be rational. The whole episode was unreal. To be talking with him like this, to have him sitting at her side, had something fantastic about it, like dreaming in broad daylight.

His fist clenched on the table. 'I'll get to the bottom of the matter. If someone has been frightening her and, by God, it looks very like, they'll live to regret crossing my path.'

'Leave it alone, Guy.' Impulsively she covered that hard fist with her hand. 'She's still very weak. There's a long period of convalescence ahead. Don't question her. Do nothing to resurrect her fears. You alone can aid her recovery. She trusts you. It is your chance to prove yourself her knight in shining armour. You won't abandon her again, will you?'

She could tell by the expression on his face that the child had become most dear to him. No longer need she stand alone, shielding Miranda from ignorance and cruelty. The realization and relief were so acute that she began to cry, without a sound, face buried in her hands, the tears running from between her fingers.

Guy put his arms about her, held her trembling body close to his heart. She cried for a long time, he consoling her and stroking her hair.

Chapter 3

'Supposing you find that you're up the gut? What'll you do?' asked Jack from his position on the moth-eaten fur rug in front of the roaring fire.

'My God, Jack, your language. Master of subtility, that's you! Were I to find myself with child, I suppose you mean?' The flames bathed Lalage's naked flesh, touching it with gold and crimson. She was on her knees, smiling down at him. 'I should tell my loving husband that I was carrying the heir he so greatly desires. He would be delighted.'

Jack rolled a mouthful of whisky appreciatively round his mouth before swallowing it. 'You *are* a bitch, aren't you?' he said musingly. 'You'd let the poor bugger live in ignorance, raising a brat that could be anybody's.'

'Not just anybody's.' She hugged her knees, staring into the blazing heart of the fire. 'I've been careful to keep it in the family. Guy, Denzil and you. If I become pregnant, and I say "if", for I use methods to prevent such an unfortunate occurrence, then the child will be a Wylde, whichever of you is the father.' She gave him a calculating glance. 'Come on, Jack, admit it. Wouldn't it give you a certain satisfaction to know that perhaps it was your son who would eventually become Lord of Beaumaris Combe?'

'Cunning vixen,' Jack commented with grudging admiration. 'You've worked it out well. Don't slip up and include your patient in the group. Raoul adores you, and he doesn't resemble a Wylde in the least. Can't have you farrowing down with a by-blow who has French blood in its veins.'

'No fear of that.' She flicked her hair from her face and lounged back on her elbows. The dancing firelight caressed the upthrust of her breasts, deep mauve shadows contrasting with the orange glow, running down across her belly to the dark triangle between her legs. 'Were you not so singularly unobservant, Jack, you'd have known that he's a sodomite, in love with that smuggler boy-friend of his. I expect they're in bed together at this very moment.'

Jack grunted, wrestling with the strong emotions of lust and

288

loathing which she had the power to arouse. Her remarks concerning his illegitimate birth were brutally accurate. Perhaps this was what lay at the core of their strange alliance; the resentful anger, the ill-concealed envy of the underdog had set a sympathetic chord vibrating between them. How well he understood that passion of hate, that longing for redress. An eye for an eye was no bad law at that!

'We're two of a kind, you and I,' he commented thoughtfully.

'Oh, no, Jack. I walk alone. I need no friend, no companion, no lover. My philosophy is simple – to stay free, to make love with anyone who interests me, and to die young whilst I'm still beautiful.' She spoke with cold restraint, without raising her voice or making a movement, her tone even, monotonous.

'I'm certain that you'll fulfil that last ambition,' Jack said with sharp irony, giving her a venomous glance. 'Someone is bound to cut your throat before long.'

'Why?' She looked at him with wide, innocent eyes. 'I am most careful not to offend. No one would wish to harm a hair of my head. Do I not conduct myself with the utmost decorum?'

'Oh, aye – when you're not gadding around in breeches,' reminded Jack, thinking what a fascinatingly amoral creature she was. Angelic-daemonic; like a terrible, plague-bringing comet.

'I may be forgiven that small eccentricity. Society likes to be a trifle shocked. It titillates their jaded palates.' She gave a careless lift of her shoulders, and Jack remembered her appearances in London and the gossip which, in his position of half servant, half confidant, had reached his ears. Oh, yes, she charmed them all, totally misleading them with her aloof loveliness, her sad story.

'You hypocrite.' There was a bite to his laughter, although he enjoyed seeing those who thought themselves his superiors fooled. 'What an act! I've seen you, driving to take tea with some snobbish dame or other, looking as pure as if you'd come straight from church where you'd been earnestly begging the saints to take you back to heaven!'

She rocked with silent laughter. 'I enjoy every role I play. Perhaps I should have been an actress.'

Jack sat up, his hand on her arm, fingering that silky skin. 'And which part d'you play when you're with me? Is it a part? Or are you sincere?' Anger and contempt were reflected in his face, but it had no effect on the hard clarity of her expression.

She shook off his hand. 'I don't know. You're a brute, Jack, and crude. You amuse me.'

'Do I indeed.' His sensual mouth was grim. 'In reality, I'd be doing mankind a service if I wrung your neck.'

'Such harsh words, Jack.' She wriggled closer, winding her arms about him, her tongue exploring the velvety rim of his ear. 'Wouldn't you miss this – and this?' Her hand had wandered to his groin.

Jack was breathing hard. 'There are plenty of other trollops,' he rasped, curbing the desire to strike her. 'Be still, woman. There are times when you sicken me.' She recoiled sharply, glaring at him. 'You haven't told me what happened to Miranda,' he went on. 'I suppose you're aware that she nearly died? Your handiwork, I'll wager.'

'I don't know what you're talking about.' Her face was masked.

'Her fright was nothing to do with you? Come off it! Don't play the innocent with me. This is Jack, who can read your rotten little soul, remember?'

'Perhaps I did scare her – just a bit.'

'My God, the poor lass,' he said sombrely. 'I hope that Guy never finds out or I wouldn't give you tuppence for your chances.'

In his experience in the debased slums of St Giles, among the boozing-kens, the opium-dens, the brothels where the lowest kind of diseased, desperate women put themselves up for hire, Jack had never met her like. He did not trust her an inch, and had not agreed with Guy's decision to bring her to Highfield Lodge. On the surface, she appeared to be satisfied that Raoul and his friend were hiding from the coastguards, but one could never tell what she was thinking. The sooner they left the better, and Jack hoped that Guy would take Lalage with him when he next went to London. Though he could not resist her, he had been disgusted at the alacrity with which she had seized upon the chance of frequent visits to the lodge, coupling with him after attending to Raoul. Somehow, it was an affront to his masculinity. The male should be the pursuer, the conquerer, not the woman.

Yet even as these thoughts flashed through his mind he was conscious of her fingers snaking up his bare leg, fondling his knee, his thigh, crafty fingers which knew just the right zones for manifold pleasure. Damn her. The witch. The infernal sorceress! To assert his supremacy, he flung her down on her back, holding her roughly, one knee jabbing between her legs, bruising the tender flesh on the inside of her thighs. He was poised there, about to thrust into her, when the door opened and Denzil walked in.

'Hell and damnation!' Jack muttered as their eyes locked and he saw the shocked look of utter disbelief which faded swiftly into anger on the young man's face.

Denzil had been transported with delight when Lalage came to nurse Raoul. He had given them plenty of scope for love-making, and because he spent more time there than at Wylde Court, he was able to avoid Guy and keep his illusions of bliss until the moment when he stepped into the shabby, dusty room. A shiver ran through him. It was as though he had been sleeping on his feet, and awakened. Everything was crystal clear to him. His glance took in each detail, weighing its tawdriness, its self-indulgence, its sordid, furtive complications which rose up like mud in a stagnant pool when a stick stirs the water.

The naked man and woman fused together in front of the fire seemed to freeze for an instant, and it could have been himself there with Lalage, and Guy walking in on them. What was the expression? *Flagrante delicto* – caught in the act – while the crime was blazing.

Because he wanted to kill her, Denzil turned tail and fled. As he ran down the staircase, the old house rattled and squealed about him, the faded hangings, rickety furniture, dust-grimed portraits flashing past with the speed of his escape. The place was ruinous and terribly cold, but outside in the yard it was colder by far. Through the dusk the frost sparkled like rhinestones, but Denzil was blind to the chill, blind to everything, flinging himself on his horse and galloping off towards the bare, windswept moors.

Molly was coming across the cobbles, basket over her arm. She halted in her tracks, staring at him with a frown, sensing his urgency, seeing trouble written all over his set face. He was riding as if chased by demons and she lingered by the door, puzzled by his violent exit, her eyes on the bleak ridges of the heathlands, where the clouds swirled and shifted in the distance.

'You are late, Mrs Smithers,' said Lalage crisply, coming out through the door, tall, regal in her cape of purple velvet, sable-trimmed, a huge muff on one arm. 'The patient requires a meal. See to it.'

'I'm aware of that, my Lady.' Molly stared back, almost as tall, very nearly as proud. She had never bowed the knee to any woman, and had no intention of setting a precedent with this foreign hussy.

Jack was at Lalage's heels, and his mother gave him a shrewd stare. He looked sheepish, despite his swagger and, knowing him inside out, Molly guessed that he had been up to something. 'I'm going to drive Lady Beaumaris to the manor,' he vouchsafed, then made a too-late offer: 'Shall I carry the basket into the kitchen for you, Ma?'

'I can manage,' she answered tartly, letting him know by the inflection in her voice, her narrowed look, that he might be able to pull the wool over other people's eyes, but not hers.

He was shuffling his feet uncomfortably, and she felt a bit sorry for him. She loved him and he was a son to be proud of in his fine clothing. She could even trace Mark's features in his face, and yet this was blurred by a certain coarseness. He was a rogue, unprincipled and immoral, she knew that, but he had never treated her badly. The rapport between them had been strong, until lately. When she had tackled him about Miranda, he had been surly, uncommunicative. She had been able to get nothing from the villagers either, never on close terms with them. If someone had 'witched' the child, they would not tell her.

'We'll be getting on then, Mother!' He attempted to be jovial. Lalage was waiting for him, that uncanny stillness about her.

'I've just seen Mr Denzil.' Molly put their reaction to the test. 'Riding towards Round Tor as if the gabble-hounds were after him. Looked black as thunder, he did.'

'Perhaps he's had a row with Lord Beaumaris,' Jack answered, a shade too quickly.

'Are you going to stand there gossiping all night?' Lalage's accented voice struck across, colder than the twilight.

Molly did not go into the house at once but watched them cross the yard and disappear into the stable. Her intuition was speaking to her, a voice she always heeded. Trouble was brewing. She could snuff it in the air.

The London winter season was in full swing. A frenetic gaiety swept through the fashionable crowd who now thronged each other's houses, attended balls, concerts and the opera. The gentlemen did their duty and escorted their ladies to every smart function, but their happiest hours were spent in another form of entertainment.

They were sociable animals, and their aristocratic clubs gave them ample scope for expressing that genial *bonhomie* towards one another which would have astonished many a wife who found her husband a boring, miserly tyrant at home. In the strictly masculine atmosphere of these establishments they could relax, complete business deals, discuss the news, compare notes about the prices of various brothels, and argue the merits of paying six guineas for a whole night in the arms of a lively, high-class whore or of giving some drab a sixpence for a quick coupling up against a wall in an alley. Gambling was the main preoccupation of these clubs where they could waste their money on silly wagers, and sit up all night mortgaging their properties on the turn of a card. Places and promotion went by nepotism and favour and it was essential for an ambitious man to be a member of one or the other. The clubs had risen originally from the popular coffee-houses. White's had been going strong for years, and Brook's had started life as Almack's in 1764, but had changed hands and name in 1778.

It was in the sacred precincts of Brook's that Ambrose met Guy one evening. It was early and not all the regulars had yet arrived. They strolled into one of the large gaming-rooms, a beautiful apartment with an arched ceiling festooned with plaster-work, scrolls and wreaths, panelled walls, fine long oval windows and a large mirror, standing fully seven foot high and five feet wide, above the marble fireplace where a coal fire roared. Glittering crystal chandeliers adequately lit the many small round tables. The chairs at two of these were already filled, and each player had a small, neat stand at his elbow on which was placed a wooden bowl to hold his money.

Robert Burgess was sitting on a damask-covered couch near the fire, reading a newspaper. They joined him, going over topics of the day, the war and the happenings in France. Ambrose expressed amusement at the fact that England had been unprepared for war and yet this did not seem to trouble her people in the least. They never for a moment doubted that they would win.

'Win? Of course we shall win!' growled a fiery old gentleman from the depths of the leather wing-chair which he habitually occupied. He had the purple-veined swollen nose and rubicund complexion of the heavy drinker, and wore an elaborate wig, thickly powdered. His cravat bore the rusty stains of snuff, and he kept a pinch between his fingers for much of the time. He glared at Ambrose, noting his American drawl and dubbing him a foreigner.

'I'm not casting doubt on your victory,' replied Ambrose, lounging on the couch, one long elegant thigh crossed over the other. 'Egad, I'm well aware that anything which looks like a fight is delicious to an Englishman.'

A flunkey stepped, soft-footed as a cat, across the highly polished parquet floor. He bowed and presented a tray of drinks. The old man snorted and took a glass of claret, still regarding Ambrose with ill-concealed contempt. 'Damned Frenchies! I hate all foreigners, particularly the Frogs. Before I learned there was a God to be worshipped, I learned that there were Frenchmen to be detested! You're American, ain't you? Dammee, one of that treacherous crew!'

'Surely, you don't hate the *noblesse* of France, do you, sir? Their sufferings are terrible,' interposed Guy, irritated by the old man's sweeping statements.

'A Frenchie is a Frenchie, whether peasant or prince,' he answered huffily, signalling to the manservant to top up his glass. 'Don't trust 'em. Never have, never will. Know how to get 'em riled though,' he chuckled wheezily. 'I just say to 'em – "remember Agincourt"! That gets their dander up!'

He banged on the floor with his stick. Several dedicated gamesters, engaged in the ritual of hazard, turned to hush him crossly. He ignored them, embarrassing Robert, for he was his uncle, Lord Delbeigh. The old could be most irksome sometimes.

'We're fighting the regicides, uncle, not the Royalists,' he shouted, trying to penetrate the solid wall of Delbeigh's self-opinionated despotism.

'A pack of bloody-minded roughnecks,' added Ambrose, amused at Robert's perturbation. 'Because cruelty and mass slaughter have won their ends swiftly, they've glorified them, calling them liberty and justice.'

'What d'you know about it, sir?' Delbeigh rested both hands on the knob of his cane and leaned forward, bleary eyes trying to focus. 'You Americans and your Boston tea-party! It should never have been allowed. You're a dandified poltroon, and I wonder that you've the confounded gall to sit in a club with true-born Englishmen!'

'You know Mr Alington, uncle,' Robert protested, with a

shame-faced grimace at Ambrose. 'He's from South Carolina, descended from the finest British stock.'

'Good evening, gentlemen,' called Augustus Sanderman, who had just entered the room. 'May I be permitted to join you?'

Before anyone could reply, the crusty old Lord gave him a fierce glare. 'God's teeth,' he snapped grumpily. 'I don't know what this damned club's coming to. Think I'll resign. The air stinks, don't-cher-know – now lawyers are granted membership! Your cravat is fit for a footman, sir! But what can one expect from a fellow engaged in such a trade? I've the misfortune to employ one myself, an unmannerly varlet who keeps his hat on his head whilst speaking to me! D'you know what they say about lawyers, Sanderman? Do you, eh? They are likened to insomniacs – they lie first on one side, turn round and lie on t'other! Ha! Ha! Did you hear that, Robert? He! He! A capital joke, what?'

Sanderman remained cool, whilst Delbeigh went off into throaty chuckles which ended in a choking spasm. His face turned puce and he thumped himself on the chest, rendered temporarily speechless, to the relief of everyone.

'Do sit down, Sanderman,' said Guy, waving him into a chair. 'I didn't expect to see you tonight. I thought you were accompanying my wife to the opera.' There had been an argument about this, for Lalage did not want to see the performance, until he had mentioned casually that the Prince would be there.

'I shall go later,' Sanderman answered suavely, perching on the edge of the seat like a fastidious sparrow. 'I understand that her Ladyship will be in Lady Mortmorcy's box. May I welcome you back to London, Lord Beaumaris. And how is the health of Miss Miranda? I was so sad to hear that she had been unwell.'

Guy's face softened. 'She is recovering, thank you. William's wife, Sally, is looking after her.'

The lawyer expressed his delight in pat phrases, but his eyes had wandered to the door where several newcomers were now standing. *Émigrés* who had escaped from that seething cauldron of revolt, taking with them little except their lives. They were quiet and grave, bereft of the benefits which centuries of privilege had given them, their eyes haunted by the horror of seeing family and friends destroyed, their King and Queen executed. De Belcourt was among them, and his eyes met those of Ambrose who gave a brief inclination of the head then turned his broad shoulder away, saying to Guy from the side of his mouth:

'Put me in irons, my friend, lest I be tempted to accept his challenge at faro. He's reckless, and gets so bloody heated when I win. There's something about him which brings out the worst in me. Odd, though he consistently loses, he never seems to be short of money.'

Sanderman was sighing over the lot of the refugees. 'They have my deepest sympathy, poor souls. How sad is their state. To what a pass have they come.'

Delbeigh had recovered, aided by a further glass of claret, but his voice was husky as he declared with mounting indignation: 'That's all very well, but do they have to invade our clubs? I don't like the way they've been received with open arms. I shouldn't be surprised to find spies among 'em. We are at war with France, dammit! I hope Burke and Pitt know what they're doing!'

Ambrose watched and listened whilst appearing to be almost asleep. In reality, he was seeking an opportunity to have a private word with Guy. He was worried about the safety of his cousin, Hercule de St Croix. Ambrose's mother had been a daughter of the House of St Croix whose father had settled in Martinique. Her brother had remained on the family estate in Brittany, and his son, Hercule, was the present marquis. Ambrose had visited him, early on in the troubles, finding that he had been permitted to stay in his chateau with his son and two daughters, living in rather straightened circumstances. Now, since the abortive uprising in the Royalist areas of Bordeaux, Gironde and La Vendée, a second wave of Terror made it imperative that the St Croixs get out fast.

Ambrose did not particularly like the haughty Hercule, for he was filled with bitter hatred against those who had contributed to the downfall of the aristocracy, making no attempt to understand when Ambrose had pointed out that there was something necessary and even good in the changes. They had debated the matter at some length, there in that gracious chateau high on its rise overlooking the peat marshes. Ambrose could not agree with him that the ideas of Rousseau, Diderot and Tom Paine were wrong, simply saying that the revolutionaries had no right to dictate what mankind should or should not do, and that there would be no peace or prosperity in France until those who had seized power had learnt the elementary lesson of decency and fair dealing.

The marquis had refused to listen to his moderate opinions, furious because the Assembly had renounced all immunities, exemptions and privileges, feudal dues and fines, tithes, the salt tax, the game laws, in fact everything which the nobility had looked upon as their undisputed right. He had been associated with Court life, and a long stay at Versailles and St Cloud had done nothing to soften his approach to the lower orders. Nothing would change him. He was too told, too set in his ways. Ambrose knew this, recognizing in him the sort of man who would climb the steps of the scaffold with a sneer on his lips, cursing the rabble. He must be saved, in spite of himself. There was his son, Henri, to consider, and the two daughters, pretty, pampered creatures of fourteen and sixteen. The Convention had now decreed that all youngsters should learn a trade. This was the best that could be hoped for them, followed by marriage to some farmer or shop-keeper. At worst, they might be seized by a drunken, inflamed mob and given to the men for sport before they were killed.

Ambrose was roused from these gloomy speculations by Delbeigh, who was still ranting on. 'They can't even hunt. A Frenchie capers about the field, and no more thinks of leaping a hedge than of mounting a breach!'

'I'm surprised that you are not attending the theatre tonight, Mr Alington,' Sanderman remarked with a sly smile. 'All the fair ladies of London will be present.'

Ambrose pretended not to have heard that remark. He turned to Guy. 'Shall we try our luck at Swobbers?' and he jerked his thumb in the direction of the faro table.

As they left to take their places among the gamesters, they could hear Delbeigh grumbling: '*Liberté! Égalité!* What consummate rot! If any of my farm-workers tried it, I'd hang 'em at their own front doors!'

Aurora and Lalage met at the Ranelagh, a favourite haunt which combined the advantages of assembly-hall and concert-room. It had a gallery round three sides, reached by two staircases, and under this were small, secluded recesses ideal for supper-parties.

They had arrived earlier than usual for the opera began at eight o'clock, and they were not alone. Half a dozen gentlemen had gallantly offered to escort them, for the company at the Ranelagh was very mixed, peers and pickpockets, honourables and dishonourables rubbing shoulders. Aurora flirted and exchanged *risqué* repartee with these handsome members of the *haut ton*, her vanity satisfied at being seen with the smartest bucks in town. It even consoled her a little for the fact that Ambrose had declined her invitation, preferring Brook's and the companionship of Guy.

She suspected that it was the prospect of seeing Lalage which had made him refuse. They prowled around each other suspiciously since the phaeton race, sometimes making contact, sometimes not. Aurora knew that he disliked Guy's wife, a feeling which she shared in full measure but, obeying his instructions, she made sure that they spent much time together. This was easy to accomplish, and the two women were the focus of attention at every gathering. Aurora was aware of an ambiguous feeling towards Lalage, drawn yet curiously repelled. Lalage won over and interested everyone she met, and it seemed that she was determined that she and Aurora should be very dear friends. This suited Aurora's plans to perfection. Above all things, she wanted to please Ambrose.

He had told her that he was still puzzled by Lalage's accent and the memory of seeing her somewhere, in an entirely different set of circumstances, the details of which continued to elude him. So Aurora watched her opportunities, and insinuated rather than urged her inquiries into Lalage's background, but no matter what subtle tactics she employed, they resulted in failure. Lalage always exercised an ever wakeful reserve with respect to herself and anything connected with her former life, persisting in her story that she was suffering from amnesia. These evasions were always conducted with sadness and passionate declarations of her fondness for Aurora, her trust in her, and with vague promises that she should be the first to know if memory suddenly returned. Aurora was as much in the dark as she had been on that day when Guy had carried Lalage to El Skala.

Filled with good food and fine wine, the ladies and two of the beaux entered Aurora's carriage whose brown exterior was emblazoned with her coat of arms on the gleaming side-panels. It had yellow velvet lining and Savonnerie carpet, soft cushions, and well-fitting window panes which never rattled. The door closed, the uniformed footmen jumped up behind, the outriders spurred on, the postillions cracked their whips, the horses plunged and broke into a canter, followed at the same rapid pace by others bearing the rest of the gentlemen.

The cold of the evening, with its light sprinkling of snow, did not affect them in their warm cloaks. When they alighted at Covent Garden Theatre, one of their escorts threw a few coins to the beggars who hung around the splendid entrance, avoiding the staves of the sturdy, liveried porters on guard. They stared at the rich going in to be entertained, eyes huge in those pinched faces, the icy wind whipping their meagre clothing about their emaciated bodies. Most of them had rags bound around their bare feet in an attempt to preserve their toes from frost bite. Those carelessly flung coins would provide a little gin, a little opium. Soon they would be unaware of cold and hunger.

Coaches jostled for place before the magnificent portico of the theatre, disgorging their fashionable occupants. Rich's opera-house had suffered a full reconstruction in the previous year, carried out by the architect, Henry Holland, who had worked on the Prince's own Carlton House. Up the steps swept Lalage and Aurora, admiring the gorgeous decorations where everything was of fawn, with green and gold panels. The auditorium was in the lyral form, solid in appearance, overflowing with carvings and fluted columns, the fronts of the boxes forming bulges like the curve of a ship's side. The cappings of these were of green morocco leather, as were the upholstered seats. The effect was grand and imposing, and the excitement of the audience rose to a crescendo when the Prince of Wales entered the Royal box. He was a musician himself, often playing the 'cello in Joseph Handel's orchestra. He insisted on the finest players and singers in any work which he graced with his presence. There was a current vogue for Italian artists, and no expense was spared. Even those who did not care for music and were only there because it was the done thing, had to cease their chatter and pay attention when the conductor raised his baton and the performance began. The Prince would tolerate no interference with his enjoyment.

During the first interval, when the fops had opened the bottles of champagne carried into the box by their servants, Augustus Sanderman slipped into a vacant seat close to Lalage, and de Belcourt appeared also. While keeping up a light-hearted stream of gossip with her escorts, and bowing and signalling with her fan to other admirers in the pit, Aurora watched Lalage, deep in conversation with the lawyer and the Frenchman. She was curious to know what Sanderman was whispering into Lalage's ear. He was speaking earnestly and rapidly but there was too much noise for Aurora to catch any of the conversation.

'Are you expecting Ambrose tonight?' Lalage inquired when, the performance over, they were alone in the carriage, bowling through the dark streets.

'No,' answered Aurora. 'He's gambling at Brook's.'

'So is Guy.' Lalage hesitated, then added: 'May I come in for a while? I'm not sleepy, are you?'

Aurora was tired but she found her bedchamber lonely and the bed itself far too wide for one person, when Ambrose was not there. Now that the glitter and glamour of the evening were over, she dreaded her own company, knowing that she would lie awake, staring at the draperies of her vulgarly grandiose four-poster, and worrying. Something had happened of such tremendous importance that it had shaken her brash confidence to the very foundations. She was pregnant. There was no doubt that it was Ambrose's child, but she could not pluck up the courage to tell him. This shamed and annoyed her. She was acting with the shrinking trepidation of a peasant wench seduced by her feudal lord. Supposing he were to scorn her? She was terrified that he would walk out of her life for ever, if he felt the trap closing.

Tilly had gone to bed. Aurora had told her not to wait up, but the fire had been banked high and the room was warm. The pug was asleep in her satin-lined basket with her puppies. They had been born six weeks before, a most exciting event. They were now old enough to stagger about, and there was the constant flurry of mopping up after them when they squatted and made puddles on the carpet. Aurora adored them, realizing soon after their arrival that this urge to pet baby creatures was nothing more than the awakening of her own maternal feelings and this, more than a missed period, had sent her in panicky flight to her physician, where her suspicions had been confirmed.

Lalage, as always, sought the warmth of the fire. 'How cold England is,' she said. 'I miss the Mediterranean sun. Do you remember Morocco, Aurora? That gloriously warm country where all the colours of the rainbow seemed to have been mixed in a vast pot and poured haphazardly over everything – over people's clothes, over the magnificent palaces and mosques, over the sunsets and the soil itself.' There was a strange, intense hunger in Lalage's voice. It made her unusually vulnerable.

Aurora shot her a glance, sensing a chink in her armour and prolonging this by agreeing with her, and adding: 'I loved to see the Rifan women, coming to market from miles around. They wore such implausible, huge straw hats covered with ribbons, pompoms and little mirrors. I meant to buy one and startle London by appearing in it, but I never did.'

'Perhaps we'll visit El Skala again one day. I'll ask Guy.' Lalage fell silent, her face shuttered once more.

Aurora poured out two glasses of wine and sat on the walnut day-bed, letting her cloak slide away from her beautiful, sloping white shoulders. Her gown sparkled with sequins. Without waiting to be invited, Lalage sank down beside her.

'Your gallants went their separate ways, I presume?' Aurora said lightly, half wishing that she had not asked her in, but hoping that the intimacy and the wine might make her divulge the content of her deep discussion with the lawyer and de Belcourt.

'Oh, yes, and I'm glad. Those two can be rather tiresome. Isn't it pleasant to be here, on our own, without the company of men?' Lalage loosened her manteau. She was wearing red velvet, very simply cut, with long narrow sleeves and a plunging neckline. Diamonds shone at her throat and ears, family heirlooms which Guy had given her.

'I like men. Don't you?' Aurora laughed, but she was aware that Lalage was in an odd mood, her movements languid, eyes bright and shining.

She shrugged. 'Sometimes I like them – sometimes they bore me. Half of them are so unskilled in the art of making love. Don't you find this so, my dear? Oh, they grunt and thrust and sweat and waste a great deal of effort, striving after their own fulfilment, expecting us to achieve it too. Most offended if we fail, due to their clumsy, insensitive handling of our bodies. Very few know how to bring a woman to ecstasy. Don't you agree?'

This was strange talk indeed, and Aurora replied: 'I like a lusty bed-fellow. There's nothing to match a virile male.'

Lalage smiled mysteriously, one winged eyebrow lifting. 'No? This has not been my experience.' Her voice was husky, and she drew a tiny phial from her reticule, flipping back the silver stopper and allowing several drops of dark brown liquid to fall into her wine. 'Will you have some?' she offered it to Aurora.

'What is it?' Aurora knew, but she was playing for time.

'Laudanum – tincture of the divine poppy,' Lalage answered dreamily, lifting the glass to her lips. 'It is wonderfully soothing. Try it.'

Aurora shook her head. She had partaken of the drug several times, enjoying the dizzying sensation and the dreams which it evoked, but she was thinking of the little creature curled in the depths of her womb. She had not intended to conceive it, but now that it was there, she would do nothing to harm it. Ambrose's child. The thought made her lips curl in a soft smile. She would tell him when next they met. To hell with his reaction. If he did not want to marry her, then she would simply retire to her country seat and live there quietly, peacefully, with her baby.

Lalage was talking, telling her about her dreams and the sweet lethargy which came with the blessing of the poppy draught. Her voice droned on, and under the spell of bodily fatigue, the warmth of the fire, the wine she had drunk, Aurora was nearly asleep. Those murmured words were like a lullaby, soothing her into a trance from which she was rudely aroused by the feel of a hand on hers.

Her lids flew open, and she met Lalage's eyes. They contained the burning ardour of a lover; hateful and yet overpowering. Aurora experienced a strange rush of tumultuous excitement, mingled with fear and disgust. It was as if a boyish suitor had found his way into her bedroom disguised as a girl. Good God! she thought. Here will be a piece of news for Ambrose!

She moved to the far side of the couch. 'I'm weary, Lalage,' she said faintly. 'My coachman will drive you to Doric House.'

Lalage continued to look at her with those compelling eyes, fringed by thick black lashes. She smiled in a kind of rapture. 'Why are you holding back?' she whispered. 'You have nothing to fear. Why not yield to exquisite temptation? I can show you pleasures that you've never dreamed existed.'

'My life is already filled with pleasure,' Aurora retorted smartly. 'I've seen most things – experimented in many ways. I'm quite certain that you could teach me nothing new.' But even as she spoke she was visualizing softness, darkness, smooth embraces shared with a being who would know her needs. Not some hard, angular male, in love with his own virility and ego, but someone with sensitive hands and lips, using sensual caresses – a soul-mate – another woman.

She was scared by this glimpse into her own psyche, shuddering from it as if it were a kind of moral leprosy. She rose quickly, and so did Lalage. Aurora thought she was going to stop her from reaching the bell-pull near the fireplace. She did not, however, watching her and smiling. A footman appeared at the door and Aurora handed Lalage her wrap.

'Goodnight,' she said firmly. 'Please do not forget that your husband and yourself are engaged to dine with me tomorrow evening.'

'Are you quite certain?' asked Molly when she opened the mill door to Dora, on that same night, down in Beaumaris Combe.

The moon was shining brilliantly and the snow shimmered with a faintly blue light from that great, full orb. It had snowed heavily on the day that Guy and Lalage had departed for London, but since then it had been so cold, with such sharp frosts, that no more flakes had drifted down from the iron-grey skies.

Dora took off her cloak and stood before the fire, lifting her skirts and warming her buttocks. 'I've no doubts at all,' she replied, and her pleasant face was unusually hard. 'You should've seen the child when her Pa and his wife came to bid her farewell. She took one look at that damn woman, and fainted clean away.'

'What did his Lordship do?' Molly bent down to smooth the fur of the big black tomcat who was rubbing round her legs.

'He seemed confused like. Mrs Sally twigged it, right enough. She just held Miranda tight, and asked them to leave.'

'And Lady Beaumaris?' Molly gave her a straight, stern look, while the clock ticked on the mantel-shelf, the cat yawned on the rag-rug, and the fire spat and crackled merrily. The scene could hardly have been more cosy and reassuring. Two simple country women, meeting to chat about the doings of their superiors.

Dora took the armchair, and her eyes were stormy. She wore an expression which Josh Appleyard would have found hard to believe of his happy-go-lucky, loving future bride. 'Oh, she just stood there, cool as you please – wearing black she were – a black velvet riding-habit. Her face were like marble, and she stared at Miranda like – like, I dunno what. His Lordship took her away, but I knowed and Mrs Sally knowed, that 'twas her that had done the mischief to the little 'un.'

'Have you brought the things I told you to get?' Molly's eyes met Dora's in a bright stare.

'Aye,' replied Dora. The cat leaped lightly on to her lap and she rubbed his fur absently. 'I got 'em, all right. What you going to do, Molly?'

'I've already done most of the work.' There was a touch of pride in Molly's voice. 'I just need those bits o' things to finish it off.'

'Finish what off? What you been up to?' Dora asked nervously. Excitement knotted her stomach and made her heart bang in her chest, and yet she felt at home in that warm, shabby kitchen where the cat accepted her as an ally. He was arching his back, rumbling with pleasure as she caressed him in that ticklish, feline place beneath his chin, his green eyes long, ecstatic slits.

'When you told me that 'twas the foreign woman what had harmed that innocent babby, I made up my mind to make a mommet,' said Molly.

'Lor', mercy me! A death-doll!' Dora's voice was filled with awe. 'Can you really do magic, Molly? They say you can, down in the village, but I weren't sure.'

'Happen I can, when it's important,' Molly replied mysteriously. She went to the sideboard and opened a drawer, taking out an object which she brought over and laid on the plush cloth which covered the table.

Dora placed the cat on the rug and stood by Molly, staring down. On the crimson cloth there lay a waxen image fashioned in the shape of a woman. 'Oh, my dear life!' she breathed, turning as pale as the figurine.

Molly's broad, strong hand clamped about her arm. 'You'll keep this to yourself,' she commanded. ''Tis a serious undertaking, and musn't reach the ears of the magistrate.'

'I won't say nothing to nobody, I promise,' vowed Dora, considerably shaken. 'It can't be wicked, can it? Not when we're adoing of it to avenge the little girl?'

'What's right? And then again, what's wrong?' Molly replied. 'I only know that a child has suffered, and it don't seem wrong to me, to punish the evil-doer. Let's get to work.' Molly was different somehow, tense, alert, her slate-grey eyes oddly alive, an absorbed, secretive smile hovering around her mouth.

Following Molly's instructions, Dora had obtained some strands of Lalage's hair, stolen from the brush left on the dressing-table in the Master Bedchamber of Wylde Court. It had been easy enough to get hold of one of her discarded gowns and snip a few remnants from it. She gave these to Molly, and they worked diligently, sewing a doll-sized garment to fit the mommet. The hair-combings were teased out and fastened to the head.

'I've performed the ritual and given it her name.' Molly sat back and looked at their handiwork with satisfaction. 'Now, the next part must be done by you, Dora.'

She added a pinch of powder to a chafing-dish over the fire, and a heady odour arose with the coiling smoke. Two more candles were lit, casting a glow on the table. She pushed forward a small carved box. Dora lifted the lid with trembling fingers; it contained several slender, dagger-sharp pins.

'Take them,' Molly instructed solemnly, 'and filling your whole heart with the fell intention of her death, stick them into the head, the heart and the vitals.'

Dora laid the macabre doll on the table and her hand hesitated over the box, then suddenly dipped and picked out a bodkin. Without giving herself time to think, she cursed Lalage with all her might, plunging one into the forehead, a second into the belly, and stabbing the final one into the chest.

She was sweating, and breathing as hard as if she had just run a mile, the strength draining out of her so that she had to sit. Molly placed her hands on the mommet, adding her own ill-wish before lifting it high and then laying it in a narrow wooden receptacle which resembled a miniature coffin, closing the hinged lid firmly.

'I'll keep it here and recharge the intention daily,' she said. 'You must think on it too, bringing your will to bear. Mind you tell nobody – nobody at all. Not even Mrs Sally. If you speak, the magic won't work.'

'I won't tell,' gasped Dora. 'But how can it work, Molly? Lady Muck be in London.'

Molly gave a deep smile. 'Distance won't prevent our deadly arrows reaching her. I can't say how it'll happen, or when – but it will – oh, yes – it will. Of course, you do realize that there will be a price?'

'You want me to pay you? I can. I've money of my own, and Josh'll give me more, if I ask him.'

Molly was putting away her magical implements, and then she stirred the fire with an iron poker. 'The payment won't be in cash, my girl. But it'll have to be made somehow. Nothing is for nothing, you know.'

'How? What'll it be? Who'll pay?' Dora was frightened. She wished that Josh was there with his strong arms, his tender smile, but she must never tell him what she and Molly had done. He was a good Christian, a regular church-goer, and he would be angry.

Molly looked suddenly tired as if some of her vitality had

gone into the thing in the box. 'I can't tell you. I only know that a price will be paid, a sacrifice made.'

Seeing the fear on her young friend's countenance, she rested a hand on her shoulder. 'Don't be frighted, Dora. It won't be you or yourn. You've done a good deed. I know it. 'Twas born out of love and concern for Miranda and Mrs Sally.'

'And you, Molly? Why did you do it?' Dora's eyes were round, her face holding a curious mixture of horror and satisfaction.

Molly heaved the kettle from the hob and poured boiling water into the tea-pot. 'For those reasons too, I suppose, and for the sake of the Wylde family, though why I feel indebted to 'em is beyond me. And a little for my boy, Jack, for I've a notion that he's got himself entangled with her. Don't know what's happened yet, but I am going to find out.'

They sat quietly by the fire for a time before Dora faced the wintry night, sipping tea and exchanging thoughts, while the cat slept and the mommet lay in its grim casket.

Chapter 4

Ambrose swept up his winnings and said: 'Gentlemen, I shall leave you now. Perchance, Lady Luck will smile on some other fortunate if I remove myself. Are you ready, Guy?'

They bowed to the company at Brook's and sauntered out into the night. Ambrose's coach was waiting and when they were inside, he tapped on the roof with his cane and the vehicle moved off. Their destination was Bedford Row, and on the way there Ambrose began to talk.

'We must get to France double-quick.' His face was carved with lines of severity, illumined by the lamps of the interior. 'The news is diabolical. The Royalist uprising ended in disaster and the leaders were guillotined at the end of October. God damn the Jacobins! They're more determined than ever to smash any resistance. Brittany has been singled out for special attention.'

'Poor devils!' Guy exclaimed. 'Haven't they spilled enough blood?'

Only a few moments ago in Brook's, Ambrose had been a spendthrift, idle fop, but that had changed dramatically now. His manner was calm, his speech quietly deliberate, filled with commanding power. 'The cities of the south do well to tremble. The Girondins are being hunted like rats. An army has been sent there, six thousand strong. They call themselves *La Compagnie Marat* – ruthless brutes who travel with their own guillotines. A monster is in charge of operations in Nantes – Jean-Baptiste Carrier by name. One of our men has just come from there. His reports of atrocities are the worst yet. Though Carrier has four engines of death working the clock round, this does not satisfy him. The *noyades* is his brain-child.'

'What the hell does that mean?' Guy muttered into the dimness of the coach, the clatter of the passing London traffic sounding almost comforting compared with his friend's gruesome words.

'Translated, it is the drownages,' that deep voice continued. 'Prisoners are herded on to flat-bottomed craft, towed out mid-stream of the Loire river and scuttled, with the wretched victims under hatches.'

'Christ! That's insane!' groaned Guy.

'Even this, and the guillotines, is not enough for Carrier. He has taken to rounding up prisoners by the hundreds, men, women and children, and massacring them with chain-shot. Another idea, concocted by him and Marat's Redcaps, is what they term the "*Mariage Républicain*". Men and women are tied together, feet to feet, hands to hands, and flung into the Loire. They delight in tethering a duke's daughter to a murderer, a marquis to a harlot, for not only *aristos* are suffering, but anyone – criminals, vagrants, gypsies and whores. Our spy said that the river is choked with bodies, the banks black with carrion crows. The Redcaps fire on the drowning people as they struggle in the water.'

'Oh, France – France! Like Saturn, the revolution is feeding on its own children,' said Guy, his voice heavy with pain and anger. 'You want us to go to Brittany? To get some of them out?'

Audacious though he was, Ambrose could see the impossibility of such action. 'No, Guy, it would take an army to stop it. I'm going to concentrate on rescuing my cousin, Hercule de St Croix. His chateau is too close to that area for comfort. A staunch Royalist, he's bound to have compromised himself, giving money, at the very least, to the cause.'

The coach stopped at the steps of his house, and they continued their conversation when ensconced in the study. As they sat one on each side of the fire, brandy goblets to hand, Ambrose outlined his plan. 'Giffe has already gone to join some of the others – Englishmen and French patriots. You know the drill.'

'I certainly do,' Guy replied, somewhat wrily. Oh, yes, he knew the complicated grapevine which existed; the inns where horses could be obtained or changed for fresh ones, sympathetic landlords risking their necks to provide food and disguises, maps and guides. On the last venture, he had driven a farm-cart for miles, with Raoul de Remiville hidden under bales of hay.

'Send for William. We'll set out as soon as he arrives.'

'And Denzil?'

'He'll sail with your smuggling friends. They must be waiting at that cove outside of Cherbourg. You know the one I mean.' Ambrose was full of vitality and enthusiasm, and Guy felt an answering excitement awakening in him.

'I'll write to William tonight. He should be here by the end of the week.'

'That's fine.' Ambrose inhaled the bouquet of the brandy, and the blue eyes regarding Guy over the rim of the glass were keen. 'Guy, what of Lalage? D'you trust her?'

'Implicitly,' Guy answered promptly, frowning a little. 'Why d'you ask?'

'You've told her nothing?'

'No. She helped to nurse the wounded *duc*, as I've already explained, but she thought he was a smuggler.'

'She never questions you? Doesn't wonder why you disappear sometimes?' Ambrose sipped the brandy.

'It never appears to trouble her, though she does get annoyed if she thinks I'm incarcerating her at Wylde Court and gallivanting off to the fleshpots without her!'

'Humm – you are to be congratulated, my friend. The only man I know who has a trustworthy wife. You must be pleased with yourself.' Ambrose was obviously dubious.

Guy's spine stiffened. 'Naturally I trust her. Would I have made her Lady Beaumaris if I didn't?'

Ambrose laughed, lightly and without mockery. 'Goddammit, you don't have to prove to me that you're a muleheaded man of principle! I accept your word on't! Lalage is as loyal as can be, but don't push it too far.'

When Guy had gone home, to send that important letter off to his brother, Ambrose went upstairs and changed. His valet was a negro, a small, wrinkled, wide-smiling man with snow-white hair. He had looked after Ambrose since he was a lad, almost one of the family. He took his master's fine clothes and hung them in the armoire while Ambrose dressed himself in a shabby, frayed at the cuffs, brown suit, with scruffy boots and grubby linen. A dun-coloured overcoat and battered topper put the finishing touches to this outfit. He ruffled his blond hair and smeared coal-dust over his cheeks to give himself an unshaven look.

Leaving the house, he hailed a passing hackney coach and, after giving the driver an address, hopped inside. They left the smart residential area and drove towards the docks on the riverside, a lurid quarter of cellars, opium-dens and sailors' hangouts, steeped in a pall of savage misery. There were few people on the streets on such a bitter night, but noise burst raucously from taverns along the way. The coach stopped at one of these, a notorious hostelry near Wapping Wharf.

Ambrose got out and paid the fare, then pushing open the door with the knob of his swordstick, he went inside.

It was a den of appalling squalor, the floor covered in churned-up sawdust, the benches and tables dirty and knife-scarred. Smoke gusted from the blackened hearth. The stink of spirits, vomit and human excrement hung thick in the air. Under the dim lamps people were slumped over the tables – sailors, workmen, tramps, a few debauched women, a cursing, rowdy bunch in an atmosphere reeking of vice and haphazardly controlled violence.

Ambrose did not linger in the taproom, he shoved his way through and mounted a set of dark stairs at the back. Coming to the room he sought, he strode under the lintel, surprising Captain Dave Chapman on the bed with a whore. She cursed. Chapman cursed. Ambrose just stared down at them, bending his height to avoid striking the beams with his head.

'Get that draggle-tailed slut out of here, Chapman,' he ordered crisply. 'I want to talk to you.'

She jumped to her feet, a scrawny, painted creature, anybody's for the price of a tot of gin. Her face was vicious, a wealth of picturesque epithets spitting from her lips. 'Who the 'ell's 'ee?' she shrieked. 'Bleedin' cheek, bargin' in 'ere!'

'Get out!' said Ambrose, with a jerk of his head towards the door.

'Not till I'm paid!' she screeched, retrieving her scattered clothing, tawdry gown, gaudy feathered hat.

'Paid be damned,' snarled Chapman, a large individual whose muscles had gone to fat, chest matted with ginger hair, arms heavily tattooed. His features were of a sour cast, head balding but with straggling greasy curls covering his bull-neck. 'We ain't finished.'

'Gawd, I give yer a friggin', didn't I?' she protested. 'Bloody 'ell! What more d'you expect fer a shillin'? A bleedin' maiden'ead?'

Ambrose tossed her a coin. She went down on hands and knees, grubbing about looking for it under the tumbled bed. 'Thanks fer nowt!' she grumbled, finding it.

'Get!' snapped Ambrose.

'Up yours!' she retaliated, sticking her stiff forefinger in the air. She stalked out, mother-naked, battered bonnet jammed on awry, her clothes under one arm.

'Jesus wept! She's got a mouth like a Billingsgate fishwife!'

commented Chapman, grinning at Ambrose. 'What d'you want, sir?'

'The usual, captain.' Ambrose dusted a chair and sat astride it, his arms folded along the back. 'I need that leaky old tub you call a boat. Is she fit to sail or has some demanding creditor taken her over?'

They talked at some length. Chapman was a seaman of polyglot forebears, and his ship sailed under American colours. The French were not at war with that country, though they had challenged most of the European states – Holland, England, Austria and Prussia. The Republicans were destroying France's credit and commerce, already on the high road to bankruptcy. Ambrose had used Chapman's services before, and intended to do so now to free St Croix. It was going to be fraught with danger, not only from the ruffianly Marats. He could get into France on this cargo ship and, God willing, escape from it with the aid of Redvers's smugglers, but once in England provision would have to be made for the marquis and his family. Spy mania had swept the land since war had been declared, with wild tales of Jacobin bandits, fully armed and disguised as *émigrés*. Pressure on the government to take steps had grown so fierce that a Bill had been introduced subjecting foreigners to stringent supervision. Ambrose would have to hide them at Holt Hall and then get them passages to South Carolina.

When Ambrose and the captain had agreed on the day, time and price, Chapman hauled himself from the mattress and began to pull on his clothes. 'We'll have to find Collyer,' he grunted. 'He's first mate, and he'll kick the crew out of the stews, punch their heads till they're sober, and get 'em on board.'

'Where is he?' Ambrose rested his chin on his crossed arms, still straddling the chair.

'Down the cockpit,' was the laconic reply.

London was not for the squeamish. There were many activities which the populace paid to watch and bet on; bull-baiting and bear-baiting, dog-fights, prize-fights and cock-fights. Wherever a contest was held, there would be punters consuming gallons of liquor. Ambrose had attended many mains. He and Guy pitted their own birds against one another, but it was the first time he had been to one in the slums.

Chapman took him through mean streets and under dark archways and hanging lanterns which swung and creaked in the wind and did everything but light the squalid obscurity. They reached a derelict-looking building which housed the pit and were at once plunged into a deafening uproar. The spectators bellowed with excitement, hurling bets, abuse and encouragement to the crowing contestants on the dirty, blood-spattered mat. Ambrose and Chapman elbowed their way to the front. There was a lull between the ending of one bout and the start of the next. Brandy bottles were uncorked and passed around, and gin purchased from the sellers who were always in attendance. There was an iron cage suspended from the ceiling directly above the pit, and a gambler crouched within, being punished in this uncomfortable and humiliating way for neglecting to pay his debts, a salutary warning to others.

Chapman found the mate, and they stood with him, elbows on the wooden supports of the ring, jostled at every turn by enthusiasts. There was much talk of the sport, the merits of various birds coming under heated discussion. The jargon would have been gibberish to the uninitiated, but Ambrose knew what they meant when they referred to 'close-hitters' and 'bloody heelers', saying that this bird had a good mouth, and that one came to every point.

The crowd were variegated, lusty and rowdy. There were several gentlemen mixed in with the rabble. Coarse faces, red with gin and gambling fever, waited impatiently for the next bout. Some began to bang on the wooden boards, whistling and cat-calling, though there were a few who stood mute, glowering blackly, having lost money they could ill afford. Their wives and dependents would go hungry next day and the landlord would have to wait for the rent.

There was a gangway leading into the shallow-sided pit, where several white canvas bags dangled on hooks. Each contained a cock, ready heeled and trimmed. The clucking of one particular bird, cocooned in his bag, was answered deeply and savagely by the others. This noisy creature was lifted out by his handler, a small, dapper man who resembled a rooster himself. He held him high, parading round the pit so that everyone might view this splendid specimen. The bird's glossy feathers were vividly patterned in scarlet and ebony, and his head was snakelike, ferocious. He was compact and handsome, and his long, iron-scaled legs had enormous spurs. He strutted on the mat, plumage ruffled truculently, his great, vigorous beak like that of an eagle.

His challenger had also been lifted from a bag, chuckling a

retort to his crow, issuing a warning. The uproar increased while the man who was organizing the betting extolled the virtues of each. He was a slick, flashy ruffian, with herons' quills stuck in his dented felt hat.

'Here you are, gentlemen!' he bawled above the din. 'Two finely matched cocks, strong, nimble and ready for your pleasure! On my right, the Bloodwing Pile, known as Hector – two years old, weighing four pounds, the winner of many mains. On my left, of equal merit, the Black and Red, called Thunderbolt. He's of the same age and weight, and has a fearsome reputation. Take your pick and place your bets!'

Shouts, money being thrust at the lad going round with the book, and Chapman laying his money on Hector, whilst Ambrose put two guineas on Thunderbolt. The pit was cleared except for the handlers who, each holding a bird, taunted them with each other's presence, allowing them to feint from a distance, then placing them down, facing one another, though the men still kept a tight grip, encouraging the birds' crowing and mantling until they were almost too dangerous to hold – then they released them.

There was a disturbance as more people came in, forcing themselves against the barrier. Ambrose did not look at them, his attention focused on the combat. The first terrific onslaught of the cocks was strikingly grand and courageous. The onlookers yelled their approval while the betting became vociferous. The birds were sparring warily, watching, dodging, looking for the first cut. In a flash of feathers they came together, beak to beak, locked in battle, then they suddenly rose up in a tremendous flurry of mingling, powerful wings and lethal heels That leap, that fire, that passion of aggressive strength were fierce and overpowering.

Great, circular metal candle-holders lit the action, flaring down on the battling birds and the sweating crowd caught up in the frenzy of blood-lust and greed. Ambrose leaned forward, shouting encouragement to Thunderbolt. Everyone was craning for a better view. The atmosphere was electric. When the cocks rebounded from the fury of that first blow, it became apparent that Hector had been hit. Blood spurted from his neck where one of Thunderbolt's lethal spurs had pierced him.

'He's been throated,' someone cried.

The handlers caught up the gamecocks in an instant, smoothing their ruffled plumes and setting them back on the mat again. They touched them with delicacy, as if they were precious porcelain, an odd action when the outcome was bound to be butchery and death. Hector was brave, and staggered towards Thunderbolt, but he was badly hit and ran like a drunken man. Thunderbolt, full of fire and irritated courage, gave a brutal finishing stroke, springing above him, burying his spurs up to their hilts in his prostrate rival. The blood fountained up, spattering members of the audience. The once-proud Hector was reduced to a scarlet-oozing, motionless bundle of feathers.

Men shouted, haggled, argued and cursed, while money changed hands and Thunderbolt was carried high by his owner, slightly wounded but made doubly fierce by his victory.

'You've won! Dammit!' Chapman was bawling in Ambrose's ear, but he hardly heard, his attention concentrated on that couple who had arrived late. They stood directly opposite him. One of them was Jack Smithers, and the other was a woman, a beautiful woman, out of place in such rough surroundings, yet her cheeks were flushed, her eyes blazing as she laughed.

Ambrose's mind was suddenly illumined as by a flash of lightning. He stared at her in that moment of terrible recognition, seeing her livid face, her cloud of black hair, her hands and skirt smeared with blood from the cock's death-agony, her harsh, strident laughter reaching him over the tumult. The scene dissolved, another superimposed on it, and he knew where he had seen her before. The cries of the gamblers became the screams of a vengeful mob, and he was there, pretending to be one of them, in Paris two years ago.

'*À bas les seigneurs! À bas les tyrans!*' they yelled, as the tumbrils rumbled over the cobbles bringing further victims. Noble gentlemen, stunned and mute by the appalling catastrophe which had stripped them bare; well-bred women, their once lovely gowns torn and grey with dirt, their hair cropped short ready for the block. Some wept, some prayed, others stood, balancing themselves against the jolting of the crude carts, staring blindly at the jeering proletariat whom they despised and who had turned against them with the savagery of caged beasts on the loose. Children clung to them, terrified eyes on that tall, gaunt death-machine which awaited them. The blade rose, glittering in the heat of that sun-drenched square. It fell and rose, crimsoned and dripping, to fall again and again, for hours on end.

Ambrose saw Lalage, as he had seen her then, in the forefront of the mob, screaming with the rest, in a fever of ecstasy as she watched the blood spouting from the guillotine in the *Place de la Révolution.*

'So you see, darling, she is one of those creatures who are as content to make love to women as they are to embrace men,' said Aurora, continuing the conversation which she had begun when Tilly awakened them with coffee next morning. Ambrose made no reply. He was sitting by the fire in a cushioned armchair, wearing an ornate lounging robe and thumbing through a newspaper. She pummelled her pillow into a more comfortable shape, her white skin and golden hair shining against the black satin. 'Ambrose!' her voice rose an octave. 'You haven't been listening to a word! I might as well address my remarks to Didi!'

He lifted a fair eyebrow and smiled. 'She'd take no notice of you either – much too busy being a mother, ain't you, gal?' He leaned over and prodded one of the wrinkled pups who had escaped Didi's eye and was crawling over the rug. She alerted instantly and padded across to snatch him up in a softly chastening mouth, dumping him back in the basket on top of his squealing brothers and sisters.

'I was talking of Lalage,' Aurora enunciated clearly, as if speaking to a slow-witted infant. 'Telling you about last night, and how she propositioned me. Aren't you the smallest bit interested?'

She was being unreasonable and touchy and knew it, but she could not help thinking that at one time he would not have been sitting there with his nose buried in some stuffy paper full of boring news. He would have stayed in bed – with her. Yet she had to admit that there were compensations in this cosy domesticity. It was as if she were his wife, not his mistress.

Ambrose laid aside his paper and stood up, giving a stretch and a yawn. 'It doesn't surprise me, honey,' he replied, smiling at her with those amazingly blue eyes. 'Nothing that lady does surprises me.' She was startled by the harsh note that had crept into his voice, then he laughed. 'Why didn't you take her up on it? I could've come around and watched.'

Though he concealed it well, beneath this banter he was deeply troubled and had spent much of the night thinking about it. What was Lalage doing in England? More to the point, how had she reached Morocco? He doubted that the story of her loss of memory was true, and he had believed her to be dead. Something had gone badly wrong with his plans if

315

such a viper as she had escaped the trap he had cunningly laid for her in France. He knew that he should warn Guy, but even his nimble mind could devise no satisfactory way of doing this. In the coach last night, Guy's angry reaction to the hint that he should beware had been plain enough. A man such as he, who had set convention at defiance by marrying as he had, was not likely to admit that he had chosen unwisely.

He longed to confide in someone, but was too wary. Instead, he sat on the side of the bed, taking one of Aurora's hands in his, and her heart flipped right over as she read something in his eyes which was astonishing. A loving warmth seemed to come from them, radiating through her. It had been almost dawn when he came to her, letting himself into the house with a latchkey which she had given him. Overjoyed as always, her arms had welcomed him. He had been chilled to the bone, snuggling against her like a tired child, and they had slept thus, each taking comfort from the presence of the other. Wordless, not even physically aroused, friends as well as lovers. In the morning, confession had trembled on her tongue and she had nearly told him that she was pregnant. Perhaps he will be pleased, she had thought, perhaps wonder and happiness will widen his eyes and he'll swing me up in his arms and call me 'baby', as he does in rare moments when his guard is down.

She had lost her nerve and said nothing. The moment had vanished, for Tilly had come into the room. Ambrose had wakened then, drinking the hot coffee and turning beneath the sheet to make love to her. She had relaxed, waiting for that beautiful moment of the joining of their bodies. Ambrose, Ambrose, there never had been, never would be anyone else but Ambrose. Her ambitions had shrunk. All she wanted was this man and his child. Nothing else mattered and, when he had taken her, she tried to tell him but he had gone to sleep again. To comfort herself, she had thought of the life within her, imagining herself large, maternal, swollen with milk, holding his baby to her breast, feeling its mouth on her nipple. The idea was so sweet that it had made her heart ache and she had turned on her side towards Ambrose, wanting desperately to share this emotion, but was afraid. Supposing he did not want her to have this baby? But it was there, growing hourly. A few more weeks and it would begin to move. How long could she conceal it from him? What would he do when he knew?

These disturbing thoughts continued to gnaw at her mind as

316

he sat there on the bed, lighting up a cheroot and speaking to her with an unwonted seriousness. 'Aurora, in a day or two I have to go away for a while.'

'Oh, Ambrose!' The bottom dropped out of her world, a wasteland of desolation spreading out before her.

'Please, darling, listen to me,' he continued in such a firm tone that she knew it was hopeless to protest. She stayed silent, feasting her eyes on every angle of his strong-jawed face. 'There's business up north that demands my attention. Hopefully, I'll not be there long.'

He paused. It was hard to be glib when she was looking at him with concerned eyes. He had thought that a little clever, wordy manipulation of the truth would have sufficed, and was horrified to find that he had been mistaken. His heart was heavy at the idea of leaving her. Tilly had pulled back the drapes at the windows and daylight streamed in, but the curtains around the bed were still partially drawn. In the dim glow, he could see Aurora's questioning eyes, her tumbled yellow hair, her tender smile which pleaded with him not to go. She had given him so much happiness, an infinity of affection and joy, and he knew that she loved him. Oh, she'd not said as much, but the signs were plain to see.

His own emotions concerning her were jumbled. Disappointment and cynicism had left traces on his soul. He had been in love several times. A great deal of pain and disenchantment had made him blasé, and he had thought himself immune to women, those calculating, greedy bloodsuckers on whom he had wasted his youthful romanticism, but Aurora was not like them. He had discovered this at their first assignation, finding it nigh impossible to visualize life without her. If love was to be worth anything it must be honest, trusting, humorous and tolerant. He believed that such qualities existed between them, but to ask her to marry him now would have been downright selfish, for he was tossing his life into the hands of fate, following that destiny which he had deliberately chosen.

He was silent for so long that Aurora dared to speak. 'Well, dearest, if it's a question of business, then I'll wait meekly for your return,' she said with a forced smile.

Those intensely bright eyes switched back to her face, and he tried to find words which would not strike terror into her. 'As you know, I'm pretty rich. There's the plantation back home – Holt Hall, and the house in Bedford Row. I bank at Coutt's, and papers concerning my property are in the desk in my study.

I've made a will. You'll find the name of my lawyer amongst the deeds. I've named you as my sole heir and beneficiary.'

As he had feared, she became terribly agitated, jumping up with a start. 'Ambrose! What a thing to say! My God, anyone would think you're joining the army, not setting off on a business trip. You haven't enlisted, have you?'

Tilly appeared at the door. 'Madame, there are several persons waiting to see you, and Julian has arrived.'

'Go away! Damn you!' Aurora shouted and Tilly, offended, twirled on her heel and marched out, shutting the door with a snap.

Ambrose chuckled, puffing at his cigar. 'Oh, now you've upset her. Isn't it time to bring in your pets? Your menagerie, with its various assorted members, which has about it the flavour of a sultan's whim?'

'To the devil with that! I want to know what's on your mind, you devious rogue.' Worry sharpened her voice, but there was a sob in it.

He clipped her around the waist, pulling her against his hard chest. 'If you'll hold your peace for a second, hellcat, I'll try to explain.' She stayed in his arms, quiescent, listening and: 'How the hell do I know what's in store for me?' he said, his lips brushing her cheek. 'Anything may happen. The roads are dangerous and alive with highwaymen. Someone may challenge me to a duel if I lick 'em at cards. I'm just telling you what I've arranged, that's all. There is one thing more. The town house. If I die, I want you to turn it into a foundling home. Use some of the money to employ decent folk to look after the brats, and pay for its upkeep. It'll give some of those poor little bastards a chance. Will you do that?'

'Yes – yes – anything you want, but don't keep talking about dying. I can't bear it!' she cried, her knees shaking while he held her tight. After a struggle, she mastered her emotions and steadied her voice, knowing that he would resent her hectoring him, but it was impossible to match his calm. 'Ambrose, don't go. Please, don't go.'

'Needs must when the devil drives,' he murmured gently. 'If I return safely, there's something else I want to ask you,' he added mysteriously, but would say no more no matter how she badgered him whilst he dressed and prepared to go out. He said goodbye and left her to fume, though his smile curled round her like an embrace.

Later, when Tilly ventured in to attire her, she found her

mistress pacing the room, swearing one moment and laughing the next, in a bewildered state of vexation.

Lalage was having her portrait painted. The artist had been a pupil of the late Sir Joshua Reynolds, and his services were much sought after by the rich and famous. His name was Francis Sudley and his studio was in Blackfriars. Jack drove her there and then went off on some concern of his own.

Sudley resided in a house which had once belonged to a nobleman. Now it was rather neglected in appearance, and the outside was in need of repainting. Lalage had already had a number of sittings, and she made her way straight to the studio. This was an immense room, for alterations had done away with the main staircase leading to the upper floor. A drawing-room ran across the front of the house, linking with the studio, and overlooking the river with its irregular shore, broken by jetties and moored boats.

As is often the case with men driven by genius, Sudley was extremely untidy. The studio was cluttered with a rich miscellany of objects, anatomical figures, copies of Greek statues, stuffed birds under glass domes. It was fashionable to be painted against a classical background, so busts stood around and there were several broken pillars, urns, carved furniture and draperies. Canvases leaned against the walls. Pots filled with brushes, a palette smeared with vivid dollops of oil-paint and bottles of thick dark varnish stood on the table, alongside dirty dishes, sticky glasses and decanters.

When Lalage came in, Sudley was standing, head on one side, scrutinizing the life-size, almost completed portrait of her which rested on an easel. He was poetic in appearance, with a dreamy gaze, though his mouth was inclined to looseness. Thick, dark curls ringed his head, and he had small hands with long, tapering fingers.

'Good morning, Lady Beaumaris,' he called cheerily, making a bow, already wearing his paint-daubed overall, ready to start. 'One more sitting and we shall be finished. What do you think of it, eh?'

'It is a truly remarkable likeness,' she observed coming to rest in front of it.

It could have been a mirror, not a painted canvas, faithful to the sitter in every detail. Sudley had sketched in a setting of dark, sombre trees under a limpid blue sky and placed her there, as if she stood in a forest clearing on the Wylde estate. She wore a white gown, fastened beneath the breasts with a red sash, the colour repeated in the shimmering silk stole which flowed over her shoulders and trailed down so that its gold fringe nearly touched the ground. In one hand she held a slender walking-cane, the handle festooned with ribbon, whilst the other clasped a fold of her dress. White satin slippers peeped demurely from beneath her hem. With skilful magic, the artist had captured her for all time. She would live for ever on that canvas, always young, always beautiful. In the future, her descendants might look at that picture hanging in the Long Gallery of the manor, seeing her there, darkly lovely, contemplative, mysterious, perhaps remarking to one another: 'Great-great-grandmother was certainly stunning! Such a sweet, sad expression – like an angel!'

An hour passed while Lalage posed and Sudley worked diligently, adding the final brush-strokes. He hummed under his breath, and took an occasional drink. Outside, the wind blew freshly, the sun shone on the frost, while the tide ran high and white sails bellied out, drifting past the windows. The traffic was muffled to a rumble, and there were glints on distant spires and domes. Lalage was disinclined to talk, lost in that reverie which Sudley had immortalized, but peace was disrupted when Sanderman and de Belcourt were announced by the solitary servant who catered for the artist's needs.

Sudley laid aside his brush and Lalage stepped down from the dais. 'A thousand pardons, sir. We are interrupting you,' said the lawyer.

'The work is all but completed. The light is fading. These winter days are so short that I shall have to discontinue. When it is dry, I intend to beg Lord Beaumaris's permission to exhibit it at the Royal Academy,' Sudley replied, absorbed in studying it from every angle.

'Indeed you should. It is very fine.' Sanderman prided himself on being something of a connoisseur. 'Lady Beaumaris to the life!'

More compliments, followed by light conversation, and then de Belcourt held Lalage's mantle while she slipped her arms into it and put on her full-brimmed, feather-loaded hat. She bade Sudley good-day, gracious and dignified, and walked out into the wintry sunshine with the lawyer and the Frenchman, saying:

'My coach awaits. May I drive you somewhere, gentlemen?'

Sanderman smiled and answered softly: 'D'you recall our

little chat of last night? It will do me much honour should you consent to meet the gentleman of whom I spoke. He has expressed the greatest possible longing to make your acquaintance.'

Lalage flashed him a glance. 'I'm intrigued. Is he an admirer? If he's a member of the social circle, I'm surprised that we haven't already met.'

'He is something of a recluse, dear lady. The frivolity of high life doesn't appeal to him. I think it would be more discreet if you dismiss your own vehicle and travel in mine,' Sanderman replied, exchanging a significant look with de Belcourt, behind her back. The *viscomte* smiled, that oily young man with the sly dark eyes and brittle, facile charm which he used, quite blatantly, for his own ends.

Before long they were seated in the carriage and leaving Blackfriars. Sanderman gave his coachman instructions and he took the road towards the parish of Chelsea, a place of quiet streets and recently built houses springing up around the church, village green and old cottages. Wealthy tradesmen found it a convenient distance from the heart of the city and, wishing to live away from the dirt and overcrowding, thought its countrified atmosphere very agreeable. Lalage had been there before, visiting the dancing-rooms of the Ranelagh rotunda, but she was unfamiliar with the street branching off from the King's Road into which the coach now turned.

The houses there were older, set well back behind shrubs and trees, surrounded by high walls which rendered them completely secluded. The carriage swung between a pair of iron gates, and rolled up a drive which twisted and turned before reaching a large, solidly built mansion. It was nearly dark now, and the evening was clear. The moon had just emerged from behind a thick layer of cloud. A fitful sheen of silver danced over the façade of the house. Lamps had been lit on either side of the central front door under its curving, shell-shaped arch. Sanderman seized the lion-headed knocker and rapped firmly.

The sound echoed away inside. They heard footsteps, and the door was partially opened. The lawyer slipped in and there was the murmur of voices, then he reappeared and ushered Lalage and de Belcourt into a wide hall, chequered in ochre and white tiles, its frescoed ceiling supported by marble Ionic columns. A stone staircase rose steeply at the far end, branching off into a railed gallery.

The man who had let them in was squat, dark, heavily-jowled and did not look like a servant. He showed his long teeth in a grin as he spoke to Sanderman with a kind of mocking familiarity. He had a slouching gait and manner, and his eyes narrowed as they darted to Lalage.

'I'll tell him you've come,' he said, nodding at Sanderman.

'No need of that. We'll go up,' snapped the lawyer.

The man shrugged. 'Suit yourself. It's your funeral.'

He was not the only person present. Several other men lounged against the walls, casual, almost indolent, but they did not take their eyes off the new arrivals. They were too independent to be lackeys and wore no uniform, yet they were not gentlemen though a couple were well-dressed. One thing they had in common – each was armed.

Sanderman managed to retain his ease of carriage and a certain air of quiet scorn as he addressed the man who had admitted them: 'Lead the way, Fripps, we haven't time to waste.'

With a knowing smirk and a brusque order to the others to keep a sharp watch for intruders, Fripps moved off up the broad staircase. It was a fine, well-lit house and the walls were hung with paintings and large mirrors in carved Italian frames. 'This is an odd establishment,' remarked Lalage to Sanderman, one hand resting on the curved banister, the other lifting her skirt. 'Your friend must be most eccentric.'

'Oh, he is, milady, he is,' he replied, smiling and unctuous. 'You'll find that he's quite an exceptional person.'

A large door faced the head of the stairs, and Fripps knocked on it. Sudden silence fanned down over the hall, the stairs, a curious silence, charged with a peculiar tense quality of anticipation. Every eye was on the door. Then from within a man's voice called to them to enter.

The room was dusky, but the fire glowed, bathing everything in scarlet. A man sat behind a large, ornate desk, silhouetted by the lamp at his back. He was writing and did not look up until his three visitors had stepped over the threshold and Fripps had gone, closing the door behind him. Lalage took a step, then stopped as if turned to stone. The colour had drained from her face and something akin to terror flared in her eyes. The hand gripping her long cane went chalky at the knuckles.

The man rested back in his chair, trailing the quill-pen between his fingers. 'So, citizeness, we meet again,' he said, in a cool smooth voice which bore only the slightest trace of accent.

Sanderman glanced at Lalage, realizing that she was so

322

stunned that she could not utter a word. 'Is it as I suspected, Citizen Latour?' he asked respectfully. 'This is the young woman you sought, is it not?' There was an eager, cringing look in his eyes, resembling that of a pet dog waiting to be patted on the head for being obedient.

'You were quite right, Sanderman,' answered Latour, smiling faintly, tapping the end of the quill against his lips. 'Most observant of you to recognize that which gave her away.'

'The ring! I noticed it on her hand as soon as I met her, and guessed that she was not what she pretended to be.' Sanderman was excited, trembling, his face flushed.

'Ah, Lalage,' Latour shook his head sorrowfully, his tone gently reproachful, like a father admonishing an obstinate child. 'You should have got rid of it. Your greed will be your downfall, *chérie*.'

She stared at that lean-visaged man with the heavy, slanting black eyes and cruel mouth. His dark hair, winged with silver at the temples, was swept back, accentuating the severity of his haggard features. He rose to his feet, meeting her stare with cold, reptilian eyes. There was nothing about him which one could pin-point as villainous; he was quite handsome, his austere clothing faultlessly tailored, fitting his form well. His manner was formal, even slightly old-fashioned, but in spite of this there was an ambience there, hinting at dank prisons and violent, deceitful dealings.

He walked towards her, reaching out a hand and touching her cheek. She shrank back, but continued to glare at him. 'Latour! You devil!' she hissed. 'D'you think I would have thrown away that sacred symbol of freedom?'

He sighed, his eyes glittering. 'Sacred symbol? Name of a dog, what a hypocrite you are! Nothing is sacred to you – neither cause, nor friendship, nor honour. You spit on such things. You are a traitoress, a corrupt creature who follows only the dictates of appetite. I gave orders that you were to be killed. Someone disobeyed me. Heads shall roll for it.'

'Why don't you kill her now, Latour?' de Belcourt cried impatiently. 'An enemy of the Reformati should be given no quarter!'

'You fool!' sneered Latour, head uplifted, eyes blazing with contempt. 'What do you know of such matters? You are an *aristo!*'

'I was!' replied de Belcourt, adding with stinging bitterness:

'A younger son, a nobody as far as my family were concerned. I found friends among other young nobles who had a strong sympathy with the doctrine of equality.'

Lalage laughed unpleasantly. 'I've met their like! Can a leopard change its spots? Can a man who betrays his own kin be trusted?'

'You betrayed yours,' Latour reminded suavely.

'They were not my kin!' Her face was white, eyes baneful. 'I have no kin.'

'And no friends.' Latour's lips curved in an icy smile. 'You forget, citizeness, that I myself was of the aristocracy. My father was among those tyrants who had oppressed the people for too long. I studied. I met brave men who convinced me that the system could be overthrown. Our cause has been victorious, and we shall spread the fierce crusading blast of revolution into every corner of the globe.'

'England is ready,' Sanderman burst in eagerly. 'The Reformati has powerful friends in the highest places – here, in Europe and America. Their money pours regularly into the Jacobin coffers. We shall triumph. There is seething unrest among the poor. They are burning to rise against their masters.'

Floating in his fevered brain was a bright vision of himself in control over a government where he held lofty sway. For years he had dabbled in politics, motivated by spite and ambition, joining the Reformati, a secret society with origins in Germany. Its aims were anarchy, power and control, and many of the leaders of the French Revolution were active members, free-thinkers whose ideals of justice had been gradually corroded. Intellectuals, like Robespierre, who had no personal wrongs to avenge, but had become possessed by the uncontrollable monster they had created, that monster of revolt which, though glutted with blood, demanded more and more.

Sanderman had thought that he was dreaming when he had been introduced to Lalage, raised her hand to his lips and saw the ring. That curious device – the crescent moon with a star balanced on the tip of one horn, the whole surrounded by a circle of snakes. He knew it so well. The sign of the Reformati, used as a brand, a seal on their correspondence. From that moment on he had watched her, though she was cunning, never giving herself away. He had made his report to their London-based leader – Jacques Latour.

De Belcourt had been in England for some time, coming over

before the war with orders to spy and stir up the street-corner agitators already aggravating the discontent among farm-labourers, factory hands and craftsmen. The House of Hanover had never been popular, and there were many who wanted to topple the German monarchy from the English throne. They could have succeeded earlier, had not their plans been betrayed to Burke who had exposed a Jacobin plot to arm a mob in Birmingham. The war had been a setback to the Reformati. Prior to its declaration, thousands of refugees had poured into England with their terrible stories of atrocities. It had been easy to infiltrate then, wily men and women busy about their anarchic work, but now a wave of patriotism was making it more difficult. Though the *émigrés* had been received with compassion, by a curious paradox that French influx had intensified popular hatred of the nation as a whole. Yet the biggest traitors lay in places of importance, men like Sanderman, and professional politicians, well-known and trusted.

'Why don't you kill her?' repeated de Belcourt stubbornly, defying Latour who was regarding him with that chilling smile. 'What use is she? A turncoat who will betray us!'

Latour did not answer him at once. He was in such a strong position in the organization that he need answer to no man, save possibly Robespierre or whoever climbed highest among the demagogues of the Convention. He was a cool, calculating visionary, who believed in his cause and the destruction of its enemies, but encouraged others to carry out the carnage. A gentleman by birth, far removed from the coarse violence of the sansculotte, one who wore fine linen and appreciated music, classic literature, good wines. The hands which signed death-warrants were manicured and perfumed, showing no trace of their bloody work. In dealing with human beings, he relied on three major weaknesses – greed, desire and fear. He had no heart and very few emotions. These were carefully controlled. The intelligence chief of the Reformati, who organized espion-age, policing and murder. He had a hard contempt for women; love was to him something peculiar and idiotic, to be used brutally in the struggle for power.

He had positioned himself in such a way that the candelabra was on the console-table behind him. Thus his face was shadowed, whilst the light fell on Lalage, Sanderman and de Belcourt. His eyes went from one to the other, one dark brow lifting slightly.

'You are too impetuous, *mon ami*,' he remarked blandly. 'I shall not kill the citizeness yet. I have work for her.'

'Work?' Lalage's eyes were narrowed, suspicious. Having recovered from the initial shock, she faced him boldly, imposing in her sweeping cape, made taller by the high-crowned hat she wore. Latour saluted her mentally. She had never lacked courage, whatever her other faults. 'Why should I involve myself further?' she added pithily. 'I have carved a comfortable position for myself.'

'Indeed you have,' he agreed, with urbane suavity. 'Lady Beaumaris of Beaumaris Combe. An *aristo* at last, eh? You've used your beauty to good effect. How clever of you to trade on that masculine weakness which believes that beautiful women should have no thoughts out of harmony with those silly, poetic sentiments which their beauty inspires. In my experience, women are harpies who will do anything for money. You, *ma belle*, have ever been mercenary and acquisitive – a true harpy!'

'You think that is what I came here for?' She was like a goaded tigress. 'You believe that I married Guy Wylde for money and position? How can you say that? We have worked together, sent hundreds to their deaths, and yet you accuse me of wishing to join the ranks of the nobility! How little you know me!'

Latour remained detached and indifferent during this tirade, as if her words were not addressed to him. He leaned against the desk, contemplating the sparkling buckle of his black shoe. She was rising to the bait as he had guessed she would. 'I know you extremely well, *mon enfant*,' he said when she paused for breath. 'A greedy creature, and a vengeful one. The revolution, for you, meant the settling of old scores. Any means justified that end.'

'What did I tell you? She's a bitch! Get rid of her!' de Belcourt broke in unwisely.

'Be still, you whelp!' Latour turned on him so violently that he jumped back a pace. His leader recovered himself immediately, but the calm spell had been banished. Like a cobra with its hood raised, ready to strike, his hypnotic eyes were trained on Lalage. 'Citizeness, you will obey me. I have orders to flush out *Le Fantom*. He's a thorn in the flesh of my government with his damned audacity, his constant interference with the course of justice. We want him. We must have him. No one knows his identity, but it is suspected that he's an English nobleman. You mix in the right circles. You will find him for me.'

A change came over Lalage. She relaxed her defiant pose, strolling to the side-table and helping herself to wine. Holding the glass between her fingers, she smiled at Latour, eyes seductive, lips slightly parted. Latour permitted himself a moment's amusement, remembering how she had once thrown herself at his head, lusting not for himself but for the power which he represented. He had repulsed her then, and he did so now, letting her know by the sneer curling his lip that neither she nor any woman stirred the remotest flicker of desire in his loins.

She read him correctly and her face froze into a hard, cold mask which matched his own. '*Le Fantom!* Don't worry, Citizen Latour. I've done what I have – come to this grey, freezing country – tolerated an impossible family – married an arrogant swine who thinks he can dominate me and turn me into a brood mare – for the sole purpose of hunting down this *Fantom*! I want him myself! I'll make him pay dearly for what he did to me!'

Chapter 5

'Here you go, princess,' said Jack, tiptoeing into Miranda's room. 'See what a kind lady has sent you from London.'

'A Christmas present?' Miranda looked up at him with lacklustre eyes, tucked into the cosy armchair close to the fire, a blanket wrapped around her.

'If you like.' He grinned down into her pale face. 'Soon be Christmas, won't it? The mummers'll be coming to sing carols, and your Grandma will have a big party up at the manor for the villagers. You've got to get better by then, haven't you? So you can join in the fun.'

'I am better,' she answered, showing little interest, then perked up a bit. 'Can I have my present now?'

'Lor', I'd quite forgotten about it!' Jack smote himself on the brow, rolled his eyes and pulled a comic face. Then he dived a hand into the breast of his greatcoat and pulled out one of Didi's pups. 'She hasn't a name yet, so you must give her one.'

Sally, standing by and smiling at them, saw the delight with which Miranda took the small animal into her arms. She had been thinking about giving her another puppy, but she had become distressed if the subject was broached, still mourning Rex. Jack, rushing in where angels feared to tread, had unwittingly completed her recovery.

'Oh, Sally – Sally!' Miranda cried, cheeks pink for the first time since her illness. 'Isn't she sweet? She likes me. Look, she's licking my nose. I'll call her Fairy. She's just like a fairy. What dear little paws!'

'Lady Mortmorcy asked me to bring it for her,' Jack said to Sally. 'She has a heart of gold, that one, though she keeps it well hidden. His Lordship must've told her what happened. I've had the little devil in my coat all the way down.' His face was rueful. 'She's not house-trained either! Thunderation! That's taking the call of duty too far!'

Sally laughed, her heart lifting, while Jack joked and entertained her with accounts of his doings in town, carefully censored for her benefit. It was good to talk with someone who brought in a breath of the outside world, far beyond the confines of Dorset. She had been shut up in the cottage for too long, nursing Miranda, seeing no one but William, Dora and Molly. The weather had not helped, the skies pewter, the air inert, laden with cold. Snow flurried the fields and lay in feathery drifts, making excursions difficult.

William had not relished the ride to London in such conditions. Sally might have tried to stop him had she not known that he was obeying the call of duty. She wished that she did not know, happier in the days of her ignorance, now beset with anxiety. Guy and William going to France, putting their lives at risk. It was horrible to be a woman who could do nothing but watch and wait, while the men went off adventuring. Was this really the thing that they cared for above all others? she wondered. William loved her, of course, but rather as a child loves its mother. If another playmate called him to take part in a dangerous game, away he went, forgetting her until he needed her again.

Denzil came to see her in the afternoon, and Dora ushered him into the parlour. His visit surprised her, for he spent most of his time at Wylde Court. Lady Charlotte was worried about him, confiding in Sally the last time they met. He was so short-tempered and rude these days, not like his usual buoyant self, his mother had declared. She feared that he was turning into a second Guy, wondering if he might be drinking too much. Sally had promised to find out what was wrong, unable to tell her that he was brooding about Lalage, never reconciled to the fact that she had married his brother. She had prayed that his work with the league would fill his mind, but one glance at his sullen face as he entered the room told her that this was a false hope.

'How nice to see you, Denzil,' she exclaimed brightly. 'Would you care for some tea? Something stronger, perhaps? There's brandy on the table. Help yourself.'

Denzil shed his overcoat, laying it on a chair. He shook his head. 'Nothing, thanks.' Then he stood awkwardly by the fireplace, unusually clumsy, knocking the poker against the coal-scuttle with a discordant clatter.

'Sit down, Denzil.' Sally pointed to a chair, unsure how to put him at ease. 'Is this a social call or can I be of assistance in some way?'

He took the seat but did not relax, hands dangling between his knees, staring wretchedly into nothingness. He looked pale and ill, as if some deep-rooted trouble was pouring a strange heaviness into his veins. 'I shouldn't have come,' he began haltingly. 'It's not right to bother you. You've enough to contend with – William gone away – Miranda sick. But, oh, Sally, I must speak to someone. I think that I'm going mad.' He sprang up and began to pace the room, driving his fist into his open palm.

'Is it the business of the aristocrats? You are frightened? Is that it?' Sally's intuition told her that this was not the trouble, but she was giving him leads, the chance to pour it out.

'No! God, if that were all!' He thrust an impatient hand through his chestnut curls. 'It wasn't so bad when she was in London, but now she has come back, and Jack with her.'

Sally could remember a time when she was afraid of him, hating his unkind teasing when they were children. Now, like a bad boy, he was wanting to make some confession, and she sat perfectly still, waiting. 'You speak of Lalage, I presume. Yes, she has come home again, and Jack Smithers accompanied her, as it was his duty to do. Why are you in such a state?'

'Jack is her lover,' Denzil shouted, then stopped short and buried his face in his hands.

'That's an awful thing to say. It can't be true,' Sally protested.

'It *is* true. I've seen them together.' He lowered his hands and his eyes were wild. 'Before they went to London, when she was at the lodge, nursing de Remiville.'

'Does Guy know?' Her first thought was for him.

'No, I think not.' There was the look of a damned soul in his eyes.

'You caught them? What happened? What did she say?' Sally was calm, surprising herself by her control. At the same time, she was not proud of the relief which swept through her – and the confirmation of something shapeless, unnamed, partially obscured, which she had experienced from the first moment she saw Lalage.

Denzil was trembling. 'She said nothing – not then,' and he told her how he had chanced upon them, lying naked in the empty room, his words tumbling over one another in the frenzy of recall. 'Later, she spoke to me – said that Jack had forced her –'

'She asked you not to tell Guy?'

He was silent for a second, then burst out: 'She threatened that if I did, she would confess that I too was her lover.'

It was a horrible moment. 'My God! You fool!' she gasped.

He sank down on the couch beside her, bowed his head in his hands and began to cry. It was dreadful to see this good-looking young man reduced in such a way. Sally had known that he was a lady-killer, overhearing giggly gossip among the maid-servants, but this shook her to the core. Adultery with his brother's wife was utterly untenable.

'I love her! I love her! Don't you understand?' Denzil sobbed.

'How can you love her when she's been coupling with Jack?' Sally said with blistering scorn, but she did understand. She loved Guy even though he was married to that treacherous woman. Love cannot be confined, dictated to or reasoned with, she knew that only too painfully. She softened, putting an arm about his heaving shoulders, giving him her handkerchief. 'Oh, Denzil, what a mess. She's not worth it, my dear.'

She hated Lalage then, hated her callousness, her overween-ing pride and vanity which had led her to amuse herself with the boy. She was one of those dreadful creatures who enjoyed stabbing adoring lovers to the heart, deliberately plunging the dagger deep, and twisting it in the wound.

'I hope that I die in France,' Denzil cried, keeping his face averted, shamed by his tears, riddled with guilt. 'What else is there but death for me now? I adore her. No matter what she does. I can't help myself. I want her – I shall go on wanting her.'

'She is Guy's wife. You can't have her! Don't talk of dying – that's wicked. Pull yourself together, Denzil. Can't you see that she's absolutely indifferent? If she loved you in return, then there might be a solution. You would both have to face Guy and ask him to divorce her. But she doesn't love you or Jack. She's ruining your life, trampling your hopes underfoot, destroying your future with the cold thoughtlessness of a child tearing the wings from a butterfly.'

He was calmer now, the handkerchief a crumpled ball in his hand. 'Everything you say is true,' he agreed dully. 'D'you think that I don't know that? It makes no difference.'

There was a hollow feeling of defeat and despair within Sally. Nothing would change him. The bitterest phrases, the sharpest irony would not alter him one jot. 'Why did you tell me?' she asked. 'What d'you expect me to do?'

'I don't know. Nothing, I suppose, but I do feel better for having spoken.'

This made Sally angry. He had eased his conscience by passing the burden on to her. Better by far if he had kept his mouth shut. The only person unaffected by this situation was Lalage, who was blind, deaf and dumb to love. It was not fair. Why should she be allowed to escape retribution? Then another thought struck her forcibly. 'You'll not mention it to Guy until this venture in France is over.'

'I shan't see him. I'm to sail with Redvers.'

Every instinct was urging Sally to go to the manor and confront Lalage. She longed to voice all the things which had been hammering at her for months – her loathing and distrust – her present conviction that it was Lalage who had nearly killed Miranda. But she knew that she must deny herself this satisfaction. Now was not the time to do it. Of far greater importance were those men who were intent on crossing the Channel into enemy territory. She must school herself to be patient for a while longer. When Guy returned the matter would have to be brought to light and, meanwhile, she would watch Lalage, biding her time, preparing to strike.

Denzil stood up and reached for his coat. His face was thinner, bonier, a man's face now, not a boy's. His crime was bringing its own punishment. Would justice be meted out to Lalage in some undreamed of way? Sally prayed that this might come about.

She went to him and, standing on her toes, kissed his cold, damp cheek. 'Dear cousin,' she said softly. 'I am your friend, remember that. Your secret is safe with me.'

'I must return to Wylde Court,' he mumbled, aware of his unworthiness, embarrassed by her kindness. 'Mamma will be waiting. I'm afraid that I've been sorry company for her of late.'

'You hope to see Lalage. No need to deny it. I too, have been in love, Denzil. I know its insanity. You will take her again, if she offers herself, even though she reeks of the stables and Jack Smithers.' Her brown eyes were immeasurably wise and filled with understanding.

She walked to the outside door with him, and watched him mount his horse. A chilly sunset lurked behind a sky of tarnished steel where the clouds piled up like giant rocks. In the distance, the thunder of the sea sounded like a presage of doom.

Lalage lay in the bath-tub in front of the roaring fire in her bedchamber, idly popping soap bubbles whilst Bethany took a gown from the wardrobe and spread it out across the bed. The armoire was full of clothes; the tallboy drawers overflowed with stockings, gloves, night-attire, chemises and diaphanous sequinned scarves. Lalage was extravagant, and even Guy frowned at her dress-bills.

When the ritual of bathing and hair-washing was completed, she sat on the stool by the dressing-table and Bethany towelled her locks. 'A pity we had to leave London, madame,' she observed as she worked. 'Just when the season was reaching its peak.'

Lalage's eyes were rebellious, her smile tight. 'My dear husband's orders. As a dutiful wife I could do nothing but obey him.'

'Of course, milady.' Bethany's skilful fingers were busy with the brush.

'You are very competent at dressing hair,' Lalage remarked, watching her in the mirror. 'Almost as clever as that foppish Julian creature whom Aurora employs. I noticed it when you first came to me.'

'I've had some experience, madame. Before I worked at Wylde Court, I was personal maid to the Honourable Mrs Duckworth, over near Warrington.'

Lalage gave her a sharp glance. 'Why were you dismissed?'

Bethany hesitated, wondering whether to lie, then she tossed her head, secure in her position of maid to this great lady. 'She said I was debauching her son.'

'And were you?'

'That would be telling,' Bethany answered pertly.

'The soul of discretion, eh?' The slanting amber eyes sparkled at her. 'I like that quality, Bethany.'

'You can rely on me to serve you loyally. Haven't I already proved to you just how trustworthy I can be?' Bethany added a jewelled comb to her mistress's curls.

'You have, and I've rewarded you handsomely. Can I also rely on that dashing rascal of a postillion who courts you with such ardour?'

'Oh, yes, he'll do anything I ask him,' came the smug, confident reply. Bethany adored every moment of her life. Many perks came her way; tradesmen slipped her bribes to bring a piece of merchandise to Lalage's notice; those seeking posts in the Beaumaris household made it worth her while to recommend them; Lalage passed over her cast-offs, and she had a whole string of lovers. She had become snobbish and greedy, and set great store by her title of lady's maid, queening it over other members of staff.

333

'I may want him to ride to London with a message. Tell him to be ready, night and day. He'll be well paid, if he holds his tongue. No one must get to hear of it,' Lalage said, rising to her feet and letting her robe slither to the floor.

Bethany dusted her with perfumed powder and helped her into a thin silk chemise. The gown followed, crimson shot-silk over a salmon satin slip, the revers trimmed with ivory lace, topped by a long-sleeved spencer, short-bodiced and buttoning down the front. Bethany rolled white stockings up Lalage's legs, fastened them with ribbon garters, and slipped a pair of crimson pumps on to her feet.

'There's someone at the door, madame,' she said, for Lalage appeared not to have heard the knock, absorbed in studying her reflection in the cheval-mirror.

'Who is it?' she called impatiently.

'Denzil,' he murmured through the thickness of the wood.

Lalage signalled to her maid to let him in, then ordered her to stand guard outside. When they were alone, he tried to take her in his arms, but she side-stepped neatly. 'God, you look awful,' she said, frowning. 'What's the matter with you?'

'Damnation, Lalage! I've not seen you alone since you arrived.'

She laughed and tapped him lightly on the cheek with her fan. 'I should think not! It wouldn't be seemly. I'm a married woman! You shouldn't seek to plough another man's field, my dear young sir.'

He growled out an oath and wrenched the fan from her, snapping the mother-of-pearl sticks in his fury. 'Damn witch! I'd like to strangle you! What of Jack?'

Her eyes flashed with anger. 'You oaf! That was my favourite fan. You'll buy me another, damn you! Well – *what* about Jack? It's no business of yours! Christ! You bloody Wyldes! You think you own the earth and everyone on it! You're just like Guy. D'you think I wanted to come back to this hell-hole? He insisted, while he's off God knows where. D'you know what he's doing? Where he is?'

Denzil was staring at her miserably. He had left Briar Cottage filled with noble intentions. They had not survived for long. Just to be in the same building with Lalage was exquisite torture. Hating and despising himself he had been unable to keep away from her bedroom door.

'I've no idea where Guy has gone.' He lied badly, unable to concentrate.

'I think you do.' Her eyes narrowed. 'Tell me, is he with another woman?'

'I don't know!' He flung up his arms in despair. 'Does it matter? I'm glad he's not here! Damn him!'

'There's something that has been puzzling me,' she said, coming closer, the soft swishing of her skirt driving him into a frenzy. 'Those Frenchmen at Highfield Lodge were not smugglers, were they? I think they were illegal *émigrés*. I've heard of those gentlemen who rescue the *ci-devants*. They always look after their *protégés*. I believe that in spite of Guy's words to the contrary, he is one of them.'

All her energy was gathered into her piercing stare. Denzil was weakening, almost mesmerized by her fixed smile, like that of a statue which seemed to express human warmth but which was cold stone. 'What would you say if it were true?' he stammered.

'I should admire him.' Her face came to life now. 'Ah, to be loved by such a man. So courageous. Like a god.'

Denzil would have given his soul to have her look at him with such admiration. The truth trembled on his lips. 'I'm not saying that it is so, but supposing – just supposing that I also belonged to such a league, perhaps that of *Le Fantom*?'

Her eyes widened, her hands reaching him. 'Denzil! D'you know him? *Le Fantom*?' He remained silent and comprehension flashed across her face. 'Denzil! Answer me! Are you suggesting that Guy is he?'

This was terrible. Stronger than the fact of betrayal and its consequences was the fear that Lalage would cleave to her husband if she thought him to be the leader. 'No – no – it isn't Guy – I swear it isn't Guy.'

'But it *is* a Wylde – don't try to hide it, I can see it in your face.' She was so fierce, dominating, strong hands shaking him, determined to be answered. He half shook his head, but was torn, wanting her to think it so, hoping for reflected glory. Her hold relaxed, eyes musing, tiger's eyes, slits of gold, eyes of the stalking beast. 'If not Guy, then who? Not you, Denzil – that's for sure.' The contempt in her voice stung him. She stilled, muscles tensed before the spring. 'William! It *has* to be William! It fits perfectly. Solid, stuffy old William! What a perfect blind – how very clever. This would explain his trips to town. I wondered why he was tearing himself away from his silly bride.'

'But, Lalage – I don't think – I mean – you could be wrong,' Denzil blurted incoherently, but his brain was whirling. Why not let her believe she had discovered the secret? What harm could it possibly do? William was head over heels in love with Sally. He'd never taken a shine to Lalage. She would never be able to seduce him. It would be safe to let her think him *Le Fantom*.

With one of her extraordinary changes of mood which stunned him, she now pressed close, perfumed fingers in his hair. 'Silly boy – you can trust me. Tell me about it, Denzil. Come, my hero, let us lie on the bed, and you shall recount your adventures. I'm on fire to hear of them. A knight must always have a lady to champion, mustn't he? My scarf shall be your favour.'

Some time later, when Denzil had gone, Lalage sat down at the secretaire and wrote a letter. She strewed sand over the wet ink and holding the sealing-wax to the candle-flame, allowed several drops to fall where her signature should have been. She pressed her ring to it. Bethany entered promptly at her summons, and Lalage handed her the envelope.

'Take this to your postillion. He must leave for London at once,' she ordered. 'Here is money. There will be more when he returns. If you fail me, I'll see that you are both dismissed with such stains on your characters that you'll never get another post.'

Bethany, shaken by the expression on her face, dipped a frightened curtsey and sped off, but she paused when she reached the stable, holding the letter up to the lantern and reading the address. Augustus Sanderman, eh? The dirty old dog! So he was one of madame's lovers, was he? She had suspected as much. Oh, her Ladyship was a sly one, all right! A woman after Bethany's own heart. She smiled knowingly, fancying herself party to another amorous intrigue, but she was not as clever as she imagined. She did not know – no one knew – that the spanking new light carriage which Lalage had wangled out of Guy was manned entirely by a disguised bodyguard of Reformati members, including the young postilion. Within half an hour the letter was on its way.

The American schooner, the *Memphis Queen,* lay anchored at Wapping Wharf. It was not the most salubrious of areas, and a motley conglomeration of people lined the water-front. Mariners wearing calico trousers, sporting tarred pigtails and round black castors, swaggered up various gangplanks, waving to wives or harlots, their voices rising above the general din.

Brusque commands from officers mingled with the curses of sweating stevedores humping cases of cargo, and the shouts of vendors who swarmed in the crowd, selling last-minute necessities to those about to embark. Merchants strolled there, engaged in earnest conversation with grizzled, weathered captains. Thieves and pickpockets practised their trade. Weak sunshine washed over the tangled masts and spars of the ships riding at anchor on the murky grey water.

Captain Chapman stood on the deck of the *Memphis Queen*, while sailors scurried about under the stern eye of the mate, porters lugged bales into place, and a davit creaked overhead. It was growing dark, the tide on the turn, the swift current attacking the heavy stagnancy of the Thames, sucking and sloshing at the schooner's bow.

He jingled the guineas in his pocket, and smiled sardonically as he considered the folly of those who had paid him so much for the doubtful privilege of being transported to a country where a man was likely to have his head severed from his neck. Mr Eli Brown was the name given by the lanky American who had come aboard an hour ago. Chapman's eyes had twinkled as he accepted that title, pretending not to know that seedy-looking fellow in the plain dark suit and Quakerish hat, his hair a nondescript mud-colour, slicked back from his long, serious face. He had been accompanied by his secretary, another lean, tall individual, as dour as his employer, and a servant who carried the hand-luggage. Two ladies were with them, muffled in flowing cloaks, bonnets and face-veils, and they had gone below immediately.

The passengers' papers had been in order and they were shown to their cabins. Now the anchor was up and the *Memphis Queen* began its journey through the misty darkness to the mouth of the river. A few hours of sailing before such a strong wind and they would sight Havre.

In the narrow, cramped quarters allotted to them, Mr Brown sat down on one of the bunks and glanced out through the thick glass porthole. The lanterns swayed on their gimbals, and it was difficult to keep balance against the slant of the floor for they had reached open water and the sea was choppy. His 'sisters' were complaining.

'Egad, Ambrose,' one of them remarked with a disparaging glance at her dowdy black dress, 'you might have selected something more becoming. I'd never dare appear at Mrs Berkeley's wearing this old tat! I'd be laughed to scorn!'

Ambrose smiled and lit up a cheroot, drawing the smoke back into his lungs, then exhaling it through flared nostrils. 'Sorry, Charlie, but it's right for the part. You're Miss Verity Brown, remember? And you, Nick, are Miss Prudence. Two very respectable spinsters, travelling with their brother to Geneva. I've brought you on this trip so that you may recover from the shock of our dear Mamma's sudden death – hence the black and those most convenient veils. You won't have to shave so often or so closely. William's our servant, so you may order him about.'

'Only in public,' warned William with a grin. He was disguised in a grey hair-piece and sober garb.

'I've worn my under-drawers, as well as these quite hideous red flannel petticoats. It's frightfully draughty,' moaned Nick, too pretty in his fair, curling wig to be a nonconformist maiden-lady.

Ambrose shot him a hard blue stare. 'Leave me to do the talking, and don't flirt with the officials in the custom-house.'

'I'm going to get some rest.' Guy stretched out on the locker and wrapped his cloak around him.

'Good idea, Mr Secretary Crabtree,' said Ambrose, easing down on the bunk. He grinned across at Nick and Charlie. 'You too, girls. Get your beauty sleep. God knows when we'll get another chance of a nap.'

By now they were excellent actors. Ambrose, who spoke the language fluently, confused the military at the landing-stage by his atrocious, heavily-accented French and his severe, puritanical manner. They were glad to give him back the passports without too close an examination, and direct him to an inn where a coach could be hired. His generosity in handing out American dollars hurried everything along smoothly. A thin, misty rain had begun to fall, turning the roads into a morass of sticky mud, doing little to alleviate the gloom of Havre.

Despite war and revolt, life carried on much as usual. Labourers went to work, shops were open and wives trudged to market with baskets on their arms and children clinging to their skirts. The poor were as wretched as ever for, when all was said and done, the furore of revolution had done little to help them escape the poverty-trap. The streets were tortuous, and smelt of stale fish and open sewers. There was a noticeable lack of noise, and plenty of soldiers about. Some wore the blue uniforms of the National Guard, others were sabre-rattling bullies of the

Compagnie Marat, sporting enormous moustaches, red caps, tricolour waistcoats and black shag trousers. No one accosted the sedate party who wended their way to the inn, accompanied by a couple of porters staggering under the burden of luggage. They passed one little knot of idlers at a street-corner who were muttering and glaring at passers-by, an oath on their lips if anyone dared to stare back, but it was too cold for them to hang about, and they shuffled off, heads bowed, hands stuffed deeply into their pockets.

The inn was kept by an elderly peasant who was in Ambrose's pay. He took them to the courtyard where a coach stood ready harnessed. On the driver's box was hunched a figure in torn coat, muffler and cockaded hat. He was puffing on a short-stemmed clay pipe, and nodded to his passengers.

'Good-morning, Giffe.' Ambrose smiled up at him before climbing into the musty interior. 'All well, I presume.'

'Going like clockwork,' Giffe announced with beaming good humour. 'The sight of gold produces miracles. Robert's gone on ahead. He'll be at the first changing-post.' He cracked his whip, clicked his tongue, and the vehicle went rattling off down the street.

They met up with Robert as arranged. He was dressed as a farmer, ill-kempt and insolent, demanding a lift as a free citizen of France. They had been travelling for hours and had stopped in a remote village to change horses. It was an unimposing hamlet, typical of others through which they had passed, filled with grey stone houses turning an almost blind face upon the world – an unfriendly, suspicious face. The weather was in their favour; though it made the going rough, it kept the people indoors. When they journeyed on, Robert was seated beside Giffe, high on the box out front.

The Chateau de St Croix lay on the edge of the forest of La Roche-Bernard, only a few miles from the water-logged peat marsh, La Grande-Brière. It was far too close to Nantes for comfort, and Robert's reports had been anything but reassuring. The countryside was flat and bleak with swamps and grasslands seen through a film of rain – ditches and miniature hazel spinneys, isolated cottages and tiny hamlets joined by narrow tracks, reeded meres and meandering waterways. There was no shelter from the winds which gusted across the boggy marshes, until they reached the great stretch of beech and oak which formed the forest.

There, on a slight rise, stood the chateau which had housed

the St Croix family for generations, glistening with that natural whiteness of the stone from which it had been built, a stone which whitens and hardens with time. It had conical-capped towers of blue-grey slate. From a distance they looked like a collection of pepper-pots. Once it had been surrounded by a moat, but this had gradually silted-up, and was now inhabited by a few monstrously large carp who propelled themselves through the slimy water with a lazy flick of huge fins. The forest had belonged to the lords of St Croix, rich in deer and boar, and the proceeds of the salt and peat marshes had flowed into their treasury, but such affluence was no more.

The chateau bore the indelible marks of four years of neglect, following the riots in 1789, when the populace of the area, inflamed by the news of the storming of the Bastille and egged on by paid agitators, had marched in a mob upon it. They had smashed windows, looted goods, raided the cellars and larders, and marched off again, screaming the popular catch-phrase: '*À la lanterne les aristos!*'

The coach rumbled across the drawbridge which no longer operated to keep out intruders. It was growing dark. Rain glimmered on the ridges of the highly ornamental roof. A dog barked somewhere, but apart from that the silence seemed virtually perpetual. No lackies came running, no grooms to take the horses; the servants, old and young, had packed up their belongings and left in the wake of the mob. Only Hercule de St Croix's faithful valet had remained, and one retainer, too old to change his ways. The chateau had always been his home, and he despised the title of *aides-ménage* which the government had conferred on humble employees, considering the name of servant to be a slur.

Ambrose hammered on the great, iron-studded door but, when no one came, he stamped round to the rear, Giffe following with the coach. They walked inside unchallenged. The retainer was nodding by the kitchen fire, starting up on seeing them, obviously told to expect guests. He hobbled ahead, leading them through a vast warren of huge, damp rooms, all showing signs of devastation. Curtains had been torn down and never replaced, the carpets were slashed, furniture damaged, and Ambrose's face was grim as he remembered how it had been on his last visit, before the Bastille had fallen, before the murder of the King and Queen. His footsteps echoed hollowly, and sadly he recalled the richness and elegance of the furnishings, the magnificence of mirrors and gilding which had once decorated the chateau. The mob had wantonly destroyed them, hacking priceless art treasure to pieces with their crude weapons.

He found the marquis and his three children living in rooms on an upper floor. What could be salvaged from the wreckage below had been used to make this apartment as comfortable as possible. Hercule had aged considerably, and he greeted Ambrose with the intense relief of a man who has struggled alone for too long. His son, a well-built, athletic-looking youth of seventeen, bowed gravely when introduced, while his sisters Josephine and Marie clung together, frightened. They were unused to strangers, marooned in the old castle, never allowed beyond the gardens for fear of reprisal.

Food was scarce, but the marquis insisted that his visitors eat, humiliated by the barenness of his table. After a crust of bread, some cheese and a glass of sour red wine, Ambrose brushed aside polite talk. 'You must leave at once,' he said, his face planed by shadows in the candlelight.

'Leave?' St Croix frowned, an arrogant expression playing round his thin-lipped mouth. 'You can't be serious? Abandon my chateau. Run before that *canaille*! Never!'

He was a handsome man, upright and haughty of posture, with fine-boned features and an aquiline nose. Ambrose realized angrily that even deprivation had not taught him the lesson of humility. 'Why the deuce d'you suppose I risked my life and that of my men to come here, if it wasn't to get you to England?' he shouted.

'I had hoped that we might defend the chateau,' the marquis replied.

Ambrose gave a bark of laughter, wondering if the strain had toppled his cousin's reason. 'Are you mad? Haven't you heard what's been happening around here? Armed troops threaten you now, not an undisciplined rabble. The Company of Marat has been dispatched south to root out Royalists and kill every man, woman and child! Don't be a fool, man. We leave at dawn. There's not a moment to lose.'

'Papa is right! We should not bow the knee to a dirty crowd of assassins!' This came from Henri, brought up to ride rough-shod over the serfs, unable to accept that those ignorant, half-starved peasants had turned on their masters.

Ambrose and Guy exchanged a glance. They were determined that St Croix would go, even if they had to knock him out, and his stupidly obstinate son. 'Listen to me, both of you,' said the American, and he started to relate in bald, unvarnished detail exactly what was taking place in Nantes and other regions of Brittany.

The marquis and Henri turned pale, and the young ladies began to weep. At the end of half an hour, all resistance to his plan had been effectively destroyed. It was as well that agreement had been reached, because the dawn appeared to be coming early – a strange dawn for the sun was rising in the wrong direction.

'That's not daybreak,' said William, staring out of the unshuttered window. 'What lies west of here?' The sky seemed to grow lighter even as he watched, spreading a curtain of crimson wide.

'The Chateau Brane,' whispered the marquis, white-lipped, his hauteur vanished.

'It's been fired!' Ambrose exclaimed, and swung into action, turning to Nick and Charlie. 'Get out of those gowns. Remember the plan?'

Long before the true dawn came, Mr Brown's party were once again in the hired coach, but with several differences. Eli Brown was still in charge and Giffe was the driver, helped by Robert, but Josephine and Marie had taken the place of Nick and Charles, St Croix had been transformed into Mr Crabtree, and Henri was now their servant. Guy and William had changed into the baggy trousers and sheepskin coats of villagers, while Nick and Charlie were disguised as labourers. Each carried the correct indentity papers for his pretended trade. St Croix had managed to keep a few horses, and the four men took these. They transported the valet and retainer to a place of safety and then separated, taking different routes to the rendezvous in Cherbourg.

Ambrose leaned from the coach window and looked back at those tall stately towers of his mother's ancestral home. The sky was peculiarly luminous and white and the sun was coming up, a fire-ball in the milky vapour. Its rays tipped the roof and turrets with crimson, reflected in every window, creating a curious illusion. It was as if the chateau was already burning.

'What are you doing here?' asked Jack from his slumped position by the log fire flaring in the grate.

He squinted across the room, but could not bring his mind and eyesight into definite focus. Everything was indistinct, floating in dust, wavering in space. The air was stale, the bed unmade, the sheets tossed anyhow. Once it had been a fine apartment, years ago when used as a hunting-lodge, but now the floor was coated with dust, there was a large patch of damp on the gilded ceiling, a corner of the arras flapped drearily in the draught, and cobwebs festooned the window-sill.

'I've come to see you,' Lalage replied, pulling off her gloves as she walked towards him. 'And also to offer my services, should you be expecting a ship-load of wounded men in the near future.'

Six candles were blazing on the table, with bottles of wine, some bread, and the remains of a chicken. Jack, in his shirt-sleeves and tight breeches, his bright auburn hair falling untidily over his forehead, sprawled in a large red velvet chair.

'What the hell are you on about?' he growled, reaching for the bottle. He had been there for hours, drinking quite alone. Though he knew that he should have remained clear-headed that night, his mind was uneasy. Sober, he must justify his actions to himself, intoxicated, no such justification was necessary. Molly had been giving him the rough edge of her tongue. Somehow she had got wind of his affair with Lalage and had not spared him. If there was one person in the world whom he feared and respected, it was his mother. He had not admitted to anything, but Molly knew and was not pleased.

Lalage took the other armchair, supremely elegant in her black riding-dress, long cloak spilling to the floor. 'There's no need to lie, Jack,' she said calmly. 'I know what has been planned. Guy and William are in France, and Denzil has gone to meet them.'

'Who told you?' He looked at her vaguely, drunkenly, aware of menace in her cool manner.

Lalage poured herself a glass of wine. 'Denzil, of course. Oh, yes – he confessed everything. Quite the little hero, isn't he? And my husband too. Who would have guessed that they'd become involved in such quixotic adventures? What of you, Jack? Why aren't you there also?'

With every word which coiled from between her scarlet lips, Jack was becoming more sober. He did not let her know this, keeping her glass replenished, watching her as she drank and wondering how much she really knew. 'I've more respect for my neck,' he replied drily. 'I'd rather be a live coward than a dead hero. I'll bet that you couldn't worm secrets out of Guy, but that fool Denzil is wax in your hands.'

She laughed, colour flushing her cheekbones, those oblique eyes shining. She threw off her cloak and jacket, temptingly slender in her white shirt and sleek black skirt, in the full pride of her youth and beauty, a queen of pleasure, the personification of earthly joys. Uncoiling herself from the chair, she went to him and sat on his knee, linking her arms about his neck. 'It was very amusing,' she murmured, fingers in his curls. 'He told me because he wanted my admiration so desperately. You don't care whether I admire you or hate you, do you, Jack?'

'No,' he answered, while his hand found its way inside her shirt, finding one firm breast, his thumb revolving on the nipple. 'I can honestly say, my dear, that I don't give a damn.'

'That's what makes you so fascinating,' she confided against his mouth, her tongue flickering over his lips. 'Don't you want to know anything about me? Aren't you interested in my past?'

He gave a sceptical grin. 'I thought you didn't have a past — couldn't remember a bloody thing. Or was that a lie too?'

She hesitated, and there was a wild, slightly insane look in her eyes. Been at the drugs again, thought Jack, there's certainly something exciting her tonight. She slipped from his lap to the rug at his feet, leaning her head back against his knees, grasping his hand and pushing it back into her shirt. 'It was the biggest lie of all,' she began, her voice low, vibrant. 'You should have the greatest sympathy with my story, for I am also a bastard.'

'Go on, tell me.' Jack was stroking her as one might soothe a savage animal.

'My mother was Greek — a peasant woman seduced by a nobleman whilst he was staying at his villa near the Adriatic Sea. Such an old, old story,' she said bitterly, 'one that brings misery to the girl, while the vile man remains untouched.' She jerked away from Jack's hand, as if her hatred of men included him. He let her talk on without interruption.

'He was the Comte de Tourzel, head of a powerful family — my father, and I adored him, till I learned what he was really like, a cruel, proud *aristo*. Oh, he was most magnanimous to me, his little Greek love-child — one of his many by-blows! I was taken to France — to his chateau. Can you imagine my joy, my high hopes? I expected to be treated as his beloved daughter, only to find myself working in the kitchen, the lowest of menials.

344

His bitch wife saw to that! I visited my mother when she lay dying, still a young woman, killed by the shame of her betrayal. She made me swear to be avenged on the *comte*. I fulfilled that vow. I watched him go to the guillotine, with his wife and his legal children. It was I who had denounced them to the mob.'

'How the hell did you get involved with Guy Wylde? Why did you pretend to have lost your memory?' asked Jack at last, neither condemning nor applauding her.

She stirred, smiling up at him. 'It suited my purpose. We lost ones learn to be cunning, don't we, if we are to prosper? I have an enemy.'

'Only one?' Jack laughed. 'I'd have thought you would have a million.'

'I've been hunting this man for a long time. My most desperate hours have been comforted by dreams of seeing him tortured – whipped with spiked thongs – hot pincers tearing out lumps of his flesh!' Her voice shook, harsh and vindictive. 'It was through him that I fell foul of the Reformati.'

'What the devil's that?'

'A group to which I have pledged myself. A powerful sect who demand unswerving loyalty. Their initiations, rites, symbols and purpose are deadly secret, and their vengeance is swift and terrible if one defaults. I want this man, and now, Satan be praised, I've got him!' The look of triumph which lit her face was hideous to behold.

'Who is he?' Jack was completely sober now.

Her laughter was savage. She had swung round, on her knees before him, and the fingers which clutched at his thighs were like the talons of a predatory bird. 'He's been hiding under a pseudonym, Jack! *Le Fantom!* The Jacobins have been searching for him! The Reformati want him! But I know his real name! Denzil told me!'

Jack bruised her wrists as he tore them away from him, holding her arms wide apart, shaking her. 'Who is it, you bitch, tell me!'

Her laughter had the ring of hysteria and her eyes were blazing, but cold, devoid of humanity. 'To think that I could have searched the whole world over, but kismet ordained otherwise. Destiny, fate – those truths I learned among the Muslims. It was my karma to be washed up into Guy's arms, setting me on the path which has led to my enemy.'

Jack was bewildered. He had never been told who *Le Fantom* was; the least people who knew, the better, was the league's premise. 'Are you saying that it is Guy?' he shouted.

'No – no, you dullard! He's much too flamboyant, too suspect! Their choice was brilliant. A stroke of genius. A quiet, solid, farming man – who would think him capable of acts of derring-do?' She leapt to her feet, laved in the scarlet of the flames roaring up the chimney, and she was breathing hard, her voice charged with an almost sexual intensity. 'It's William! He's *Le Fantom!*'

Jack knew instinctively that she had got it wrong. In her obsessive determination to find *Le Fantom*, it was as if she had clutched at any straw. There was no logical reason why he should be so convinced of her mistake. As she had said, someone as unlikely might well be the ideal candidate, yet it did not add up. 'William?' he said doubtfully.

'Yes, William, dolt! He's in France now, isn't he, along with my dearly beloved husband, freeing more bloody *aristos*? They'll find a hot welcome in Cherbourg. I've informed the Reformati.'

The enormity of this took a second to sink in, then: 'You've betrayed them? William, and your own husband?' breathed Jack.

Her mirth rang through the room, a chilling, merciless sound. 'He means nothing to me. Surely, you'll join me in wishing to see the destruction of the Wylde brood? With any luck, they'll get Denzil too! Won't that please you, Jack? I'll be mistress here if they die. We'll have the run of the place. No one shall stand in our way.'

'What makes you think I'd share anything with a vicious bitch like you?' he regarded her levelly, wondering to what further depths of iniquity she could possibly sink.

She flung herself down beside him, head back, face upturned to his. 'Don't lie to me, Jack. You want me. I know you do. Don't you understand, the Reformati will forgive me now that I've got *Le Fantom*. They would have killed me otherwise. Now I shall rise high in their esteem. You've no idea how powerful they are. The revolution will spread to England, and those who have been loyal will be put in positions of the greatest authority. We'll be among these, rich and omnipotent. There's nothing we can't achieve together, and I must have you by my side. What do a few lives matter?'

Jack's eyes ran over that perfect face which concealed such

346

terrible depravity – the living portrait of cold beastliness, ruthless enough to commit foul crimes and cruel enough to laugh at them. She was so swollen with hubris and self-glory that she did not notice his close scrutiny or lack of enthusiasm.

'This organization – the Reformati. Have they many members in this country?' he asked quietly.

'They've friends everywhere,' she nodded eagerly. 'Sanderman is one of them, and de Belcourt. I'll introduce you to our leader, Latour, when we get back to London.'

Her arms were round his waist, and she pressed her body into his, between his spread thighs. She was smiling, eyes languorous, lips pouting for his kisses, certain that she had won him over. Though it made him want to gag, Jack gave them to her, then said: 'So, sorceress, you think you've been mighty clever, capturing *Le Fantom*, snitching on your husband and all?'

She wriggled closer, passion rising. 'Rejoice with me! Drink to the Reformati and to the downfall of aristocrats and all who aid them!'

Jack hit her, once, twice, thrice. With each blow, her head jerked back with a force which could have snapped her neck. Blood began to stream from her nose. 'You filthy whore!' he snarled, and hit her again.

She was a strong woman and, surprisingly, had kept her feet, but was momentarily stunned. Astonishment and hatred twisted her bloody face, and in a lithe movement she had stooped and grabbed the poker from the hearth. 'Keep away from me,' she warned, balancing it like a sword.

Jack lunged but, using both hands, she raised it. The room spun, sickening arcs of fiery stars whirling as he took the full force of her blow on the side of his head. Jack staggered, and she sprang for the door, shouting: 'I thought you had more spunk! I was wrong. You're still the Wyldes' lick-spittle!'

He took a step forward, weaving on his feet like a drunken man, then the room erupted as she flung open the door. Three men burst in, running at her bidding, her henchmen ordered to protect her by Latour, to protect but to also see that she did not give him the slip.

'You want him?' shouted the foremost, a large hard-featured bully flourishing a cudgel.

Lalage stood back against the wall, her slit-pupilled eyes like those of no earthly woman. 'Yes. Take him. He won't join us, so get him to Latour as a hostage.'

The last thing Jack saw was her face, a great bruise already purpling on her cheek, before another cracking blow precipitated him into darkness.

Chapter 6

There were soldiers at the barricade across the road just beyond Cherbourg. Giffe saw the blue uniforms appearing out of the dusk, the dull light glinting on muskets and sword-hilts. There was a wagon just ahead of them and he drew on the reins, slowing his team as the bar was lifted and the cart moved off along the road.

The coach approached and a sergeant, broad-shouldered and officious, came abreast of it, passing the steaming horses and pausing to look up at Giffe. 'Your papers!' he demanded.

Taking his time and seeming perfectly at ease, Giffe fumbled in the pockets of his capacious ragged overcoat and finally produced a wad of documents. The sergeant thumbed through them. 'They're quite in order, captain,' said Giffe respectfully. 'An American gentleman, his sisters and two servants, travelling from Switzerland, and going aboard a Norwegian vessel bound for New York.'

'I'm a sergeant, not a captain,' reproved the guard, not unpleased by the mistake.

'Not for long, I'll warrant. A fine soldier like yourself will quickly rise through the ranks,' said Giffe with bucolic earnestness.

'These seem to be correct.' The sergeant smiled and handed him back the papers. He signalled to the men at the barrier. 'Pass on, citizen.'

This situation had met them along the route from St Croix, and Giffe was beginning to congratulate himself. If luck continued to hold, by morning they would be safely aboard the *Mayfly* and homeward bound. Cherbourg was a thriving port, and granite-built, grey-slated houses dotted the quay, alongside the noisy, smelly fish-market. Boats, heavy with their catch, were speeding for the shore, rising, dipping in the swell. Giffe, watching them from his perch on the coachman's box, wondered if Captain Redvers was out there somewhere, waiting for nightfall and the chance to put in at the cove. He said something to this effect to Robert, huddled beside him in his role as assistant driver.

Ambrose led the party into a waterside tavern and booked rooms. As they went through the taproom, he noticed a pair of men wearing the broad-brimmed hats of Breton peasants, and two more, taller than the rest, clad in disreputable garb, scarlet caps cocked over scruffy hair, knees poking through tattered trousers and torn shirts clinging to their wide shoulders. With loutish bravado, they had taken the centre of the floor, bare feet thrust into straw-lined sabots, one smoking a pipe, the other quaffing a mug of ale. They gave the newcomers furtive, suspicious glances, muttering blasphemies and spitting on the ground in their direction. Satisfied that each member of his troop was now present, Ambrose walked past as if he had never seen them before in his life.

The room was long and low, lit by a lamp which swung from a rafter and belched out fumes, adding to the reek of garlic, rancid grease and human sweat. The inn was as shabby and unwelcoming as its customers, a few down-at-heel men, some women and several children. On one corner was a wide plank which served as a counter, cluttered with jugs, bottles, slices of bread, cold meat, wedges of cheese and many mugs. The landlord, surly and ill-favoured, stood behind it. A Republican slogan, badly spelt and scrawling, dribbled red paint across the wall at his back. Ambrose took his sisters and servants to a shadowy trestle table and ordered a bottle of wine. He was apprehensive. Had he been a dog, the fur would have been rising along his spine. Hercule was a hot-head, likely to react should anyone make a slighting remark about *aristos*. So far, Ambrose had been able to curb him, but he longed for the moment when they could slip away to the cove.

A few more people shambled in, mostly men taking their habitual glass before going home. A serious bunch who spoke in hushed tones, glancing around furtively as if fearing that spies lurked. They had slaughtered their feudal lords, but it seemed that in so doing they had merely taken on another yoke. Gone was the salt and freshness of Gallic gestures, freedom of expression and noisy rhetoric. Conversation was low, desultory, each wary of his neighbour.

Ambrose's nerves were taut, the responsibility of the St Croix family weighing on him. Josephine and Marie had obeyed him without demur, but the men were anything but pliable. Henri resented having to dress and act like a servant, and the marquis was far too rigid in his role of secretary. Ambrose was certain that their performances would not have deceived a blind idiot.

He glanced at his pocket-watch. Had enough time elapsed so that they might go to their rooms without arousing suspicion?

He decided that it had, and was about to suggest it when suddenly there came an ominous noise from the street, the heavy tramp of boots and the rattle of muskets. 'The Marats!' someone shouted, and the customers began to get to their feet, fumbling with their belongings, terrified. 'The Marats! There's a troop of Marats outside!'

Women's shrill trebles mingled with the curses of the men, and children wailed. The Marats were feared and hated, far too fond of rebel-hunting and not too fussy who they arrested in the process. A patrol could start a brawl which might end with deportation or death. Men started to slide towards the door but they were too late. It crashed open and soldiers crowded through the entrance. Weapons clanked, boots clumped across the stone floor, orders were barked above the shouts of men trying to flee, being caught and dragged back. There were dull thuds as gun-stocks met skulls and bodies fell.

'This is a peaceful inn! We do no harm!' quavered the landlord, wringing his hands in anguish as he cringed before the hulking Marat leader.

'I'm looking for escaping *ci-devants*. Have you seen 'em? Don't lie to me, dog, or I'll have your tongue torn out!' roared the captain, glaring around with his great sabre in his fist. Of typical peasant stock, he strove to counterbalance his lack of brain by brawn.

'*Aristos?* Here? Oh, no, your Excellency –' The landlord was white with terror, his fat body seemed to be disintegrating with it.

'Search this bloody pest-house!' shouted the captain, aiming a kick at him. His men went into action. There were splintering crashes, furniture went flying and they attacked the door with their musket-butts and smashed several windows, just for the hell of it. Boots thudded up the staircase, and the din continued from aloft.

Some of the troopers were herding people into the middle of the room, taking names, ungentle in their handling. Ambrose and his companions were screened by a low partition, and not noticed until last. Then the captain stopped in front of their table. 'What have we here?' he bellowed.

'We are Americans,' Ambrose replied calmly.

'Show me your papers.' The captain thrust his head forward. His eyes, set near his hooked nose, had a squint, his lips were thick and moist and his breath stank of alcohol. 'American, eh? We'll soon see if that's true.'

In that instant, one of those tall, lanky oafs who had been eyeing Ambrose since his entry suddenly bounded from the troopers and knocked against the hanging lamp. It fell, scattering oil and broken glass, plunging them into total darkness. In the pandemonium which followed, Ambrose seized Josephine and Marie by the hands, opened the rear door, and pushed them out.

The alley was dark and the wind whipped down it, bitterly cold. Making certain that Hercule and Henri were following, Ambrose rushed the girls along, crossing a square where a plane tree creaked and stirred. The houses were shuttered, blind. The cobbles gleamed, wet, slippery, and the uproar had died into the distance.

Ambrose took the road away from the quay, a lonely road, bordered by stunted trees, bare branches leaning away from the perpetual sea-breeze, spreading out like stiff strands of hair. The air was filled with brine. A low rumble as from far-off artillery carried the threat of storm. The sea and land were black, the sky smeared with menacing copper. Another low rumble shook the heavens, the whole night filled with foreboding attuned to Ambrose's mood. He glanced back. Two figures, ethereal as ghosts, could be seen – the marquis and his son.

'My God, we've been betrayed!' panted Hercule.

'That clumsy lout who doused the light –' began Henri, panting and furious.

'Was Guy Wylde! He did it deliberately,' snapped Ambrose. 'Help your sisters. We must hurry.'

The tattered clouds were tearing across to mass together, meeting with a guttural roar. Brazen lightning split the darkness, and they saw the pale glimmer of each other's faces. Ambrose and his cousin exchanged a stare. Though related by blood, they were alien. Hidebound Henri, as fanatical as the Jacobins in his own way. Ambrose unsheathed his sword-stick, making for the cliff edge, seeking his men in that swirling, wind-torn gloom. His boots skidded on mud as he went down the steep incline. The sea boiled, seething, limitless, flinging its waves against the rocks. Somewhere out there the *Mayfly* was waiting. He heard the angry roll of thunder, looking up at the ominous sky. A great white undulating mass hurled itself in front of him, enveloped him in a stinging, wet embrace, then withdrew down the beach. Where the devil were the others? He

352

screwed up his eyes, seeing two faint spots of gold on the sea. The *Mayfly*! It had to be! The rowing boat would be there, in the pounding surf.

Musket-fire rattled from the port. Shouts, the drumming of hooves, rose above the storm's rage. The marquis was running along the shore with his children. There was a moment of utter confusion as Ambrose headed for the spot where the boat should be. The Marats had found the cliff-path, but the men they were after got there first, tumbling headlong down. Ambrose heard Guy's voice as the Marats came on. Hand-held flares cast a lurid glow, the flames streaming back in the wind, hissing, spluttering. Giffe and Robert stopped, swung round and fired volleys. Two Marats went down. Ambrose saw the huge form of Redvers wading through the swell. Ignoring the rain of bullets, he and Denzil carried the girls to the bobbing craft, manned by skilled oarsmen. Giffe had formed his men into a tight line, backs to the sea, facing the oncoming soldiers.

Henri had leapt in after his sisters, but his father suddenly ran forward, snatched up a sabre from a dead body, and rushed them, hacking and slashing, crying: 'Death to the Republic! Long live the King!'

A musket-ball smashed into his chest. He fell backwards on to the sand. The sea ran over him, sucking, dragging at his corpse, bearing it into the heaving water. Henri stood up. The boat swayed dangerously. 'Father! My father! Save him!' he yelled, his voice thin against the cacophony of the storm gods.

Redvers forced him down with a mighty hand. 'Too late, son. Be still, or we'll capsize!'

William stood firm, shoulder to shoulder with Guy. He knew a moment of supreme unity, of ecstatic joy, fighting at his brother's side, firing into the panic-stricken mob of Marats. He heard the hiss of a bullet as it passed close, and the percussive thud of a report. He was about to fire back when there sprang another flame, a second shot. Lightning exploded inside him and he staggered, hands at the gaping hole. He refused to believe it. He couldn't have been hit! His spirit was wrenched from him in one great cry. Guy caught him as he fell.

Suddenly Sally came broad awake. She sat bolt upright, a horrible sense of fear, a feeling of emptiness around her. Guy! she thought. Guy! Guy!

The candle had gone out and the room was black, cold too.

Dawn was not far off. She fumbled and found the tinder-box on the bedside table. Never had she been more thankful to see light than when the wick flared and her room swung back into perspective. She had thought she was dead, entombed in eternal darkness.

She was shivering, still in the toils of a horrible nightmare which, try as she might, she could not recall. They would be returning soon. The clock gave the time as five-thirty. Her heart hammering, she rose, doused her face in the freezing water in the china basin, dressed and combed her hair. She shuddered with that stillness and waiting which was answered by someone calling her name.

The casement opened under her fumbling fingers. White mist swirled in, pungent with salty seaweed. She could see the bare trees through it, the sky a shade lighter, but could not guess who stood below until he spoke again.

'Come down, Sally. Don't wake the servants,' said Guy with a terror-inspiring urgency.

She flung her cloak round her as she ran, with him in a few seconds, stupefied with relief. He was safe, real and solid, his hands gripping hers. 'What is it, Guy? What has happened?' Her voice trembled.

'It's William. He's dead.'

'He can't be.' Her mind rejected it, but her heart knew that it was true.

His arm came about her, steadying her. 'My dear girl – will you come? He's at the lodge.'

She tried to walk but her knees buckled. He swung her up and carried her to his horse. She was seated before him, his arm pressing her to his chest, the powerful beast moving under them, cleaving through the darkness, the mist. It entered her nostrils and lay upon her lips, sour, stifling – like death. The nightmare came back – a black horse, a black rider, galloping across the Styx to Hades. William was dead and she had woken with Guy's name on her lips. Shame lay, a cold stone, in her breast.

She stood in the lower room of the lodge. Dawn was stealing in, making the candles pale and sicken, its chill fingers tracing over the weary faces of the people gathered there. Sally's eyes went to the thing stretched out on the refectory table. It was covered by a cloak. Guy's hand was at her elbow, and he gently lifted back a fold. At first glance William seemed to be asleep, but Sally knew that this was not so. His features had stiffened,

354

the skin waxen, like those effigies in the chapel. Gone was the warmth from within. There was no one there – nothing.

Voices came faintly, as though muffled by a thick layer of wool. She could not make sense of a word – their mouths moved in their strangers' faces. They seemed to circle her, an odd collection of people in rough, wet clothing – some men, and the shadowy figures of two girls. Someone, she thought it was Guy, pushed a beaker of rum into her hand. The liquid burned her throat – heat radiated from the hearth, but she could not stop shivering.

Through the misty confusion, a face swam before her. It was Ambrose Alington, his manner grave, his bearing so dignified that she hardly recognized the foppish colonial who had come to her wedding. It can't be happening, she thought, this fantastic meeting, alive with weird quirks and ripples. I must still be dreaming.

'I'm so sorry, Mrs Wylde,' his voice reached her, his eyes grave and compassionate. 'This is terrible. Tonight, we lost one of our best men.'

'What are you doing here?' She should be saying something else, she knew – weeping, breaking down. She stared at him with wide, dry eyes.

A wry smile touched his lips. 'Sometimes I help these fellows out. Guy tells me that you know about it.' His hand was on hers. 'Look here, can you talk to the youngsters? Their father was killed as they escaped.'

Henri was on the settle by the fire with his sisters, all three exhausted, totally bewildered. Sally gazed at them blankly, then her eyes went to Robert Burgess, whom she knew slightly. A brawny middle-aged man with a fierce face was fixing a makeshift bandage round his arm. There were two others, younger, ragged, wearing strange-styled hats, who stood with them, advising. Denzil was immobile by the table, staring fixedly down at William, like a man in a trance.

Ambrose's smile was encouraging, his arm steadying her. Gathering her wits by degrees, she rallied, as he had hoped she would. He did not know her very well; they had exchanged only a few words in the past, but he instinctively recognized her qualities. Wise in so many ways, he had seen from the start how things stood between her and Guy, no matter how they pretended. In his opinion his friend had been a fool not to have snapped her up long ago, instead of getting entangled with such as Lalage. While he introduced her to his cousins, his agile mind was working on the problem of Guy's wife. It had plagued him since the revelation in the cockpit, and he had watched her as best he could, yet never by word or deed had she shown herself to be other that a beautiful butterfly intent on frivolity. He had begun to doubt his own perception. Perhaps he had been mistaken, and Lalage simply bore an uncanny resemblance to the leader of the Megaeras. He had heard it said that each person has a double somewhere. It was true that he had never actually met that notorious woman, only seeing her at a distance, acting as he had through hearsay and interviews with several of her victims.

He had been living in Paris at the time, playing the part of a student, a Jacobin sympathizer, though engaged on espionage work. News had reached him of a woman more bloodthirsty and vindictive than the worst of the men. It was she who had roused those bestial, vicious Furies, fanning the flame of hatred against the Austrian Queen. Tales were repeated of her perversions, her love of torture and butchery. Eventually, he had set a trap for her, aided by other underground fighters. Greater even than her other lusts was that of avarice. Through this, he had implicated her in an act of treachery to the Reformati, that most mysterious, deadly sect of which he had been able to discover very little.

Old memories, most of them bad, rose like bile in his mouth. He was aching with fatigue, too distressed by William's death for clear thinking, even his stubborn strength sapped, but there was something niggling insistently – something out of order. 'Has anyone seen Jack Smithers?' he asked his subdued followers.

His crisp question shocked them out of their torpor. They looked at him, riveted by his black-cloaked, commanding presence. 'Hell, no,' answered Robert, cradling his injured arm which had been sliced by a Marat sabre. 'That's damned odd. He should have been down on the beach when we landed. Where the devil's he hiding?'

'Drunk, and snoring in a tavern, I'll wager,' commented Giffe, who had been acting the doctor, now fixing a scarf round Robert's neck as a sling. 'Or fumbling some doxy's petticoats,' he added. The old soldier thought Jack sloppy, lacking in discipline and duty.

His words penetrated that blackness in which Denzil had existed for hours. His mind was malfunctioning. Nothing was valid, part of him locked in time on the sands, hearing

William's sudden cry, seeing his face contorted as he collapsed. Now Jack's name rang out loudly. Jack, that rival who had obsessed his thoughts during the dark, stormy Channel crossing. Jack, who had remained in safety, undoubtedly in Lalage's company. Jealousy, like some foul entity, had gnawed away at his vitals. Denzil had experienced fear on the beach – the stark reality of bowel-estranging terror. The shots, the flames, the uniformed Marats – this had been no game, no heroic fantasy. He had never seen men die before. And Jack had not been there, he'd stayed at home – Jack, who should have died in William's stead.

Shock had divorced Denzil from rationality. He had no control over the words that came from his stiff lips. It was as if someone else spoke them, a voice outside himself. He moved jerkily, and the surprise was as great as if the corpse had suddenly come to life. 'You want to know where Jack is? Why don't you ask Lalage?'

'What are you driving at?' Guy glared at him while the whole room held its breath.

Oh, no, Denzil, no! Sally begged mentally. Not now! Not in this bleak hour of grief. Be merciful.

'If anyone should know his whereabouts, then it will be her,' Denzil went on, driven remorselessly by his devils.

Guy was very still, watchful. 'Why? What odds is it to her?' He knows, Sally thought, sensing it in the air which crackled between the brothers. He's known all along, but his pride refused to allow him to face it.

'Ha!' Denzil's white face expressed bitter mirth. 'She thinks you're away – thinks she's safe. I expect Jack's in bed with her – your own bed in the Master Chamber. He's her lover.'

In a reflex movement Guy was across the room and had him by the throat, shaking him as a terrier shakes a rat. 'How dare you! How dare you! Lalage and Jack – you lie!'

'It's true! I swear it!' Denzil gasped through the stranglehold on his cravat, drawing ever tighter till sparks and spirals danced against crimson in his brain. 'It's been going on for weeks. They mock you behind your back!'

Guy's face was suffused with dark colour, veins throbbing at his temples, hot blood beating relentlessly, urging him to kill. 'Liar! Goddamned liar!' He squeezed harder, instinct urging him to crush the life from this impudent brat who had dared put into words his own gut-felt fears and suspicions.

Ambrose flung himself on them, using force to prise away

that murderous grip. 'Take it easy, Guy! He's your brother, man!' Denzil sagged against the table, choking, tearing his shirt open at the throat. No one else moved, frozen with horror. Ambrose, fists still clenched round Guy's arms, looked from one angry Wylde to the other. 'For shame – have you no respect?' He jerked his head towards the table. 'William lies there cold, and you brawl!'

'I'm telling the truth,' gasped Denzil, and Ambrose did not doubt him. It slotted into place perfectly. 'You must believe me, Guy.'

'I'll believe nothing till I have proof.' Guy's face was grey and he looked old, shoulders slumped now that the first hot rage had left him, eyes burning in hollow sockets.

'What proof d'you want?' The boy demanded desperately. 'Will nothing satisfy you till you catch them fucking – as I have done?'

The seas of the North Pole could not have been more chilling than Guy's eyes as they met his, holding, hypnotizing him. 'You've seen them?'

'Yes! God help me – yes!' Denzil wilted, sinking his face into his white, cupped hands.

'Why didn't you tell me before?'

'I couldn't!'

'Why, Denzil? It was your duty, if she was wronging me.' Guy was unaware of it, but his voice was that of their father.

Memories of childhood rebukes from that stern, disapproving man who had considered him a milksop, spoiled by his mother, finished Denzil completely. He cracked asunder, throwing himself at Guy's feet. 'Kill me!' he implored. 'Kill me! You have the right! Jack is not the only one – I too have known her! I can't go on living with that! Kill me – end my misery!'

Guy was stunned, incapable of speech, but Ambrose was not. 'You spineless fool!' He bent and hauled Denzil up, furiously angry and uncompromising. 'God, you've chosen your moment, haven't you? What a time for confessions! You'll have to live with the knowledge of your adultery! Dammit, d'you expect to absolve yourself by prompting Guy to end your life? That would be too easy. You've got to go through hell, boy, and maybe come out of it a man.'

'Far better if Guy were to shoot that blackguard, Jack,' put in Robert, appalled by Guy's devastation.

'It's not the same. Don't you see – what I've done is so much worse? Guy is my brother.' Tears were running unchecked down Denzil's cheeks.

'You forget. He's Jacks too,' reminded Ambrose grimly.

Denzil had forgotten, somehow he always did, unable to look upon Jack as in any way related. 'Jack's a rogue! He's crude about women. He hasn't worshipped her, as I have!' he shouted wildly, as if this would offer a kind of mitigation. Though sincere in his frenzy of grief, shame and guilt, in an odd, warped way he felt smug – the overbearing Guy had not had her to himself after all – for once he had been baulked of his will. In a turmoil of conflicting feelings, he added dramatically: 'Perhaps Guy will forgive Jack, but no one will forgive me.'

Guy got a grip on himself, squaring his shoulders, deliberately feeding his rage. He loomed over the cringing Denzil, enormously alarming in his shaggy sheepskin cloak. 'Stop snivelling, you wretch! I shan't kill you. Battle with your conscience and I hope it destroys you!' He turned on his heel and strode towards the door.

'Where are you going?' Ambrose's clipped accents arrested him.

'To find her!' he flung back.

'No, Guy, not yet. Matters have to be settled here. You can't walk out like that. You have to break the news of William's death to your mother.' Ambrose went up to him, resting a hand on his shoulder, making him look at him. He was still his commander on whose actions so many lives depended. No matter what personal tragedy or heartbreak, this must not be forgotten. 'I think you should tell her the truth. Alas, you'll be obliged to lie in public. I advise you to give out that he was killed in a shooting accident early this morning, but Lady Charlotte has a right to know how it really happened. Perhaps it will soften the blow if she knows that he died in a good cause.'

'You are right,' Guy answered dully. 'I'll put him across my horse and lead him home, then call the doctor.'

'Denzil, you'll go as well, and comfort your mother. You too, Mrs Wylde.' There was no question but that they would obey him.

Sally rose, leaving Josephine and Marie. Ambrose stood there like a god, power flowing from him into her. She gazed up into his resolute face with its strong, hard lines, her cloak held about her with one hand, the hood fallen back from her long, pale hair.

359

'I'll slip in so that no one knows I've been here,' she replied. 'Guy must send someone to wake me with the news.'

'Capital. I'm sure that I don't have to impress upon you the extreme secrecy of all this,' Ambrose smiled at her kindly. 'In the normal course of events, I wouldn't dream of making such a disclosure, but you are quite exceptional, my dear Mrs Wylde – the widow of a man I was proud to call friend.' He lifted her hand to his lips in salute of her courage.

'And you, Ambrose? What are your plans?' There was something eerie about Guy's statue-like stance, green eyes glittering in his frozen face.

'I'm expecting a carriage from Holt Hall at any moment. I shall take Henri and the girls there, our friends too. They can rest, change and generally tidy themselves, then travel by stage-coach to London. My destination is Dover.'

'You're returning to France?'

'Yes, almost at once. You're aware of the next operation I've planned.' He was brisk, efficient, and Sally gazed at him in awe.

'Then I'll see you in London, after the funeral.'

'God willing,' Ambrose nodded, and turned away to give an order to Giffe who leapt to attention.

'The work must go on, Guy.' Sally touched his hand. It was like ice. 'It is what William would have wanted.'

In the cold light of the wintry dawn, Guy took William home to Wylde Court for the last time. Everything went as he and Ambrose had planned. No one thought it strange that he and his brother had met for early fowling. Guy's movements were notoriously erratic, he came and went at will. Dr Rowsell was sent for, and examined the body gravely. There was absolutely no cause for doubt. Death had been instantaneous, a most regrettable misadventure when William's gun had exploded, sending the bullet into his chest. This was what Guy told him and Rowsell, knowing and respecting the most powerful family in the area, did not argue. Sally came down, wearing a night-gown and peignoir, feigning shock, but there was no pretence about her grief, this was all too genuine.

It was some time before Guy could get away. Though he made Denzil go to their mother, there were Boxer and Miss Potter to see, the whole horrified staff to calm. An hour passed and at last he mounted the staircase, slowly, heavily, making for the Master Bedchamber. He had particularly ordered that

Lady Beaumaris was not to be disturbed, saying that he would tell her of the accident himself.

Bethany was hovering at the door, but he dismissed her, opening it quietly. The curtains were still drawn, the room washed with pearly light, and Lalage lay sleeping in the four-poster. Guy walked across and stood looking down at her. Her dark hair was spread over the pillow, lashes making dusky wings on her cheeks, a sheen of moisture on her lids, one hand tucked beneath her head. Her olive skin gleamed, breasts moving with the gentle evenness of her breathing. He remembered the magic of their first meeting, his delight on discovering that she was a girl, her innocent, elusive charm, and the hopes he had had of finding happiness with such a beautiful creature. Gone, all gone. For a long time he had known it. Denzil had merely given shape and substance to his doubts.

She stirred, as an animal will in sleep, sixth sense telling it that it is being watched. Her lids fluttered. She turned her head and those strange eyes were looking up at him, a direct, clear glance, unclouded by slumber. Controlled, wary, then meeting his gaze candidly. No nymph escaped from a mountain pool could have been more ingenuous. She stretched out her arms to him, the white lace sleeves of her nightgown falling back over the smooth flesh.

'Guy! You've returned! What a wonderful surprise!'

He did not go to her embrace, considering her coldly. He saw a change flicker across her face, surprise perhaps, and something else which he could not decipher, before he went to the windows, pulling aside the curtains, letting in the greyish light.

Silhouetted against it, he turned to her again, and his eyes widened. 'My God! What have you done? Those bruises!'

They had not shown in the semi-darkness, bluish smudges on either cheek, the swollen lip. 'I took a tumble from my horse,' came the instant response. Then she smiled, stretching languorously, pouting a little. 'Guy, I'm so pleased to see you. I've been so lonely. Come to bed, darling, you look tired. Did you ride all night, simply to wake me? How gallant.'

'A fall from your horse, my dear? How very unfortunate. For a moment I thought you might have had a row with one of your lovers – not Denzil, I imagine, he's much too forbearing. Jack, now, has ever been ready with his fist, and has no gentlemanly compunction about hitting women.' His eyes were like green steel in his lean, haggard face, his sarcasm cutting.

Lalage sat up, dark curls tousled, eyes feline. 'Denzil? Jack?

What is this? Have you been at the bottle again? If so, go away until you're sober. I'll not listen to your drunken insults.'

He took a step nearer, but she held his gaze without flinching. 'I am sober. Where is Jack, Lalage? I am told that you would know.'

Lalage swung her long legs over the side of the bed and got up, maintaining her dignity. She reached for her robe, but his hand snaked out, preventing her. The angry colour flamed into her damaged cheeks. 'Guy, give it to me. Your mood is foul and I intend to ring for Bethany. Kindly leave the room.' As he took no notice, she added: 'I've no idea of Jack's movements. I've more to occupy my thoughts than in wondering what a stable-hand is doing.'

'Stop lying!' His tone froze her, as did the expression on his face. 'Denzil has told me everything – about him, and about Jack.'

Lalage recovered her poise. 'Oh, Denzil – silly boy. I was half expecting this. He threatened to lie about me to you if I continued to refuse his advances. He fancies that he's in love with me, you see – a bad case of calf-love, I fear. He'll get over it. You surely can't believe him, darling.' She yawned behind her hand, giving him an arch glance. 'So much bother about nothing. Really, Guy, you can't be serious? You know what he's like – a spoilt brat who throws a tantrum if he can't get his own way.'

Once, he would have laughed with her, bewitched and believing, but her every word, every gesture was now convincing him that Denzil had spoken the truth. It was as if her mask had been stripped away, revealing the rottenness beneath. For answer, he seized the low neckline of her nightgown, his nails marking her skin. The fabric resisted for an instant and then yielded to his force. In one movement, he had ripped it from her, tearing it open, and tugging the single garment from her. As he released it, it fell to the floor, leaving her naked. Lalage did not move, out-facing him, but he was blind to the splendour of her body, seeing not a woman but a hideous demon, as ugly as sin.

'You bitch!' he ground out. 'You're bad – bad to the depths of your being. If ever there was an evil woman, it is you. Of some people, one can say that they're corrupt to the bottom of their souls. Of you, I say that you're corruption itself, without a soul!'

'Guy!' she exclaimed, and he was satisfied to see that she was shaken. 'You don't mean that. How can you say such a thing of

362

me? Some stupid tale your jealous brother has concocted. You're too shrewd to believe it, aren't you?'

'To be frank, I don't care much any more.' She could not reach him, any power she had once had over him had vanished. 'It's finished, Lalage.'

'What are you going to do?' He knew what she was thinking, weighing up her position, calculating how great a settlement she could expect if he ended the marriage. She began to bargain. 'You have absolutely no proof of my adultery. I don't admit to it for one moment. You can't divorce me. Think of the scandal.'

The sordidness of the situation pressed agonizingly in on him. He wanted nothing more than to escape from her presence, hating to breathe the same air, nostrils sickened by her cloying perfume. He turned away, instinctively seeking the door, needing to fill his lungs with strong fresh air. 'We'll speak of it later, and if you seek monetary gain, you'll conduct yourself decorously over the next few days. I want no trouble from you to add further to the tragedy which has struck this family.'

'Tragedy?' Her voice sharpened, and he heard the light fall of her bare feet following him. 'What d'you mean?'

He paused, looking back over his shoulder. 'William is dead. We were shooting together early this morning, and his gun misfired, killing him.'

He heard the hiss of her indrawn breath, flashing a glance at her face. The expression he saw there was one of intense interest. 'William? Dead?'

'Yes. You seem pleased. My God, d'you hate me so much that you are glad? William never harmed you.'

She was on the defensive at once, skilfully turning this against him. Her eyes narrowed, and a sneering smile twisted her mouth. 'Ah, I see it all now. Your accusations are nothing but a ruse to get rid of me. William is dead and Sally is free. You now hope to be able to carry on your affair with her, divorce me and make her your wife. D'you think I haven't noticed, haven't seen the way in which she looks at you with her great cow eyes? But it won't happen, Guy. I'll see you in hell first. You'll never get shot of me and that bitch will never be Lady Beaumaris!'

Knowing that he would murder her if he stayed, Guy fled from the room and did not stop running until he reached the garden. There in the peace and coolness of a sheltered spot beyond the terrace, he leaned his arms against an old, mellowed wall, and buried his face in them.

William's body was laid in state on a bier in the Great Hall, following family tradition. Candles burned in tall brass holders at his head and feet, to remain lit night and day. The farmers, estate-workers and villagers filed past to pay their respects and leave wreaths of holly and evergreen.

There had been a fall of snow that morning; this had half melted during the day, but frosted over when the sun went down. The roads were treacherous, icy, but this did not prevent people calling continually to offer their condolences. William had been popular in the district, and his sorrowing young widow was there to receive those quiet, respectful friends who had no idea that she was controlling herself with the utmost difficulty. For William's sake, for Guy's and Lady Charlotte's, she must not break down.

The Dowager kept to her room, and she was extraordinarily calm. Her face lit up when she saw Denzil, safe and well, and he went to her, lifting her pale hand to his lips. She looked shrunken beneath the frilly white lace cap, her silvered chestnut hair in two thick plaits each side of her head. Chalmers's hands were shaking as she poured tea into delicate Wedgwood cups with an arabesque border. Her eyes were pink and her nose was red and she sniffed continually, far less in command of herself than her mistress.

'Dear William,' Charlotte sighed from her wing-chair, where she sat with a shawl about her shoulders and a rug over her knees. 'God rest his soul. Such a good son. Ah me, the passage of time. The old days are gone for ever. You tell me he is dead, but only a moment ago, or so it seems, he had been crawling on this very carpet while I jingled his rattle and made him chuckle. He was a beautiful baby, much more handsome than you, Guy. You were a great roaring monster! Most unlovely!'

'Naturally, I would be, Mamma,' Guy answered with a thin smile. He loved her, but could not help viewing her with animosity. Even now, she was enjoying the drama, surrounded by people. That was meat and drink to her – to be surrounded by attentive people. As long as they did what she told them, she asked for nothing more.

'When I was a girl, I had little contact with my parents,' she went on, eyeing her captive audience. No one dared say her nay, not even Guy, in her role as the mourning mother. 'I saw them infrequently, accorded them respect. They were distant, formal. It was not the done thing for a great lady, like my mother, to have much to do with her offspring. Childhood then was a stage in life to be passed over quickly, but by the time you boys were born, things had changed. Oh, yes, children had become fashionable. Of course, nanny cared for you, but you did spend time with your Papa and myself. Do you remember?'

Guy remembered. Being dragged in from some absorbing game, washed and dressed up in stiff, uncomfortable clothes, in such a vile temper by the time his nurse had whacked him and polished him that he was usually very badly behaved in the drawing-room. He had hated being cooed over and patronized by his mother's lady friends, hated being forced to stand still and recite poems to them. Most of all, he had hated posing for the portrait painter. Reynolds had executed a picture of him. There it hung on the wall now, staring back at him – a sullen child of eight in a blue velvet suit. My God, Guy thought savagely, the artist's bill had been for one hundred and fifty pounds! I should have been the one paid for the exquisite suffering and embarrassment it caused me!

'I think I can honestly say that there existed not only respect but affection in your feelings towards us,' Charlotte said smugly, well and truly launched on this sentimental journey down the memory track. 'I was better informed on child-care than my dear Mamma. That odd writer, Rousseau, had published a book in which he advised that infants should not be wrapped in tight swaddling bands. He said that their limbs must be free, with nothing to cramp growth and movement. Every one of my friends had read it, so our babies wore light, pretty frocks – very much kinder to tiny tots.'

'He also applied this logic to the minds of men,' Guy said sardonically. 'Liberty was not confined to children's clothing. Hence the upheaval across the Channel. I'm shocked to hear you praising such a man, Mamma.'

Charlotte closed her ears, refusing to be cheated, enjoying imposing her personality on them, taking the lead. 'That's of no matter, Guy. I'm speaking of this family. The Wyldes! Our dear son William has forfeited his life, helping to fight tyranny. I am proud of him – proud of you all.' Inspired by this sense of family honour, she went off at a tangent. 'We'll show them that we're not to be dictated to by a pack of unruly tub-thumpers! How dare they shout about their rights? What rights? Burning ricks – causing riots! That damned John Wilkes has a lot to answer for. D'you know, his squinting radical face has been plastered over mugs, jugs – even tea-pots? Given pride of place on the shelves of the workers! Disgraceful!'

'Don't distress yourself, Mamma dear,' soothed Denzil, falling back into the cosy position as favoured son. He sheltered behind it. Mother did not know about Lalage and him – she must never find out. She loved him and he basked in the warmth of her approval, vowing to be a better person from now on. He was filled with loathing for himself. He was sensual, ungrateful. He would give up women. Perhaps he might enter the Church. Mamma would like that.

She was dabbing at a tear with a minute lace kerchief, and placed her thin, ring-laden hand on his arm to assure herself that he, at any rate, was still with her. Let Guy glower and gloom till doom's day, she had her beloved Denzil.

William was laid to rest among his ancestors in the crypt. After the funeral, Sally walked away a widow indeed – time merging, overlapping. Not so long ago she had left the chapel as a bride, admittedly not a happy bride, but a woman with some status, none the less. Now she had nothing, except Briar Cottage. Soon she would be alone there with Miranda and the servants, for Dora was to marry Josh in the New Year. Lady Charlotte was already putting out feelers. She wanted Sally to give up the cottage and return to the manor, telling her how much she missed her, confiding that Chalmers drove her to distraction. Sally stubbornly entrenched herself in her determination to do nothing of the sort. She liked her freedom, her independence, and had no intention of accepting the Dowager's slave-chains again. She had already tried the pathetic approach, and Sally suspected that a lengthy battle of wills lay ahead.

The only thing she wanted to say when in her company was: 'William left a child, you know. Your first grandson –', but such things are best left unspoken. Perhaps Lady Charlotte already knew, closing her eyes to Danny's parentage, as she did Jack's.

Sally slipped away unnoticed, while the clan of friends and relatives were in the Great Hall, drinking sherry with that reverent, strangely light-hearted attitude people reserve for such occasions. Beneath the platitudes there lay a kind of wild relief in knowing that they were still alive and someone else had just been interred, not themselves. They had successfully put off the inevitable confrontation for a while longer. Sally could not bear it, for she had been the focal point, the dead man's widow. The Wylde family feeling was everywhere, claustrophobic, accentuated by the common bond of loss; the house, the servants, the dogs, horses and peasants, all became adjuncts. This was the way the Wyldes had always operated, like a tidal-wave, sweeping everything before them. They might detest one another, never have a good word to say in each other's defence, but let danger threaten from outside and they closed ranks.

Lalage had been constantly on view, magnificently and dolorously attired in drifting black. She had swept towards Sally at the funeral, arms outstretched, crying: 'Oh, my poor girl! So recently wedded, and now a widow! My heart breaks for you!' Unable to stop her, Sally was drawn into a perfumed embrace. Lalage had never touched her before, and she had stiffened in revulsion.

'Thank you, Lalage, I appreciate your sympathy,' she had said coldly and stepped out of her reach.

Sally went to the stables and found a gig. She drove down the wide avenue between snow-sprinkled lawns and skeleton trees. Somewhere a peacock screamed, a lonely sound in the crisp, still air. Dora was looking after Miranda during her absence, but she had been home several times, not surprised to find that the child had already known William was dead. Illness had increased her sensitivity, and Sally accepted her 'sight' as a normal part of everyday life. Miranda would be so pleased to see her and to hear that she would leave Briar Cottage no more.

Her connection with the manor was ended. William had provided for her generously, and Guy contributed a substantial monthly allowance for Miranda. There would be no financial worries, but her heart ached for William, and she was filled with useless regrets. The horse clopped along the ice-rutted lanes leading away from Wylde Court. Saffron clouds drifted across a milky sky, and the sun was low, sulky, turning hanging icicles to sparkling flames. Sally's fingers were numb on the reins. It will be so cold in the crypt, she thought, but at least the sexton had not had to hack up clods of rock-hard earth. William would not feel the cold.

Hot tears burned her eyes, tears she had been unable to shed before. She still could not quite believe that he was dead, although she had seen him lying in his coffin, and had led that melancholy procession through the churchyard. Surely a personality such as his could not have disappeared entirely? Yet where was he? She could not give credence to the notion that he would be content to spend eternity amidst clouds and hosts of white-robed angels playing golden harps. It was illogical. She had kept this to herself; Lady Charlotte was happy to think him in heaven, and who was Sally to question her simple faith? She found herself wanting to discuss this with William, which was quite absurd. How could she talk to him about his own death? He would have laughed, had he been able to hear her, and probably recited some comic epitaph to lift her spirits.

The horse's ears, his brown mane, the twisting road beyond, were blurred by tears. William would come no more to Briar Cottage, and she must begin the painful task of sorting through his things, all those insignificant personal effects which had made up his existence. Sally wept, the recognition of his goodness, his patience and forebearance coming too late. Too late. The saddest words in the language of mankind. Now she could never tell him – never say – 'I almost loved you.'

The road wound up to higher ground where Sally could see for miles on this clear winter day. Somehow, gazing at the view which he had loved so much, her grief abated and tranquillity possessed her. The hills receded one behind the other into the distance, mauve and grey-blue, capped with snow, those ancient hills where once the Romans had mined for lead. The wind tore across the open land, and Sally was glad of her warm cloak, long scarf and gloves, her cheeks and nose stinging from its lash. A kestrel hovered above a hedge; rocks and crows beat upwards on great, ragged wings before wheeling down into the gaunt treetops. The bleating of the sturdy sheep carried a long way. She reined in, comforted by the familiarity of the land-scape. Much of its beauty lay in the contrasts; one could ride from the port to the open heights, could be lost in sunken lanes, soused in sudden unexpected streams, gaze at the smooth, sculptured fields which caught every change of light, and see the hollow where, tucked into itself, lay Beaumaris Combe.

Danny will live here and love it as his father had done. Sally took heart at the thought, drying her eyes and clicking her tongue so that the patient cob moved on. The track led downwards now, nearing the trees. The wind rustled the frosty branches and the last dead leaves fluttered down, withered and blackened, to join their fellows on the forest floor. The quiet was absolute, but Sally felt no fear, finding the isolation of the winter woods held more beauty for her than in the blaze of summer glory. It suited her mood.

Peace was shattered by the sound of hoof-beats. She glanced over her shoulder and saw a woman galloping down the slope of the hill, wild against the stark scenery, her cloak flying out, a whip in her hand. She took the ditch in one smooth leap, and caught up with the gig. Sally did not stop, but Lalage slowed her horse to a walk, bringing it alongside.

'I thought you were still entertaining the mourners to the funeral-meats,' Sally said without looking at her.

'I needed to ride. That house! My God, so much talk of death!'

This woman, this creature who had lain with Guy's brothers, unscrupulous, uncaring. Why are we here together, in the odd, rusty light of winter? thought Sally. I hate her. I've always hated her. I lied to myself in the beginning, thinking that I wanted to be friends with her, but I was ready, oh, so ready, to be her enemy. She turned her head and studied Lalage's face. She had never looked more beautiful, alive with some secret triumph. A strange, unusual beauty, in some antagonistic way appealing to her senses, so that she understood why Denzil had forsaken honour to possess her, and Guy's reason for making her his bride.

In that snowy dimness, it was as if she saw her for the first time, in all her richness of colour, her tricorne hat with the plume, her raven hair, the fascinating wickedness of her face, in the full pride of depravity. Sally shuddered, disgusted, yet in a dark, profane corner of her being there stirred a faint spark of envy. What woman worth her salt did not secretly yearn to be a cold, alluring temptress?

The wind swept down from the moors with demon shrieks. It tore the snow from the naked branches, powdering them as they rode beneath. 'What do you want?' asked Sally.

Lalage smiled, eyes veiled by her lashes. She flicked at her skirt with her whip. 'I've come to warn you. You won't get Guy. I know that Denzil has been bad-mouthing me. Guy is very angry. I suspect that you've been pot-stirring too, but I'll not be cast aside. He can drag it through every law-court in England, but I shall refuse a divorce. I have friends who'll help me, and if he's not careful, I'll start inquiries into William's death. He may find himself being charged with murder. After all, it is only his word that it was an accident. His motive is obvious. He wants you.'

She was vindictive and evil. If crossed she would not hesitate to plunge them into a cess-pit of scandal. The damage that she could do, even if proven guilty, was frightful. 'You can't hope to win. Guy and I have never been lovers, whereas you – Jack will support Guy – Denzil too!'

Lalage laughed confidently. 'Jack has disappeared, and

Denzil will obey me. D'you think he'll hesitate to betray his brother if he believes that I love him?'

'Jack will return, he always does.' Sally gripped the reins tightly, lest she should strike that sneering face.

'Not this time,' said Lalage.

'How can you possibly know that? Don't pin your hopes on his absence. Jack has gone off before, but he always comes back.'

There was nothing more to be said, and yet there was everything. Layers of deceit, layers of meaning, one obscuring the other. Was Lalage receptive to the things Sally's mind was screaming? Did the words 'bitch! Heartless bitch!' vibrate in her brain? She longed to shout: 'You harmed Miranda! You stole the only man I've ever loved!' but she refused to sink to Lalage's level.

Lalage hesitated, a slight frown between her brows, as if indeed picking up something from the ether. Then that empty smile curved her lips again. 'Be careful what you do, Sally, if you don't want Guy to swing.' She wheeled her horse around and kicked him into a gallop, taking the hill at a rush, silhouetted between the trees for a moment, black against the white cold sky, before disappearing over the brow.

Several nights later Sally sat in her parlour, looking at the moon rising through the haze. The quiet disturbed her. The house was full of sleep and silence. Dora and Molly had been so kind, but they were treating her as if she was some delicate invalid who must be protected at all costs, and their usual frankness was missing. She had overheard an odd snippet of conversation, entering the kitchen unexpectedly. They had stopped at once on seeing her, looking shifty, hurriedly changing the subject.

Molly had been saying: 'I told you that there would be a price.'

To which Dora had replied: 'Mr William paid with his life, d'you mean?'

Later, when Sally leaned over to kiss Miranda goodnight, the child had touched her face gently, the puppy snuggled under the covers beside her. 'Don't worry, Sally,' she had said. 'The doll will take care of everything.'

Her gaze had rested on the gorgeous wax 'baby', sitting at the end of the bed, staring vacantly with its blue glass eyes. It had yellow curls of real hair and a wonderful set of clothes, an exact replica of a lady of fashion. Aurora had sent it down by mail-coach from London. Did Miranda refer to that doll? Sally could not be sure.

Her imagination was playing tricks. The cottage was too full of memories and, at each turn of the stair, she half expected to come upon William, to hear his voice, smell the crisp outdoor air which had always hung about him. It was late and she was tired, and she could have sworn that she heard footsteps in the hallway, the hair rising at the back of her neck, waiting to see his wraith drift through the door. She was not afraid. His ghost would not reproach her. Maybe he had come to make certain that she was safe. The door opened and a tall, dark figure stood there, but it was a man of flesh and blood.

'I had to come,' said Guy, closing it behind him, confused and astounded to see her face suddenly spring to life at the sight of him. 'I couldn't go without speaking to you. Forgive me. I frightened you.'

She rose and took a step towards him, though unaware that she did so, eyes searching his features, tender as a mother's caress. He was leaner, and his facial bones, always prominent in the Wyldes, gave shadows and lines to his cheeks and eyes. His thick, dark hair emphasized his pallor. He gave the impression of a man with his back to the wall.

'You're welcome, Guy, at all times,' she replied. 'But where are you going so suddenly?'

Her voice was sweet and cool as a mountain stream, so refreshing after the day-long chatter at the manor, soothing his agitation which had been increased with the arrival of the post. He met the intense, absorbed devotion of her gaze and was greatly touched, realizing that she loved him. The bitter-sweetness of it was too much, following the disasters which seemed to be crowding on one another. He was still reeling from the blow of Lalage's infidelities; it would take years before he could trust a woman again – perhaps he never would. Yet he needed to talk to someone about the latest development.

'I must go to London in the morning,' he said, and his tone of voice sent her into near-panic.

'Oh, Guy – not more danger? Haven't you done enough?' Keep calm, she counselled herself, don't add to his troubles.

She took his hat, his gloves, his whip, while he shrugged off his overcoat. 'Dangerous, yes – most dangerous,' he muttered, spreading his hands to the fire, feeling the letter in his pocket burning like a branding-iron.

Sally went to the table and poured wine, bringing over two matching goblets, chalice-shaped, of cloudy pink glass outlined in gilt. Her finest glasses, but only the best was good enough for him. She let him drink, then gently questioned. 'What has happened?'

In answer, he felt in his breast pocket and pulled out an envelope, handing it to her. It was of the finest-quality paper, as was the letter inside. He nodded to her to read it. The writing was as elegant as the sheet it covered, but its content sent a chill stabbing through her. 'Lord Beaumaris,' it began formally. 'We are holding Jack Smithers as a hostage. He will be returned to you in exchange for *Le Fantom*. Return to London immediately, where you will receive a further communication on this matter.' It was signed 'Latour'.

In silence, Sally read it through twice more, the words printing themselves indelibly on her mind, then: 'My God,' she whispered. 'Poor Jack. What are you going to do? *Le Fantom!* You are associated with him?' A thought struck her, too terrifying to bear contemplation. 'Guy! It isn't you? You're not *Le Fantom?*'

'No.' Guy took the letter from her, scanning it again, as if seeking a solution to the dilemma. 'But I work for him.' He lifted his eyes to meet hers, shaking his head as he did so. 'No, Sally – I'll not tell you who he is. This might put you in peril.'

'But Jack – you can't let him die. Does Molly know about this? She's concerned about his absence, I can tell, though she goes about her work cheerfully enough.'

She was so calm, and Guy admired her for that, thinking: she has spirit, a Wylde by birth as well as marriage. He recognized in her a strength and mastery closely allied to his own. 'I've told no one but you. Molly came to see me shortly after the letter arrived, almost as if she had sensed it. I managed to fob her off. She thinks he's on a mission for me. I shall save Jack, if I can, but the decision rests with my leader.'

'This man – Latour. D'you know who he is?'

'No. A Jacobin, I presume. *Le Fantom* will know. There's no time to lose.'

'And Lalage? She'll travel with you?'

His face darkened, fists bunching involuntarily. 'Oh, yes – I want her where I can see her – the faithless slut!'

Sally had had no opportunity to talk with him about her, to gauge the depths of his anger. 'What action will you take concerning her? You can't harm her. She is your wife.'

372

'My wife?' His voice was grim. 'No more. I shall never sleep with her again.'

Life beat up in Sally in a released fountain of joy, and she filled her eyes with him. His face was so beautiful, stern and serious, his build so fine, his legs in their beige breeches and riding-boots so handsomely shaped, his eyes angry and hurt. She had dreamed so often and so fiercely of being alone with him in the night darkness, but now there were still so many barriers between them. William was hardly cold in his grave – Jack was in terrible danger, and Guy about to risk his life to save him.

'Will you divorce her?' she asked quietly, all her heart, her soul, in her eyes.

He looked up at her from the couch by the fire, his face drawn and exhausted, hair tousled, falling over his forehead. 'I don't know – I can't think clearly.'

She came closer and stroked back the lock from his brow and, with a weary gesture, he leaned his head against her breasts. It was as if he was her child. 'Oh, Guy – my poor Guy.'

'How soft your hand is,' he whispered. 'I've not slept for days. Perhaps I shall do so now.'

Chapter 7

'Will you marry me?' shouted Ambrose as he strode through Aurora's bedchamber and into the dressing-room beyond.

She had her head in the wash-basin, and Tilly was pouring water over her hair. 'What?' she screamed back at him, thoroughly startled for she had not expected to see him yet.

'Get the soap out of your ears,' he laughed, leaning on the door-jamb and admiring her rounded backside as she bent over, the satin of her negligée outlining the delectable curves. 'I'm asking you to be my wife.'

At that she straightened, folding a towel turbanwise around her head. 'You don't mean it?' she scoffed, cushioning her heart which would break if he was jesting.

'I damn well do!' He seated himself on the edge of the bath, drawing her between his thighs. 'Leave us, Tilly, there's a good girl,' he added to the maid, winking at her over Aurora's shoulder. Tilly beamed and curtseyed and took herself off.

'You crazy man!' Aurora half laughed, half sobbed. 'Where have you been? Why didn't you let me know you were back in London? What a fright I must be!'

'You look wonderful.' He held her firmly and kissed her long and deep, so that all protestations melted, leaving only the bright shining star of his proposal. His smile was warm and tender, and he put her away from him for a moment. 'Do I take it that you don't want to marry me?' he teased.

Alarmed, she clung to him. 'I do – oh, so much! I thought you'd never ask. But there is one thing –' she paused and her blue eyes clouded. 'In all fairness I must tell you of it. I'm with child.'

'Capital!' he grinned. 'That'll give us a head start. I warn you that I want at least six sons and six daughters. I won't insult you by asking if it is mine.'

'You know it is. I love you – you insufferable bully!' She was so deliriously happy that she was shaking from head to foot.

'Hey, calm down, love – mustn't harm the boy. It is a boy.

I'm certain of it.' He hugged her and kissed her again, then said: 'Get dressed quickly, we are going to the theatre. Don't ring for Tilly. I'll help you.'

'My hair!' she wailed. 'Julian is coming to dress it.'

'Damn Julian! Ruffle it up a bit more – set a new mode. God, you're lovely! What's the time? Hell, let's go to bed. If we leave here at seven o'clock, that'll be soon enough!'

Aurora was awakened from a blissfully happy sleep. Ambrose was prodding her gently. They were lying snugly in her outrageous silver four-poster. She yawned and stretched and wondered if the baby would be born beneath its ornate, purple tester, murmuring something to this effect.

'Guess it will, unless you happen to be brought to bed at Holt Hall,' he said, his hand coming to rest on her belly, caressing both her and the unborn in one gentle movement. 'Wouldn't that be just fine? An Alington coming into the world under the roof of the old home. When is it due to arrive?'

'In June,' she sighed dreamily. 'The time of sunshine and roses and midsummer.'

'We'd better get hitched mighty soon. Let's announce our betrothal tonight – at the party after the performance.' He could feel her heart fluttering against him, and she lay laxly, as if her body was disjointed, loose and heavy with love. He leaned down and kissed her open mouth, her warm moist mouth with its drooping red lower lip.

They talked while she dressed, and Aurora was very persistent in her questions, saying: 'I don't believe a word of that cock and bull story you told me about having to go to the cotton-mills up north!'

She was seated on the stool, wearing a chemise trimmed with fine lace and narrow ribbon, one leg crossed over the other as she carefully rolled on her fragile black silk stockings. They were so transparent that they acquired a subtle tone of dull, silver grey against her flesh.

'You have beautiful legs.' Ambrose had also risen and put on his clothes, and now sat regarding her from the day-bed.

Aurora met his eyes and caught her breath. 'You are quite remarkably fine too, sir,' she managed to say, feeling wobbly at the knees, chiding herself for being such a lovelorn ninny at her age, but there was no denying that Ambrose had surpassed himself that night, clad in lilac and silver, with a large black cravat, a tightly buttoned jacket and soft boots of Cordovan leather. His hair looked shaggier, more flaxen than ever, and he exuded that air of careless elegance which transformed him into a dandy.

Was he more than that? Aurora wondered yet again as she prepared herself. This did not take long as she wore very little: a celestial blue slip and an overgown of white jaconet bordered with a Greek key pattern. With its décolleté neckline and extremely high waist, the bodice was only four inches deep, barely covering her breasts, and the sleeves were short puffs. Aurora shivered, and Ambrose smiled.

'You must be frozen, honey! Ah, but fashion is a severe taskmaster. You poor, suffering creatures, wearing Mediterranean-type clothing in a European winter!'

Aurora pulled a face at him, and fastened a pearl necklace about her throat, then hooked matching earrings into her lobes. She combed her hair out loosely and touched her cheekbones with rouge. A cashmere shawl in a bold Paisley print, a flowing Russian mantle of sapphire velvet lined with white satin, which Ambrose gallantly held for her, and she was ready to go.

But there was something she was determined to say, before losing him to his friends. She looked up at him, yielding to one of those impulses which so often arose in her, often wisely, sometimes not. She put her hand on his arm. 'Why aren't you frank with me? Your mysterious trips – they are not to do with business, are they?' She took a deep breath, then brought it out in a rush. 'I think that you are one of those rash fellows who band together to aid the *aristos*.'

Ambrose was coolly taking snuff. 'Really?' he exclaimed, with a quirky smile. 'What an absurd notion, my love. You've been reading too many novelettes. Can you really see a lazy man like myself, who likes an easy life, dashing backwards and forwards across the Channel? La, it would be so tedious! Damned dangerous, too!'

His eyes, heavy-lidded, bright blue, looked down into hers. His was such an attractive face, strong-jawed, belying the indolent smile. He was cunning, well able to deceive the world, but not the woman who loved him.

'*You* are *Le Fantom!*' she said, with a sudden intuitive flash.

Any lingering doubts vanished. Ambrose, taken aback, was incapable of the smallest attempt at clever parrying. It seemed unnecessary to lie. Aurora loved him. They were to be married, so: 'Well, well – so you're not just a pretty face,' he said slowly. 'How very bright of you, but don't forget that curiosity killed the cat.' He dropped a light kiss on her nose. 'You are right. I am *Le Fantom*.'

Now that she had the truth, terror stabbed her. She swayed towards him, flinging her arms about his neck. 'Oh, Ambrose! How mad – how brave! My dear – the danger!' She buried her face in his cravat.

It was impossible to tell whether it was pregnancy which had aroused this new, raw sensitivity in her or simply that she had learned to read every line on his face, every expression in his eyes. During his absence she had been unable to shake off the conviction that he was the spectre who defied the Jacobins. Brooding about it whilst he was gone, she was now torn in two by pride and fear.

'I'll tell you everything as we drive to the theatre,' he said, and picked up his cloak, *chapeau bras* and sword-stick.

Before they reached the door, Tilly appeared. 'Lord Beaumaris is here to see you, sir. He says it is urgent.'

Ambrose frowned. 'Guy? I thought he was in the country. Wait here, Aurora. I'll be as quick as I can.'

Guy was waiting in the study across the hall. Without any preliminaries, he told Ambrose exactly what had happened, showing him the letter, and another which had been delivered to Doric House when he arrived there that afternoon. Ambrose read them through without a word, his hands flat on the table, staring down at those two innocent-looking sheets which were his death-warrant. The second one instructed Guy to be at Covent Garden Theatre that evening, accompanied by *Le Fantom*. They would be met. There was a simple warning that on no account were they to inform anyone or attempt to have others follow or aid them. Again, this was signed by Latour.

'Who is he? What is he?' grated Guy, sombrely attired in mourning black.

An odd smile touched Ambrose's lips briefly, and his eyes were honed to a cutting edge. 'Latour? Someone I've been wanting to meet for a long time. He's a big noise in that mysterious society who call themselves the Reformati. Slippery as an eel, doesn't always use that name, of course.'

'He's a Jacobin?'

'Oh, yes – at least for as long as it suits him.'

'And the Reformati? I've heard you speak of them, but not much.'

Ambrose shrugged and heaved a sigh. 'I don't know much. I've tried to ferret out information, but their followers are too loyal or too scared to give anything away, mostly the latter. The sect is very powerful, very cruel – stopping at nothing to gain their ends. Latour was an *aristo*. He's a renegade, a human vampire, by all accounts.'

'My God, and this is the man who holds Jack! You can't do it, Ambrose! I won't let you! You can't sacrifice yourself!'

Ambrose was calmly returning him the letters. 'Do we sacrifice Jack in my stead? He's your half-brother.'

'And one of my wife's lovers!'

Seeing the anger, the bewildered torment in his friend's eyes, Ambrose clapped him on the shoulder. 'Come on, Guy, get a hold of yourself, man. It's not in you to let him die as a cheap form of revenge. We've got to help him, and you know it.'

'But you, Ambrose? In exchange for him? It's impossible!' Guy groaned. 'We must tell the others – arrange for them to trail us.'

Ambrose shook his head. 'Useless. The place will be swarming with Reformati spies. We've got to go through with it alone. One false move and Jack's a dead man.' He drew a small pill-box from his waistcoat pocket, removed the lid and held out some tablets to Guy.

'What's that?'

'Poison,' Ambrose said, then as Guy drew back, shaking his head, he added: 'Don't be a fool. Take them, conceal them somewhere, but make sure they're easy to take if need arises. Guy, these people are ruthless. When I lived in Paris, there was a man who came to me with information. It concerned a Reformati member – a woman. Several days later, I found him in a disused church. I've never seen such mutilation. He had bled to death – emasculated, then crucified above the altar. These poison tablets are instantaneous. I want to be good and dead before they cut off my balls and nail my hands to the timbers.'

'God, Ambrose, there must be a way out of this,' Guy protested, taking the proffered pills and slipping them into his pocket.

'Does anyone else know?'

'I've told Sally.' Guy did not have to explain this to his friend. Ambrose knew him better than he knew himself.

'You've said nothing to your wife?' Ambrose was putting two and two together and coming up with some disquieting results. The Reformati? The *tricoteuse*? He'd been a fool not to take action, giving Lalage the benefit of the doubt.

'I'm not speaking to her more than is absolutely necessary. She's my wife no longer!'

The Theatre Royal, Drury Lane, was the oldest of London's many playhouses; the first legalized establishment of its sort to be given the power and glory of a Royal Charter, back in the seventeenth century. It had undergone many changes since Nell Gwynn danced there and captivated King Charles II. A magical place, rich in atmosphere, the Mecca of every aspiring actor and actress, still patronized by crowned heads, with its army of powdered-haired footmen in Royal livery. People who would have died rather than be seen in a low, common music-hall, went there in shoals.

A tragedy was being performed that night, with Mrs Bracegirdle in the leading role, and the entrance was crowded. Aurora and Ambrose chatted amiably to friends, the lofty, classically designed vestibule resounding to dozens of cultured, light tongues. Ambrose played the flippant, witty fop, but found it hard to adjust to this tinsel society with possible torture and death waiting him.

'Been out of London, have you, Alington?' queried one slender, pale young man, flipping open the jewelled lid of his snuff-box. 'Taking the air at Holt Hall, I'll wager.'

'Went there to get some decent food.' Ambrose held up his quizzing-glass and stared coldly at him. 'Having a dreadful time with the servants in my town house. Damned rogues, the lot of 'em! As for the rascally chef! Rat me – God sends meat, but the devil sends cooks! Give me trout from my own stream, a grouse from my own moor, and an apple tart from my own orchard, and I'll ask for nothing more.'

'Can't abide country life myself,' the dandy replied with a shrug and a polite sneer. 'All that space, rough winds and greenery! Sink me, if it ain't tiresome! Rarely visit my estate if I can avoid it. I know it's considered awfully smart to wander in the fields and meditate on the wonders of nature, but I see sheep and cows as machines for turning grass into mutton and beef – nothing else, my dear chap.'

This evoked laughter, frothy as a *soufflé*, with careless smiles, the flutter of fans and the sparkle of gems but, like Ambrose, though not for the same dire reason, Aurora found it unreal. She had listened, speechless, as he had recounted some of his adventures and broken the news of William's death, while they drove through the dark streets. So Lalage had seduced Denzil and been Jack's paramour. This had not come as a surprise, but the hard quality in his voice as he spoke of France had chilled her blood. He had been so graphic in his description of life there that she had almost experienced the alarms, the sudden hungry roar of the mob, that loud knocking at the door which spelled fate. As if there, she had smelt the foetid stench of the squares where the guillotine reigned, and seen the narrow alleys where gangs of Marats went about their business of terror.

How could such things be happening just a few miles over the sea? It was horrible, incomprehensible, so far removed from the glittering theatre. It made Aurora terribly afraid, and she slipped her hand into Ambrose's palm. He had warned her that there were plots to rouse similiar rebellion in England. She wanted to run away, to find a little church somewhere so that they could be married that very night – wanted to beg him to take her to America at once, to endanger his life no further. Her fears would have been doubled had she known the purpose of Guy's calling at her house. Ambrose had not told her, dismissing it as a matter of small moment.

She saw Guy's tall head above the throng near the entrance. He waved, and was soon standing with them, accompanied by Nick and Charlie, whom she had once despised but now viewed with a kind of awe. A space had cleared around them, for people were beginning to enter the auditorium, seeking their seats.

'Where is Lalage?' Ambrose asked.

'She has a headache and has retired to her room,' he replied, with a lift of his eyebrow.

'Indeed? Poor thing. Such a pity she'll not see Mrs Brace-girdle. I understand that she is quite, quite splendid,' Ambrose said, glancing round the rapidly emptying foyer. He noticed that the fop who had been speaking to him earlier was still there, chatting with a couple of others.

Guy was glancing at Aurora, and Ambrose said: 'You must congratulate us, my friend. We are to be married.'

Guy gave a delighted grin. Any animosity between them had long since vanished. She was sorry for him, married to such a bitch. 'I'm so happy for you both.' He shook Ambrose by the hand and bowed to her.

The country-hating dandy had come closer, backed by his friends. He tapped Guy on the arm. 'Lord Beaumaris, may I have a private word with you?'

Good God! thought Ambrose. He's one of them! Guy turned,

meeting the cold eyes in that supercilious face. 'Sir? Do I know you?'

'Indeed, yes. We played cards at Brook's not long ago. Shall we withdraw outside? Bring your companion with you.'

Nick and Charlie were hovering on the lower steps which led up to the boxes, giving the group questioning looks. 'This is it,' Guy muttered to Ambrose.

Ambrose eyed the fops through his glass, saying languidly: 'Heavens, Guy – what have you been doing? Is there to be a duel, perchance? Have you been tardy in paying a gaming debt?' Without waiting for an answer, he smiled at Aurora, giving an apologetic moue. 'A thousand pities, my love. Go to your box with Nick and Charlie and enjoy the show. I'll come to your house when this tedious business is done.'

She glanced nervously from her lover's face to Guy's, then to the three men waiting for them. Music swelled from inside the theatre. Soon the curtain would be rising. Something had happened, she felt it in her gut, wanting to do anything to delay him, but knowing that she must not. This is how her life would be from now on – the anxiety, the crushing sorrow of parting, the ecstatic happiness of reunion. He would go, whatever she said, so she gave him a brilliant smile, smothering her torment, learning the hard lesson of bidding him goodbye cheerfully.

Lalage stayed in her bedchamber until she was quite certain that Guy had left the vicinity of Doric House. She had already given Bethany the evening off. Guy had looked in before he left for the theatre, and she had been lying in the middle of the great bed, a cold compress on her brow. In a stilted manner he had expressed the hope that she would soon recover, and informed her that he would not disturb her again. There had been little contact between them since the morning of William's death, and she could only speculate on what his plans for her future might be. She had seen Denzil and berated him unmercifully for telling his brother about her affairs with Jack and himself. He had been wretched, shamefaced, terribly upset about William. He was so weak, bringing out the worst in her. She loathed weakness. Questioning him carefully, she had established that he had said nothing about her knowledge of their involvement with *Le Fantom*. Guy's rage stemmed from her unfaithfulness – nothing more.

When the sounds of Guy's departure had gradually died away and the house became quiet, she got up, drank a glass of wine mixed with opium and took some clothing from the armoire. It was the costume she had worn at the phaeton race. She smiled at the memory, a slow, triumphant smile. She had every reason to be pleased with herself. *Le Fantom* was dead and she was about to be rewarded. Determined, single-minded, nothing on earth would stop her carrying out a plan of action once she had decided upon it. Every ounce of energy, each beat of her heart pulsed to that purpose. She dressed with feverish haste, then flung open the doors which led out on to a balcony. The room was at the back of the house, and she leaned over the stone balustrade, looking down, her mouth set. There was light enough for her to see the water-pipe which ran from the roof to the garden below, and the passage beyond leading to the stables.

She threw a leg over the parapet, found the pipe and clung to it, then began to descend. When nearly at the bottom, she jumped, falling on hands and knees, startling a night-prowling cat who ran for the nearest tree and scrambled up it. Lalage held her breath, listening to hear whether the noise had disturbed the watchman. There was no sound but the hoot of an owl. The rooftops were black against the rising moon, and the stars sparked in the frost-bound sky.

Keeping well in the shadows, she went to the stable. Guy had taken the coach, complete with driver and footmen. The grooms were in the cosy little snug at the back. She could hear them singing drunkenly and arguing over cards. She spoke to her horse softly while she saddled him, then led him out, stroking his nose. When they reached the street she swung up on to his back and, digging in her heels, hair flying, was away towards Chelsea.

It was extremely dark, and the scattered lamps made the darkness even denser when once outside their individual radiance. No one heeded the cloaked figure galloping by. There were still people about: horsemen, and coaches bowled along the wide roads of Mayfair, but the traffic thinned in the outlying parishes where folk retired early behind shutters and locked doors. The merchants who occupied these substantial houses feared robbers, and posted hefty menservants armed with muskets, but Lalage feared nothing. She did not know the meaning of the word, her mind streaking ahead to her meeting with Latour. Her eyes shone and she laughed up at the moon. He would be there, waiting for her. She had smuggled a message to Sanderman.

The cold ride thrilled her, the feel of the powerful animal surging forward, responding to her hands, her whip. The knowledge that *Le Fantom* was dead had been exalting her for days. She had succeeded against all odds. Alone, unaided, beholden to no man. It was best that way – she liked to be alone, needing no one. The wind was rising, soughing in the branches on each side of the road which led to Latour's mansion. A wild wind, tearing at her hair, her cloak, seeming to catch her up and toss her high among the myriads of swirling, diamond-dusted stars. The opium was peaking within her and it was good. She laughed again, savagely, loudly, and whipped the black. He shot through the gates and up the driveway to where the light above the porch beckoned. She was still laughing as she flung the reins over a post and took the steps, two at a time, battering on the door with her stock.

'Wake up, you lazy bastards!' she shouted. 'Let me in!'

The men on guard either recognized her voice or had been told that she was coming. The door opened at once and the ugly face of Fripps grinned at her. She brushed past him contemptuously, her fierce eyes abruptly checking the whistles of admiration which Latour's guards started to make. Without pausing she stepped lightly across the hall and ran up the stairs. It was as if she already owned the house and every man in it.

Sanderman and de Belcourt were with Latour, but he snapped his fingers to dismiss them when Lalage entered. He remained standing, his palms flat on the top of his desk, staring at her. Without waiting for an invitation she seated herself in a carved chair, one long slim leg thrown over the arm, insolent as a St Giles gasconnader.

Latour's eyes burned in his cadaverous face which was as pale as the linen at his throat. 'Well, citizeness, you wish to see me?'

Lalage was unconcernedly playing with the lace at her cuff. 'Certainly, Citizen Latour. I carried out my part of our bargain, now what do you propose doing for me in return?' she replied, with a taunting glance.

The room was warm and well-furnished as befitted the businessman whom Latour purported to be. This suited him, for he appreciated comfort, the finest wines and the best food. Not for him the misery of the poor whom he professed to support. He recalled Lalage's love of mind games, and how she had enjoyed pitting her wits against him in the past. A smile flickered across his thin lips, and something akin to admiration glowed in his pupils.

'I deliberately chose to see you alone,' he said in his soft, sibilant accent. 'Thus, only we two shall know what transpires.'

'How wise of you.' Lalage was feeling her power, testing it, rejoicing in it. 'Such a secret is valuable. There are many who would have paid a king's ransom for *Le Fantom* and I, only I, enabled you to kill him.'

His fingers drummed lightly on the table top. 'My dear child, and who are you suggesting *Le Fantom* was? Give me his real name.'

Lalage leaned her head back against the cushions, smiling and confident. 'You received my letter, didn't you? You arranged the ambush in Cherbourg. He was killed there. It was William Wylde.'

He permitted himself a faint smile. 'Ah, I see. And if I were to tell you that you were mistaken?'

She sat up then, limbs coiled to spring, eyes glittering. 'Mistaken! Is this some trick by which you think to cheat me?'

'No trick, I fear. Yes, I had your letter and yes, I sent word to the authorities in France. The Marats were ready to apprehend *Le Fantom* and, for a while, I too thought that he was dead. But recently prisoners have been spirited away from the strongest, most heavily guarded gaol in Paris. Such a clever, daring escape could have been carried out only by *Le Fantom*. He is still alive. You named the wrong man.'

Her face was contorted with rage. 'You lie! You want to go back on your word to spare my life – to make me your fawning thing, prepared to do more dirty work out of fear. My information was worth a great deal of money and you want to avoid paying me. Well, Latour, it won't work! I know too much about you. I can inform on you to the English authorities and see you hanged as a spy.'

'Your threats are extremely foolish,' he countered gently. 'I hold your life in my hand. I've but to summon my men.'

'You wouldn't dare!' She was beside herself with fury, recklessly defiant.

'Dare not! To me?' The lean, ascetic face hardened and the black eyes were devoid of pity. Her mockery diminished his authority, insulting one who would not tolerate insults, yet he continued to speak as if to a friend, his voice intimate, persuasive. 'You should not try my patience too far. We made a bargain. Your life in exchange for *Le Fantom*. Admit that you were wrong. William Wylde was one of the men who work for him, but he was not *Le Fantom*. However, you did well to send me Jack Smithers.' He sighed, but something evil peered out from between his narrowed lids. 'He's an obstinate young man, but we managed to coax him into confessing that his master, your husband, is in cahoots with him.' A chill had crept over the room, and his magnetic eyes held hers. Latour and his thugs were inventive in devising methods for loosening stubborn tongues.

They were interrupted by noises below, men's voices, footsteps coming up the staircase. Lalage was on her feet, and Latour found himself staring down the barrel of a small pistol. 'What the hell's that?' she demanded. 'Another of your tricks?'

'Child, child – put that toy away,' he soothed, unmoved. 'Unless I'm mistaken, you are about to meet your husband and the real *Fantom*.' Someone knocked on the door and: 'Enter!' Latour shouted.

Guy and Ambrose had been roughly handled after being bundled into a closed carriage in a side-alley near the theatre. Disarmed, wrists bound, then blindfolded. Now the scarves were whipped away from their eyes, and the first person Guy saw was Lalage. The sudden dazzle of candlelight half blinded him, but through it he stared across the room at her. For an instant he thought that she too had been captured, then realized that she was armed.

'What on earth?' he began, then was silenced by the look on her face. It was the expression of a baulked demon, and she was staring not at him but at Ambrose.

'You!' she hissed, head up, eyes slanting and very bright. 'You are *Le Fantom*? My God – *you!* The American fop-doodle!'

A faint smile quirked Ambrose's lips. 'And you, Lady Beaumaris, are an imposter!'

Latour was speaking swiftly to the men who surrounded his prisoners. 'This is the man? You're certain?' There were half a dozen of them, cloaked, armed, including those who had apprehended Guy and Ambrose in the foyer of the Theatre Royal. He came closer, staring up into that watchful, smiling face. 'So – they tell me that your name is Ambrose Alington. Is this correct?' A slight trace of emotion, even excitement, lit his cold features.

'It is. I guess that you're Latour. I'm warning you, my government won't take it lightly if I'm harmed.' Though trussed and at a disadvantage, there was nothing cringing about Ambrose. His mind had never been more keen, taking in the room, the men, seeking an avenue of escape.

'Your government won't know anything about it, until it's too late,' Latour mused, smiling a thin, triumphant smile as he caught and held Ambrose's eyes.

Lalage was at his side, the silver pistol jabbed against Ambrose's waistcoat. 'Oh, Latour, let me play with him for a while,' she begged. 'I want to see him squirm – to hear him scream! You owe me this!'

His eyes were colder than ever, the lines about his thin-lipped mouth deepening. 'I owe you nothing! He's mine!' He paced slowly round Ambrose, thoughtful, considering. 'Any sport enjoyed at his expense shall be mine, and mine alone. You've given us a great deal of bother, *mon ami*, and shall suffer accordingly. After which, your destination will be Paris, where your public execution will provide a grand spectacle for the mob, if they don't get hold of you on the way and tear you limb from limb!'

Guy recovered from the shock of seeing his wife. 'Lalage, why are you here? What part are you playing in this?'

Ambrose answered for her. 'She's one of them! I've suspected it and was a fool not to have acted sooner.'

Bewildered, stunned, Guy shouted at Latour: 'Where's Jack Smithers.'

'Of course – your bastard brother. You wish to see him? That can be arranged,' answered Latour, giving an order to one of his men. 'Get him up from the cellar at once.'

'You'll let him go, and Guy also, now that you have me?' Ambrose watched Latour as a man watches a deadly viper.

Latour sighed and took a pinch of snuff, using a silk kerchief to dab at his nostrils. 'What would you do under like circumstances, my dear *Fantom*? Would you free enemies who know so much about you?'

'But this was the arrangement? You struck a bargain.'

'And I shall retract – in the interests of my cause, you understand.'

'You are entirely without honour, sir!' Ambrose said, keeping him talking, fighting for time.

'Entirely,' Latour inclined his head. 'Honour is for the weak. Honour has put you in the position you are now – my prisoner.'

Two men entered from a side door, half dragging, half carrying Jack. When they released him he fell heavily and lay on his back, groaning. He was half naked, filthy, his face hardly recognizable, eyes inflamed slits above a broken nose, mouth swollen grotesquely where he had bitten deeply into his lips in agony. His hands were useless, covered in coagulated blood, the fingertips raw, nail-less stumps.

'My God!' breathed Guy, making a lunge towards him but hauled back by the guards.

'Is he dead?' Ambrose was deadly calm.

'Not quite.' Latour flicked fastidiously at his cravat, eyeing the tortured man.

Lalage swaggered over until she stood above Jack, hands on her hips, looking down at him. 'Faugh! What a stink!' she jeered. 'You're lying in your own filth, Jack! How degrading for such a fine stud! Never mind, you've lost your fingernails but not your manhood. They won't tamper with that, until I give the order. Perhaps I'll pickle it in brine – a keepsake – to remind me of good times, eh?' She bent closer, hissing fiercely: 'You dolt! Why didn't you do as I wanted and saved yourself needless pain?' Straightening, she aimed a vicious kick at his cracked ribs. Jack yelled, shuddered and then lay silent.

At that moment there came the sudden smashing of glass and instant uproar from downstairs. Shots rang out – men were shouting and there was the noise of running feet, the clash of steel meeting steel. The guards leapt for the door, wrenching it open and Ambrose, who had been quietly working his hands free of the bonds behind his back, jumped for the candelabrum, knocking it over and shrouding the room in darkness. 'Come on, Guy!' he shouted, and they ran through the door.

There was a guard outside, but Ambrose felled him with a chop at the throat, seized his sword, cut Guy free, lunged at another man as they pelted for the stairs and tossed his assailant's weapon over to his friend.

Men were fighting in the hall. Two lay dead and one was dragging himself into a corner, leaving a trail of blood on the tiles. 'Look! There's Robert – Giffe – and Denzil!' exclaimed Guy. Then there was no time for talk as they rushed into the mêlée, the acrid smell of gunpowder flaming in their nostrils. The light from the great chandeliers shafted down on naked swords, running like bright blood on the razor edges as Guy engaged de Belcourt, and Ambrose, swinging his weapon like a cleaver, fell upon another of the guards. Sanderman cringed in the doorway of the salon, his arms flung up as Denzil covered him with a pistol. Giffe, with a ferocious roar, threw himself on

Fripps, disarming him with a mighty sweep of his cutlass. Fripps leapt for the stairs, halfway up before a bullet hit him. He spun round, swayed, then toppled down.

De Belcourt spared him one glance, then renewed his attack on Guy, desperately trying to beat down his blade. Guy deflected the blow, driving him back with massive, wheeling strokes. The Frenchman retreated, step by step. He was pouring sweat, his face twisted with fear. Then with a single, flying lunge Guy drove his steel into the spy's neck. The blood sprayed up from the pierced jugular vein. De Belcourt poised for an instant, crumpled and pitched forward on to his face.

The fight was short, brutal and final. None of Latour's tough, seasoned veterans remained alive. Ambrose's men rested, chests heaving, some mopping at cuts. A silence filled the house, rendered more acute by the recent furore. Ambrose glanced round the shambles of the hall, noting that a dozen of his band were assembled. He grinned across at Denzil, whose pistol was jabbed into Sanderman's back.

'That was well done, young Wylde. But how the deuce did you find us?'

'Through the Jew – Leitchman!' Denzil's face seemed to have matured amazingly. His voice rang with the confidence which Ambrose expected of the Wylde brood. 'He came to Doric House, very alarmed because he'd been passing close to the theatre and had seen Guy and an unknown companion being hustled into a coach at gun-point. He'd been lurking there to catch Guy or Jack – something about forged passports. Anyhow, the upshot was that he found me instead. He's not a bad old rogue, seemed keen to help, though I did reward him well. I told him Jack had vanished, and asked him if he'd heard anything down the grapevine. He mentioned a house in Chelsea, apparently his burglars had cased it with view to robbery, but found it too heavily guarded. It was a long chance, but I rounded up the others and came here, risking a charge of breaking and entry, rushing the place front and rear. Thank God I did!'

'Interfering puppy!' Latour shouted from the head of the stairs. 'I swear I'll see you walk to the guillotine, along with your brother and *Le Fantom*!'

He stood there, his gaunt face white with fury, Lalage acting as a shield, his gun pressed against her temple. Ambrose stared up at him, and he answered: 'Come down and fight me! Our meeting is long overdue!'

Latour did not move. 'Take one step and I'll shoot the woman!'

'Do it!' challenged Guy, blade dripping with de Belcourt's blood, in hand. 'It will save me the job!'

'Guy! Help me! He took me prisoner – trapped me – made me obey him!' Lalage cried.

'Lying bitch!' he snarled.

With a sudden appalling dissonance, the great pier-glass at Latour's back shattered. Giffe had fired at it. In the split-second pause as Latour swung towards it, Lalage dived out of his reach and Ambrose took the stairs. His voice rang out, sharp as the steel in his hand.

'Fight, you dog! Fight *Le Fantom!*'

With an oath Latour wrenched his sword from its scabbard and lunged. Ambrose was ready, his weapon coming to life, flashing as the light rippled along its length. Steel scraped on steel, hissed and rasped, darts of flame caressing each blade, spurting from point to point. Ambrose parried, but he did not attack. He was smiling grimly, waiting, alert for his enemy's next move, the swords kissing, sliding in a husky whisper. Latour lacked his opponent's patience, determined to show what speed could do. He thrust wildly, seeking an opening, but meeting that same baffling, almost lazy guard.

Suddenly Ambrose was upon him, driving him back along the corridor till Latour recovered his balance and counter-attacked. Nothing he could do enabled him to break through that calm, taunting defence. They were at the top of the stairs again, and Latour realized too late that he had been deliberately manoeuvred into this perilous position. He snarled viciously, losing command of himself, and Ambrose's chill smile deepened, his dazzling point pursuing him unmercifully, everywhere at once. Its tip touched Latour's cheek, light as a kiss, opening the flesh to the bone. Next it stung his neck, his hand, his brow, leaving a trickling trail in its wake, an irritating wasp, goading Latour into carelessness. Again and again he left himself open to the death-blow, but remembering Jack, Ambrose did not intend to finish him off quickly. Let the wretch sweat! Let him suffer as he had made others suffer. He must see death coming, and know that he was about to plunge into the pit of hell without being shriven. No one would send up a prayer for his black soul.

Ambrose shook his head to rid it of perspiration trickling from his hair into his eyes, and Latour slipped to one knee, his sword stabbing upwards. The shooting steel entered Ambrose's shoulder. He took an instinctive step back, knocking up the blade, the hilt of his rapier catching in Latour's. With a lightning twist, he tore it from Latour's grasp. It shot through the air, curving high before dropping to the hall below. In a reflex action, Ambrose lunged, transfixing Latour's chest, leaning on the blade, using all his strength to ram it home. With a throttled cry, Latour clawed at the quillon pressed against his ribs, the blade skewering him. As Ambrose withdrew it, Latour stepped backwards into space and hurtled down the stairs, his skull smashing on the marble flooring.

Guy rushed up the steps and seized Lalage, frog-marching her to the hall. Ambrose ordered his men to search the house and make certain that every one of the gang was dead. His shoulder was bleeding, an ever widening crimson stain spreading over his silk jacket, and Guy said: 'Get to a surgeon. Have that looked at!'

'Later,' Ambrose replied, panting heavily, his hair dark with sweat. 'There's still work to do.' He glared sternly at Sanderman who was cowering under the stern Denzil's pistol. 'I'll inform the constables that we found spies here. You, sir, will stand trial at the Old Bailey! Tie him up, Denzil.'

'Yes, sir!' Denzil answered with a wide grin, and he and Robert bundled the lawyer into the salon, using the curtain-cords to rope him to a chair.

'You can't send me to Newgate Gaol,' Lalage protested, struggling fruitlessly in Guy's grasp. 'I'm your wife! Think of the disgrace! I should deny it. No one would believe you.'

Even now she showed no fear, refusing to recognize that she had reached the end of the road. Guy tightened his grip, hurting her, staring at that beautiful, savage creature who had hood-winked him. Cold, heartless, she laughed at corpses, mocked death and suffering, glutted herself on blood, and he had once thought her to be so innocent, so badly used. This was the bitterest blow of all, wounding his pride. He did not yet know how, but she had betrayed him. Had he been the only one involved it would have been bad enough, but Jack had been tortured, his friends endangered and William slain.

'Did I say anything about you being charged as a spy?' he answered coldly, eyes burning in his pale face. 'I shall deal with you myself.'

She laughed softly and rubbed her cheek against his sleeve. 'Oh, Guy, I knew that you wouldn't harm me. We'll go home, forget this. When I explain, you'll understand that I was a victim of circumstance. I love you. We're one, aren't we, darling?'

His hand shot out and seized her by the throat, fingers closing, digging in like live things with a purpose of their own. She choked and clawed at his face, leaving bloody scratches, but he did not release her, bending her backwards, backwards, till it seemed that he would snap her spine. 'Love!' he grated. 'You know nothing of love, you inhuman devil! I want the whole story! I'll have the truth from you – now!'

He let her go, knocking her back against the panelling. Stunned by the blow, massaging her bruised throat, hatred and an animal ferocity possessed her and she screamed: 'Hear it then! Hear it and be damned!'

Alert for any tricky move, Guy watched her, murderous in the white heat of his anger. 'I'm waiting! Speak, bitch!'

She was like a wildcat in a snare, lips drawn back over her teeth, eyes blazing. 'I'm Greek, bastard daughter of a French nobleman. I hated him! Hate all the *aristos*! I joined the Reformati, determined on their downfall. I was powerful among them, leading the women, all would have been well, had it not been for *him!*' She stabbed a finger at Ambrose. 'Oh, yes – *Le Fantom* was the bane of the Jacobins! We couldn't find out who he was, try as we might. We never met, but I knew that he was my enemy. He sent a message to Latour, telling him that I had accepted a bribe from an *aristo* in return for setting him free. The Reformati are without mercy. He knew I would be killed. But the assassin was an idiot and bungled the job! It was easy to persuade him to take me to Marseilles, so that I might slip on to a boat and go back to Greece. All I had to do was give him my body.'

'You whore!' Guy hit her again. Her head cracked against the wall, but she did not stop talking, an insane light in her eyes, blood trickling from her cut lip.

'Oh, Lord Beaumaris! Such a noble gentleman! My gallant knight!' she mocked, as if hungry for him to vent his rage on her. 'All men are vile. Greedy, lustful – like filthy dogs! Even you – St Guy! That *canaille* who should have murdered me was afraid of what he had done. He sold me to slave-traders, and I was shipped to Morocco, and bought by a perverted old goat of an Arab, who fancied himself in love with me and made me his favourite wife! Ha! What an honour! I spent my days being bathed and perfumed for his pleasure – a pleasure that he could never quite attain, no matter what aphrodisiacs or novelties he tried.'

Her face was loathsome to Guy, shorn of the beauty with which he had once endowed it, now holding a curious quality of ferocity and cold beastliness. 'What devilish fiend amused himself by bringing us together?' he muttered.

She laughed, loudly, coarsely, and Ambrose who was standing by cursed himself for not recognizing her when they were first introduced. As she stood there, defying Guy, defying them all, she wore that same crazed expression which had been hers at the guillotine in Paris. It was her cropped hair, her meek manner which had deceived him, coupled with his respect for Guy's judgement.

'Fate – call it what you like!' There was a ring of delight in her voice. She was enjoying the havoc, pleased to see Guy floundering in the wreckage of his lost illusions.

'How did you come to be in the sea?'

She was smiling, that sly, self-satisfied smirk which he had grown to hate. 'I was found in bed with someone else. The Arab was impotent and the handsome slave-boy wasn't. The old man wanted him too, he liked pretty youths. It was pique as much as jealousy which prompted his revenge. The slave was fourteen, and beautiful. Carelessness on the part of the eunuch guards had made them think he wasn't old enough to endanger the harem. They put that right when they caught us. He was castrated then and there.'

'And you?' Guy felt numb, hoping that his mind would refuse to register more. He was wrong. Pain seeped through his system like poison.

'I was flogged, my head shaved, and then I was flung into the sea from the high wall of the *seraglio*. I thought my end had come, but the devil looks after his own. You rescued me, dear husband.'

The hall was quiet and still. Away in other parts of the building there were bumps and crashes as the men went about their work, but here they stood in the eye of the hurricane, a timeless space where each faced the other with the masks stripped off.

'So it was a sham – a lie,' Guy said slowly, the truth stark and terrible.

'I had to find *Le Fantom*. I wanted his death. You were English. It was rumoured that he too came from England. You were rich and titled, and that suited my purpose admirably.'

Lalage was poised there, head up, battered and bruised, ringed by enemies, but unrepentant.

'You never loved me – never intended to play your part as my Lady or give me children.' Guy spoke like a man living a nightmare.

'No.' Her eyes slanted up at him. 'What are you going to do, Guy?' She sounded confident, expecting that he would be unable to resist her.

'I'm going to kill you,' he replied.

She drew back violently, her face blank with shock. Then she made a bolt for the salon door. Guy was too late to stop her, running in, hearing a crash as she hurled herself through the window. Ambrose was behind him, and Guy launched himself out of the broken casement, heedless of the glass lacerating his hands. He could hear Ambrose close at his heels and slowed a little, fingers closing around the butt of the pistol which his friend pushed into his hand. The moon was high, casting purple shadows on the bushes and trees. There was no sign of her, but as they rounded a corner, they heard the sound of hoof-beats on the drive.

'Damn!' exclaimed Ambrose. 'She mustn't get away.'

There were lights in every window, the front door hanging crooked on broken hinges. The horses tethered out front jingled their bits, breath like fog in the frosty air. Guy took one, foot in the stirrup, already swinging into the saddle, as with a grunt of pain from his wounded shoulder Ambrose heaved himself on to another. The cold cut Guy's lungs like a knife, freezing the sweat plastering his forehead. He dug in his heels, spurring the beast forward, galloping through the gates, then slowing, wondering which direction Lalage had taken. The clouds passed from the face of the moon and he caught sight of a horse and rider, some way ahead, making for the river.

There was nothing in his mind but the determination to catch her and the blistering shame of his own pride which had brought such dishonour. He saw himself as if in a distorting mirror, grotesque, hideous – damning his own soul, damning every member of his family by his headstrong association with that hell-hag whom he had taken to wife.

He was gaining on her, though her animal was fast. The street was deserted under the pale, cold moonlight, and he had a clear view of her. Then, aware that he was following, she suddenly urged her horse over a hedge and, without pausing, Guy did likewise. The way was rough and he began to curse as he hit the loose stones, fearing that his mount might stumble and throw him. Banks of cloud shrouded the sky again and, for a moment, he thought that he had lost her. She seemed to see in the dark, forging ahead regardless. The wind was strong and the clouds fled before it. The scene was like a picture viewed through frosted glass, with the trees of ebony sharpness. Guy heard the river not far away, and saw the wall which followed it, built high against flooding.

Lalage stopped abruptly, turning the horse's head this way and that, but she had come to a dead end. Houses blocked her path on one side, Ambrose and Guy on the other. She slid from the saddle, a slim, tall black figure, running up the stone steps which led to the top of the wall. Reaching the summit, she turned, facing Guy, features shadowy, faintly glimmering in the half light. He raised his pistol and fired.

The sound echoed and re-echoed. Lalage staggered, stretched her arms once towards the sky and then disappeared over the brink. Ambrose and Guy reached the spot together, staring down the long drop into the swiftly flowing Thames. It was running full, and tossing up little white waves. She had vanished without a trace, the current swirling onwards to the sea, carrying her back to that element from which Guy had stolen her, a year ago in Morocco.

His madness left him. The moonlight seemed to absorb it. He did not move or speak, gazing at the dark water. Ambrose too was held quiet in that awesome moment. Blackness swallowed all as the clouds veiled that staring, pitiless moon once more.

Chapter 8

Miranda's voice reached Sally, sweet and clear. 'Papa will be home for Christmas.'

Sally was in the kitchen, helping the cook to prepare for the festivities. There was much to do, and this was a blessing. Only sometimes when she paused in her labours did thoughts of William take command. No one had been more just, more decent than he, she knew this, missing him, weeping for him, but at the same time awash with anxiety for Guy. It was over two weeks since he had set out for London.

Miranda danced in through the door, the pup frisking around her legs. 'Did you hear what I said, Sally?' she asked, going straight to the table where the cook gave her a mixing bowl to scrape.

'I heard you, darling, and I hope you're right. It would be lovely to have him here, wouldn't it, and Denzil too? But there's been no letter, and it is Christmas Eve tomorrow.' Sally smiled at the child, her heart overflowing with thankfulness. Miranda was so healthy now, pink-cheeked, sturdy, fully recovered. They watched over her, of course, herself, Dora and Molly, and the only outings permitted were in the gig, where she was swaddled in rugs and furs, but there was no reason to fear a relapse. If anything, Sally was more worried about Molly who was desperately alarmed by Jack's long absence, shaking her head dolefully and saying that she kept having bad dreams about him. Miranda often took her hand, gently reassuring her that Jack was alive and Papa was taking good care of him.

The Dowager had invited her to bring Miranda to Wylde Court for the Yuletide celebrations. Sally supposed that she should go, because Lady Charlotte was fretting for Denzil, and also she wanted to be with Cecily and Barbara who found Miss Stanmore dull company. At the same time she was determined to delay till Christmas morning, wanting to spend a while at Briar Cottage, to hang garlands of holly and mistletoe there, just as she would have done had William been alive.

There was something disturbing about the atmosphere of the manor these days. Though the Dowager wore black, as did they all, she appeared to have recovered from the blow of her son's death with remarkable speed. Neighbours came and went at Wylde Court with an easy frequency unknown in the past. It was a female-dominated community now. Perhaps the suddenness with which she had been brought face to face with death had made her acutely aware of her own mortality. Whatever the reason, she could not bear to be alone, as if finding silence eerie and threatening.

Sally had called there on the previous day, but had not remained long, conscious of something distasteful in the hectic fever which possessed everyone as they planned the revelry. Chalmers had been in fine fettle, chattering animatedly with Lady Charlotte and several lady callers, while Miss Potter and Mr Boxer stood by, awaiting their instructions. They were discussing a dance which was to be held in the Great Hall. Not long before, William had lain there on his funeral bier, and yet they would soon be dancing on the same spot. Sally had felt her face freezing as she listened, though they did have the courtesy to hush a little when someone happened to notice her, but this was soon forgotten again as the irrepressible excitement welled up.

It seemed that the Lord of Misrule would reign triumphant in the traditional way, to organize masques and plays and every kind of diversion. Visiting mummers would come stamping in, disguised in weird costumes, to caper and dance and act out their ancient ritual of death and resurrection, as they had done for centuries. Carol singers would bang on every front door in the village, or group on street corners under their lanterns, and each house would shine with a multitude of candles for the Feast of Lights.

'It will be fun, won't it?' Miranda was saying, helping the cook to make Imbals, a shortcake of fine flour mixed with pulped fruit, rolled out thinly before being baked and iced with sugar.

Sally knew that she must conceal her sorrow, her longing for solitude, and enter into the spirit of it. This is what William would have wanted. 'Great fun,' she agreed, setting to work on an elaborate marchpane, using a bundle of birch twigs to whisk the ingredients before pouring it into a carved wooden mould to set.

In the evening she helped Miranda to wrap gifts. She was a generous child, and had spent much time with the pedlar who had been invited into the kitchen with his pack of trinkets. Now, seated on the hearth-rug in the nursery, she exclaimed over each treasure, while Sally knelt beside her with scissors, coloured paper and ribbon. The little pug thought this to be some game designed purely for her amusement, and Miranda's laughter pealed out at her antics. Sally watched them romping in the soft light of the high, thick-clustered candelabrum on the table and, just for a while, she forgot her troubles, the child's joy, her tingling excitement and anticipation communicating itself to her.

For the Dowager they had selected a magnificent, domed pincushion, covered in red plush, over which were worked white glass beads to form a floral pattern. Denzil was to have a silver-gilt snuff-box; Cecily, a set of oval cards with pictures of flowers printed on them, and Barbara, who had developed an irritatingly pious turn of mind under Miss Stanmore's influence, was being given a devotional book.

'And this is for Papa,' Miranda said breathlessly, hands cupped round a globular glass paper-weight. She gazed ecstatically into its shiny depths in which were buried, like layers of flies in amber, small gaudy objects, vastly magnified, and resembling sections of jam-rolls and sea-anemones. 'Isn't it lovely? I've kept the best present for him. Well, almost the best – yours is nice too, but I'm not telling what it is.'

'Indeed, young lady! Well, I hope he'll arrive in time to receive it,' Sally replied, but not too eagerly.

Miranda's face was serious, rather reproving. 'I've already said he's coming.'

Sally put an arm round her, holding her tightly against the ache in her heart. 'If you're convinced of it, my love, then I'm certain he will.'

'He'll be alone, apart from Jack and Denzil. She won't come here again. She's gone. The sea never gives up – it claims its own.' Miranda's voice was dreamy but content.

The puppy disturbed them, leaping upon the paper, worrying and attacking it, and after that there was laughter, the parcels completed, then hot milk for supper and Miranda being put to bed. Sally kissed her, settled the guard securely round the fire and blew out the candles. Then she went softly to her own room.

She had a few presents of her own to wrap and hide from Miranda's inquisitive eyes, but this did not take long and the clock told her that it was not yet eight. She could hear the jolly voices of the staff down in the kitchen, and envied them. They would be drinking ale and eating mince-pies, sampling the cook's culinary efforts and dreaming of the feast to come. Josh would call in later, and Dora's eyes would sparkle in the lamp-light while he teased and wooed her, anticipating a happy future.

Depression could be held at bay no longer, and Sally sank down on the bed which she had shared with William. It was a beautiful bed with reeded, fluted columns, delicately carved with acanthus leaves, chosen for her by him, in the same thoughtful way that he had planned the whole house. She had not been happy in her marriage, but had grown accustomed to him, warmed by a sense of companionship, used to thinking in terms of 'we', rather than 'myself'. It was hard to adjust to single life again, but this she must do. Pointless waiting for Guy. He had given no indication of loving her, not even a hint or a vague hope. Yet this was not quite true, and she sighed deeply, remembering how he had come to her the night before he left for London.

She had held him in her arms while he slept, hardly daring to move a muscle lest he woke, unaware of the passage of time, listening to his even breathing, allowing herself the forbidden joy of brooding over him. She had pressed her lips to his forehead, tasting the salt of his skin and then, light as a butterfly's wing, had kissed his mouth. There had been no one to see, and she had submitted to her weakness, tracing over his features with her fingertips, thinking how young he looked in repose, the hard lines softened, the lips fuller, no longer curled in mockery, the dark lashes like shadows on his cheekbones. Pity had ached in her, and a terrible feeling of responsibility. It had made her raw, spiritually naked, vulnerable to suffering, and yet she had gloried in the painful pleasure of it, folding the barbs of love to her heart.

Guy had slept soundly for a long time, his head pillowed on her breast, whilst she had lain on the couch, aware that the fire had died down and the candles were guttering. Even had she been tired, she would not have wasted a precious second in slumber, exalted and cloud-high with happiness, the dull ache within her, constantly there, eased by the pressure of his body against hers. For those few rapturous hours, he had belonged to her.

He had awakened just before dawn, and she smiled now, remembering how anxious he had been to leave quietly, afraid that the servants might hear. That had been the last she saw of him, waiting for news, watching the road, restless, uneasy, certain that something dreadful had happened.

Would he ever come again? Or was she fated to live on memories? She went to the window, twitching the curtain aside and staring out. The night was rough and wet, the wind rushing madly over the moors, carrying driving sleet. He'll not ride from London in this, she reasoned. No, he'll wait until conditions improve. There was another horrible possibility for which she had already braced herself – perhaps he had relented and forgiven Lalage. The more she dwelt on this, the more convinced she became that this is exactly what he would do. Lalage would emerge triumphant, returning with him, as beautiful and dominant as ever.

Guy was so proud, and that obstinate hauteur would prompt him to deny that he had been blind to Lalage's alley-cat morals. He would justify this in some clever way, and in doing so acquit himself of being duped. His vanity would demand it, and his wife's allure would win him over. Bitterness welled up in Sally. The thousand contradictory emotions of love, despair, anger, jealousy and susceptibility combined to obscure her judgement. Intuition gave her an insight into his character, and she probably knew him better than anyone, but pain made her harsh and unjust towards him too.

The clock chimed nine, and Sally was no nearer to achieving peace of mind than an hour before. She decided to fetch up a bottle of wine and get drunk, follow the example of men who managed to find solace in it. Opening her door, she listened for a moment. The servants' voices were further away. They had retired to Dora's sitting-room to continue their carousal.

It was dark and she regretted not bringing a candle, hearing the vigorous hiss of sleet beating against the windows. She felt her way along the passage and there, at the head of the stairs, she ran into him in the gloom. His hands held hers in the first shock of contact. They were wet. He was wet. His lips were ice-cold as they found hers, and Sally was stunned – yet it was no surprise. The kiss might have lasted an hour or a second. She was cold, but from the inside, her breathing shallow and difficult. She had wanted this, yearned for it, but the intensity of that yearning now served to stultify.

She could see the pale blur of his face, the heavy hair tossed back as if wild fingers had played with it. Snow powdered his shoulders, the breath of the trees and the deep night emanating from him, fresh and pungent.

'Where is Lalage?' she whispered, overwhelmed by his closeness.

'I shot her.' She could feel his hands trembling. Without weighing her words or aware of anything but comforting him, she said: 'It doesn't matter. Don't think of it.'

In the half glow and stillness, his voice was low. 'I've been a blind fool, chasing after pinchbeck, when the real gold lay under my very nose.'

'We can't talk here.' She could not concentrate on what he was saying. 'Come to my room.'

'No!' There was horror in the sharp denial. 'This is William's house. I'll take you to the lodge. Will you come?'

Sally delayed long enough to pick up her cloak and run to Dora's parlour, sticking her head round the door and asking her to listen for Miranda. She registered her servants' blank, astonished expressions at the eccentricity of going out after dark in such weather. No doubt she would have to avoid subtle questions in the morning, but she did not care. Swiftly, silently, Guy led her by the hand through the house and into the garden. His horse was at the gate and he lifted her to the saddle, mounting up behind, riding hard amidst the whelter of sleet and darkness. They were lone figures on the landscape. The whole white-swirling country seemed naked, punished by the ice-scented gale.

When they reached the lodge, they left the horse in the stable and ran for shelter. Guy had a key and they were soon inside. It was cold and deserted, echoing uncannily, the wind whistling between gaps in the floor-boards, the roof, walls and windows. Guy strode into the drawing-room, striking a match, his face red in the sudden glow. He lit a candle and, holding it aloft, took her upstairs.

'This is a grand old place,' he said, opening the door of a room which she had never seen before. 'I'm going to have it repaired and put to rights, after we are married.'

'Married? I don't understand.' She stood quite still in the centre of the floor, the sleet melting on her face, her cloak dripping.

'Not yet, of course.' He did not look at her, finding some kindling and concentrating on getting a fire alight in the wide, highly ornamental stone hearth. 'Lalage is dead. I'm certain of it, though her body has not yet been found. I shot her, but she fell into the river and was borne away.'

Bewildered by his words, keenly aware that he had brought

her to the room in which he slept when staying there, Sally sat down, trying not to stare at the bed, fixing her attention anywhere but there. The room was clean, and in a better state than the rest of the house, giving an idea of how it must have been in its prime. Above the dark oak panelling were frescoes of pastoral scenes. The ceiling was picked out with gilding, inlaid with further colours, faded red and deep blue, edged with cream medallions. Though threadbare, the chairs had coverings of velvet with shaggy fringes, but it was the giant four-poster to which her eyes kept returning. The curtains were thrown up over the ceil, exposing its great width, with carvings at the foot and the Wylde coat of arms painted at the head.

The fire was blazing and Guy heaped more wood on it lavishly. She left the chair, dropping down and warming her numbed hands. 'Tell me what happened in London,' she said. 'Is Jack safe? And what of *Le Fantom*?'

'Jack is safe, and home with his mother. *Le Fantom* too, escaped. Ah, but Sally, I have Lalage's blood on my hands, wicked though she was. I've become a creature of the night,' he replied, almost as if to himself. 'I fear the light of day, casting such shadows as I go that nothing, I think, could prosper near me. Sometimes I feel that I am cursed. I'm half afraid to hope that we will marry, and expect to pay dearly even for the comfort of your smile.'

Sally was startled by the change in him, having always known him as cynical and mocking. This gloom was alarming. She could not plead for his happiness, for that would mean pressing her own case, so she said: 'Far better to avoid such ideas, Guy. Tell me about it.'

He was kneeling at her side, and gave her a sideways glance. 'Before I do, get out of those wet things lest you catch cold.'

His clothing too glistened, and he began to strip, his body ruddy in the firelight. Soon he was completely naked, hanging his things over a chair. Sally hesitated, becoming more confused by the second, but she could see the sense of his advice and undressed slowly, partially concealed by the blanket he handed her. He flung another, toga-fashion, around his muscular frame, and she was relieved when his masculinity was hidden from her sight – shy, frightened and desirous.

He began to pace the floor, thrusting a hand through his hair, pulling back the locks from his brow. Then he started to speak rapidly, sometimes turning towards her as if his emotions must find an object, sometimes communicating in low tones, at others throwing his words into space, making his indictment against the mysterious powers who had ruled his fate.

Sally listened in silence, her quick imagination picturing each incredible event. Ambrose was *Le Fantom*! Lalage a spy! 'I can't believe she could have been so false,' she whispered when he paused. 'And Jack – oh, poor Jack! How horrible!'

'Every word is true.' He stared at her sombrely, wondering if he was about to make another classic error. Could he trust her? Was it possible that he might make a happy union at last? What insanity, and yet what sweetness. She was bathed in gold, the flames flickering over her face, turning her skin to molten bronze, her hair to dusky fire, but she was unconscious of her beauty, making no attempt to seduce, as Lalage would have done.

'What of the powers-that-be?' She was so earnestly concerned for him. 'How did Ambrose explain away several dead bodies in that house in Chelsea?'

Guy linked his fingers with hers. '*Le Fantom*'s activities are approved in high places. They know that he and Ambrose are one and the same man. He had but to drop the word "spies" into the right ear for difficulties to be smoothed over.'

'And what have you told society? I presume that no one knows she was the biggest traitor of the lot!' The iron had entered her soul, her hatred of Lalage, alive or dead, feeding within her like a foul maggot. She could not hide her bitterness.

His eyes were troubled. He felt himself to blame for corroding her faith in human nature. 'At first, I said she had gone away for a while. Then Aurora, in whom we had confided, told her hairdresser that Lady Beaumaris had eloped with a lover. It was all over town the same day, though none have dared tackle me about it.' He came closer, gazing down at her with such a serious expression that her heart contracted with love and longing. 'Oh, Sally, I hate to see that hardness in your eyes. It is over. I am sane again, and I beg you to marry me. Will you?'

She shook her head in perplexity, tears thick in her throat. Oh, the fever and pain of love. Even now she could not believe, dared not hope that he was sincere. 'Why? Why me? Is it because you are lonely and unhappy, or because your self-esteem has been so badly hurt?'

He was angry then, scowling at her. 'None of these things. Have done with this nonsense. I expected straight dealings and plain answers from you. You love me, don't you?'

'Yes.' It was pointless denying it. 'I have always loved you. I married William when I had lost you to her. I was tired of being alone, sick to death of spinsterhood. William loved me and I was fond of him. Had he lived, or had you been happy with her, I would never have told you.' Her voice broke and she struggled not to cry. 'I can't believe that you would want me. I'm plain, no longer very young.'

'Plain!' There was genuine astonishment on his face. 'You, plain? My dear girl, you are beautiful! I didn't know that I loved you until I heard that you were betrothed. It came as a great shock. Somehow, I had always felt that you belonged to me, but was blind to the truth. You are my friend, my love, my kin. Why, compared to you, other women are either fools or wantons!'

He caught her to him with both arms, dragging her against him while he kissed her. This time it was a kiss of need and passion. His mouth opened hers, and his tongue caressed her with a shock of delight which melted the last of her resistance. The warmth and pressure of their bodies fed something within each of them which had been hungry for too long. He withdrew his lips, holding her a little away, so that he might look at her. Sally was too confused to do other than follow her instincts. He too seemed endearingly bewildered, this hard man who had always been so sure of himself.

'I want to be your wife, Guy, more than anything,' she murmured, clinging to him. 'But this can't happen for at least a year. I must respect my mourning period, and no one knows Lalage is dead. I can't wait any longer, darling – I'll be your mistress. Take me now.'

'Oh, Sally, you wonderful woman.' Guy lifted her up in his arms and carried her to the waiting bed, his face close to hers, his voice tender. 'My mistress, beloved of all others, with whom I shall share delights in private, until the day I can claim you as my legal bride. It will be our secret. I'll come to you whenever I can. I love you, Sally – now let me show you how much.'

Sally responded to him as she had never done with William. He was no longer the aloof cousin with her the humble recipient of his bounty. They were man and woman, alone in the night, alone on a high peak of passion, unrestrained by convention, so close that it seemed their bodily shells fell away, leaving naked soul to naked soul. Later there would come questions and planning, probably arguments, but now they thought of nothing but the fusion of their flesh, and when at last the shattering fulfilment of the senses was fading, they still lay locked together. Guy cradled her in his arms, fondling the gold silk of her tangled hair, and Sally pressed herself to him, her lips moving tenderly over his face.

Who can explain the force which draws two people together? she mused sleepily. It is more, much more than just physical attraction. Lying there, with the warmth of his body radiating through her, she wanted to share every aspect of his life, to know his heart, his fears, his dreams. It was the beginning for them, the start of something so delicate that it must be tended lovingly during the coming months, taking root and flourishing strongly so that nothing could destroy it. Understanding would come, and with it forgiveness, but now there was no yesterday, no tomorrow, only the present where they could drown in each other.

In the terraced garden a group of people were gathered beneath the spreading branches of a cedar tree. Beyond that patch of welcome shade, the sun blazed down on stone steps and balustrades. The air was potently scented with roses, jasmine, thyme and lavender. On such a day Wylde Court seemed to slumber, lulled by the rocking, dreamy call of the wood-pigeons deep in the encircling woods.

'Devil take me,' reflected Ambrose. 'I sure am going to miss England.' He was sitting on the grass at Aurora's feet, soaking up the sun, wearing a pair of cool cotton breeches, his torso, legs and feet bare.

'We'll come back sometimes,' she said, ruffling his bleached hair. 'I fully intend that our daughter shall know the delights of London life, as well as those of Charleston.'

Seated in a wicker garden-chair, wearing white and shaded by her frilled parasol, she looked across the lawn to where Miranda and her sisters were teaching the baby to walk. Miss Stanmore hovered uncertainly, issuing nervous instructions which they ignored. Ambrose and she were frequent visitors to Dorset now that Guy and Sally were married, but in a week they were sailing for America where, as young Mrs Alington, she must face his haughty aunts and inquisitive relations. Aurora was a supremely contented matron these days, her wildness tamed, still madly in love with her husband. The child, named Christabel, had been born at Holt Hall during the summer of the previous year.

'It'll be good to go home, honey – there's so much for you to see, and I want to show off my lovely wife and daughter. She's a

404

real charmer, ain't she? A terrible flirt already, just like you.' Ambrose stretched lazily, tired from his swim, lying on his back, hands laced under his head, gazing up into the azure sky.

'Don't worry about the house in Bedford Row. It'll be safe in my care,' remarked Denzil, lifting his face from the daisies he was piling into the lap of Elizabeth Compton's pink silk dress. She was a wealthy, malleable girl whom Lady Charlotte was trying to foist on to him. He reached up to stick one or two flowers amongst her mousey curls, a process to which she submitted with an unattractive blush.

Denzil was not interested in her. He was one of those unfortunate beings who find heart-wounds very hard to heal. Lalage's death had affected him deeply, though he recognized the justice of it. Yet, even though knowing every aspect of her wickedness, he would sometimes sit, staring into the distance, fancying that he saw the ghost of his lost love, that woman who had brought short joy and lasting sorrow into his life. By his prompt action which had saved Guy, Jack and Ambrose, he had redeemed his tarnished reputation, but having lost one brother and seen another broken by torture, Guy refused to allow him further dealings with the league. For a while Denzil had remained at home, but had soon grown weary of his mother's demanding company. During a stay in London he had made a new circle of friends, inviting them to Wylde Court on lengthy visits. Down had come batches of favoured companions of the moment, youthful philosophers, exquisite dandies or perhaps serious lads of earnest political views. The Dowager adored entertaining them, but Guy found them a tedious bore. Denzil had started to cultivate loose flowing locks, open collars, flying cravats and, to his mother's horror, trousers.

When Guy married Sally, causing raised eyebrows as they had not waited a full year, Lady Charlotte had moved into the Dower House with Chalmers. He had made it brutally plain that Sally should be undisputed mistress of the manor. Denzil did not go with her, manfully resisting storms and sulks, determined to keep his own apartment where he could do exactly as he pleased. Ambrose and Guy had decided that something must be done about him, not satisfied to see him idling away his time and falling into bad company. He had much to give, and Ambrose had craftily involved him in plans for the large property he had purchased in London with the intention of turning it into an orphanage. The preparations were completed now, and Ambrose was going to open it formally before he sailed. Denzil was to be in charge over the kindly couple selected to care for the homeless children.

The scene in France had changed so dramatically that Ambrose's part there was finished, *Le Fantom* laid to rest. Giffe and Robert had volunteered for the army, while Nick and Charlie were betrothed to heiressess. The Reign of Terror had ended when Robespierre lost his popularity and went to the guillotine.

'It's down to the French now,' Ambrose said, discussing the matter with Aurora and Denzil, while Elizabeth listened, open-mouthed. 'Everything has turned topsy-turvy there. It makes one wonder if there's any logic in death and destruction.'

'Julian was telling me only the other day, about the strange new fashions being adopted by the *demi-monde* in Paris,' Aurora added, holding out her arms to Christabel who was tottering towards her. 'Everyone has gone quite mad, it seems, and there's evidence of luxury springing up again.'

'Of course there is,' Ambrose observed cynically. 'The *aristos* couldn't bring much out of the country, so their mansions were left standing, filled with treasures and unguarded. A lot of people have made money out of the revolution, and the chateaux have found new occupants – members of the *bourgeoisie*.'

'It is quite ridiculous,' Denzil flashed angrily. 'There are balls and soirées being held with as much extravagance as in the days of the King. What of the peasants, I'd like to know!'

Ambrose was on his feet, throwing his daughter high while she shrieked with laughter. 'I suspect they're as wretched as ever. 'Tis the place-hunters, the profiteers who coined money out of the shortages who now prosper.'

'The well-bred women who saved their necks by marrying tradesmen are having a wonderful time, so I understand,' Denzil grumbled, still worrying about injustice. He half admired, half hated these survivors who danced the nights away. 'They're saying that every fashionable *citoyenne* is pregnant.'

'Good heavens, how extraordinary!' exclaimed Aurora with a laugh. 'Having slaughtered so many, I suppose they hope to relace them with little Republicans.'

Exhausted by romping with his demanding child, Ambrose flopped down on the grass while she bounced energetically on his chest, a fair-skinned imp who already had him under her well-sucked little thumb. 'Can't put you straight on that one, my love,' he grinned at his wife, the tenderness in his eyes warming her like wine. 'But I do know there's a new street-group – young men who despise red caps and shaggy woollen clothing. Sansculottism is old hat! As hateful as death, apparently. These are an up and coming breed of dandies, who wear their hair plaited at the temples and knotted into a pigtail at the back. Some call them the Muscadins – others the *Jeunesse Dorée* – Golden Youth.'

'They sound interesting,' Aurora murmured, stirring the warm air with her fan. 'Where did they spring from?'

'Who knows? Relatives of the persecuted perhaps? It may be nothing more than the usual rebellion against the views of their elders which comes up in every generation.' Ambrose, glad that Miranda had collected Christabel and taken her off to play, rolled over on to his stomach, stuck a blade of grass between his teeth and chewed as he mused. 'They riot and demonstrate, and carry clubs loaded with lead. Any *Tappé-dur* or Jacobins they fall in with get beaten up.'

'And the Convention tolerates them?' Denzil was baffled by the ever-changing face of politics.

'Sure, they do. The Gilded Youth, with their semi-military outfits, are viewed with delight. The Republic love the army, don't forget, and their forces are growing strong. I'm afraid England is in for a lengthy war.'

'At least these young men have drawn the teeth of the Jacobin monster,' commented Denzil knowledgeably, receiving an admiring glance from the demure Elizabeth.

'There's a deal of trouble in Paris. Trade's in a state of flux, people queueing at bakers' shops, everyone either bickering, brawling or waltzing. The Jacobins are gone, hooted and hustled by the hungry mob and the swaggering Muscadins,' continued Ambrose, stretching out a hand and caressing Aurora's sandalled foot, smiling up at her, his long lashes, black at the base and tipped with gold, casting shadows on his bronzed cheeks. 'The Convention keeps its seat amidst the chaos, and Paris has risen again, demanding bread and a Constitution, just as it did five years ago, when Louis and Marie Antoinette reigned. Life goes around in circles.'

Sally had been busy in the house, but now she left it to join her guests. She passed between the stately flower-beds where masses of geraniums flaunted their gaudy scarlet amidst the hollyhocks, lupins and foxgloves. White syringa starred the shrubbery walls where a gate gave access to the herb garden.

She walked slowly, drinking in the tranquillity; bees bumbled heavily over the spicy plants, filling the air with hum and stir. Butterflies loitered on bejewelled wings, and she pointed one out to the baby which she carried.

'Look, Phillip, isn't it pretty? Can you smell the herbs? What d'you make of it, eh? You should be keenly interested, my dear, for it will belong to you one day.'

Phillip stared with the wide shining eyes of the newborn, but he made no answer, being only two weeks old. He was a fine boy with a crest of thick black hair and eyes which might well retain their present shade of blue. It was like falling in love all over again to cradle her child in the crook of her arm, and Sally smiled and watched him, her favourite occupation since his birth. His little hands were folded against his bib, and that spell-binding baby-odour crept into her nostrils, enslaving her even more.

He was pink and wonderful and comic, full of character already, a miracle of creation who demanded nothing but her milk and her love. He had arrived suddenly and unexpectedly when she and Guy had been spending a night at Highfield Lodge, their retreat from pressures at the manor. He had rushed to the mill and fetched Molly, flouting convention and insisting on helping with the delivery. Most irregular, of course, giving their neighbours something else to gossip about. Sally had wanted him there, taking comfort from his calm strength when the pains came swift and hard, sharing that splendid moment when the child came into the world and they knew they had a son.

Sally had been quite unprepared for the torrent of love which had swept her as, naked and squalling, Phillip had been placed in her arms. She had not thought it possible to love anyone as fiercely as she loved Guy, but now there was this little person on whom to lavish her passion. Only two weeks ago, yet she felt that she had always known him. Sensitive to his every need, she seemed to remember what it was like to be a baby, utterly helpless, with no language save a cry. If left lying on an uncomfortable fold, he couldn't move; if he had an itch, he couldn't scratch – a pain, and he was unable to ease it, entirely at the mercy of a race of giants. She had engaged a nanny, but guarded Phillip devotedly, training the woman herself.

Life had not been easy during those months when she and Guy had been forced to keep their love a secret. Only the blessing of their infrequent nights together had made it endurable. It had been sheer torture to meet him in public, where his very regard for her made it incumbent on him to treat her ceremoniously. To have openly singled her out for notice would have been tactless and tantamount to disaster. The strain on both of them had been tremendous. In spite of knowing his reasons, it had hurt her to see him when they could not be alone, giving him back coldness for coldness, and mocking formality for his grave courtesy. He had proved more patient than she, soothing her in those blissful snatched hours of privacy.

There was an awful time some two months after Lalage's disappearance, when Guy was suddenly called to London. On his return he sought Sally, weary from the journey and the ordeal he had faced. 'She's dead,' he had said. 'I'm certain of it. I had to identify a body which had been dragged out of the water, where the river joins the sea at Chatham. It was badly decomposed – the face was gone, tattered bits of flesh clinging to the skull, but the hair was still there – curling, black – Lalage's hair. What finally convinced me was her ring – the one which Sanderman had confessed carried the Reformati seal – it was still on her hand. I told the authorities that it was my wife's body, and she was placed in the family vault in Highgate Cemetery. The newspapers were full of it – Lady Beaumaris had been murdered by an unknown assailant. Now there's nothing to stop us marrying, Sally.' But there was, and both knew it. Propriety had to be observed.

Eventually the wedding had been announced, midst consternation and reproaches from the Dowager, to which they paid no heed. It was unusually soon after the deaths of their respective spouses, but they could afford to wait no longer, for Sally had discovered that she was pregnant. Now followed the happiest time in her life and she bloomed in her contentment, totally at ease when the league disbanded and Guy gave up those perilous runs to France. They buried themselves at Wylde Court, seldom in London, re-discovering the joys of their mutual ancestral home. Sometimes they rode out together, round the estate or up to the moors to watch the ever-changing colours patterned by drifting clouds, or again wander on the smooth yellow sand, listening to the thunder of the sea.

Sally rarely thought of Lalage, though occasionally she would find her feet leading her to the Long Gallery where Francis Sudley's painting had been hung. Guy had reluctantly given it wall space, hating any reminder of his second wife, but he could not avoid it, always careful to speak respectfully of her when outsiders were present. The portrait had been placed in a dark corner of the gallery where he did not have to look at it if he passed that way.

It gave Sally a prickling sensation down the spine to stare up at her one-time rival. It was so lifelike, yet gave an entirely false impression of angelic beauty. Only a person who had known her well would be aware of something odd in those slanting eyes which seemed to follow wherever one moved. Cruel mockery, perhaps? A challenge? And at times, when Sally was tired and the day was dark outside, filled with mist or driving rain, she would start, fancying that she heard the rustle of silk and Lalage's light step at the door.

Engrossed in her thoughts, nursing Phillip, she was not aware that Guy had opened the gate. He paused, silently watching her. The sunlight bathed her, and the breeze fluttered her white gown, making it cling to her limbs, now throwing into shadow, now revealing the curve of her bare ankle. Her corn-gold hair fell loosely down her back, and the strong light seemed to have melted into it.

It is not unusual for a man, whom love has betrayed and left stripped, to turn to religion for consolation. Guy had not done this. Instead, he had turned to Sally. Too often disappointed by women in the past, the appearance of love in maturity had come in sweetness and joy and a bewildering upheaval. It was like an earthquake, flinging up new heights and baring unknown depths. He was happy, almost dangerously so, afraid to tempt the gods. When Phillip had been born, Guy dared to believe again. The stars in their courses had had a strange influence on him, but now they were making atonement.

'Sally, darling – there you are,' he said, missing her though they had been apart for only an hour at most.

She spun round, greeting him with a wide smile. He raised her hand and brushed it with his lips, then she felt his arms about her like wings, his shadow encompassing the baby and herself in a protective embrace. He had been swimming with Ambrose, and carried his shirt across one shoulder, clad in nankeen breeches and thonged sandals. He was as deeply tanned as Ambrose, but whereas the American's skin was golden-brown, his was a rich coffee shade. Sally looked up, admiring him, and he carefully took Phillip from her, liking the feel of that tiny body fitting so perfectly into the curve of his arm.

'Isn't it a glorious day,' she exclaimed. 'I've never seen the old place so beautiful.'

'To me, you make it beautiful, even when it's raining,' he replied, while she tucked her hand into his elbow and they started to walk towards their friends. 'Did you see the dawn? It was spectacular. The dawn of a night which had never become really dark. It reminded me of Africa. I'll take you to Morocco next year, when Phillip is old enough to be left with his nanny.'

Morocco. The name had a fatal ring. Guy had found Lalage there, and as Sally thought of this, it was as if mists shrouded the earth, robbing the scene of living light, dulling the tints of flower and turf, contracting the horizon. She shook this off. Lalage would come no more to Beaumaris Combe, but the wounds she had inflicted would never be entirely healed. Sally stiffened her spine and agreed to accompany him, though she could not bear to be parted from Phillip, beginning to understand the strong pull between maternal and romantic love. Her first duty lay towards her husband. He must never take second place. She would go with him to El Skala, see those blue waters from which he had saved Lalage, setting in motion a chain of strange events. By so doing, she might be able to lay the ghost, once and for all time.

Jack, strolling from the direction of the stables, saw the group beneath the tree and, at the same time, noticed Guy and Sally emerging from the herb garden. His body had healed under Molly's nursing, but the inner scars remained. He would never forget what he had suffered at Latour's hands nor forgive the part Lalage had played. It was as well that Guy had killed her or he would have done it himself. He and Ambrose had become firm friends, and he was looking forward to going to America with him. Ambrose had told him so much about the opportunities which awaited a strong, resourceful man in that vast country of untapped wealth, fully prepared to sponsor him. It would be hard to leave Molly, but that old reprobate, Tom Redvers, had retired from smuggling and made an honest woman of her at last, so she would not be alone. America was not the end of the world, he had assured her. Fast sailing ships made the Atlantic crossing with ever-increasing frequency. It was Ambrose's intention to return to England often, to re-open Holt Hall which he was leaving in the care of trustworthy retainers.

As Jack neared his friends, and the half-brothers to whom he had grown closer, his mind ran on concerning his mother, recalling an incident which had happened shortly after his arrival home. He had entered her kitchen unexpectedly early one night, and found her bending over the fire.

'What you up to there, Ma?' he had asked, for she was busy burning something. It was melting in the flames which lapped greedily around it, blue-green and purple. Just for an instant he had imagined that the thing had a vaguely human form, had seen pieces of charred fabric and a few strands of black hair.

Molly's eyes had flown to him, then dropped to his bandaged hands. 'Oh, I'm just getting rid of something that's served its purpose,' she had replied mysteriously. Jack had experienced a chilly spasm of uneasiness. Molly was a deep one, all right. He had learned long ago not to question her activities.

Ambrose hailed him, and they began to go over details of their journey again. There was a picnic in progress on the lawn. Footmen had come out to spread a white damask cloth on the table, and there was champagne and cut glass goblets, crimson and gold china, floury white bread fresh from the oven, wafer-thin slices of ham, yellow cheese and firm primrose pats of dairy butter stamped with the Beaumaris crest.

Aurora took one look at the great dish of strawberries, the jugs of clotted cream, and declared loudly that she simply must resist temptation as she was already too plump, then proceeded to demolish two large helpings. 'I declare that I'm so hungry these days, I'm beginning to suspect that I'm *enceinte* again,' she said with a wry smile, but her eyes were twinkling.

'Splendid! You're doing your duty as a good wife should,' answered Ambrose complacently.

'What an unfeeling rogue!' Aurora declared, addressing Sally, as one mother to another. 'D'you know what he said to me after I'd been delivered of Christabel?' Without waiting for an answer she rushed on: 'He told me that he was exhausted, to which I replied: "You're exhausted! How d'you think I feel after hours of labour?" He had the enormous cheek to say: "Why do you feel tired? You've been lying in bed all through it!"'

Sally laughed, and the men threatened to go down to the tavern if they were about to indulge in childbed reminiscences. The two women were friends now, brought together by the dangers their men had faced, and by their children, but some-times Sally would remember that Aurora had been Guy's mistress. It was disturbing, and she found it hard to imagine

412

them making love. Flighty though she appeared to be, Aurora had eyes for no one but Ambrose.

Philip was hungry, and Sally sat with her back to the bole of the tree, opened her bodice and suckled him. He was always hungry, it seemed, and she needed him as much as he did her, to relieve the surging pressure of the milk. When he was replete, and had had his back patted to bring up the wind, she laid him in the rush-woven basket which the villagers had presented to her.

'He looks so much like you, darling,' she murmured to Guy, who was resting in the shade beside her.

'Really? I didn't think I resembled a red-faced, wrinkled little old man,' he teased.

Cecily was picking daintily at the strawberries, a lovely girl, already conscious of the opposite sex, flirting artlessly with Ambrose who always made a fuss of children. Barbara was still plain, still rather devout. In the autumn they would be going to Bath to board at a finishing-school. Sally would miss them, but was thankful that Guy had made this decision for they were becoming difficult to handle. Miranda, tall and skinny, would always be with them; her body was developing but her mind remained childlike. She worshipped her brother, and his coming had filled the gap left by Danny when Dora moved into Josh's farmhouse.

The spruce young nanny came to take Phillip indoors where she would place him in the old oaken cradle which had sheltered a succession of Wyldes. Miss Stanmore ushered her charges away, insisting that it was time for their nature walk. Cecily grumbled, declaring that she did not intend to spend the evening pressing boring wild flowers, but Guy spoke to her sharply and she flounced off.

July hung over the meadows where the long grass lay in swathes, and the soil split and crumbled in the heat. The trees were at their greenest, casting great blocks of shade. It had been a long, gorgeous day, busy yet lazy – high summer over garden and sea, cornfields and moorland. And now evening had come; the fires of sunset cooled, and a deep pink sky brooded over the teeming earth, lit by the sickle of a young moon which had hung, ghostlike, in the air the whole afternoon.

Gathering up their belongings, still laughing and talking, the others dawdled back to the house to change for dinner, but Guy and Sally lingered. 'Shall we take a walk?' he suggested.

They left the garden hand in hand, wandering through the

413

woods towards the cliffs, drawing in the luxury of the stillness, the cool fragrance, the glory of advancing night. Guy put an arm round Sally, pulling her close as they stood looking down at the gently heaving sea, curving along the edge of the cove far below. It was molten on the horizon where the rapidly disappearing sun had turned the sky to amber.

His mouth found hers. She was warm and yielding, his wife in every sense of the word. 'No regrets?' he whispered.

She shook her head, gripping him almost harshly. 'Oh, no – I'd do it over again, a hundred thousand times! My only regret is that we've wasted so much time.'

He compressed his lips, frowning. 'That was my fault, not yours. I married two other women before I finally discovered that I'd been entertaining an angel, unawares. I suppose that, in some weird way, I've Lalage to thank for making me lift the veil of my blindness. It was a tragedy that William had to be sacrificed to do it.'

The thought of William and Lalage made Sally shiver and, thinking that she was cold, Guy took her shawl and placed it round her shoulders. Warmed by this protective gesture, Sally knew that her future would be filled with such affection and understanding. A safe love, free from passions as evil and destructive as those which had driven Lalage, that enchantress who had cast such a fearful spell over each of them, until Guy had found the courage to return her to the jealous, possessive sea.